My Blue Suede Shoes

Also by Tracy Price-Thompson

1-900-A-N-Y-T-I-M-E

Gather Together in My Name

Other People's Skin

Knockin' Boots

A Woman's Worth

Proverbs for the People

Chocolate Sangria

Black Coffee

Also by TaRessa Stovall

The Hot Spot

The Buffalo Soldiers

Other People's Skin

Proverbs for the People

A Love Supreme

My Blue Suede Shoes

Four Novellas

TRACY PRICE-THOMPSON and TaRESSA STOVALL

ATRIA PAPERBACK
NEW YORK LONDON TORONTO SYDNEY

A Division of Simon & Schuster, Inc.
1230 Avenue of the Americas
New York, NY 10020

This book is a work of fiction. Names, characters, places, and incidents either are products of the author's imagination or are used fictitiously. Any resemblance to actual events or locales or persons, living or dead, is entirely coincidental.

ATRIA PAPERBACK and colophon are trademarks of Simon & Schuster, Inc.
Designed by Davina Mock-Maniscalco
Manufactured in the United States of America
ISBN 978-1-61129-475-0

CONTENTS

EDITORS' NOTE

It shouldn't hurt to be a woman, and as sisters in this great country, it is our collective responsibility to ensure that our daughters and sons know this statement to be absolutely true. Violence and abuse manifest themselves in a myriad of ways, and there isn't always a raging red flag to alert us that someone we know or love might be in pending danger.

My Blue Suede Shoes seeks to shed light on various forms of abuse in relationships and to heal these hurts by focusing on the root cause of the abuser's behavior and having him or her take responsibility for instituting the necessary self-change.

Whether it be child abuse, physical abuse, sexual abuse, or emotional abuse, domestic violence in any of its many manifestations is simply wrong, and as a people we must acknowledge it when we detect it in our communities and then take active steps to assist the victims in obtaining the help they need to remove themselves from relationships that cause them harm.

But help mustn't only be provided for the victims of abuse. Many cases of domestic violence are perpetrated by those who have also been abused themselves. Causing pain to others thus becomes a vicious cycle, one that is difficult to break without intervention and assistance.

In this second volume of our Sister-4-Sister Empowerment Series, we not only seek to illustrate various aspects of domestic violence and abuse, we also strive to understand the motives behind the behavior and to find methods of eliminating the abuser's need to inflict pain on others. It is our hope that the stories we've penned for this important volume of fiction are eye-opening and thought provoking in ways that are beneficial to you in your daily life.

So, as you go about your lives, may each of you place an arm of protection around your sisters and brothers in need, while praying for them the same safety, comfort, happiness, and protection that you seek for yourselves. May you be blessed with the utmost peace and balance, and as you navigate the harrowing roads to self-awareness and determination with CC, Zana, Charmaigne, and Monique . . . please . . . if you run across a sister who's in trouble, don't turn your back on her. Empower her! Be a *Sister 4* your *Sister*. Share a copy of this book, and give her a pair of blue suede shoes.

Peace and balance, Tracy and TaRessa
www.empowerourselves.org

DESIREE

BREAKIN' IT DOWN

COOPER

Chapter ONE

Fantastic show, CC!"

Smiling expectantly, the producer handed tall, stylish Cornelia Christine Smart a bottle of Evian. The popular host of the TV gossip show *Breakin' It Down,* CC opened the bottle and took a swig before extending a handshake to her guest.

"Thank you, Mr. Combs. I'm sure your new line of clothing will do well in this town. Especially now that you've been seen on my show."

Mega-rap star and designer Sean Combs raised his eyebrows. "Yes, they would have never heard about me if it weren't for you!" He laughed good-naturedly. "Thanks for the publicity."

Stepping off the set, he walked into the gaggle of screaming women who had lingered for an autograph. CC Smart frowned as she watched him whip out a pen.

"Can someone get those people out of the hallway? It's a fire hazard!" she yelled as she yanked the lavaliere mic from the lapel of her sapphire St. John knit suit. Grabbing her bottled water, she breezed by her wiry, freckle-faced producer. "Out of my way, Josh," she said. "You didn't go into my dressing room while I was on the set, did you?"

"No, ma'am. Just like you ordered. No one's been in there. And there hasn't been a peep from your daughter, either."

"Good," said CC, breathing easy. "She's probably sleeping off the cold medicine I gave her." Then, changing the subject, she added, "Who've we got tomorrow?"

Josh Clark consulted his clipboard. "We still got a call in to the mayor about his impending divorce. Oh, and a call in to Aisha Robinson. But she's been ducking us since that shoplifting rap."

"Forget the mayor. He's been creepin' for years. That's not news. I want Aisha to come on the show. She needs to explain why the wife of an NFL player caught a case in Saks." CC turned and wagged her French-tipped finger in her producer's face. "I want her fat ass on my set tomorrow morning. No excuses. Everybody in this town answers CC's calls. Everybody."

"Yes, ma'am."

"I've got to take Alizé home. Let Sidney handle the run-down meeting."

Josh nodded. "Yes, of course. Your daughter looked pretty sick when you brought her in this morning. You don't need to come back in today, we can handle it."

"Of course I'll be back. She's just got a cold." At her dressing room door, CC paused. Josh looked at her, expecting more orders.

"What are you waiting for? Get that thieving bitch on the line," she said, dismissing him impatiently. Patting her meticulous weave, CC waited for Josh to turn the corner. Then, looking around surreptitiously, she opened her dressing room door.

It was just as she'd left it. On her dressing table, a tube of Mocha Promises foundation still sat open after she'd hurriedly applied it that morning. She always did her own make-up, hair, and dress—she didn't trust the employees at the station to keep her secrets. Beneath her flawless complexion were dark, ugly blotches. Her ebony, bone-straight hair once belonged to a poor woman in India. Her ample breasts had cost her a small fortune.

She quickly straightened up the table. She hated for her workstation to be a mess, and that included her dressing room. She was known in the station to throw a fit when the staff left lipstick-rimmed coffee mugs on their own desks too long.

It took no time to organize her dressing table, but still her stomach felt antsy. She tried not to think about her daughter, Alizé, whose sniffling and whining had almost made CC miss the interview of a lifetime. Bigger than Mr. Combs and his new urbanwear.

She'd worked for a month to land that morning's story. "Soul Killa" was the latest designer drug flooding the port city of Norfolk, Virginia, and she'd had the first, groundbreaking interview about its devastating effects. It was with a woman whose thirteen-year-old son had just died from an overdose. The interview had gone perfectly. The woman had melted into tears on the set. CC made a point to hug the woman maternally and let her own eyes well up in sympathy. And then, out of nowhere, the woman had fingered her son's pusher. Said his name loud and clear. Live. On air.

Then she had followed that segment with an interview with Sean Combs. Wow. Her show had "Emmy" written all over it.

But the show almost hadn't happened. This was the morning that her seven-year-old brat, Alizé, had decided to pull another one of her stunts. Faking a cough just to get out of going to school, the kid had dragged her ass so slow she'd missed the school bus.

Selfish bitch, CC thought. *After all I do for her.*

She threw her BlackBerry into her saddle-colored Coach purse and began to gather up her notes for the next day's show. Suddenly she heard a tiny whimper. Her temper flaring, she got up and stomped to her coat closet, throwing the door open.

There, at the bottom of the closet beneath the coats, the seven-year-old sat holding her knees to her chest. She flinched as the door opened, raising her hands instinctively to protect herself.

My Blue Suede Shoes

"Didn't I tell you to shut the hell up?" CC whispered behind clenched teeth.

"I *was* being quiet, Mommy," said the child. "No one heard me in here, I promise."

CC could see that Alizé had been crying. *Good for her,* she thought. *I bet she won't miss that bus again!*

Sweat blotted the child's forehead, and her dark, brown eyes were sunken with fever. Her thick braids were fuzzy and unkempt. It had been days since CC had had time to re-braid them.

"Just get up," CC said. "I'm taking you home, and then I've got to get back to work. If I hear another peep out of you, I'll slap you to the middle of next year."

Suddenly there was a knock as Josh entered excitedly.

"Great news, CC! Aisha just called back and said she could show up. She said no one else is letting her tell her side of the story. I still have to talk to her attorney, but . . ."

Josh's voice trailed off as he looked from CC to the closet. What was the little girl doing in there? Instinctively, he took a step back, realizing he might have just crossed CC Smart—something no one ever got away with.

Caught off guard, CC quickly recouped. Seeing that her lapdog producer was already intimidated, she surprised him with graciousness.

"That's fantastic." She smiled plastically. Then, bending down, she helped Alizé to her feet. "When I came back in here, she was sound asleep on the floor. Poor thing! Must have nodded off after hanging up her coat. Feeling better, sweetie?"

Alizé nodded without making eye contact with Josh. She stood like a wooden toy soldier as CC bent and hugged her tightly.

"All right, Josh," said CC. "I have to get some food in her stomach. I'll be back in no time."

"That's okay, CC," Josh said. "She looks pretty sick. Maybe

we should plan a rerun tomorrow. Call me if you end up at the doctor's office."

CC spun around. "She's fine. I'll be right back—count on it."

CC quickly dumped her daughter off at home, microwaved a packet of ramen noodles, and gathered a change of clothes for the evening.

"Eat up; I've got to get back to work," she said. "And while I'm gone, drink plenty of liquids and stay in bed. Don't call me—I've got a meeting after work."

Back at work, she settled on the next day's guests and changed for the evening. Jumping into her sky blue Cadillac Roadster, she sped toward the waterfront.

For the blacks who lived in the port city of Norfolk, Virginia, history was full of shuffling and reshuffling of their destinies to suit whites. In the colonial period, the city had thrived on importing slaves from the West Indies and exporting the fruit of their labor—tobacco, peanuts, and cotton.

In the 1800s, Virginia had been unsure what to do with the growing number of free blacks in the state. In its first program of "Negro removal," the state decided to ship them all back to Africa. A Norfolk-born, black freeman, Joseph Jenkins Roberts, had made the best of it. He became the first president of the Republic of Liberia.

As she turned down Main Street, CC smiled to herself. Downtown Norfolk was undergoing a major redevelopment, which meant more Negro removal. But this time not all the Negroes were being broomed out. *This* Negro had gotten in on the ground floor of the funky, chic Gentry Square, with its ivy-covered lofts and renovated town houses.

Of course, not all Negroes were created equal. Her new, upscale neighborhood was still within walking distance of the projects. CC couldn't wait until they swept out all of the hood rats on Temple Street. Or maybe the low-lifes would destroy themselves with guns and drugs—that would save everyone the trouble. As soon as the projects were gone, her property values would skyrocket.

CC turned onto Waterside Drive and headed toward the new Ellington Hotel overlooking the Elizabeth River. A group of black investors had built the project and spared no expense. Now, only four years later, the gamble had paid off. The Ellington was the hub of the city's political and social life. It also had the metro area's only five-star restaurant, the Poseidon.

The ladies' lounge at the Poseidon was swirling with Caribbean blue glass, mosaic tiles, and sleek stainless steel. CC leaned carefully over the sink, trying not to let the splashes of water on the counter stain the front of her coral Donna Karan jacket.

"Sloppy bitches," she muttered, tossing back the thick fall of her weave.

The dark-skinned, heavy-set restroom attendant stood against the wall, her bored eyes surrounded by plump moles. When CC cast her an impatient glance, the older woman jumped to attention and swabbed the area with a thick terry towel embroidered with the symbol of Poseidon—a pitchfork.

Satisfied, CC shooed the old woman away, then pulled her sequined cosmetic bag from her evening clutch. The reception for the new chairman of the board of TechTel was in full swing outside. He was reputed to be an elegant man, one of the few African-American CEOs of a Fortune 500 company. *Black and single—ripe for the picking,* CC thought as she eyed her face in the mirror.

Carefully, she painted Lovesick Ruby lip color along the Cupid's bow of her mouth, then dabbed the pout of her bottom lip with Sunrise Shimmer. She blew herself a kiss and smiled with satisfaction. The lounge attendant stared at her in the mirror, but when CC caught her eye, the woman looked down at her shoes.

Spritzing herself with Invitation, CC closed her purse, satisfied. On her way out of the lounge, she tossed a five-dollar tip on the floor. She didn't wait to see if the attendant bent down to pick it up.

Outside, the room buzzed. Even though the Poseidon was full of Norfolk's elite, the crowd parted for CC, the statuesque black woman who'd dared to wear a coral-red pantsuit to the business reception. She ruled over the room like Nefertiti, pausing every few steps to plant mock kisses on the cheeks of the deal makers and power brokers.

"CC!" fawned Joe Hudsen, the chief of police. "Nice show today."

She smiled as if he vaguely pained her. "Do something about that Soul Killa stuff flooding the streets, Joe. If not, I'm going to have you answer for it on my show."

The chief's face went red, and his affable grin disappeared. He solemnly patted CC on the shoulder as others watched the exchange with amusement. No one ever knew where CC Smart would plant her fangs. He laughed nervously. "CC, you're always on the job!"

"CC! Glad you could come!" gushed the bubbly Jeannie Chambers. As TechTel's public relations hack, Chambers had pulled the reception together. "Have you met our new chairman yet?"

"I was working my way toward him." CC cast a sidelong glance at the police chief and added, "I got sidetracked."

Chambers enthusiastically took CC by the arm and pulled her to the front of the queue that had lined up to meet the new CEO. "He's going to need an introduction to Norfolk's black community," said the veteran publicist. "I want you to think about having him on *Breakin' It Down.* He's awesome on television. Not only is he handsome, he's—"

CC felt the vibration of her cell phone beneath her jacket. Her heart leapt—maybe it was her producer, giving her a heads-up on breaking news for her show tomorrow.

When she looked at the number, she froze. It was Alizé.

CC's mood darkened as she tucked the phone away without answering it. That child was like an anvil around her neck. It seemed she had a sixth sense—every time CC was about to have fun, do a blockbuster interview, or meet the unmarried head of a Fortune 500 company, Alizé had a way of throwing up roadblocks.

"CC?" Jeannie Chambers called. "This is Maxwell Cortland. Mr. Cortland, this is the hottest media personality in town: CC Smart."

CC tried not to gaze too long at the smooth butterscotch of the man's clean-shaven head, the seductive amber of his eyes, and the sexy fit of his Brooks Brothers suit. "Pleased to meet you, Max," she cooed.

CC watched as his eyes, nearly glazed from shaking so many hands at the reception, suddenly locked upon her. No one else in the room had dared to call the multi-millionaire anything other than Mr. Cortland.

"The pleasure's all mine," he said, bowing slightly, his hands resting comfortably in his pockets.

"Allow me to give you a *real* introduction to Norfolk," CC said. "You know where to find me—I'm at WAVE-TV 22."

He nodded, a smile playing around his smooth lips. Like a viper, CC knew exactly when to strike and when to retreat. Without another word, she walked away, her ample hips swaying in her wake. She knew without looking that his eyes were glued to her backside.

Her phone vibrated again. CC made a grand gesture of pulling it from her pocket, hammering home how important she was. Who else would dare chat on the phone at such an important event? But seeing it was her daughter again, she silenced her cell.

Alizé would pay for this.

The child had already missed school pretending to be sick. When CC was dropping her back home this morning, she'd noticed how Alizé had perked up at the hope of them spending a "sick day" at home together. Further proof that the child was just faking illness to get attention.

"How do you feel now?" CC had asked as Alizé slurped the last of the noodles.

Making her way to the bar, CC remembered how Alizé had put down the bowl slowly, grinned like a clown, and said sweetly, "I feel better, Mommy."

Furious, CC had slapped the bowl from Alizé's hand. The child's eyes bulged wide as she dropped to the floor, shrieking. "If you feel so good then why did you pull that stunt this morning?" CC had screamed. "You could have made me miss the biggest story this year! What the hell is wrong with you?"

"I'm sorry, Mommy!" the seven-year-old cried. "I thought I was sick!"

"You thought? You *thought*? Well, look, bitch. There's no one but me to pay the bills around here. If you want a roof over your head, then you play hooky on your own time. Got that?"

The child had remained on the floor, curled up like a trembling bug, while CC threw the bowl in the sink. To punish Alizé, she had herded her to her bedroom and wedged a chair beneath the knob.

"If you're so sick, get in the bed and stay there until I get back," CC commanded.

"What if I have to use the bathroom?"

"Hold it until I get home. If you can't respect my needs, then why should I give a damn about yours?"

Once at the bar, CC ordered a cosmopolitan because it matched her outfit. She tried not to think about Alizé's bogus phone calls interrupting her important work at the party.

"Great show today," came a voice over her shoulder.

CC looked up to find Reverend Marcus Turner peering at her. With his outdated salt-and-pepper Afro, he was the head of Mt.

Olive A.M.E., a small black congregation on Temple Street. The reverend had been leading protests against the gentrification of Norfolk's downtown, arguing for more affordable housing rather than high-priced town houses like CC's. She had never met him in person and wondered how a jack-leg preacher even got on the guest list for the reception.

"Thanks," she said drolly, taking her drink and scanning the room for a better conversation.

"Hope you stay on the issue. Drugs are tearing our community apart."

"I know," CC said. She waved enthusiastically at the head of the school board.

"You have a lot of power," the reverend said, blocking her escape. "You have to understand how to use it."

She smiled curtly and scurried away. But for some reason, his words sent a shiver through her.

Power? CC knew she had power, but deep down, she wondered who she'd be without it. Power made people fawn over her, indulge her, applaud her. But how many people truly cared about her for who she was inside?

Suddenly the party wasn't fun anymore. CC refused offers for a nightcap at Tobacco Row. Instead, she gave the valet a twenty-dollar bill and drove her Roadster home.

Arriving at her two-story brick town house, CC could see something wasn't right. Lights were on all over the house. If Alizé was still locked in her room, who had turned them on?

She was rattling the keys at the front door when it opened by itself. Shocked, CC looked up. "Lola? What are you doing here?"

"Where the hell have you been? We've been trying to reach you all night!" CC's mother, Lola Smart, opened the door wider. Her gray hair was tussled and her tea-colored complexion had gone sallow.

"Where's Alizé ?" CC asked.

"She called me on her cell phone and I caught the bus over here right away. She was where you left her, barricaded in her room. She'd vomited all over her bedcovers, poor thing. And her temperature was one hundred and two."

CC hid her shame with heightened concern. "Alizé? Alizé!" she called from the living room. "Are you all right, honey?"

"She's sleep now, Cornelia. I changed her sheets and gave her some medicine."

CC turned to her mother. Suddenly she felt like a child herself, small, backward, and unworthy. "Why didn't anyone tell me?" she whispered.

Lola scoffed and shook her head. "Alizé said she tried to call you on your cell phone, but no one answered. Eventually she called me. She couldn't get out of the room to even let me into the house to help her. Good thing her latchkey is hidden outside."

It was too much, going from the heady reception where everyone feared and respected her to this moment, where everything was CC's fault. "Alizé plays games, Lola. We both know that. I had no idea that she was really sick."

Lola shook her head but held her tongue. CC angrily took off her three-inch Ferragamos. Muttering, she confronted her mother. "Don't even talk to me about what I should have done," she seethed. "You don't know what I go through with that child every day. She's so headstrong and manipulative. I'm doing the best I can."

"By leaving a sick seven-year-old in lockdown? Baby, why didn't you just call me if you needed someone to watch her this evening?"

It was more than CC could stand. "*Baby*? I'm not your baby, so don't call me that, Lola. I'm not going to take a lecture on motherhood from a crack-head. Got that?"

Lola sat down, resigned. It was an old argument, one that she was tired of having. "Cornelia, look at me," she said quietly. "I can't do anything to change the past. I was a bad mother. I was an addict. I can't make that up to you—ever. I've been clean for twenty years. I'm here for you now, and I can be here for Alizé. You just have to let me in."

CC sat deliberately on the sofa and clutched a pillow. She rocked gently, trying to not to come undone. She wanted to beat Lola, blacken her eyes, close her fingers around her throat.

She tried counting silently to herself. She was frightened by the volcano inside of her that was constantly on the verge of exploding. Her feelings were getting harder to control, more explosive and instantaneous. With every promotion, every five-hundred-dollar suit, every man whom she lured and threw away, she'd thought she'd finally transcended that the dark spot on her soul.

But the darkness always resurged. No matter how much Cristal champagne she sipped from Waterford flutes, memories still haunted her of eating federally-funded breakfasts during the school year—and scrounging the hot, putrid city garbage for food in the summer. No matter how many Louis Vuitton handbags she owned, she couldn't shake the terror of not knowing whether her mother would return home this week, or the next. No matter how many vacations to Turks and Caicos with rich boyfriends, she could not erase the night the officials came to her doorstep to throw her into foster care.

No matter how many liars and self-righteous hypocrites she exposed on her show, she couldn't hide the truth of her own life: The great, refined, educated, confident, hard-hitting, award-winning CC Smart was the just the nappy-headed, skinny, discarded, unlovable daughter of a crack whore. She didn't even know her father's name.

"Cornelia? You all right?" Lola asked, biting her nails nervously.

Was she all right? No. No, she wasn't. But she didn't need the help of the woman who'd abandoned her when she was ten. "You can leave now," CC said robotically. "I can handle it from here."

Lola hesitated a moment, then smoothed the wrinkled cotton of her housedress. "All right, then," she said. "Whenever you need me, I'm a phone call away. Any time of day or night. You just call me, hear?"

Those were words she used to long to hear from her mother. But now they only struck anger and resentment. "Get out," she whispered.

Lola left, closing the door quietly as if she were escaping a sleeping tiger. As soon as she was gone, CC melted into tears. Afraid of her own sadness, she wiped them away as quickly as they came. Picking up her shoes, she tread quietly upstairs.

She listened for a moment outside her daughter's bedroom, then tiptoed in. The room smelled of bile, sweat, and the Vicks VapoRub that Lola had slathered on to help the child breathe. CC put her hand on Alizé's forehead; it was sticky with heat. She reached above Alizé's yellow-ruffled bed and pulled back the curtain to open the window. A faint breeze wafted inland from the river, encircling the room. Alizé stirred in her sleep.

CC leaned over the child, tempted to plant a gentle kiss on her cheek. But some jealous part of her soul wouldn't let her. Instead, she left the room feeling sad. As she took one last look before closing the door, she noticed how the moonlight cast a pearly glow across Alizé's gingerbread skin. With her thick curl of innocent lashes, the child reminded CC of herself thirty years before, holding tightly to slumber—the only time she'd ever felt safe.

Chapter TWO

Josh Clark knocked on the dressing room door. "Ms. Smart? Twenty minutes. Do you want to talk to the guest before we go on?"

Inside the dressing room, CC dabbed the sweat that beaded on her brow. She'd barely slept after the encounter with her mother. She wished the witch would stay out of her life, but ever since she'd adopted Alizé, Lola had been trying to push her way back in. What did she think this was, "Big Mama's Family"?

That morning, Alizé was still asleep and feverish when CC got up for work. She'd meditated for twenty minutes, trying not to let her daughter's illness push her over the edge. When the housekeeper, Dorethea, arrived, she gave her the health insurance card and fifty dollars.

"Take a cab to the doctor's office if Alizé looks worse," CC said. "I've got to get to work, but I'll call you later."

Dorethea had been hesitant, but CC darted out before she could ask any questions. At work, she'd tried to calm the anxious palpitations of her heart with a nip of vodka. The alcohol just made her sweat.

"I'm coming, Josh!" CC yelled through the closed door. "Chill out."

She swished out her mouth with Scope, hoping to mask the alcohol, then went to the green room. Inside sat Aisha Robinson. When CC saw how distraught the woman was, her own nerves subsided and her confidence burgeoned. This was going to be easy.

Aisha stood when CC opened the door. "Thanks for having me here," the guest said meekly. Her black, velvet skin was streaked with tears. She was skinny as a runway model, giving her the unfortunate appearance of one of those large-headed, wide-eyed waifs on the Save the Children infomercials.

The wife of Heisman Trophy winner Lenard Robinson, Aisha had once waited tables while hoping to break into show business. Her marriage to the talented running back for the Baltimore Ravens was like a Cinderella story. While her husband traveled, she remained in Norfolk where she'd been raised. Now she was a socialite, sitting on boards of hospitals and children's philanthropies.

It was a shock to the community when she was arrested inside Saks with three thousand dollars in clothes and jewelry stuffed into her Gucci travel bag. At first she claimed that she'd picked up the wrong purse in the dressing room, but the store security cameras told another story.

A top-flight lawyer had gotten the charges bumped down to petty larceny. After receiving probation, Aisha had disappeared from public sight. Now she was back, speaking for the first time about what happened.

And it was all on *Breakin' It Down*. Another coup for CC Smart.

CC took the woman's hand. "Thank you for coming," she said sweetly. "You're very brave. I know this is a hard time for you, but people are waiting to hear your story. You'll help so many with your courage."

The woman nodded and followed CC onto the set. As soon as the camera came on, CC snapped into her television persona—the fearless, confident journalist who told it like it was.

She deftly allowed Aisha to start the story where she was comfortable. The quick rise to the top. The pressures of celebrity. The terrible fear of success. The miscarriage and grief. The thrill of stealing little things. The way it made her feel alive again.

"It wasn't about money," Aisha said, weeping openly while CC held her hand. "I was so lost, so sad. I stole things for the high of getting away with it. I just wanted to feel something again."

CC listened, but the story didn't ring true for her. CC herself had experienced much of what Aisha Robinson had been through: a meteoric rise from the bottom, a public lifestyle, money. But she never ripped off department stores. She never pretended to be an upstanding pillar of the community while catching a case for stealing.

"Are you saying that you aren't responsible for what you did?" CC asked.

Taken aback, Aisha stopped sniffling. "No! I'm just trying to—"

"What kind of role model do you think you are? Are you telling children that if you're rich, you can get by with anything?"

Blindsided, Aisha stiffened. "I didn't come here to make excuses, CC. I'm here to shed light on a problem that countless Americans have. Kleptomania—"

"Were you sick or just greedy? When you were arrested, you had seven hundred dollars in cash in your purse and platinum credit cards. Why would someone who has everything steal?"

"That's what I'm trying to say, it's not about the money—"

"No, it's not. It's about being ghetto. In your mind, you're still that tacky girl from the Bay End Projects with a gangsta mentality. What you can't afford, you'll take."

From a hidden reservoir, Aisha pulled upon a store of poise. She stared silently at CC, then said quietly, "You know, CC, I've been in rehab for a month trying to figure out why I've hit rock bottom. You might be right. Maybe feeling like I didn't deserve all the good things that happened to me was part of it. Maybe that's because of the poverty I grew up in. That's no excuse. And that's what I'm here to tell all of my supporters, my friends, my family, and most of all the kids who look up to me and my husband. You can rise above your circumstances, but you have to do it by honest, hard work and by sticking to your values. You don't have to steal, lie, or cheat."

"Thank you, Aisha," CC said. Then she turned to the camera. "And thank you for watching. I'm CC Smart, breakin' it down."

No sooner had the camera shut off than the audience erupted in applause. As interns led the audience out of the studio, Josh bounded over to congratulate her. "Good job, CC!"

CC beamed and turned to shake Aisha's hand, but the woman turned her back and regally left the set. Shrugging, CC patted her producer on the back. "Excellent job, Josh! You keep this up, and we'll have a network show one day!"

"Thank you, Ms. Smart."

"CC, that was brilliant," said A. J. O'Connor, the executive producer. "I watched the whole interview from the control room. Hard-hitting, pointed—you didn't let her off the hook. I can't wait to see the ratings."

CC beamed as O'Connor turned to the staff. "Okay, everyone, since it's Friday, lunch is on me! But be back to work this afternoon—you've got another show on Monday!"

On cloud nine, CC strutted back to her desk to check her fan mail. The adrenaline of the show, the applause, the staff adoration all made her mood soar. She felt electric and invincible.

Her thoughts suddenly turned to the handsome CEO, Maxwell Cortland. She wondered how long it would take him to contact her. Closing her eyes, she imagined his broad shoulders and full lips.

The chime of her cell phone jarred her out of her reverie.

"Missus Smart?" It was her housekeeper, Dorethea. "I'm with Alizé at the hospital. I done what you told me. She was so weak this morning she could hardly eat, so I brought her in. The doctors need to talk to you . . ."

This was not her daughter's hysteria or her mother's meddling. This was the real thing. CC grabbed her purse and scurried for the car.

CC arrived at the emergency room and demanded to see Alizé immediately. When she reached the child's side, she wasn't prepared for what she saw. Alizé lay with a tube in her nose, struggling to breathe. Her light brown skin had gone gray.

"Oh, Dorethea!" she gasped, covering her mouth.

The stoic housekeeper got up and relinquished her bedside seat. "She kept asking for you, Missus Smart," Dorethea said. "I told her you'd get here soon."

CC reached over and pushed back one of her daughter's braids. "Alizé? Darling, can you hear me? Mommy's here now." Alizé opened her eyes a sliver and faintly moved her head. "Yes, that's right," CC comforted. "I'm here now."

In that moment, CC thought about the day she'd first held Alizé in her arms. How, for the first time in her life, she'd felt complete. She'd had such high expectations that her new daughter would fill that empty place inside of her. Everyone said she was so brave to adopt a child on her own. Deep down, CC felt the baby was adopting *her,* choosing CC to be her mother. She'd never felt so wanted, so loved, so proud.

Over the years, the reality of parenting had set in. Alizé turned out to be needier than CC had imagined. Instead of feeling completed by a child, CC was depleted by the colicky infant. Over the years, the demands never let up. Alizé was a high-strung toddler, an inquisitive pre-schooler, and a whiny first-grader.

Now here Alizé was, swaddled again like a newborn, pliant and adoring. CC felt warmed by a wave of tenderness.

"Ms. Smart? The doctor will see you now," the nurse abruptly interrupted.

CC snatched some Kleenex from the bedside. "Okay," she sniffed. "Dorethea, thank you for bringing her in. I had no idea she was so ill. You're a blessing."

Dorethea nodded curtly. "Yes, ma'am. Do you want me to stay?"

"No, you can take the rest of the day off. Thanks again."

The nurse showed CC to the doctor's office. As she entered, she struggled to regain her composure. She felt off-balance, vulnerable.

Without so much as a "hello," the doctor dug right in. "Mrs. Smart, I have to tell you, I'm deeply concerned about your daughter's condition." The portly, pink-faced physician remained behind his desk. The office walls were plastered with diplomas and certificates.

There was something about his demeanor that raised her defenses. "I prefer Ms.," CC said, feeling a slight tinge of shame that she was still unmarried.

"Ms. Smart, then. Your daughter is seriously dehydrated. She's got pneumonia."

CC's eyes widened. Why hadn't Alizé told her how bad she was feeling? If only she'd known, she would have—

"Were you aware that she was ill when you left for work this morning, *Ms.* Smart?," placing emphasis on the *Ms.*

"Well, I knew that she had a stomach ache. That's why I—"

"I'm afraid that your housekeeper can't authorize treatment."

"Well, I—"

"It would have been better if you'd brought her in yourself."

What was this crazy man implying? Struggling to remain dignified, she answered calmly. "Dr. Tate, I adopted Alizé when she was a baby, and I'm a single parent," she said, trying to assuage any delusion that she was a trashy baby-mama. "I don't have a partner I can rely on. I had to go to work, so I made arrangements for my daughter to get the proper care until I could get here. Here I am. Is she going to be okay?"

"Well, I noticed some bruises on her back and buttocks."

CC's heart pounded. "She's at that age where her arms and legs are so gangly. I went through a clumsy period when I was a girl, too."

The doctor didn't look up at her but scribbled on Alizé's medical record instead. "And how old is she? Seven? She only weighs fifty pounds."

CC's laugh rang hollow. "She's so picky. I can't make her—"

"She's malnourished, Ms. Smart. We don't see a lot of that these days unless there's been some . . . problem."

CC froze. Was he trying to accuse her of abusing her daughter? Certainly she was a strict disciplinarian. And Alizé had always bruised easily. But abuse? No way. Could she help it if her daughter was so jittery that she often refused to eat? Or that Alizé wouldn't even bother to feed herself when CC worked long hours? What was she supposed to do—force-feed her?

CC stood up. "Dr. Tate, I don't know who you think you are, but obviously you don't know who I am. I'm CC Smart, the most powerful journalist in this town. What are you trying to accuse me of?"

"Ms. Smart, I need to ask you to take a seat." Already pink, the doctor's jowls went lobster red. "I'm not accusing you of anything. I just said—"

"I know what you said, Dr. Tate. Let me advise you to think twice about what you say about CC Smart. I'll have your license so quick you won't know what hit you."

Chapter THREE

From across the table, CC smiled coyly at Max Cortland. They sat in an isolated corner of the deck at the exclusive Lighthouse Bistro. As the sun set, the water of the Elizabeth River calmed. In the cobalt sky, the lonely evening star shimmered. A slight breeze lifted CC's gauzy yellow skirt.

"Cold?" Max asked, noting her involuntary shiver.

CC leaned toward him assuredly. "I could be warmer."

Laughing with his amber eyes, Max scooted his chair around to CC's side of the table, so that they both faced the lingering sunset. When he put his arm around her shoulders, she noticed he smelled like clean linen . . . with a hint of spice.

"Better?"

It was her turn to smile quietly. Better? How could he know that this was the best thing to happen to her in a long time?

Max had called her three nights after they'd met at the Ellington—just as CC had hoped. Her heart pounded with joy, but she'd played it cool. He asked her out, but she'd told him that Alizé was sick and she had to be home in the evenings. He'd hesitated awkwardly. CC knew that he was surprised that she had a child. Before he could speak, she added quickly: "It's just the two of us at home. I can't leave her alone."

CC heard Max sigh on the other end of the phone, relieved that she wasn't married. "Of course," he'd said graciously. "I hope she gets well soon. Call me when you can."

CC could hear his respect for her motherly devotion. It made the sacrifices of the past three weeks tolerable. Alizé had been such high maintenance since she came home from the hospital. It seemed that she was never going to get out of her miserable sick bed and get back to school. At night she coughed and moaned that her chest hurt. CC tried to be patient, keeping her daughter plied with liquids and antibiotics, just as the doctor ordered.

Seeing Alizé in the hospital bed had rattled her. Sometimes CC still got chills thinking about what would happen if she lost her daughter. She didn't want to be alone again, without anyone to love her.

But as Alizé slowly emerged from danger, CC felt herself stifled by the child's incessant demands: the sleepless nights, the thick sputum to clean up, the meals to fix. A tight knot of resentment lodged in the bottom of her stomach. Who had been there to take care of her when she'd been feverish with measles? No one. When was Alizé going to learn to hold her own?

Lola didn't help matters. She called nearly every day, checking on her granddaughter. CC took pleasure in telling her mother that Alizé was improving and that they didn't need her help. After each call, CC felt exhausted and angry.

Sometimes the pressure got to be too much. After working all day, she couldn't bear going home to the depressing, needy prison of her town house. She missed being able to go to happy hours or be the center of attention at a reception or chat with elected officials over dinner. After the first week, she began to worry she would fall off the public's radar.

More than once, she'd sped home, fed Alizé, spooned her medicine, then tip-toed out to the Power Basie, a jazz club near Ocean View. Last Sunday, she had left Alizé tossing in the bed while she attended early services at Greater Mt. Olive Baptist Church. What would folks say if she wasn't there sporting her latest Versace suit and Georgia Hughes hat?

After three weeks, Alizé had finally been able to go back to school, and CC had breathed a sigh of relief. "It's the end of September," she warned Alizé. "Put on a sweater, and don't take it off today."

"But Mom, it's seventy-five degrees outside!" Alizé had whined.

CC was at the end of her rope. The last thing she needed was for that kid to get sick again. "Do what I said!" she'd yelled as she jerked Alizé's arm into a shabby brown sweater. "I mean it."

The child—her limbs even thinner, her skin still the sickly color of dishwater—made herself a peanut butter sandwich, put it in her Hello Kitty lunch box, and moped off to school. Elated to finally get back to her regular schedule, CC drove her Roadster to work with the top down.

That day should have been a good one, but it went from bad to worse. On the show that morning, she grilled Chief Hudsen about why the department wasn't stopping the flow of Soul Killa into the city. He'd given her a condescending smile, then informed her that the City Council had just approved a three-million-dollar budget increase so that the police could address the problem. Taken aback, CC quickly recovered.

"I'm glad that I was able to put enough pressure on City Hall for you to get extra funds, Chief Hudsen," she'd said graciously. "You'll have to come back and let us know how Operation Save Our Souls is progressing."

As soon as the show was over, she tore the staff a new one for not doing their research. The senior producer was given thirty days to find another job.

That wasn't the end of it. She had to lay out Josh for not making sure her Evian had been refrigerated, then warmed back to room temperature. She could always tell when it hadn't been chilled properly by its slightly bitter taste. Then there was the lazy-ass intern who hadn't sorted her mail correctly.

When her cell phone rang late that afternoon, she barked, "CC Smart."

"Did you forget about me? Can you go to dinner tonight?"

It was Max. Suddenly, the pressures of her day melted away. She had yet to go out with him, but already his voice made her go soft on the inside. She was sure that, unlike the countless other jerks she'd dated in Norfolk, he was The One.

This time, she promised herself to take it slow. What was it that Marcus had said before he'd dumped her last year? "Your love is like quicksand. One toe in, and you suck a man all the way down to the bottom."

Those words had hurt, and she'd made Marcus pay for them. She'd gotten his office assistant to accuse him of sexual harassment on *Breakin' It Down*. Not the kind of press you're looking for when you're Norfolk's leading gynecologist.

Still, his angry words had made her reconsider her strategy when it came to men. "I'm not free tonight," she had lied to Max. "How about Thursday?"

So there they were, almost a month after their first meeting at the Poseidon, sitting on the river on a late-summer night, the stars now dotting the darkening sky. His strong arms made her feel small. Safe. Loved.

"Whatchu thinking about?" he asked, sipping a latte.

Her heart fluttered. She couldn't let him know what she was really feeling. Men never wanted to know what was on her mind. Every time she told them, they ran away.

She sat up rigidly, forcing him to remove his arm from her shoulder. Turning to face him, she deflected his bid for intimacy. "I was wondering the same thing. What's on *your* mind, Mr. Cortland? Do you miss all the ladies you left behind in New York?"

From interviewing hundreds of people in her career, CC could sense when a question hit the soft underbelly. The corner of his mouth twitched slightly. His eyes went flat, as if he were hiding behind a memory.

Son of a bitch is married, CC thought. She felt her spirit shrivel. Thanking God she hadn't let him make a fool out of her, she gathered her embroidered lemon meringue shawl. "I guess I should go."

She started to stand, but Max took her wrist and pulled her back to her seat. She wanted to resist him, beat him with her shoe, scratch his eyes out. But he took her hands in his, brought them to his lips, and kissed them gently. When he looked at her again, she noticed how his eyes were shimmering in the candlelight.

"My wife died last year," he said softly. "Breast cancer. I'd known her since we were in college." He swallowed deeply, then went on. "We had a brownstone in Manhattan, and it was such a lonely place after she was gone. We never had kids." He smiled ruefully. "I always wanted them, but between the investment bank and her charitable work for children with AIDS, she was too busy.

"I couldn't stand the empty house without her. I decided to move our offices down here, where I'd grown up. At least I could go fishing, sit on the beach," he smiled sheepishly, "and maybe meet a nice southern girl."

CC was dumbstruck. His openness was both welcoming and shocking, like the cold splash of the Atlantic on an August day.

As someone who had been lied to much of her life, CC knew raw honesty when she heard it. She thought she craved it, but now that it was in front of her, it felt too big. "I—I didn't know," she stammered.

"Don't feel bad," he said. "I thought you'd heard—you always have the scoop on everybody. The moment I met you, you reminded me so much of Carolyn. Your drive, your power, your commitment to correcting injustices with your show. And you also have a daughter. That takes even more dedication."

"She's adopted," CC blurted. It was important to let him know that she was even nobler that Max had imagined—and that there was no baby daddy waiting in the wings.

"Adopted?" Max nodded as if she'd just confirmed his deepest suspicions. "That's just like you, isn't it?" he said.

The sun dipped below the horizon as an electric silence buzzed between them. Max reached for her face to draw her close, CC took his hand and moved it to her waist. Feeling his soft lips against hers, she thought about how perfect she was for him.

And how she had kept him from discovering, at least for the moment, the sewn-in tracks of her fake hair.

"Ms. Smart, here's your mail," said the squeaky blond intern. "Just the way you asked me. Personal mail here, unopened. I opened your fan mail and responded to most of it. Here are your invitations to speak—I'll schedule the ones you want to accept."

CC nodded, barely looking up from her computer screen. She noticed that the intern wasn't going away. "Put everything over there" She waved at a clear spot on her well-ordered desk.

"Um, well, where do you want me to put this one? I thought it was junk mail, and I accidentally opened it."

CC stopped typing. The intern's eyes widened, as if she'd

just knocked on the door of the Wicked Witch of the West. Whenever CC detected cowardice in someone, it always tempted her to squash them. Or at least say "Boo!" to see them scurry away.

Not this time. As the intern nervously held out the opened envelope, CC felt a gathering dread. "Thanks, Emily," she said. "I'll take that."

The intern handed CC the letter and skirted away. CC slid it into her suit pocket, then took her mug of organic dark roast and strode to her dressing room. Behind closed doors, she sat in front of the mirror and read the letter.

"Dear Cornelia Smart," it said. "We have tried to contact you at your home address without success. This letter is to inform you that you have defaulted on your equity loan. If you do not pay the $50,000 loan in full within 30 days, we will begin foreclosure proceedings. Please contact our office immediately."

The room was suddenly hot. Beads of sweat mottled her Mocha Promises foundation. She lifted the dark hair from her neck and fanned herself with the letter.

She'd bought in on the ground floor of the Gentry Square redevelopment. In fact, when it became widely known that she lived there, Norfolk's buppies flocked to the urban outpost. The value of her home had doubled in only a few years. Why not take out an equity loan to buy the Cadillac Roadster that she deserved?

She'd meant to save some of the money for Alizé's private school tuition, but she'd had to refresh her on-air wardrobe. Plus, after the show had gone from weekly to daily, she'd started taking *real* vacations. One year, she'd gone by herself to São Paulo, another year to Paris, maxing out her credit cards. The interest rates kept climbing right when Alizé's tuition became due. Because of that brat, she was buried in debt.

She'd managed to rob Peter to pay Paul, but she couldn't keep up with the payment. CC partied less. Stayed out of Saks. Actually wore a gown that she'd worn last year to a fundraiser. Sold some of her jewelry. She tried to catch up on past-due mortgage payments. But the bills kept climbing.

Now the pressure was mounting, but she refused to buckle. She would think of something. She fired Dorethea, pretending to be unhappy with the way the woman dusted. She thought about pulling Alizé from the expensive Norfolk Country Day School, where the tuition was a small ransom. But that would raise eyebrows. Above all else, she had to keep up appearances.

In the two months that they had been dating, CC had thought several times about telling Max her problems. Certainly he'd have connections in the financial community who could bail her out. Then she remembered how much he admired his wife's acumen as an investment banker; she didn't want to seem stupid by comparison.

Now they were going to foreclose on her house. She wondered if that skinny little intern had read the letter before giving it to her. CC's body went hot, like she'd been struck with a bolt of lightning. What if the intern blabbed it to the rest of the staff?

CC looked for a bottle of water, but there was none in her dressing room. She stomped to the door. *"Josh!"* she yelled. Her producer came running. "What did I tell you about my water?"

"Sorry, CC," he said. "We were done with the taping for today. I didn't know you'd need more water this afternoon."

"What, am I only allowed one sip a day? Am I supposed to go around here like a camel?"

"No, no, of course not. I'll be right back."

"Shit. Forget it," she said, fanning herself furiously. "Look, I have another question. What do you think about that intern?"

"Who, Emily? She's great. She's studying journalism at William and Mary. Smart girl—"

"I don't like her," CC said. "She keeps going through my personal mail. I've asked her a thousand times, and look!" CC held out the opened envelope.

"Well, I'm sure we can work that out. If you want, I'll deal with your mail, Ms. Smart. I'll handle it."

"Damn straight you will," CC said. "Fire her."

Chapter FOUR

Max stood with CC on the brick steps of her town house. A chilly drizzle fell in the night. "Aren't you going to invite me in?" he asked.

CC's heart clutched. She loved the way Max adored her. But now, more than two months into their relationship, he was pressuring her. "I told you, Max, I don't want Alizé to see me with men. Not until I'm sure about us."

"How much surer do you have to be?" he asked impatiently. "CC, we've been dating since September. You won't even sleep with me. I'm a grown man, I have needs."

She wanted nothing more than to wake up in the morning with Max Cortland in her bed. In fact, a quick marriage might end all of her financial woes. But how could she sleep with him and let him touch her fake breasts, fondle her fake hair, see her without makeup? Would he still love her?

She needed to string him out longer until she was sure about him. To get him to ease up, she summoned fat teardrops. "Max, please," she sniffed. "You're just getting over the death of your wife, and I have a daughter to raise. This is all too soon."

He kissed her gently in the autumn rain. "Okay, Ms. Smart. I'll never be accused of coming between mother and child. But I'm warning you, there are a lot of women beating down my door. I can't wait forever."

He held her close, and she didn't want him to let go. "Good night," he said solemnly. "I love you."

She stood on the porch and waved as he drove away. Fumbling with her keys, she let herself inside.

At once, the smell of old potato peels, bacon grease, and rotting bananas assaulted her. She hung up her coat in the front closet and kicked off her shoes so that she would be able to find them there later. Shuffling through inches of discarded mail, magazines, and old grocery bags littering the floor, she made her way to the kitchen.

Standing at the sink was Alizé. Even though it was past midnight, the child was still in her school uniform, trying to wash the mountain of dishes that had accumulated over the past weeks.

"Mommy!" she exclaimed. "I wanted to surprise you!"

CC looked forlornly around the kitchen. Open boxes of Kellogg's Corn Flakes, pizza boxes, tuna fish cans, yogurt cups, and pots dried red with spaghetti sauce littered the floor, counter tops, and table. The sight of it all made CC feel sick. "I wish you had started earlier," she mumbled. "I'm going to bed." CC slogged through the trash, dirty clothes, and rotting food that covered nearly every inch of the house.

"Okay, Mommy," Alizé chirped. "I'm going to wash *allll* of these!"

Things had started to get out of control as soon as she'd let Dorethea go. Her worries over money, the stress of work, and the pressure of her relationship with Max had made her shut down. It was all she could do every day just to keep up appearances. Once at home, she ate out of cans and dropped them on the floor. She took off clothes but never had the energy to clean them. She ordered Chinese take out, but didn't bother to throw away the empty cartons. Every day, she promised herself that she'd clean up the next day. That day never came.

The mess had accumulated so gradually, it was out of hand before she knew it was happening. Now she just told herself that it didn't matter. Who cared about the dust, the ants, the smell? As long as she looked good when she left the house, it was nobody's business what lay behind closed doors.

In her bedroom, she pushed aside a stack of magazines and flopped down, fully dressed. The last thought she had before falling to sleep was "I have to buy some new clothes."

On Monday morning, CC got up extra early. These days it took more time to get ready, since she had to sniff through several garments before finding anything wearable. Coordinating her shoes and purses had become impossible. Instead, she stuck to a single pair of basic black Pradas and matching purse. That would work until spring arrived. And because most of the food in the kitchen was spoiled, she had to allow time to stop on the way for coffee and a muffin.

"Alizé!" CC called from her bathroom, where she stood on moldy towels and dirty Kleenex while putting on her make-up. "You'd better get to the bus stop!"

In the mirror, she caught the reflection of Alizé standing behind her, tears streaking down her face.

"What now, Alizé?"

"I don't have any clean underwear."

"How is that my problem?" CC grilled the seven-year-old. "Did you do laundry?"

"I didn't have any money. And there's no detergent."

Her daughter's words stung like an accusation. CC's blood boiled. "Look, bitch, if you want clean clothes then clean them! I'm trying to hold this family together, for Christ's sake. Can't you do anything for yourself?"

Alizé backed away from the door. "I'm sorry, Mommy. I can just wear some dirty panties."

"Oh, no you can't," CC said, furious. "You put on your uniform and go without any underwear. That'll teach you to do your laundry!"

Alizé began weeping. "Please, Mommy, I'll do my laundry after school! I promise. I can't go to school without underwear. What will I do in gym class if my skirt flies up?"

"Tough shit," CC said, putting finishing touches on her blush. "You should have thought about that all weekend."

"Please, Mommy . . ."

"Shut the hell up, Alizé! I'm sick of your constant whining! Go put on your uniform. I'm waiting. And you'd better not put on any underwear."

The little girl scampered to her room. CC waited at the front door, tapping her foot impatiently. "Hurry the hell up! I've got to get to work!"

Alizé, dressed in her rumpled uniform, walked slowly into the kitchen. CC watched as her daughter rummaged through the trash on the floor and found a half-eaten apple and an old slice of pizza. She wrapped them gingerly in a used plastic bag and put them in her lunch box. "Okay, I'm ready," she said, pulling on her jacket. Her long braids were frizzy and full of lint.

"Let me see," CC said.

"What?"

"Let me see."

Tears flowing anew and her face blushing red, Alizé slowly lifted her skirt to reveal her bare body.

"Okay," CC said. "You're going to school like that for a week. You have to learn to live with the consequences of your actions. Now get out there and catch your bus. And stop that stupid sniveling."

CC drove happily to work with the radio blaring in her convertible. For some reason she felt powerful again—like an athlete after a good, hard run.

The director's fingers silently counted down: Three, two, one!

"This is CC Smart, and you're watching *Breakin' It Down*. Today, a groundbreaking interview. The whole city was shaken last year when Tidewater High's star girls' basketball player, Tameka Johnson, was gunned down in a drive-by shooting. It was the night they'd won the state championships. Tameka was popular, beautiful, and headed for the University of Virginia. Instead, she was buried in her basketball uniform.

"Pressure from my show has caused the police to focus on the ravages of the dangerous drug Soul Killa. Last week, they arrested Tameka's killers. Evidently, the suspects had been targeting Tameka's mother, Keisha Johnson. Keisha was a Soul Killa addict and prostitute who owed her pushers money. She was devastated by her daughter's murder. Since then, she's gotten clean and has formed an organization at the Bay End Projects to help get the drug off of the streets.

"Join me in welcoming Keisha Johnson to the show!"

The studio audience clapped as Keisha came onto the stage. CC looked her up and down. *She's from the same ghetto where Lola lives,* she thought. *The same place I grew up.* The woman was wearing tattered tennis shoes, threadbare slacks, and a Tidewater Mermaids sweatshirt. Her hair was in tight, neat cornrows. As CC smoothed out her new Oscar de la Renta skirt, she wished she'd made the woman go through wardrobe. Keisha Johnson was making the set look bad.

"Keisha, how does it feel to be responsible for your own daughter's death?" CC asked bluntly.

The woman looked down humbly. "I can't sleep at night. Every time I close my eyes, I think about Tameka. I pray and ask God why He took her and let me live."

"Good question," said CC, wondering what Lola had been thinking those many dark nights she'd left CC alone at home. "Why *did* God let you live?"

"I will have to answer to God for that one day," said Keisha. She had a quiet self assuredness that made CC angry. This woman was a whore, an addict, and a murderer. What right did she have to sit on this stage and be so righteous?

Slowly, the woman continued, "The only way I can make sense of what I've done is to make sure it doesn't happen to another child. That's why I've formed a group of volunteers. We're patrolling the Bay End Projects and offering kids after-school programs . . ."

CC could barely hear what the woman was saying. She was taken back to the moment when she was almost sixteen and Lola had come to claim her from foster care. By then CC had been tossed from foster family to foster family for six years. Six years of forgotten birthdays, hopeless Christmases, school plays where no one was in the audience to clap for her. Six years of empty chairs at mother-daughter luncheons, father-daughter dances, and parent-teacher conferences.

How did Lola think she'd ever make up for that?

Josh's voice came to her through the Telex in her ear. "Ask her how the viewers can support her programs!"

CC jumped slightly, then recovered her composure. "That's interesting, Keisha," CC said. "And what if my viewers want to help? What can they do?"

Back in the saddle, CC listened as the woman asked for the public's support.

"Thank you, Keisha," said CC. "That's our show for today. This is CC Smart, breakin' it down."

As the members of the audience rose to their feet, CC bowed. The applause surged as Keisha Johnson waved good-bye. "Good luck, Keisha!" someone roared. "You go girl!" someone else called out.

Annoyed, CC waved for the engineers to come take off their mics. She gave Keisha a brusque handshake, but the woman wouldn't let her hand go.

"Ms. Smart?" she said hesitantly, holding out a gift-wrapped box. "I brought you a present to thank you for having me on the show. I've heard so much about you. I always wanted to meet you."

CC's irritation softened. "You didn't have to bring me a gift," she breathed. "Why don't you come to my private dressing room?"

As they entered, CC noticed the extra bottles of Evian. Josh's job was safe for another day. "Would you like some water?" she offered.

"Uh, no thanks, ma'am," Keisha said, gazing around the room as if she'd just entered a shrine.

CC looked at her watch. "So what can I do for you?"

To her horror, the woman sat down on the sea foam sectional sofa and placed the gift on the coffee table. *Is this woman about to kick back and make herself at home?* CC wondered. *I have important things to do!*

"I keep thinking the pain will stop," Keisha said, "but it doesn't. And to make matters worse, I don't drink or do drugs to numb out anymore. I have to live fully with what I've done."

CC wasn't listening. Instead, she wondered what was inside the box. *Probably something tacky,* she thought. *Why doesn't she get to the point?*

"In some ways, I didn't know any better," Keisha continued sadly. "My mother pimped me out for drugs when I was only thirteen. I got pregnant with Tameka when I was sixteen. She never really had a chance, but she was making it. She was a star." Giant tears slid down the woman's face. "I never missed any of her games. Even when I was high."

CC felt an unexpected clutch in her throat as the woman continued.

"When Tameka got accepted to college, I quit the street. I was going to be the mother of a college graduate. On that day, I wanted her to be as proud of me as I was of her. So I quit. And you know what? Tameka supported me. She opened her arms wide and told me—" the woman's voice cracked— "even though I didn't deserve it, she told me that she loved me.

"The next day, she was dead. It was her birthday. Some thug-life pusher gunned her down because he was mad at me for getting out."

The woman was weeping now, but beneath her sorrow, there was a sliver of pride. "You asked me out there why I go on living. Tameka told me she loved me. That's the reason I've chosen to continue living."

CC felt weak-kneed. There it was again. The hard, unflinching face of truth. The kind of refreshing honesty that CC craved with her soul. Yet when she was in the presence of truth, it always filled her with terror.

Off balance, she sat down beside the woman. Why hadn't she noticed before how much Keisha's eyes reminded her of Lola's?

"You've done a great service to me and to the children of Bay End," Keisha continued, wiping away her tears with the back of her hand. "If there's anything I can ever do for you, just let me know. I'm sorry for taking up so much of your time. I just wanted you to have these. I had bought them for Tameka's birthday. I can't bear to look at this box anymore, and I thought maybe you could just keep it. Keep it to remind yourself of how blessed you are. You still have your daughter to cherish."

The woman handed CC the gift, then left quietly. When CC lifted the lid, inside was a brand-new pair of blue suede tennis shoes.

After Keisha left the dressing room, CC couldn't concentrate. She thought about calling Max to see if he could get away for a quick lunch at the Pirate's Cove. She even toyed with getting a hotel room and seducing him. The tension was mounting all around her. She wanted to be held, reassured, loved.

Before she could get the nerve to call him, her phone rang. It was the principal at Norfolk Country Day wanting to know if CC could come to the school; she needed to talk about Alizé.

"What's happened? Is she all right?" CC asked, alarmed.

"She's okay," said Olivia West, who'd been the principal there since God invented dirt. "But I'd like to chat with you in person, if that's convenient."

CC loved the way the rich always put their demands in terms of polite choices. "I'll be there at two," she said. She quickly closed out her appointments, threw the box of shoes into her car, and zipped onto the freeway.

Chapter FIVE

Norfolk Country Day School was located down a wooded lane near the place where the Elizabeth River pours out into the Chesapeake Bay. Established in 1902, it did not admit black students until 1978—and that was under threat of a lawsuit. Since the 1990s, it had become more diverse ethnically but not economically. The students who went there were of the area's blue-blooded elite.

CC had wasted no time pulling strings to get Alizé admitted into the pre-school. Despite her sullen, pouty demeanor, Alizé had done fine in the first grade. CC had worried that the child might prove to be stupid—who knew what genes she had inherited from her birth parents? Instead, Alizé was an intense learner, eager to please her teachers and a natural with numbers. She had only been disciplined once this year, and that was for taking a book with her into the bathroom and forgetting to come out with the rest of the students.

CC wondered what Alizé had gotten into now.

At the end of the shady trail sat the school, looking suspiciously like a plantation house. CC drove up to the visitor's parking lot smugly; there were plenty of old white men rolling over in their graves as she clicked her heels up the steps.

"Mrs. Smart, so good to see you again," Ms. West said courteously. There it was again: the assumption that she was married.

"Good to see you, too," CC replied, her smile masking her insecurity.

Ms. West cleared her throat uncomfortably. CC noticed that the older woman was more nervous than CC was. That was a good omen. If there was going to be a battle, CC could easily gain the upper hand.

"Well," said the principal, patting her silver hair and avoiding eye contact, "I wish the terms of this visit were more pleasant."

"What is it, Ms. West?"

"Your daughter has been, shall we say, 'inappropriate' in class."

"Excuse me?"

"What I mean is that . . . it seems she's come to school without wearing any undergarments. She was caught lifting her skirt during kickball."

"She's seven years old, Ms. West. What are you trying to say?" The principal blanched white. CC pressed on. "Did you ask my daughter what was going on?"

"Well, no. We called you immediately. We thought you would like to know."

"Know what? That she's a perverted flasher? That she was propositioning other children for sex? Is that what you think of all black people, Ms. West? That they are hyper-erotic animals?"

"Oh heaven's no! That's not at all what I—"

"Isn't it? Why would you pull me away from work for this bullshit, then? Where is my daughter? What have you done to her?"

"Mrs. Smart, I want to assure you that—"

"Just get her in here."

Alizé crept into the principal's office five minutes later. Her whole face was red and swollen from crying. She slumped guiltily against the door.

"Alizé, do you know why you're here?" the principal asked.

"I didn't have on any panties in gym class," she whimpered. "I didn't mean it. I'm not a bad girl."

"Come give me a hug, darling. What in the world happened to your underpants?" CC asked sweetly.

The child didn't move but looked from one woman to the other, like a cornered mouse before two leering cats. "I had an accident in my pants," Alizé lied. CC smiled with relief. The child wasn't going to tell on her. She breathed deeply and felt a sudden compassion for her daughter. It was just as she'd always imagined: CC and Alizé against the world.

"I was scared I'd get in trouble, so I took my underwear off," the child continued. "Then I fell down during kickball and everyone saw." She covered her face in shame. "I didn't want anybody to know."

CC gathered Alizé on her lap and cuddled her against her firm breasts. "Don't worry, darling. I know it was an accident. It's okay."

Ms. West sank behind the desk, her voice less certain. "She's come to gym class other days this week with no underwear on."

"Says who?" CC shot angrily. "Look, lady, I see what's going on here. Someone is out to get my daughter. They've got her so upset, she's wetting her pants. Instead of accusing her of lewd behavior, and instead of pulling me out of my job, you would do better to figure out who's harassing my child. I suppose it's no coincidence that she's the only black child in her class."

"Now, wait a minute!"

"No, goddammit, *you* wait a minute. Don't you ever call me back to this school to tell me some stupid-ass story about my daughter. If you do, I'll sue this school for every penny it's worth. Do you hear me?"

The principal stood shakily behind her desk. "You don't have to raise your voice, Mrs. Smart. I understand you perfectly. Alizé? Why don't you go home with your mother and start fresh tomorrow? And please make sure you're appropriately dressed in the morning."

"C'mon, Alizé," CC stood self-righteously. "Let's get out of here."

She snatched Alizé by the hand and strode to the car. The mute girl perked up when she saw the shoe box on the passenger seat. "Is this for me, Mommy?"

CC looked at her daughter's gleaming eyes and childish anticipation and realized how close she had come to being humiliated by the school. Behind that child's simple smile were the roots of CC's destruction. Every time she pulled her life together, there was Alizé hauling in authorities to poke and pry into their personal lives. Alizé was a bad-luck charm. She was the crack in the perfect façade that CC presented to the world.

Now the brat had the nerve to ask if CC had bought her a present! Infuriated, CC grabbed the box and threw it into the backseat. "Hell, no! Why should I buy you a present when all you do is find ways to humiliate me in public?"

Something hideous rose up in CC's soul. She lashed out at her daughter, slapping her face and punching her in the chest.

"Mommy! I'm sorry!" Alizé shrieked. "Please stop! Please!"

A tangle of dark emotion blinded her. Only the other-worldly terror in her daughter's voice made CC stop.

When her mother paused, Alizé quickly opened the car door and fell onto the pavement, crying.

CC stared at her own hands. What was she becoming? Keisha Johnson's sad face appeared before her. *At least you still have your daughter to cherish*. The words echoed in her head.

"Mom?" CC whispered, suddenly a little girl again. "Mom, please don't leave me."

Dazed, she accidentally leaned on the horn. Its rude blare jarred CC back into reality. She quickly looked at herself in the rearview mirror, wiping away her smudged makeup with a Kleenex. "Get in the car, Alizé," she said, drained. Alizé, now standing near the curb, hesitated. CC gave her a genuine smile. Cautiously, Alizé smiled back, then climbed in. The little girl's quick forgiveness filled CC with remorse. She hadn't meant to beat her daughter. Where had all that anger come from?

From now on, she would do better, she promised herself. She'd never lose control like that again. "Buckle up your seat belt, baby," CC said. "Let's go buy you some new underwear. Would you like that?" Alizé nodded tentatively, any hint of childlike joy fully extinguished.

As they drove away, CC noticed that one of the blinds in the school office window fell back into place.

At the mall, CC berated a sales clerk in Saks after the clerk said her credit card had been declined. Taking her daughter by the hand, she went to Sears and spent her last twenty dollars on a hot dog for Alizé and some new underwear.

By the time they got home, both were exhausted. CC cleared a place on her nightstand for the box of blue basketball shoes, then went into the living room to watch TV. Alizé usually spent time alone in her room. But that night, she was especially needy, clawing her way over the garbage into her mother's lap. Soon they both fell asleep.

CC dreamed of medieval castles—complete with lookout towers and heavy drawbridges—melting into sand and being swept out to sea. The dream left her nauseous and weak. She awakened the next morning to make herself some coffee but couldn't find the coffee maker in all the mess in the kitchen.

When Alizé arose rubbing her eyes, CC noticed the fresh purple bruises on her arms. There were red welts on her cheeks. CC sank to the floor. She couldn't send the child back to school like this.

"Mommy, see? You don't have to be sad today." There was Alizé in the kitchen, lifting her skirt and showing off her new underwear.

Barely able to speak, CC said quietly, "I think you need to stay with Lola today."

It took all that CC had to call her mother. Lola asked no questions but said she'd be there immediately.

"No!" CC objected quickly. She had stopped noticing the piles of filth in her house. Now that her mother was on the way, CC realized that she could never let anyone see the way they were living. "I'll bring Alizé to you."

"Are you sure?" Lola's voice was full of questions. CC had always refused to go to her mother's home in the Bay End housing projects.

"I'm sure," said CC. She wanted so much to add the words "Thank you," but she couldn't make herself say them.

CC dropped Alizé off and zipped away before Lola could ask about the marks on her daughter's body. At work she tried to put the last few days behind her and concentrate on the show. But she was distracted and often let the guest take control of the interview. The taping was a flop.

Knowing that the best defense was a good offense, CC demanded a meeting with the executive producer after the show. She took a swig of courage from her flask of vodka, then went into his office.

"A. J., we need to talk," she pounced as soon as she entered his office. "I shouldn't have to pay for my own hairdresser, makeup, and wardrobe. Those are necessary expenses for the show."

He stared at her, confused. "CC, we offered to pay for a stylist when you started. You refused. You told me that you wanted to take care of it yourself and you'd write it off."

"That was before *Breakin' It Down* became the top-rated morning show," CC argued. It was suddenly hot in his office. She was desperate to get her hair done, but she'd bounced two checks to her hairdresser. Now the woman wouldn't even take her calls. "I have to be styled 24/7 now. My public appearances are part of the publicity for the show. You need to be paying for that."

A. J. laughed. "I agree with you, CC. But honestly, it's not in our budget for this year. We'll see what we can do in next year's budget."

"I don't think you understand," CC said. "Find the money or I'm out of here."

"What? You can't be serious! CC, you're putting me in a bind here. Be reasonable."

In fact, this was no time to be reasonable. Her hair was a mess. She was behind on her car note. The bank had begun foreclosure.

Then there was Alizé. The dean of attendance had called to ask why the child was absent. CC had ranted that she didn't know whether she would allow her daughter to return to the racist Country Day School. There was something in the dean's calm reaction that let CC know the threats rang hollow.

"You've got a week, A. J.," CC said. "Make it happen."

She left the office to meet Max for lunch.

"What's wrong?" he asked as their meals arrived. "You look . . . terrible."

"Thanks a lot," CC mumbled, pushing her salmon around the plate half-heartedly.

"CC, you haven't been yourself lately," Max began as if he'd prepared a speech. But CC's mind was stuck on what he'd just said. Actually, she was being more "herself" than she'd ever been in her life. She'd let her hair and makeup go. Instead of being strong and strident, she was quiet and unsure, like the little girl locked inside of her. Max was getting a glimpse of the real CC Smart. And just as she feared, the real CC Smart was unlovable.

"You haven't heard a word I said, have you?" Max said.

"What?"

"CC, I don't know what kind of games you're playing," he said, throwing down his napkin. "I'm very attracted to you, but you keep pushing me away. I have no idea what's going on. Here I am offering you my love and support if you would just open up to me, and you tune me out. What the hell is that about?"

He stood up. CC reached for him, but he moved away. "I can't be in a relationship alone," he said. "Don't call me until you're ready to let me in."

CC shrank down in her seat. People were staring. She wondered if this would hit the gossip columns—"CEO of TechTel stomps out on television's CC Smart"!

"Will there be anything else?" the waiter came, holding a pitcher of ice water.

"Yes," she said curtly, handing him her plate of uneaten salmon. "I need to see the chef. This fish was like a hockey puck. I'm not paying for it."

Surprised, the waiter nodded and took the plate back to the kitchen. CC's heart pounded. She had no money to pay the bill.

Chapter SIX

Lola kept Alizé until the weekend. When she finally brought the child home, CC met them at the front door. Alizé darted past her mother into the house. Lola started to follow, but CC blocked her.

"Aren't you going to let me in?" Lola asked, surprised.

"I can't. Actually, I'm on my way out."

Lola eyed CC suspiciously. "CC, I'm a recovering addict. I've told more lies than there are stars in the sky. I know something's wrong. What's going on? I saw the marks on Alizé. I know that's why you had her out of school this week."

CC felt like she was at the top of a roller coaster about to plunge to the ground. Trying to keep her composure, she reached into her bag of tricks, turning fear into a shield of lies. "I didn't want to tell you," CC began. "You know the guy I was dating, Max Cortland? Well he's not as nice as he seems on the outside. He grabbed Alizé because she spilled a milk shake on his suit. He really hurt her. I threw him out and broke it off with him. I didn't know what to do."

"Oh my God!" Lola exclaimed. "That's horrible! Alizé didn't breathe a word! Did you call the police?"

"No!" CC gasped. "I can't call the police. He's a powerful man."

"You're a powerful woman, CC. You don't take crap from anyone. I can't believe you'd let a man attack your daughter and get away with it."

"Could you please just lay off?" CC now tried on the mask of indignation. "You keep telling me you're here to support me. I rely on you for a change, and this is what I get? You weren't there when I was Alizé's age. You don't get to run my life now."

Her mother backed down the steps as if she'd been physically slapped. "I see," she said. "I have to go."

Relieved that her mother wasn't going to try to give her a hug or a kiss, CC breathed easier. "I'll talk to you later."

The weekend was long and uneventful. She'd pushed away Max and Lola, so there was no one to ask prying questions. No one to judge her. No one to force her into fakeness.

Alizé danced warily around CC, monitoring the mood in the room before venturing a conversation. Mostly, she stayed in her room talking to herself and reading. On Saturday afternoon, CC climbed into bed. Her head throbbed, so she drew the blinds. When she dozed off, she thought she heard a little girl's voice coming from the box of shoes on her nightstand—the tennis shoes that Keisha had given her.

She woke, sweating. The box sat where she'd left it, silent and unopened.

"Mommy? I made you some dinner." It was Alizé's voice she'd heard. The little girl held a bowl of rice sprinkled with sugar and a mug of tepid water with a used tea bag floating in it.

CC smiled, her headache subsiding. "Thank you, baby," she said. This was how she's always imagined it would be. Mother and her adoring daughter, together. "Did you fix yourself something?"

Alizé cast her eyes downward. "I'm not really hungry."

CC ate the dry rice hungrily, while Alizé prattled about Dora the Explorer and the school's follies. "I'm going to be a bunny," she said proudly. "Can I go back to school on Monday? I promise to be good."

CC nodded and sipped the tepid tea. "Yeah. I don't want you at Lola's anymore."

"What's in that box?"

CC followed Alizé's eyes to the shoe box. Something about the child's covetous gaze threatened CC. "It's mine," she said gruffly. "A guest on my show gave it to me."

"But what's in it?"

"Alizé, why do you always have to push it?"

The child jumped up and ran from the room. CC was about to chase her and give her a good shaking, but her head reeled. She curled back into bed. When she woke up, it was late Sunday morning. She'd slept through church.

Wednesday should have been CC's finest hour. Chief Hudsen came back on the show to report that the department had busted a major drug-smuggling ring. Thirty million dollars of Soul Killa now lay in the evidence room at headquarters. Hudsen credited CC's crusade along with Keisha Johnson's organizing work in the Bay End Projects. The case had been cracked by an anonymous tipster after watching the interview on *Breakin' It Down*.

As the cameras rolled, CC's tired body reverted to muscle memory. She was sharp, funny, direct, and tough—as always. Once the show was over, she felt like a woman with a split personality, barely able to recognize herself as the confident person in front of the camera. CC's executive producer, A. J., watched the whole show offstage. Afterward he patted her on the back and promised to find the money she'd requested for her make-up and costuming.

Make-up and hair weaves were far from her mind. All she could think about was the letter. It had arrived by certified mail from the Virginia Department of Child Protective Services. "We request an in-home interview with you on Wednesday evening at 7 P.M." CC had called the state office and demanded an explanation. Added to her humiliation was the fact that she couldn't make the call in private from her cell phone. It had been cut off.

"Credible claims have been made that Alizé Maria Smart is being abused," the clerk on the other end of the phone had said. "A social worker will come and talk to you about it. Frankly, you'd be arrested right now if you were anybody else."

"What do you mean?" CC had shrieked. Then, remembering she was at work, she'd lowered her voice. "Who made those allegations?"

How many people had smiled in her face but told lies about her behind her back? *My mother, that bitch,* CC thought. *And Max . . . the hospital . . . the housekeeper . . . the school.*

The woman had hung up without giving her any further information. Now CC couldn't focus on anything—not even her fan mail. Social workers would be at her house that evening. A heavy fog descended. Her feet felt like they were made of stone. She chugged coffee without complaining that it wasn't her special-ordered, organic dark roast. When the caffeine made her stomach quiver, she switched to vodka.

"You don't look so well," Josh said that afternoon. "Maybe you should go home."

Instead of squashing him like a roach, she nodded quietly. "I think I will."

Grabbing her purse, CC walked out into the drizzle. Tipsy, she lumbered to her blue Roadster. But when she got to the handicapped space where she always parked her car, it was nowhere to be found. She walked in circles, unable to believe that her car had been towed by the police. She'd parked there illegally for years, but the police had always looked the other way for CC Smart.

"Shit," she said, flagging a taxi to the police station.

"I'm sorry, Ms. Smart," the desk officer said apologetically. "We don't have your car. I just checked the log."

"What?" she asked in disbelief. Nervous, she pulled on the nappy edges of her hair weave. Then she self consciously hid her hands; her chipped fingernails were in desperate need of a manicure.

"No ma'am, sorry. We don't have your car."

"Oh, my God, somebody must have stolen it!" CC cried. Then suddenly it occurred to her. Somebody had indeed taken her car—the repo man.

"Do you want to file a police report?" the man asked helpfully.

Swaying, she collected her purse and turned away. "No, I just remembered, I let my boyfriend borrow it."

Before she could get out of the door, she thought she heard the officer snicker, "I'll bet."

CC wished she could call another cab, but she didn't have much cash left. Instead, she thought about calling Max. No, not

Max . . . but who else was there? Here she was, the most powerful woman in Norfolk, stranded in the rain with no one to call for help.

Just then, the Colley Avenue bus ambled down the street. She'd taken the bus a million times as a foster child, roaming the streets searching for her mother. Without thinking, she ran for the bus stop, clomping drunkenly in her pumps. Just before she got there, her heel jammed in a crack in the sidewalk, sending her tumbling.

The bus driver pulled up and opened the door. Leaning out, he asked, "Miss? Are you all right? Were you running for this bus?"

CC wanted to scream at him, but her armor of hostility was shattering. In its place grew a humbling shame. She nodded weakly, and he waited patiently for her to pick herself up and get on the bus.

Sitting up front, she ignored the din of people on the bus and investigated her torn nylons and skinned knees. The driver gazed at her in his rear view mirror. "Hey! Aren't you CC Smart?"

It was like a lion's roar in the jungle; the bus fell silent. There was not even the tinny throb of an iPod.

"Yes," she said loudly, straightening her back and arranging her purse. "There have been a lot of complaints about the rudeness of city bus drivers. I wanted to see for myself. And guess what, young man? You pass with flying colors. I hope all of your colleagues are this courteous. If not, they'll hear about it on my show."

The driver grinned. "Thank you." When CC hobbled off near Gentry Square, everyone on the bus gave her a standing ovation.

It was nearly five by the time CC made it home. The social workers would be there in two hours. How was she going to clean her house?

In the pouring rain, she fumbled with her house keys and pushed her way inside.

"Alizé!" There was her daughter, standing on top of the mess on the foyer floor, dancing and singing to herself. On her feet were the blue suede tennis shoes.

As soon as she saw her mother, Alizé went ashen.

"What the hell are you doing?" CC screamed. "Didn't I tell you not to touch that box? Those are mine!"

"I just wanted to see," Alizé whined. It was too late. CC pounced upon her, knocking her to the ground. She snatched the shoes off her daughter's feet and began to beat her with them.

"I told you not to touch them!" CC screamed, her mind separating from her body as she pummeled the child. The emptiness inside her had become too huge. The walls of her life were crumbling. She'd lost her man. She'd lost her car. She'd nearly lost her house and her job. She was ten years old again. Penniless, homeless, and unworthy.

And now her daughter, for whom she had sacrificed so much, was trying to take even the little things that mattered. The shoes had been given to her by someone who still adored her. "You stay the hell away from my stuff, do you hear me? Stay the hell away from me!"

Suddenly CC realized that Alizé wasn't moving. "Alizé?" she said, backing away. "Oh, God."

Standing, she kicked off her broken pumps and put on the tennis shoes. They were almost a perfect fit. Leaving the door open, she wandered back out into the rain.

CC walked and sobbed, not knowing what to do or where to go. Soon, the neighborhood went from brick town houses and trendy lofts to run-down liquor stores, two-family flats and storefront churches. Somewhere in the distance, a dog barked. A car zoomed by, the stereo bass pounding like a heartbeat.

"Hey, Shorty, you ain't gone sell no ass wearing them shoes!" a man hanging out of the passenger side yelled with a laugh as he sped by in a souped-up Malibu.

Maybe my mother was right, CC thought. *Just get high and forget the pain, the failures. Who do I think I am? I'm nobody.*

"Yo, Lovey," a man slid from the shadows, blocking CC's path.

"Whatchu doin' on this side of town? You lookin' for some Soul Killa? It's tight around here, but I got some for a pretty lady like you."

CC looked up. A stranger had called her pretty. She smiled. "How much?"

He was about to answer when CC heard a woman yell from across the street. "City Boy—izzat you? Didn't we tell you never to show up in this neighborhood again? I'm calling the police right now, I swear before God!"

The man laughed out loud and ran in the other direction. The woman came running over to CC. "Ma'am, are you okay?"

CC turned to answer, but the woman exclaimed, "Ms. Smart! What are you doing in Bay End?"

CC tried to see the woman's face, but her eyes would not focus.

"Ms. Smart, you remember me! It's Keisha Johnson. Where's your raincoat? And why are you wearing my daughter's shoes? What's happened to you?"

All of a sudden, CC thought she heard another voice. Like the wail of a mother whose child had been torn from her clutching arms. A broken woman calling out, "Cornelia! I'm coming back for you! Hold on . . ."

Delirious with grief, CC fell into Keisha arms, sobbing, "Mama? Is that you?"

Keisha tightened her arms around CC. "No, Ms. Smart. I'm not your mother. But I know where she is."

Chapter SEVEN

The women at the Bay End Reclamation Club scattered when Keisha entered the community center dragging along a woman in crisis. There was a coat over the woman's head, who was sobbing and trembling. The woman seemed to be on some kind of high; she was babbling about her mother.

The Reclamation Club members had seen it so many times before—rape victims, women who'd been evicted, mothers strung out—at some point, they'd all come through that door.

"Get some warm blankets!" said Keisha ordered. "Kim, you get her some hot coffee—black. Shauna, find some dry socks for her feet. I'm going to put her in my office where I can try to talk to her."

Keisha rubbed the woman's shoulders to keep her calm and slowly guided the woman to the office while the rest of the volunteers buzzed into action.

"You just sit here," Keisha cooed. "Everything's going to be all right."

CC obeyed. Someone stuck a Styrofoam cup in her hands. Slowly, she sipped the warm, bitter coffee without complaint. Keisha helped CC step into some dry hand-me-downs. She hadn't worn second-hand clothes since she was a teenager. They were clean and warm; she was grateful.

"Okay, I hear you found another one wandering the streets," Lola Smart said, marching into the office. "I have the intake forms right here. Is she high?"

Keisha said nothing as Lola took her first look at the new client.

"CC!" Lola cried. "CC, is that you?"

At the sound of her name, CC raised her head slowly and gazed upon her mother. She smiled "I knew you'd come for me."

Lola pulled CC into her arms. For the first time since she was a little girl, CC didn't pull away.

"Dear God," Lola prayed, "thank you for answering my prayers."

"She was wandering around the streets in the rain. I was coming back from the store when I thought I saw City Boy trying to sell a woman some dope. I yelled at him to get away from her and saw that it was CC."

"Jesus," Lola breathed. Taking her daughter's face into her hands, she asked CC directly, "Are you on that stuff, too? What's happened?"

CC blinked. Where was she?

Lola tried again. "CC, are you high?"

"No," CC said, clutching her way back to reality. "No, I was just walking. I'm in trouble, Mama. I don't have anywhere to go."

Lola got on her knees and held CC's hands. "You don't have to be afraid anymore. You got me. Tell me what's happening."

CC opened her heart. She told her mother about her fears, about her financial disaster, about losing Max. She told her about the squalor in her house, about feeling on the verge of collapse and thinking, even for a minute, that drugs were her only way out.

"CC, you haven't told me anything I hadn't already figured out," she soothed. "I love you anyway. I'm just glad you are able to trust me to support you." Lola held CC's face close and looked into her eyes. "But you haven't mentioned the most important thing: Alizé."

Alizé. Soon the social workers would find the little girl where CC had left her—on the garbage-strewn floor. She covered her face with shame and began to sob.

"I didn't mean it!" she cried. "When Keisha talked to me about the loss of her daughter, I realized how much I loved Alizé. I wanted to protect her. I didn't want her to get hurt."

"What are you talking about?" Lola asked, alarmed. "Where is she? Has your boyfriend done something to her?"

CC looked into her mother's eyes. "No," she said. "He never touched her. It was me. I'm the one who hurt her."

Lola and Keisha listened as CC revealed her darkest secret. She'd been abusive to her own child. She'd done unspeakable things. She was out of control and didn't know how to stop.

Just moments before, she'd beaten the child and left her on the floor.

"What?" Lola jumped up. "Why didn't you say something right away? Keisha, call an ambulance! We've got to get to Alizé!"

Keisha ran to get her car while Lola helped CC stand. As they left, a woman at the center said, "Ain't she that woman on TV?"

"No," said Lola. "She's my daughter."

Keisha drove as Lola cradled her daughter in the back seat. The windshield wipers sloshed the cold rain. As they neared Gentry Square, CC was filled with fear again. "No," she said. "I can't face them."

"Who?" Lola asked.

"Child Protective Services. They were supposed to interview me at seven. They're already there by now. They've already found Alizé."

"Slow down," Lola said to Keisha. Then she turned to her daughter. "Now, Cornelia, I want you to listen to me. I know what it's like to hit rock bottom. Because I was out of control, I lost you, I lost my freedom, I lost my mind. However dark it is, I'm here to tell you that you can fight back. You will survive this.

"Maybe God had me go through what I went through so that I could be here for you in this moment. I will not leave you. But you have to walk this path on your own two feet. I can't take the steps for you. Today is the day you become your own woman. You've pretended to be brave all these years. Now it's time to prove it to yourself."

CC braced herself for her old feelings of anger and resentment at her mother. Instead, she nodded; her mother was right. No matter what had happened to her in the past, the moment to change things was now. "Okay," CC said. "Let's go."

By the time they drove up, the rain had stopped. A squad car was parked outside of CC's town house, along with a car from the Department of Social Services. The door was hanging open, and the garbage inside had spilled out onto the steps. A mobile van from her own television station was parked on the lawn. As the reporters noticed her sitting in the car, they dashed toward her.

"CC, what happened to your daughter?" asked a senior reporter she'd worked with for years. "Why was she at home alone?"

"CC! CC? Tell us, who reported you to Social Services? Is it true that you were abusing your daughter?"

CC winced at their questions. "Where is Alizé? Is she all right?"

"Move back, everyone. This is a crime scene." It was Chief Hudsen. "Ms. Smart, we found your daughter inside with a concussion. I'm going to have to take you in for questioning." He looked uncomfortably at the cameras, then whispered in her ear, "I hate to do this, Ms. Smart, but we're going to have to handcuff you."

He moved away and let a detective cuff her and lead her to a squad car.

As the cameras flashed and the reporters barraged her with questions, CC looked back toward her mother. Lola nodded, then tearfully covered her heart with both hands. CC took a deep breath and got into the backseat of the cruiser.

Chapter EIGHT

Josh Clark counted down, "Three, two, one."

"Good morning, this is *Breakin' It Down*. I'm your guest host, Keisha Johnson." Keisha smiled broadly into the camera. "Today we have the interview you've been waiting for all summer.

After three months in jail and two months in treatment, it's my pleasure to welcome back to the stage . . . Cornelia Smart!"

The studio audience went wild. Backstage, CC listened to the applause. She remembered when that kind of adulation used to be her drug, her way of numbing the pain inside. Now the sound made her nervous—would she be accepted after her child abuse conviction? Would people believe that the powerful CC Smart was really a severely depressed and delusional girl in need of treatment?

Uneasily, she walked out toward the stage. Her natural hair was short and full of dark corkscrew curls. Her make-up was light, revealing something the television audience had never seen before: her playful freckles. She wore a plain blue cotton top and comfortable jeans. On her feet were a pair of blue suede tennis shoes.

Without the mask of bravado, she felt tiny and unsure. Her eyes locked on Keisha's kind face, and she blocked out the rest. All through her trial, therapy, and community service at the Bay End Reclamation Club, Keisha had stood by CC without judgment.

Keisha began, "Tell us, Ms. Smart—"

"Cornelia. My name is Cornelia."

Keisha smiled awkwardly. This was her first time guest hosting in the new slot the station had opened up for community issues every week. "Cornelia, then. We all know that you served three months in jail for second-degree child abuse. And you lost your home, your car, and your job. Your fans are wondering how you're doing now."

"Thank you, Keisha," CC said, full of poise. "You've mentioned all that I lost, but you haven't mentioned all that I found." Her eyes grew misty, and she gazed down. "I had gained fame and notoriety, but I had lost myself. I took it out on my daughter rather than taking responsibility for my own situation.

"I'm so grateful that my mother was there to take custody of my daughter while I got help. I pray that one day Social Services will find me fit to have my daughter back." CC's voice cracked.

"But until then, I'm here to talk to you about what I've learned. It's not okay to hit your children, call them names, make them feel stupid or ashamed. It's not okay to abandon them or to bully them. Parenting is a serious God-given responsibility, and it's time that our community took it seriously."

CC's eyes glanced over the audience and settled on the face of a friend. "Many people walk away from those in need," she continued. "But I want to publicly thank Max Cortland, who is also a survivor of childhood abuse. Not only has he stood by me, but he has donated ten thousand dollars to help the women at the Bay End Reclamation Club."

Keisha smiled supportively and asked one more question: "Why are you speaking out now?"

"I've learned that there's no shame in failing, there's only shame in not learning from your failures," said CC, holding her head high. "Abusers and the abused endure violence in quiet shame. I wouldn't ask for help, and I almost killed my own child. Shame kept me from facing my own demons. As a part of my recovery, I have to speak out to help stop the cycle of violence. I'm here today," she said looking straight into the camera, "because Cornelia Smart is finally ready to break it down . . ."

TRACY

BROTHERLY LOVE

PRICE-THOMPSON

Chapter ONE

Tick. Tick. Tick.

Zana gripped the edge of the sink and moaned. The bathroom was hot. Humid. Darkness descended, and she held fast to the hollow ticking of her watch. Footsteps sounded. Heavy. The door creaked open and the light switch was flipped. She squeezed her eyes closed as brilliance flooded the room.

"Hey, Z, what's up?" He sounded mildly curious. "Why was you sitting in the dark?" He paused, and then his voice took on a different tone. "And why you sitting in here butt-naked?"

He stepped deeper into the room and the dampness clutched him.

"Zana? Z-baby? What's up, girl?"

There was concern in his voice now. Fear too. Zana heard it clearly, and even through the wet haze of her pain she hated to worry him.

Tick. Tick. Tick.

The second hand boomed its way around the face of her watch. She closed her eyes and pressed her forehead to the cool sink, concentrating on the ticking sound and fighting to remain conscious.

"Oh shit!" he cursed and stepped fully into the bathroom. The floor was slick and wet beneath his feet, the tub half-full of rose-colored water. His eyes darted back to Zana who was perched naked on the closed toilet seat. Her head was slumped against the porcelain and her firm breasts stood free. He noted her smeared, gaped thighs and the assortment of items strewn across the floor.

An unbent wire hanger. Cotton balls. An open bottle of rubbing alcohol.

"Zana, *no*—" Realization hit him hard, and he moaned as he reached for her. "No, baby girl, no! What in the hell did you *do*?"

She opened her eyes again and tried to catch her breath. Fire sliced through her midsection and she bit back a cry. Her naked booty was warm and wet on the toilet lid. Slick. Slippery. The sound coming from her watch grew louder. That bad boy was almost gonging now. She wanted to cover her ears, but her stomach cramped all the way down to her tailbone.

"Shit! You was preg—? Why didn't you tell me, Z?" He grabbed a hand towel from the wall rack and pushed it between her legs. He held her close. "Hang tight, baby girl. I'ma call an ambulance . . ."

"No . . ." she whispered. "Don't . . ." Her breath was hot on his neck. Sour.

"Damn! You shoulda came to me, Zana. To *me*. Now people gonna be coming all up in here. Getting up in our business . . ."

Hot tears fell. One slid into her pleading mouth.

"I'm sorry. Please don't call nobody . . ."

He looked down at his hand. The towel he'd pushed between her legs was soaked, and now he was crying too. "I gotta call the ambulance, Zana," he sobbed. "I gotta get you to the hospital. Your shit is real bad. Oh man . . . look at all that . . ."

Zana raised her head from the sink and looked first at him and then toward the mess on the floor that had his full attention.

Her watch persisted.

Tick! Tick! Tick!

Uh-uh, Zana realized as she stared at the trails of dark liquid rolling down her legs.

Not the tick-tick of her watch.

Pap! Pap! Pap!

The dripping of blood.

Don't tell them nothing . . .

His whispered warning came from what seemed like eons away. But even the desperation in his words couldn't obliterate the papping sound of blood. *Her* blood. Blood that seeped between her naked thighs, pooled on the toilet lid, then splattered down to widen the crimson tide that roared on the bathroom floor.

Regina Wilson thumbed through the stack of folders on her desk, then selected one and opened it.

"Craziness," she muttered as she read from a report. Brookshore Hospital was located in one of the most impoverished and dysfunctional neighborhoods in Brownsville, Brooklyn, and its social work department had long been understaffed and overwhelmed. Not only did the hospital have problems attracting seasoned workers to its rolls, the caseload was crippling and the turnover rate was astounding.

Regina skimmed the first page of the report, then passed it to her boss, who sat across from her desk and was working down a pile of pistachio nuts.

"Please tell me what this world is coming to," Regina asked, shaking her head, "when we have folks out there who are still trying to give themselves abortions with coat hangers?"

"Not folks," Tanya Thomas corrected her. "Girls. Scared young girls."

"You mean young girls who aren't too scared to have unprotected sex but then turn around and find the heart to jam a piece of metal between their legs and puncture their uteruses?" Regina ran her fingers through her thick tangle of micro braids and sighed. "I just don't get it," she said, nodding toward the folder. "Seventeen years old and she almost takes herself out. Good gracious! The dark days of cloak-and-dagger back-alley, dim-light-basement abortions ended a long time ago. We have free clinics all over the place these days, T. She didn't have to do this."

Tanya shrugged and crunched down on a shell and extracted a small green nut. "Well," she said, chewing, "maybe she was one of the girls who never got the memo. Who knows why people do the things they do? We've seen worse than this, Regina. It's not up to us to figure out how our clients arrived at their issues. We get paid to help them get past them. That's why we became social workers, remember?"

Regina smirked. "And that's why I took my behind back to college, too, remember? Night school was nobody's joke, and there were times when I seriously wondered if I could cut it with all those math and science classes. But a degree in social work can't hold a candle up to a degree in chemical engineering. I'm out of here at the end of the month, Miss T. My new job at H. Gathers and Brighthouse is calling me, and I swear I can't wait to answer. A thirty-thousand-dollar raise, my own office, and none of the drama and madness that's always on the menu around here. If I have to deal with one more half-dead client who I can't help, or who doesn't want my help I'm gonna get down on the floor and holler."

"Well don't stretch out just yet," Tanya said, flipping through the folder. "We still need you around here. I bet this girl does."

"Whatever," Regina shrugged. "I don't know how much she needs me, but you're right about one thing. I've seen a couple of stunts like this before. In fact, I could write the script: Hot young cutie sneaks out to play with fire and panics when she gets burned. The love she thought she was in goes right up in the flames. The baby's daddy is in denial. He's out on the corner slinging action and denies he's ever touched her. Yeah, our cutie on the ward upstairs might be fast in the tail, but she can't be all that smart. Instead of telling her parents and accepting responsibility for her mistake, she tries to fix it by grabbing a coat hanger and half-killing herself. That's craziness for real."

Tanya balked. "Come on now, Regina. I know you've been through a whole lot around here, but read the full report. This client had no parents to turn to. They were both killed before she turned twelve. The girl is an orphan."

"Well, that means she's probably a ward of the state and there should have been a caseworker assigned to help her. I bet she lives in one of those group homes over on Bristol Street, huh? Those digs fall right between a crack house and a frat house. That girl was probably doing whatever she wanted, whenever she wanted. She lost her cool and panicked when she got exactly what she went looking for."

"Wow . . ." Tanya stopped cracking nuts and stared at her coworker. The beating her friend had taken hadn't left many physical scars, but a whole lot of emotional damage had definitely been done. Regina was beautiful and looked nothing like the stereotypical do-gooder that usually came to mind when people thought of social workers. She was tall and curvy, and had fine features and the smoothest honey-toned skin that Tanya had ever seen. Regina was the kind of woman who drew attention, but she also had a big, generous, and compassionate heart. A heart that Tanya knew had become jaded and hardened from fighting what many in their field believed was a battle against societal ills that simply could not be won.

"Thirty-one years old, and already you're almost burned out on this profession," Tanya said sadly. She'd been so grateful years ago when Regina had applied for the job, and she'd hired her immediately. Regina had been exactly what the social work department needed. She was young, stylish, and had good street smarts. The population of at-risk clients in Brownsville was getting younger and less educated each day, and Regina related well with the clients in their demographic area. They responded to her because her background was similar to theirs, and Regina always seemed willing to meet the client on his or her own level, which in the past had gotten her in way too deep.

"You think I'm *almost* burned out?" Regina said.

Tanya sighed. "Okay, you're totally burned out, Regina, and that's a crying shame. I remember your first day on this job. You were so eager to get out there in the field and really change the world. It's painful to see some of the changes the world has effected in you."

Regina shrugged. "Yeah, well, seven years of sloshing in the cesspools of New York City has a way of skewing a person's perspective, you know? But I'm still young, Tanya. I'm young enough to wipe the grime off my shoes and do something different with my future. Believe me, I don't see my new job as just a simple career change. I'm leaving here so I can save my own life."

"Well," Tanya's voice was gentle, "self-preservation is the first law of nature. Try to remember that when you get upstairs on the ward. Who knows? The life that needs saving most may not be your own."

"Hey, busy lady!" a brown-skinned sister with a gorgeous smile and shoulder-length red locks greeted Regina at the nurse's station. "You're almost out of here, huh? How much longer are you gonna be with us?"

Regina smiled. Anitra Daniels was always a sight for sore eyes. No matter how far Regina was buried under her caseload, Anitra's bright smile always seemed to beckon her toward sunshine. "I'll be around until the end of next month," she said, patting her friend's shoulder as she reached for a medical chart. "There's not a whole lot I'm gonna miss about this place, but I sure will miss you."

Regina walked down the hall slowly, favoring her right foot as she read an excerpt from the doctor's notes and headed toward her new client's room. Seventeen years old. Massive blood loss. Two transfusions. The paramedics on the scene had worked fervently to maintain her blood pressure, and the girl had nearly bottomed out twice before they could get her into the operating room.

That was five days ago, and now, as Regina stood in the doorway of the open-bay ward and tried to pick out which of the broken young women lying in the hospital beds was her latest burden, she almost wept. Seventeen years old! *Just until the end of next month,* she reminded herself, using the words as a mantra to help give her strength. *I only have to deal with this madness until the end of next month.*

Regina walked down the middle of the room between the rows of beds in search of her young client. It was pretty noisy for a sick-ward, and the air held quite a few aromas that Regina's stomach could have done without. She scanned the figures in the beds, discounting some by the process of elimination. Many of these women hadn't seen seventeen in more than a decade, and others had broken limbs, black eyes, and time-hardened faces. A few talked and laughed loudly among themselves, and one patient grunted and grimaced as she sat straining upon a bedpan. To Regina's surprise, one or two were actually sleeping peacefully through the chaos.

Near the end of the row, however, lay a quiet sheet-covered form, propped up on one arm. Her back was to the room, and her bed had been pushed all the way against the wall. A vase overflowing with brilliant roses sat on the window sill, and three "Get Well" balloons were taped to the wall.

Regina's designer heels clicked unevenly across the floor as she made her way over to the bed. Although the patient's face was partially covered by the sheet, tendrils of soft brown hair lay fanned out on the pillow.

"Zana Williams? Is your name Zana Williams?"

It took so long for the patient to answer that Regina wondered if the girl was asleep. But something told Regina that she was standing in the right spot, and when she glanced at the nursing chart clipped to the footboard her suspicions were confirmed.

"You're Zana Williams, right?"

"Who wants to know?"

The voice under the sheet held a definite street edge, but it was also a lot younger and softer than Regina had expected.

"I'm Regina Wilson. I'm a hospital social worker. Can we talk for a few minutes?"

"What me and you got to talk about?" Sullen. Challenging.

"We can talk about anything you like," Regina answered. "Life, family—"

"Nah, I'm straight," the girl cut her off. "I don't talk to strangers."

Regina sighed. "Look, I know what happened to you."

"No you don't."

"Well, I know what you did to yourself. I've got to write a report about your emotional status. I have to give an assessment before they'll discharge you from the hospital. We need to talk, Zana. It doesn't have to be a long-time-no-holla type of chat, but if you want to leave this funky roach-trap anytime soon, then we need to talk."

Regina waited. She'd made a connection with her urban lingo, and she could tell the young girl was turning things over in her mind, trying to decide how to make the encounter work in her favor.

"All right," the girl agreed after a few moments. She pulled the sheet back and exposed her face, and Regina was stunned at the raw beauty and vulnerability that greeted her. The girl sat up in the bed and gathered her soft hair at the base of her neck and twisted the ends. Intelligence mixed with cunning shone brightly in her eyes as she stared back at Regina. "What you wanna talk about, lady?"

~

"You were unconscious when they brought you into the emergency room. How much do you remember about what happened before that?"

Regina leaned forward after asking her question and pretended to jot something on her notepad. Hospital regulations prohibited staff members from sitting on a patient's bed, not that Regina would have done so anyway. The nurse's aides were spread so thin on their shifts that sometimes days went by before a patient's sheets could be changed. Once the girl had agreed to talk Regina had been reluctant to leave her side, but standing on her bad foot in four-inch designer heels wasn't going to cut it, so she'd gone back out to the nurse's station and snagged a folding chair from Anitra, then dragged it to the girl's bedside.

"I don't remember a whole lot of nothing," the girl said, and Regina moved her pen and took note of the evasiveness in her tone. "You know, I got like bits and pieces of stuff in my head. Lights and noises. My stomach was hurting like hell. I remember that."

"Were you alone when you—when this happened?"

The girl nodded quickly. "Yeah. I was by myself. Nobody else was there."

"What about the father?"

Regina was hit with an icy stare in response to that one.

"What about him?"

Defensive.

"Did he help you do this?"

"No."

"Was he there?"

"Did I say he was there? I just told you I was by myself, right? I did it alone."

Regina frowned slightly, then nodded. She could dig it. Hardball and head games. That's how girls in this hood usually played it. Zana glared at her from the bed. She'd smacked the handball straight into Regina's court and was ready to hit a killer if Regina imposed her will and decided to lob the ball back.

"How well do you know the man who fathered your child?"

Zana shrugged and looked away. "He's just some dude. I know him from around the way."

"Did he know you were pregnant?"

"Nah." Quieter.

Regina studied the young girl. She was a looker, for sure. And even beneath the baggy hospital gown Regina could make out the full but pert breasts, the thick, shapely hips, and the small, youthful waist. With a body like that, the neighborhood boys were probably after her in droves. The neighborhood men, too.

Regina decided to come from a different angle.

"What high school do you attend, Zana?"

"Brooklyn Tech."

"Wow, that's awesome! They have a very competitive admissions policy. How'd you get in?"

"How do you think I got in? I took the specialized tests just like everybody else," Zana snapped.

"Well, you must have scored pretty high," Regina said, impressed. "I wanted to go to Tech myself. But I had to move uptown right before school started, so I went to Bronx Science instead. Still, it took me two tries to get in way back then, and I'm sure the tests haven't gotten any easier."

Zana nodded. "I scored pretty high on my tests. I chose the engineering track and earned enough points to attend four specialized schools. I ended up choosing BT because they have a bomb handball team."

Regina laughed, noting the girl's diction change. "Engineering? Your IQ is probably off the chart for your age, and you made an important educational decision based upon a handball team?"

"Yeah, I sure did," Zana said slickly. "I love handball. But what about you? You went to a top school too, and all you ended up being is a social worker. I guess you made a few poor decisions yourself."

The laughter disappeared from Regina's lips.

"Check this out," she said slowly, her voice tight. "Don't get it twisted, little sister. I didn't get into social work because I didn't have any other options. I got into social work because I really wanted to help people."

Just that quick the girl had flipped the script and placed Regina on the defense. "I could have done something else with my life," she continued, "but I *chose* to help other people try to do something better with theirs."

The girl looked Regina over from head to toe and then smirked. "Please. You don't even look like a social worker."

Regina laughed. "What's a social worker supposed to look like?"

"I don't know," Zana shrugged. "Old. Fat. Busted clothes and run over shoes. You know the type."

"No, I don't know the type. You can't base someone's looks or appearance on the roads they decide to take in life."

Zana cut her eyes. "I know you didn't just say 'appearance'! You up in this stink-ass room carrying a clipboard and iced out wearing Jimmy Choo spikes and Fontana skirts and slinging that real expensive Chinese hair all over the place—"

"This is my hair," Regina interrupted. "My *real* hair."

"Whatever," the girl said coolly. "Sling on, then."

Check yourself, Regina cautioned. *Stay professional.* She regrouped quickly, then turned the tables until the leverage was hers again.

"So look at you, Zana. You're beautiful. You're almost too pretty to be real, and you're smart, too. I'm checking you out, little sister. Half the time you talk like a hoodrat and then two sentences later you start to speak like you actually have an education. That's what I call a chameleon." Regina gestured toward the array of patients in the beds. "What are the odds of a brilliant young girl like you ending up in a room full of broken-down women like these?"

"Hmph," Zana smirked. She rolled over and turned her back on Regina, dismissing her as she fell back into her hood lingo. "You can go 'head with all that bullshit psycho-babble. You don't know nothing about me, lady. And I'ma make damn sure it stays that way."

Chapter TWO

The next morning Regina woke up in a funk. She wasn't exactly sure what kind of bug had bitten her on the ass, but it must have been a big one because she went to work with a scowl on her face and her mood stayed dark all morning.

"It's getting close to lunch," Tanya said, glancing at her watch. "We're doing the cafeteria today, right?"

Regina looked up from her notes and sighed. She hated the hospital cafeteria, and not simply because the food was bad. "Yeah, I guess we are."

"We could always get a frank with red onions from the man on the corner. Or walk down to the pizza shop."

Regina shuddered. "If I never eat another one of those dirty franks it'll be too soon. And pizza gives me heartburn."

"Girl, please. Everything has been giving you heartburn today," Tanya mused. "I tell you what. You're due upstairs on the ward in ten minutes. How about I order us a salad and some hot wings from Antonio's? His lettuce is always nice and fresh, and if I put the order in now it'll be here waiting when you get back."

"That'll work," Regina said, gathering her folders and sliding a pen into the pocket of her Anne Klein shirt. "And for the record, Miss T, not everything gives me heartburn. I actually felt pretty good until it was time to come to work today."

"Well, we love you too, Miss Regina," Tanya grinned as she picked up the phone to place their order. "We love you too."

Regina peeked at her notes as she rode the elevator up to the eighth floor. She'd spent the morning running all over the hospital, and she still had seven patients who needed to be seen after lunch.

Zana Williams was the last client on her morning schedule, and although Regina really didn't believe Zana was a threat to herself or anyone else, she still hadn't figured out why the girl had put her life on the line like that when abortions were entirely legal and often performed for free.

Regina was hoping their second meeting would go a little bit better than the first one had, and minutes after dragging a chair over to Zana's bedside Regina learned that despite the poor judgment that had landed her client in the emergency room, the girl actually had a little something on the cap.

"You're a senior, right?" Regina asked. Zana was sitting up in bed. There were two get-well cards propped open on her night table and a fresh floral arrangement on the window sill. "Pretty flowers," Regina murmured. Several colorful balloons had been tied to the headboard and were hovering above them. "Have you thought about college yet?"

"Yep," Zana said, nodding proudly. "I thought about it, applied for it, and I've already been accepted at several good schools."

"Oh, yeah?" Regina asked, one eyebrow raised. It was hard to imagine the young sister could be resourceful enough to get herself into a bunch of different colleges, yet couldn't find herself one abortion clinic in the entire city of New York.

"Which ones?"

Regina was prepared to hear her mention a few of the local digs like Baruch, New York City Tech, Manhattan Community, or Lehman, and she was stunned by the list of schools that tumbled out of Zana's mouth.

"Princeton, Washington University in St. Louis, Stanford, and MIT."

Regina chuckled. If nothing else, the girl had a damn good imagination.

"Those are all really great schools, Zana, and you certainly have some great goals. But really, which schools are you considering?"

"I just told you, Princeton, Washington University in St. Louis, Stanford, and MIT! What? You don't believe me? Just because I'm laying in this bed and you're sitting in that chair, I gotta be the one who's busy frontin' and lying?"

Regina shrugged. "I never said that."

"Well you actin' like it!"

Regina shrugged again. A spade was a spade.

"For your information, I'm about to graduate with a 4.0 grade point average," Zana said crisply, her diction standing up. "I scored a 1515 on my SAT, and I've taken seven advanced placement classes. I've been inducted into the National Honor Society, I have two scholarships from the National Society of Black Engineers, and for three years straight I've been the highest scorer on my school's competitive math team."

She gave Regina an "in-ya-face!" look. "So in five years when I'm sitting pretty with a graduate degree in engineering and earning big change, you'll still be sitting on your ass in the social work office swinging that horse hair and wearing cheap designer knock offs."

Regina stared hard at the girl, then pursed her lips tightly. She knew what the problem was, and after working with hostile black folks for the past seven years, she also knew how to fix it. She thought about the client who had come in her office and threatened her with a hole puncher, then tried to steal her purse. And the pretty sixteen-year-old mother who had tugged her heartstrings so hard that Regina had given the girl her home phone number. The girl had looked up Regina's address on the Internet and sent her boyfriend and his homeys over to jack her up her one morning as she left for work. She hated to even think about the idiot who used to come to her counseling sessions wearing nylon gym shorts and sporting a raging hard-on. Tanya had caught him masturbating outside of Regina's door one afternoon, and that had been the end of his social services at Brookshore Hospital.

Unfortunately, Regina had suffered the ultimate violation too. She had tried her best to help someone, and it had turned out all wrong. The terror she had lived through was a constant reminder of what kind of world she was living in, and she had vowed never to get deeply involved in any client's drama again. From that day forward she'd learned to simply provide her clients with the services she was paid to provide and keep it moving.

Zana was still giving her the eye.

"I'm sorry," Regina said quietly. "I didn't mean to imply that you were lying."

"Well, you did."

"And again, I apologize. Truly. It was inappropriate on my part, and you should be very proud of yourself for having what it takes to get into all those awesome schools. Any one of them would be a great choice. They'd all get you out of New York City and provide you with a top-notch education at the same time."

Crossing her arms, Zana gazed out the window, and after a long moment she said, "Well, I did get accepted at a school right here in New York too, Columbia, and that's probably where I'll end up."

"Why is that?"

Zana sighed. "It's not because I didn't get accepted at all those other schools, because I really did. But I don't want to leave home. I'm staying here."

Regina wanted to jump up and scream, to warn this child-of-the-ghetto that the hood was *not* a home! If Zana was telling the truth, then she was one of the rare gems who had a real shot of making it up and out. The child was being offered an opportunity to transcend the boundaries of her birth and reach for something more.

Regina had strong feelings about what was right for this girl, but past experiences warned her to play it cool.

"You told the medical staff that your parents were dead, is that right?"

Zana's attitude changed instantly. The girl uncrossed her arms and rolled her eyes. "Yeah. I went through all that with them already. My folks got killed."

"So who do you live with?" Regina asked gently. "I thought maybe you were in one of the group homes that opened on Bristol Street last year, but your home address is not even in this hospital's jurisdiction. The only reason they brought you here to Brookshore is because you got hurt on the same night that there was a big club fire on Flatbush Avenue, and Kings County's emergency room was full. I had to send them a request for your medical records."

"I live with my brother. He takes care of me."

"Oh really? How old is he?"

The girl's shoulders went up and down. "I don't know. He's around twenty-five, I guess."

"That's pretty young to be raising a teenager," Regina replied. "It says in your file that your parents have been dead for about five years. Have you lived with your brother all of that time?"

"Not all of it," Zana said, turning to look out the window again. "I was in foster care for a minute, but my brother came home from the service and got me out of there. He was in the military, in Iraq, but they let him out so he could come back and take care of me."

"That's awesome," Regina said, impressed. In an age where young black men thought less and less of the black women in their lives, it was heartening to hear of a brother who not only loved his sister enough to sacrifice his career for her but who honored his parents by giving up his own dreams to raise their minor child.

"He must really love you."

"We love *each other,*" Zana answered quietly. "My parents raised us that way."

~

Two days later Regina found herself embroiled in a heated conversation with the director of a local outpatient drug treatment facility over a client who had been non-compliant with her treatment plan.

"Let me tell you something, Regina," Libra Jackson said without an ounce of pity in her voice. Regina had worked with Libra very closely over the years and knew firsthand that the hard-charging administrator was a caring soul but seldom pulled any punches. "You practically begged me to find a slot for this girl. Yeah, she's a single mother with very limited resources, but we're trying to run a facility here, and we're already severely overcrowded. I gave her a chance, and she messed it up. So what's your problem?"

"My problem is that her drug treatment plan is court-mandated! If you kick her out she goes straight to jail. The judge will issue a warrant for her, and the cops will ship her off to Rikers Island."

"That's not my problem," Libra responded. "And it's not yours either, sweetie. The only reason I made room for her was because you're my girl and you asked me to. I had to terminate someone else's treatment early in order to give your client a slot, and in return she screwed herself and she screwed you too. I'm sorry, Regina. If your client can't show up to help herself, then she's probably not ready to stop getting high. Maybe this chick belongs in jail."

"But she has four little kids, Libra . . ." Regina pleaded. "And nobody to watch them. If she goes to jail they'll go into foster care. Don't you care about keeping those kids out of the system?"

"No," Libra answered bluntly. "Not more than their mother cares about keeping them out of it. Who knows, sometimes foster care is the best thing that can happen to a child. Keeping kids at home with their drug-abusing parents can sometimes be the worst thing for them."

Regina was more disillusioned than ever when she hung up. Even in a helping profession like social work and social services, there weren't enough people who truly gave a damn about the direction a person's life took. The system was bogged down in so much red tape that nothing substantial got accomplished without an act of Congress, and likewise, the clients didn't seem to care enough about themselves to seize opportunities for self-improvement.

"Here," Tanya said, patting her shoulder and handing her two large envelopes. "You're not going to win every battle, Regina, but at least you're still fighting."

Regina made a doubtful noise in her throat and accepted the mail. "Medical records from Kings County and Unity Hospitals," she said, extracting the documents. "And three reports from the New Lots Avenue Health Clinic. For that young girl. Zana Williams." She shrugged. "They could have kept them. The client is being discharged soon."

"This morning, in fact," Tanya agreed. "I got an e-mail request asking us to close her file out this morning because her guardian wanted an early discharge."

"Oh yeah?" Regina's eyebrow went up quizzically. "How come nobody told me?"

Tanya shrugged as she continued to sort through the mail. "I don't know why you weren't told. Like I said, I got an e-mail. Have you checked yours this morning?"

Regina frowned but admitted, "No. I haven't. I've been so busy trying to negotiate bed space and arrange transportation dockets that I totally forgot to log on."

"Well, check it. I'm sure the request is there."

Regina didn't answer. Something in the girl's medical records had caught her eye, and she felt herself go cold inside.

"Go ahead," Tanya urged. "Check your e-mail and see if you were included on the send list."

"Nah," Regina shook her head, her eyes flying across the page. "That's all right." If what she was reading was true, then she didn't have time to boot up a computer and wait forever to log on. "I take your word for it, Miss T."

Chapter THREE

Regina half limped, half jogged up the stairs to the fifth floor. She had bomb curves, but she was naturally fit and athletic too, and months ago she had purchased a treadmill that sat in the middle of her living room. She had always loved the little bit of nature that New York City provided. Running gave her a high, and she had actually finished three marathons, but that was before a couple of shady clients had forced her to give up running outdoors.

She skimmed the photocopied records she'd received from the clinic and the two local hospitals and sighed. There could be a perfectly good explanation behind everything in the reports, Regina knew. Sometimes what you thought you knew was very superficial, and when the truth was revealed you found yourself way off base. Regina might have recently earned her engineering degree, but in her heart she was a social worker. And according to the hospital reports, over the past five years at least one nurse at each facility had expressed mild concerns about Zana Williams.

Right now Regina's radar was ringing off the hook. She could be onto something real, or she could be barking up a dead tree again and setting herself up for the ass-whipping of the century. But the radar was *ringing*. Was she just supposed to ignore it?

Okay, jackass, Regina cautioned herself. *Remember what happened the last time you called yourself helping somebody who didn't want your damn help.*

Regina had already completed four counseling sessions with Zana, and although she'd felt the girl was being very guarded in her answers, that wasn't unusual for a kid who'd gotten pregnant and wanted to get rid of the baby. Regina thought she might have achieved a small rapport with Zana by apologizing for insulting her during their first session, but still. If the girl had something to hide, she was smart enough to know where to hide it. Besides, Regina had been once bitten and was now forever shy. She'd learned her lesson about sticking her nose too deep in other folks' business because there wasn't a damn soul who could protect you if one of your clients crossed the line and decided they wanted a piece of your ass.

On the ward, Zana sat with her legs dangling toward the floor. She looked even prettier today, Regina noticed as she lugged a chair down the ward and over to the girl's bed. As usual, it was pushed up against the wall, as though Zana wanted to keep a lot of distance between herself and the other patients.

"You're looking great today," Regina said with a big smile. Zana wore lip gloss and light mascara, and her wavy hair hung past her shoulders in big, loose curls. The teenager grinned as Regina positioned her chair near the foot of the bed.

"Yeah, I feel great too. Nice shoes," the girl said, pointing at Regina's feet. "You've got bomb taste because those babies are slamming."

"Thank you," Regina beamed. She might be living on a social worker's salary, but she still liked to look good. She glanced down at her brand-new blue suede shoes. They had a shiny gold buckle at the top, and she wore a navy Donna Karan suit that had big gold buttons shaped like buckles down the jacket front and a smaller one at each wrist.

Zana grinned. "What size are those? I have a fly suit that would go perfect with them."

Regina smiled. "These are a nine."

"Oh well," Zana shrugged. "They're safe on your feet, then. I wear a size seven and a half."

"So, are you ready to go home?"

Zana laughed. "Hell to the yeah!" She glanced at her ward-mates. "I can't stand sleeping around other girls. I hate it."

"Didn't you have sleepovers when you were younger? You know, with all your girlfriends, where y'all stayed up late eating pizza and laughing and stuff?"

"No! I never hang hard with females like that!"

"Well," Regina said with a smile, "what about when you go off to college? You'll live in the dorms, right? That means you'll have at least one roommate. Maybe even two."

"I don't know about all that," Zana answered. "Like I said, I'll probably choose Columbia. That way I can stay at home, sleep naked in my own room, and take the train to school every day."

Regina pursed her lips slightly but didn't push it. She knew from experience that remaining in New York for college was a bad decision for most high school graduates. It was important to get out of that comfort zone, to get out of the distinctive New York enclave with all of its nuances, in order to fully appreciate what the rest of the world had to offer.

"Well, at least you have options, Zana. You've been offered full scholarships at some of these schools, right?"

Zana shrugged. "I got full scholarships at all of them."

Regina was astounded. This girl had a chance to escape the confines of the city and broaden her horizons, but she obviously had no one to guide her toward the gate.

Regina looked down at the papers she still held in her hands. She was burning to ask Zana about a few of the illnesses she'd been treated for, but the last entry had been over a year ago, and had no bearing on the girl's case at hand.

Mind ya bizz, Regina told herself. Her job with Zana was basically done. Just because the girl was academically gifted, it didn't mean she was smart. Hell, Zana had already proven that by virtue of the fact that she was a client. In this urban environment, most girls Zana's age were already screwing. But the smart ones refused to screw without using a condom, and even the stupid ones didn't go around trying to give themselves abortions.

"Can I get dressed now?" Zana asked. "My brother is coming to pick me up on his lunch break. My doctor already said I could leave early."

Regina nodded. There was a lot she wanted to say, but her professional parameters and the scope of her duties and responsibilities were clear. She'd been tasked to assess whether the girl posed a risk to herself and whether or not there were any underlying problems that could have led her to mutilate herself and abort her unborn child.

"I just didn't want it," Zana had replied both times that Regina had asked. "I mean, I'm sorry it happened and I know I should have gone to a clinic, but I got scared. I started drinking, and then I just did it. I didn't tell nobody, I didn't ask nobody for help, I didn't even think about it, I was like the Nike commercial. I just did it."

Regina knew she had to take the girl at her word. She carried her folded chair back down to the nurse's station and plopped down beside Anitra, who looked up from her work with a bright smile.

"Crazy day already?"

Regina nodded. "Pretty rough. I've already argued with three outside facilities, made about seven calls, met with five clients so far this morning, and I have five more scheduled for this afternoon. I have yet to check my e-mails, and I still have two days' worth of notes to post to the files, but I need to find reliable home health care for one patient and arrange some kind of outpatient drug treatment for another one. But that's a typical day around here. The drama never ends."

Anitra nodded. "At least little mami in there is going home today. That's one less folder in your caseload."

"Yeah, but I just don't know . . ." Regina mused. "She's been treated at other hospitals, too. Not for anything as drastic as this, but other things . . ."

"Wow, she's so young. I would hope she's never done anything like this before."

Regina shrugged, her cynicism taking hold. "Well, even if this is her first time, my caseload isn't going anywhere. She'll just be replaced by another client who's just like her. It would be even worse if she ended up back in here again in a couple months herself."

Anitra shuddered. "Let's pray she's learned her lesson. A lot of women around here are homeless or on drugs or both. They wait until they're banging down death's door to come into the emergency room. They don't have anyone to turn to or anyone who cares about them, but this girl is different. If my trifling husband had brought me half the flowers and balloons and cards that her brother has been bringing her, I'd have never put the bum out."

"Is her brother around here a lot?" Regina asked.

"You mean does he visit her often?" Anitra nodded. "Every day. Sometimes twice a day on my shift alone."

"She's a lucky girl and doesn't even know it," Regina said wistfully. "She lost her parents at a very young age, but she's seen some blessings too. She's extremely smart—intelligent enough to get accepted to a high school that rejected *me*—and she's beautiful and can be well-spoken when she wants to be, too. That's a big plus in these parts."

"She should be graduating soon, eh?"

"Next month," Regina replied. She swept a braid back from her face and nodded. "She's got some really great scholarship offers too, or so she claims."

"She has so much going for her!" Anitra exclaimed. She glanced toward the ward and shook her head sadly. "It's hard to believe she wasn't smart enough not to get pregnant or to take care of herself in a safe way."

Regina could only agree. "I know. It seems a bit strange that she'd put herself through something so dangerous and traumatic, but we can't forget that she's a product of this environment. No matter how smart she might be, she's still living in a dumb world. If she's not careful, she could end up like the rest of these wom—"

Regina was left with her mouth hanging open when a tall young man emerged from the elevator and strode toward the nurse's station. Anitra elbowed her as a signal to take notice, but there was no way Regina could have missed him. He was devastatingly fine, with gorgeous eyes, smooth skin, and a well-trimmed goatee.

"Good morning, ladies."

He smiled, and Regina got lost in his clean white teeth and the deep cleft in his chin.

"How you doing, Mr. Williams?" Anitra said brightly. She stood up and beamed at the young man as she retrieved a folder from a stack. "Good to see you today. I just got my hands on your sister's discharge instructions, so you're right on time."

The young man smiled again and nodded.

Regina took a moment to size him up. He was model material,

that was for sure. Tall. Clean cut. Well maintained. Eye candy. There was something rugged about him that gave balance to his natural good looks, and even though she couldn't see all of him, one look at his muscular shoulders and bulging biceps told Regina the rest of his body would be just as thick and well sculpted.

"Hi," Regina said. She came from behind the desk and extended her hand. "I'm Regina Wilson. Your sister's social worker."

His smiled widened. "Yes, Miss Wilson. I'm glad you're here." He took her hand and held it for a moment. "I'm Zeke Williams. Zana told me all about you. I was planning to stop by and visit the social work office before I left."

"Oh, really?" Regina asked, surprised.

"Yes," he said. "I wanted to thank you. For helping Zana get through all this."

Regina nodded. "It was a pleasure getting to know your sister, Zeke. She's a beautiful and intelligent young lady. I'm sorry I had to meet her under these circumstances, but I hope she'll make better decisions about her life in the future. Starting with her choice of colleges."

"She told you about that, huh?" Zeke grinned. "I was surprised by all the offers she received, but then again I wasn't really surprised. Zana's got our mother's looks and our father's brains. She's a brilliant girl, and as you've probably already figured out, once she sets her mind to do something, she does it."

"I can tell," Regina agreed, nodding. "I tried to encourage her to accept one of her out-of-state college offers, but she seems pretty set on staying in New York. Personally, I think it's a bad idea."

Zeke's smile disappeared, and Regina caught a hint of something cold in his pretty eyes. "Personally? I didn't know this thing was personal with you, Miss Wilson. I've dealt with a few social workers before. Aren't you supposed to keep it strictly professional?"

Regina stammered, "I didn't mean—I'm sorry, I was just saying—it was only my opinion—" She jumbled all her words, caught completely off guard.

Zeke laughed "Relax." He patted her shoulder and gave her a friendly, reassuring squeeze. "I'm sorry, Miss Wilson. Sometimes I play too much. You don't have to apologize for looking out for my little sister. I appreciate any kind of guidance you can give her. Zana doesn't have a lot of friends, and there's only so much that I can tell her. She can probably use all the womanly advice she can get."

Regina smiled with him, but she was still unsure.

"I'm serious," Zeke said, still laughing. "Please, please, *please* don't take offense to what I said. I swear I was just joking. In fact, I've been telling Zana the same thing you told her. That she should go to a school as far away from here as possible. Do you know how live it would have been if I'da had a shot at Stanford or MIT or any one of those schools with a full ride? I mean, I got decent grades in high school, but I was nowhere near as smart as Zana is. She has a chance at getting the best education money can buy, while I graduated from high school and ran straight to the Marine Corps. How could I *not* want my baby sister to jump all over an opportunity this sweet?"

"Whew!" Regina said, obviously relieved. "You had me going for a minute there, I gotta tell you." She smiled brightly at Zeke, whose gorgeous face was full of good nature. "I'm glad we agree, not that it might matter to Zana. Like you said, she has a mind of her own and she has to choose her own path, but at least she has a brother like you who has her back and can encourage her to make good decisions."

Zeke nodded. "I'm doing my best, Miss Wilson. People are always talking about how I gave up all my own dreams to come home and raise my sister, but I don't see it that way and I don't regret a minute of it. Me and Zana were raised to be real close, and taking care of her in this way is what my folks would have wanted me to do. It's exactly what they would have expected from me, and out of love for Zana and love for them, I do my best."

Chapter FOUR

It was Saturday morning, and the streets were rain-slick from an early-morning shower. It was barely eight o'clock, but Regina had been up for hours. After running three miles on her treadmill and cleaning her bedroom and bathroom, she put a load of clothes in the washing machine, took a hot shower, then sat down to jot a few lines in her journal as she waited for her favorite stores to open on Fulton Street, where she planned to catch a few sales and satisfy her shopping jones.

Taking her journal from a desk drawer, Regina crossed her legs Indian-style and got comfortable in her cushioned window seat. Putting her intimate thoughts on paper had never appealed to her in the past, but that was just one more change she'd made after going through so much trauma the year before. Today, she got scared by the slightest things. She was paranoid to the max. Small sounds in her apartment, random glances from strangers on the street, she questioned everything. Small stuff that would have rolled right off her in the past could now send her fear factor shooting off the radar.

It was her boss, Tanya, who had given her a journal and suggested she begin writing things down so she could not only release her pain into the universe but also have a record to chronicle all the hurdles she'd conquered on her journey to healing. "But be careful, Regina. Don't just put your fears and doubts on paper," Tanya had warned her. "Write about your dreams too. Your hopes, your joys, and all the good things life has brought you."

Regina wrote slowly, her long, slanted script filling up a whole page in a matter of minutes. She was nearly drained by the time she was finished. The other tenants in her small apartment building were beginning to move around, and the sounds of laughing children could be heard and the smell of frying bacon was in the air.

The last few sips of her coffee had grown cold, but Regina gulped them down anyway. Although her writings had dredged forth old doubts and pain, the 40-percent-off sale that Macy's was advertising would go a long way toward exhilarating her. Regina loved to shop. Just the anticipation of hunting down and nailing a bargain was enough to lift her mood, and fifteen minutes later she was dressed and downstairs, hailing a taxi to take her across town to the Fulton Street Mall.

Macy's was packed to the rafters, but Regina didn't care. The swelling crowds were a mandatory part of the experience. After all, what bona-fide professional shopper wouldn't turn out for first dibs on a bargain?

An hour and a half later Regina was floating above the ground. Not only had she found two dresses, a wrap skirt, and a denim pantsuit that was dressy enough to wear to work, she'd been approached by a store clerk who was giving out coupons for an additional 10 percent off of all sale merchandise.

A 50 percent savings was enough to send Regina's excitement level up to the sky. She found a cart with a half-broken wheel and piled her purchases inside as she looked around for more bargains.

She examined a tiny Coach purse that was barely big enough to hold a small wallet and a makeup case, and it was still priced at $150.00. Regina did the math in her head. Of course they'd marked the prices up in advance of the sale, but a 50 percent discount put the purse right back within her reach. She had tossed the purse into her cart and was struggling to turn her lame shopping cart around when something snagged her eye.

The shoes. *Her* shoes. The deep blue suede slingbacks with the big gold buckle. Regina was standing in front of the rack before she knew it. The whole area had been ramshackled. Mismated shoes lay crooked and sideways on the shelves, and some dangled by the heels while others had been abandoned to their fate on the floor.

Regina grabbed the shoes that had caught her eye, and hurriedly turned them over. Size nines. *Narrow. She wears a seven and a half,* Regina remembered, as her eyes skimmed the rows in search of a smaller size.

She spotted the shoe in the next-to-last aisle. It was on the floor, propped against a knee-high brown winter boot that looked big enough to fit a man. Regina scooped the shoe up, then almost squealed out loud when she turned it over and peered at the size. It was a seven and a half.

Yes! She thought as she skimmed the rack looking for the shoe's mate. Regina took her time walking up and down the row. She looked at each and every shoe, but none matched the one she held in her hand. After scouring the last aisle, she turned around and walked back toward the first row. The early-morning crowd had picked over and tossed aside so many sale items that there was no telling where the other shoe had landed. *It's gotta be here. They couldn't have sold just one shoe,* She reasoned, eyes scanning.

They collided head-on, Regina and the woman who held the matching blue shoe. Both of them had been so focused on their search that neither saw the other until it was too late.

"Oops!" Regina laughed. She reached out to steady the other woman and was greeted with a cold, steely look. "Sorry about that," Regina said. "I guess we need to watch where we're going."

"*You* bumped into *me,*" the woman said with hostility in her voice and in her eyes. Regina took a step back. The woman was of average height, with tan skin and killer curves. Regina pegged her to be in her twenties, and she was dressed in a form-fitting Baby Phat tank top with matching deep-pressed Capri jeans. Her hair was short and stylish, with every end perfectly curled and bumped, and her fake eyelashes looked like they had been expertly applied.

She stood holding the shoe Regina needed in one hand and defiantly rested the other hand on her curved hip. Girlfriend was an urban shopper, Regina could tell. Every item she had on had been carefully selected and coordinated, from her flashy jewelry down to her hundred-dollar sandals.

The woman continued to glare at her, and Regina noted the long, tri-colored fake nails and the green contact lenses in her eyes and understood exactly what kind of person she was dealing with. A hood rat extraordinaire.

Regina shrugged and backed off slightly again. "Sorry. It's packed up in here. They're having such a hot sale . . ." She let her words trail off, but it was easy to fill in what Regina had deliberately left blank: Get over it. Shit happens.

"You have my shoe," the woman said. She held out her hand. "That's the one I was looking for when you bumped into me."

Regina frowned. She wasn't trying to get into it with anybody, but neither was she trying to give up her shoe.

"Actually," Regina said sweetly, surprising herself as she held her hand out as well. "You have *my* shoe. I was looking for it when *you* bumped into *me*."

A storm cloud seemed to gather in the woman's eyes. She took a step closer, pushing up like she was threat, but Regina had already retreated as far as she was willing to go.

"I had the damn shoe first!"

Regina nodded. "And I had this one first."

The girl rolled her eyes. "Fake hoes just kill me. All these damn shoes up in here, and you wanna get a beat down over one? Don't start no shit you can't finish, okay?"

Regina almost laughed. Fake? *The hair, the eyes, the fingernails . . . probably the tits and the ass too . . .* The pot was talking killer trash about the kettle! Staring at the angry woman, Regina expected to be filled with fear, but for the first time in a long time, she wasn't. She wasn't afraid, she wasn't intimidated, and she wasn't giving up her goddamn shoe!

Regina let it all hang out. "You have to bring ass to get ass, baby. Haven't you heard? I don't want to fight you over a shoe, but if you come at me I'm not gonna back down either. Now if you'd like, we can call a salesperson over and ask if they have any more like these in the storeroom, but I have just as much right to this shoe as you have to that one, and I'm not giving it up."

The girl smirked, then angled her chin. "Well what size is the one you got?"

"It's a seven and a half."

The girl glanced at the shoe she was holding, then looked back at Regina with hard, narrowed eyes. "Bitch, you real lucky I wear a nine," she said. She drew back and flung the shoe hard. It sailed past Regina's head and went flying down the aisle. "Because if I coulda got my foot in this seven and a half I'da shoved it up your ass by now."

The shoe landed somewhere behind Regina, and a woman standing in the aisle yelled "*Hey!*" and started cursing. Regina had flinched a little when the shoe torpedoed past her face, but she kept her feet planted and didn't move. Moments later the crazy woman gave it up. She called Regina another fake bitch and gave her the finger. Regina watched her sway her hips out of the aisle. She was barely gone when Regina bolted in the opposite direction, weaving through the crowd of shoppers as she searched the floor, glad she didn't have to fight her way out the store and determined to get her hands on that size seven and a half blue suede shoe!

Regina slept in late the next day. Tanya had called and invited her over to play a few games of Bid Whist with some friends the night before, and they ended up running Bostons and setting bids well into the night.

"I'm going to Zana Williams's house tomorrow," she told Tanya after everyone had left. Regina was rinsing out a few glasses while Tanya wiped off the card table. Her friend turned around at the news.

"Why are you going over there? You closed her file out last week, didn't you?"

Regina nodded. "Yeah, I did. She's good to go as far as our office is concerned. But she graduates from high school in a few weeks. I picked her up a little gift, and I want to drop it off to her."

"This isn't getting personal with you, is it, Regina? I don't have to remind you about what happened the last time you got involved with a client, do I?"

Regina shuddered, reliving her traumatic encounter. She'd been jogging around the track at Betsy Head Park in broad daylight when two hoodrats from Riverdale Houses jumped her from behind. They'd put a knife to her throat and dragged her out of the park, then threw her into a raggedy car where a man Regina had never seen waited behind the wheel. Those chicks had beaten her into the middle of the next week. Regina ran her hand along the side of her neck, the area where the knife had sliced her, the raised scar that she now wore her braids slung over her shoulder to cover. Months later she could still feel the warm blood as it spurted from her body and soaked her shirt. They'd pushed her into the trunk of the car, and the man had driven fast. Regina had been terrified and hysterical, and somehow between her attempts to kick her way out of the trunk and the baseball bat they beat her with, her right ankle had been broken.

And when the car stopped and the trunk was finally opened, it had gotten even worse.

"There, bitch!" Regina's client, Tricia Walsh, had spit down on her. Regina had been good to the girl. Damn good. She'd taken a liking to Tricia and felt sorry for her young daughter. Regina had eaten at the girl's house and hung out with her family members. She'd helped Tricia's mother get a job and had even given the woman designer clothes to wear right from her own closet. And at that moment Tricia was cursing her out and repaying Regina in the way she knew best. The girl was damn near standing on Regina's bleeding neck, crushing her windpipe. "That's what you get for being so damn nosey and getting somebody fired from their job! How the hell Derek supposed to take care of his damn daughter now?"

It had been an honest mistake, Regina had tried to explain. Tricia's five-year-old daughter had been referred to the hospital's social work office for unexplained vaginal bleeding, and even though Regina really dug Tricia's family, she had recommended that charges of child molestation be brought against the little girl's father.

Somehow Derek Lewis had been cleared by the Department of Youth and Family Services, but as a result of the investigation he'd been fired from his job as a school bus driver, so his girlfriend and her sister decided to take his lost wages out on Regina's ass. Not only had they beaten and cut her, they'd stood by and laughed as the driver of the car, a big, greasy, wild-eyed monster who would forever haunt Regina in her nightmares, had unzipped his pants and sexually assaulted her too.

"No, this is not personal, and hell no, you don't have to remind me," Regina told Tanya, her voice high and harsh. Her ankle started to throb. "How in the world could I ever forget?"

The next day Regina attended a midday service at Brownsville Baptist Church, then caught a cab over to the Crown Heights section of Brooklyn immediately afterward. The driver had no problem finding the address she'd given him, and Regina was relieved to find that Zana and her brother lived off the beaten path, on a narrow, tree-lined street that was congested with parked cars but seemed quiet and peaceful nevertheless.

Regina paid the driver and walked up to the front of the large private home, the bag containing Zana's gift dangling from her hand. The house had been remodeled and partitioned into small apartments with separate entrances, and Regina noticed a small planter filled with wildflowers right outside Zana and Zeke's door.

Regina rang the bell several times.

It was still pretty early in the day and Sunday-quiet, but Regina figured even if you'd partied the night away on Saturday, most people were up and at it by Sunday afternoon.

She pressed the bell again and waited. *You should have told the cab to wait,* she chided herself. As far as Regina knew, she could have been standing in front of a bogus address. It was going to be a hump back to a major street to flag down another cab, and since she'd come straight from church she wasn't exactly dressed for the hike.

Again, Regina rang the bell, and listened and waited. With each second that ticked past, her options were becoming pretty clear. It was either use her cell phone to call Black Pearl or Myrtle Cabs or another urban taxi service, then wait around for them to show up, or dig her feet into her shoes and get to trucking out to a main intersection to flag one down.

Regina rang the bell one last time for the road, then whipped out her cell and dialed the number for Zana that she had programmed into her phone. Seconds later, to her surprise, the jingle of a ringing phone could be heard coming from inside the house.

Holding the phone to her ear, Regina was startled to hear stomping footsteps approaching the door.

"Who the fuck is it?" a man barked and flung open the door.

Regina swallowed. She stood face to face with Zeke Williams, and he looked nothing like he'd looked the last time she'd seen him.

Zeke was still as fine as all outdoors, that much was for sure. He was also naked from the waist up; his smooth, muscled body damp, coated in a thin sheen of sweat.

"What the fu—" Zeke cursed and tried to slam the door shut, but Regina stuck her good foot in the crack.

"Um—" she stammered, peering inside as Zeke peeked around the door, hiding his body. Regina had only seen him for a second, but that was more than enough. His neck had looked thick and corded, and while his naked stomach rippled, his shoulders and arms bulged. And that wasn't the only thing that was bulging on him either, Regina had noticed. She hated that she'd looked, but it had been, *bam!* Right there in her face. The moment Zeke had opened the door, Regina's eyes had swept over him, past his sweat-filmed chest, down past the thick line of curly black hair that descended from his navel, and then stopped at the huge knot in his gym shorts.

"Hello?" A breathless voice came from behind Zeke and sounded in Regina's ear at the same time. She'd forgotten she was on the phone, and hearing her call answered from two different directions made her looked straight into the living room of the house.

Zana lay on her stomach right there on the sofa. She was facing away from Regina with her feet crossed at the ankles and aimed up toward the ceiling. Her back was bare, and she was almost as naked as her brother, except for a white thong and a pair of spiked red heels.

"Get the fuck outta here!" Zeke spit, still hiding, then swung the door on her foot hard enough to chop it off.

Regina yelped and dug her shoulder into the door as Zeke kicked at her toes. Regina was in pain, but she held her own. Her foot was jammed in there good, and she wasn't moving until somebody told her what was going on. But even without verbal confirmation Regina knew her eyes weren't lying, and she also knew something else too. She knew some damn body was about to have a serious fuckin' problem, because sticking out from under Zeke Williams' gym shorts was one of the biggest erections Regina had ever seen.

To call Monday morning blue would have been a giant understatement.

Regina had raged all of Sunday and halfway through the night. It was only out of exhaustion that she'd managed to close her eyes and catch a few winks right before dawn, and now, sitting across from Tanya, Regina's nose was sweating and her blood pressure was once again soaring sky-high.

"You're lucky he didn't try to kill you," Tanya said. Her face was pinched with worry and her hands flitted about, smoothing her clothes.

"Shit," Regina answered. "That fool is lucky I didn't try to kill *him*! The way he jacked up my foot and got up in my face?" She pursed her lips. "He's lucky he didn't get maced! I told you the next time one of these crazy clients tried something with me I would end up in jail, right?"

Tanya shook her head. "Now, Regina—"

"Now Regina, my *ass*! I took an oath to help those in need, but nowhere did it say I had to let the needy do me in. I'm telling you, T, he was cold busted!"

"You don't know that. There could have been other people in that house. Maybe her boyfriend."

"It was just them two—"

"Did you look around inside?"

"I told you, he wouldn't let me in! He grabbed me by the face and pushed me off his property. I told him I was calling the cops, and he told me the cops wouldn't get there fast enough to save my ass!"

"You take too many dangerous chances, Regina. You could have been hurt or even killed. Nobody besides me even knew you were going over there!"

"I wanted to give the girl a gift, that's all, Tanya. I saw something I knew she'd like, and I figured since she was graduating with honors it would be nice to show her that I was proud of her, that's all."

Tanya sighed. "Maybe you should have called first."

"I tried! I already told you! I did call. Hell, she was trying to answer my call while I was standing right behind her, looking at her half-naked butt twirling her feet up in the air!"

"Goodness," Tanya sighed again, then shuffled through a stack of unread folders on her desk. "Our caseload is already more than we can handle. This is going to open up a whole new can of worms around here, and since you weren't there on official business it might be difficult to justify committing our limited resources."

"I'm a social worker 24/7," Regina replied. "With me, it's official all the time."

"Your job was to determine whether or not this patient was a continued threat to herself or others, Regina. Christ! The kid gets pregnant by some bum and gives herself an old-fashion abortion. Young girls get pregnant every day. Sure, not all of them go to such drastic measures to hide their mistakes, but it happens. You closed the case on this girl when she was discharged from the hospital. Maybe you should have left it at that."

Regina gazed at her friend for a long moment. This job was a killer. Tanya's skin was blotched and pimply, she was grossly overweight, her hair needed re-braiding, and her clothing was worn and outdated. Stress and long hours had grinded a beautiful, hardworking and caring woman down nearly to the bone, and it hurt Regina's heart to hear such a devoted advocate place her workload above investigating the possible abuse of a child. *I'll never let a job do that to me,* Regina swore. Her days on this job were numbered, and she was steadily counting.

Spring was doing its thing when hoards of young people began pouring out the doors of Brooklyn Technical High School. The demographics of the school had changed over the years, and where there had once been a majority of white students in attendance, Regina now saw a wave of Asian students and a smattering of black and Hispanic students as well.

She stood against a parked car and watched the teenage girls flow outside wearing tight shirts and swaying their hips as they sauntered into the warm afternoon in search of lunch. Some laughed among themselves or chatted into cell phones with gross animation, while others clung to tall, gangly boys, brushing their breasts against hard male arms in an age-old attempt to impress and entice.

Regina scanned the crowd, searching for an exceptionally pretty black girl with soft long hair. They spotted each other at the same time, and Zana shot Regina a nasty look before turning her head and striding off in the opposite direction.

"Zana!" Regina called, taking off behind her. The girl picked up her pace and Regina was forced to jog a few paces to catch up to her. "Zana, wait," she said, grazing the girl's shoulder. "We need to talk."

The hood was all over the girl as she whirled around and shook Regina off.

"Don't be fuckin' touching me!" Zana hissed. "You don't know me like that, lady. So don't put your goddamn hands on me!"

"I know what's going on," Regina said softly, ignoring the tough talk.

"You almost got your ass kicked yesterday," Zana said. "Accusing people of something crazy like that. You lucky both of us didn't jump on you."

Regina swallowed hard, remembering how scared she'd been when Zeke mushed her face with one hand so hard he almost broke her neck.

"Stay the fuck away from me and my sister, you hear? If I catch you anywhere near her," he'd said, muzzling Regina's face with his big, strong hand, "I'ma *plant* your ass, you feel me?"

"I think your brother has a problem, Zana. And I can help you, if you'd just let me."

"Help me what?" the girl yelled. "*Your* life might be fucked up, but I'm doing *great*! My brother raised me the right way. I'm laced and fly, I stay pampered and pressed. Plus I've got a 4.0 GPA, remember? I'm set to be the valedictorian of my class, and I have great scholarship offers. My future looks real rosy, baby. Maybe you're the one who needs some help."

"Urinary tract infections at twelve . . ." Regina said softly. "Chlamydia at thirteen. Genital warts at fourteen and NGU at fifteen. Those kinds of vaginal infections don't just pop up in a young girl. They have to originate somewhere. Just because you go to several different hospitals for treatment doesn't mean all your records can't be pulled."

A dark look had fallen over Zana's face, and rage and defiance shone in her eyes.

"Please," Regina said quietly. "Zana, please. I'm not trying to hurt your brother, but you're only seventeen, and if I even suspect he's responsible for what you've been through, I'll have to report him."

"I ain't been through no more than anybody else has."

"Who were you pregnant by, Zana? Was it Zeke?"

The girl exploded. "Are you crazy?!? What the hell do you have against my brother? He's the best damn thing that ever happened to me and you wanna get him locked up? What? He's so young and hot you wanna get at him? You want some of that good stuff for yourself?"

Regina shook her head slowly. "It's not about him, Zana. It's about you. About protecting you."

"My brother has been protecting me since I was twelve years

old! Who the hell do you think fed me and took care of me? When my parents died, Zeke could have kept it moving in the Marines and never looked back. Instead, he came back here. He came back for *me*. He came and got me and gave me a home, a life, and did everything my parents would have wanted him to do. And now you're trying to accuse him of something that could get him locked up?"

"It could," Regina agreed softly. "You don't turn eighteen for six more months. If he gets arrested you'd have to go back into the foster system at least until then."

"Lady, what in the hell do you want from me?"

"I want to talk to you, Zana. That's all. I just want us to talk."

Zana sighed and put her hands on her hips but didn't answer.

"Just a few times a week," Regina blurted. "You don't have to tell your brother, and we can meet anywhere you want. Talk to me a couple of times a week and I'll hold off on telling the police what I saw."

"You didn't see a damn thing."

"Oh, but I did," Regina said firmly. "I saw enough."

Chapter FIVE

Regina had arranged to hold her first session with Zana in a small back office in the social work department.

"Technically, you should be seeing patients on the ward," Tanya warned her. She vigorously disagreed with the whole set up, and had urged Regina, in the absence of any proof, to either bring charges against Zeke Williams or leave his sister alone. "If anybody asks, you might want to tell them that Zana is being seen as an outpatient, you hear?"

Regina had told Zana to arrive by three. "It's either talk to me, Zana, or deal with the authorities," Regina said, laying down an ultimatum. "That means we involve the police, social services, and the Department of Youth and Family Services. Your brother teaches music to middle school kids, right? You can talk to me, or he can talk to the man. Take your pick."

Regina's stomach was in knots as she watched the clock, hoping the girl wasn't going to call her bluff. Truly, all she had were her suspicions to stand on. Despite what she'd seen at Zana's house that day, there was no real evidence to say that Zeke was sexually abusing his sister. Regina had discreetly asked a few questions around the community and had even called Libra Jackson at the rehabilitation clinic, since she was an active community resident in Crown Heights, and asked her if she knew anything about Zana and Zeke.

"That's one hell of a young man," Libra had said with pride in her voice. "I knew his mother back in the day. Sister was a doozy, a floozy, and a boozy! But when her and her husband got burnt up for messing with somebody's drugs, Zeke came home from the service and he started bringing Zana to our church and raising her right. He gave up everything for that little girl, you know. That boy did as a child what his parents couldn't or wouldn't do as grown people. He's one we treasure around here, Regina. I wish we had a thousand more just like him."

Others who knew Zeke, from the social worker who counseled kids at his school to the old Puerto Rican lady in the lunchroom, had said basically the same thing. Anytime his name was so much as uttered, a bright light shone in someone's eyes and he was praised from head to toe. Regina wasn't surprised. Zeke was a charmer, hiding behind a façade. He had everyone blinded, including his sister.

At precisely 3:20 the door swung open and Zana Williams walked in. She was dressed in a light-blue-and-brown pantsuit and wore matching sandals and carried a small leather clutch in the exact same shades.

"I'm here," she said to nobody as she stood posing in the middle of the room. There was a hard look in her eyes, and her lower jaw was set. "You said I had to be here, right? So I'm here."

Regina wanted to be gentle with the girl, but they were running out of time. Zana needed to focus on her scholarship offers and give the colleges a definitive answer. If she waited much longer and missed the deadlines then the awards could be rescinded and she'd be trapped in New York—under the control of her brother—for who knew how long.

Regina came right on out with it. "Has your brother ever touched you inappropriately, Zana?"

"Hell no! He's my brother, stupid. He loves me."

"Has he ever done anything to you that was sexual in nature?"

"I said no."

"When I came to your house that day, you were lying on the couch, almost naked. Do you normally expose yourself to your brother that way?"

"We're *sister* and *brother*. We live together, so we've seen each other half-dressed before. All siblings have."

"Has your brother ever penetrated you? Did he have sex with you?"

"I'ma tell you one more time, lady. My brother loves me. We love each other. We take care of each other. Now, somebody like you might see something nasty in that, but I don't. My brother is a good man. He helps everybody in our neighborhood, and he gives me everything I need—"

"Are you," Regina demanded, interrupting forcefully, "having sex with him?"

For a moment it looked to Regina like Zana wanted to hit her. The girl glared at her with her chest heaving, seething with anger and indignation.

"It's a good thing Zeke doesn't know I'm here. He'd rain on your ass."

"Tell me," Regina demanded. "Or tell the police."

Silence. Anger.

"You's a nasty old heffah," Zana said finally, then laughed mockingly. "Trying to start some shit just because you're jealous. You need to get yourself a man. You need to get a damn life, lady, that way you can stay out of mine. Instead, you over there seeing all kinds of dirt where there really is none. I wonder why? Could it be because there's something real dirty that you see in your own self?"

The second and third sessions didn't go much better, and it wasn't until the end of their fourth session that Regina found a small piece of common ground that she and Zana could both stand on.

"So how'd you do on your project?" Regina asked. She sipped from a glass of cold raspberry tea and motioned for Zana to sit down across from her. For the past two weeks they'd been meeting at a Starbucks downtown instead of at the office, and as usual, the stunning teenager had made quite a few heads turn as she came through the door. The girl had whip appeal, there was no doubt about that. Today she was wearing a hot pink skirt and a matching jacket, and her firm young body was swollen and bulging in all the right places. Regina shook her head. She'd been counseling Zana for weeks, and by now she knew that Zana liked to flaunt her luscious body and adorn it in stylish, expensive things. Somehow her brother managed to keep her looking top-shelf from head to toe, and grown men salivated after her curvaceous young flesh like horny stray dogs. But Regina also knew that mentally and emotionally, Zana was still a kid. She liked rap music, writing poetry, and she also liked indulging in sweets, so twice a week Regina had a cold caramel frappuccino and a warm slice of pound cake waiting for her young client.

Even though she was burning with the belief that Zeke was an abuser, Regina had decided to take things slow with Zana. She'd eased up on all the harsh, direct questions, although she remained convinced that Zeke was showering his sister with a whole lot more than brotherly love. But the girl was obviously not ready to admit what was going on, and part of that was because of her youth and vulnerability. Regina knew what it felt like to be left alone in the world without any family. She understood that Zana was clinging to her brother because he was the only solid thing she had in her life, no matter how twisted their relationship had become. Regina's ultimate goal was to help Zana see the reality of her situation for herself. The girl had a treasure chest of wonderful opportunities awaiting her, and it was now Regina's personal mission to convince Zana to accept an out-of-state scholarship and get the hell away from her brother.

So when Zana had shared the details of an upcoming engineering project with her during one of their meetings, Regina had immediately recognized some similarities to a paper she'd recently completed in grad school. She'd seized upon this commonality and quickly offered to help Zana work on the project twice a week at Starbucks. And even though Zana was still giving her a little street attitude, working on the project together seemed to bring them closer to common ground.

"I got an A," Zana said, grinning despite herself. She was still maintaining a semi-hostile façade during their meetings, but beneath all the tough talk Regina was constantly amazed at the girl's brilliance and ingenuity. "My teacher said the references we made to the infinite sink were well outside of my academic scope, and he was really impressed." Zana took a bite of her warm cake, then looked directly at Regina. "So thanks," she said quietly. "I appreciate you helping me out."

Regina nodded. "No problem." She swirled a few pieces of ice around in her cup. "I'm just glad I could remember half of that stuff. I just got my engineering degree a few months ago, but a lot of the calculations are so complex it's easy to forget a step or two along the way."

"It didn't seem like you forgot any of that stuff," Zana said with a hint of respect and admiration in her voice. "I can't wait to finish college and get in with a top engineering firm. Maybe a company like Exxon Mobile or something."

Regina laughed. "You're worrying about a job after college already? You gotta get out of high school first, girl! But," she said quietly, taking another sip of her cold tea, "if you choose the right school in the right location, in a couple of years you might be able to get an internship that'll help you land that dream job. Have you been thinking more about your scholarship offers?"

Zana shrugged. A chill was suddenly about her. "A little bit. Like I said before, I'm probably going to Columbia."

"It's a great school, Zana. An excellent school. But it's in New York, and that means you'll be stuck here in New York. Have you at least checked out the dormitory?"

"Why would I wanna live in a dorm, Miss Williams? My crib is laid out. I have a big room, a plasma TV on my wall, two closets full of hot clothes, and a refrigerator full of food. You think I'd give up all that to go live in a little shoe box with some chick I don't even know?"

"But that's a big part of the university experience!" Regina exclaimed. "A college dorm is an exciting place to be, Zana. You have your freedom and lots of room to make your own decisions, but you're not completely on your own, either. It's a stepping-stone from your childhood to your future, Zana. You really don't want to miss out on that."

Zana crumpled her napkin in her fist and looked out the window.

"I know what you're getting at, and you ain't a bit slick." She crossed her arms under her breasts and gave Regina a cold, steely look. "I'm not moving, and I'm not leaving my brother. So you can quit with all that fake cheerleading. I'm happy right where I am."

"You're in a bad spot, Zana," Regina insisted. "I know you can't see it, but you are."

"Maybe my life looks bad to you because you don't have a life of your own. Why can't you just mind your damn business and stay out of mine?"

"I'm in a helping profession. I help those who need it, even when they don't realize they need it."

"Try helping your damned self."

"I think Zeke does things to you that are wrong, Zana. I know you don't want to see your brother behind bars, but he has no right to touch you in that way."

"You said a few weeks, right? I agreed to see you for a few weeks, and then we're done, right?"

Regina sighed, then nodded.

"Good," Zana said. She sipped the last of her cold drink and rose from her chair. "Because I'm about tired of this shit. You need to give it up, lady, because you're way off base. Just give it up."

"We'll meet at my office next week," Regina called out to Zana's retreating back. The girl never even acknowledged her as she sashayed toward the door, throwing her cute hips left and right. "At my office, okay?"

Zana kept moving as Regina sat rooted in her chair. She sighed and shook her head as several grown men openly salivated as they watched sexy little Zana strut out the door.

Chapter SIX

"One more week, huh?" Tanya asked. She was watering a row of plants as Regina entered the office, and turned to give her friend and co-worker a tired smile. "I don't know what we're going to do without you around here, honey. I still haven't gotten the okay to advertise your position, so things are about to go from bad to worse."

Regina gave a wry smile. "I sure hate to leave you with all this on your hands," she gestured around the cluttered room. "Have you talked to the higher-ups about maybe getting somebody from psych to fill in here temporarily?"

Tanya frowned. "They're short-staffed over there too. There's nobody to borrow from."

"Well, I've just about cleared up all my backlog," Regina said, rubbing her eyes. She'd been working twelve to fifteen hours each day to prepare for her departure, and even though she'd practically moved a small mountain of work off her desk, at a busy hospital with patients being admitted each day, casework was a never-ending cycle. "With all the old files closed out, at least you'll only have to deal with the new cases."

"Thanks," Tanya said. "I really appreciate everything you've done around here over the past few weeks. I know how badly you want to leave us, Regina, and to throw yourself into the workload like that—especially when you didn't have to—was really good of you. I'm going to miss you, sister. And not just because you're a wonderful social worker but because you're a wonderful woman and a wonderful friend."

Regina saw the tears forming in her boss's eyes, and she struggled to hold back her own.

"No, thank *you,* T. You've taught me a lot over the years and helped me get through some of my darkest days. A big part of who I am, I owe to you."

It was in this somber mood that Regina greeted Zana when she sauntered in for their last counseling session. Regina had helped many clients during her time at the hospital, and she was proud of her record and felt good about being able to make a difference in so many lives. But Zana's case was a bitter reminder that not everyone could or wanted to be helped. Regina took Zana's refusal to escape her situation as a sign of professional failure, and quitting her job without resolving what she believed to be a serious case of abuse left her with a deep sense of personal defeat.

Zana waltzed into the room on a cloud of expensive perfume. Her hair bounced and swayed like it had just been done ten minutes earlier, and the girl was dressed in a navy blue pantsuit that Regina knew had cost at least five hundred dollars.

"Wow," she said, admiringly. "You look really nice, Zana. Are you going someplace special today?"

Zana shrugged, still sullen. "I've got some plans. So I can't be up in here chatting all day. Let's get this started so we can get it over with."

"Oh—" Regina said abruptly. She reached under her desk and pulled out a plastic bag. Smiling, she leaned across the desk and handed it to Zana. "I'd forgotten all about these," she said as Zana gave her a puzzled look, then took a shoe box from the bag.

Zana extracted a shoe from the box and stared at it with begrudging pleasure.

"Your cute blue suit reminded me of them. I wore a pair just like this one day while you were in the hospital and you said you liked them, remember? These are a seven and a half, exactly your size. They match your suit to a tee, too. Go ahead. Try them on."

"This is the outfit I was talking about too!" Zana said, kicking off her shoes. The ones she'd worn were expensive and tasteful, but they didn't do her get up the same kind of justice that the shoes Regina had bought her did.

"Yeah, these babies are fly as hell!" Zana said, giving Regina a genuine grin. She walked around the small office, trying to eye her feet from all angles and smiling as she modeled the shoes.

"How do they look on me?"

"Hot," Regina admired as the gold buckled caught the light and shined. "They look like they were made for what you're wearing. I don't think you could even find another pair of shoes to match up any closer."

"Well, thanks," Zana said when she finally sat back down on the sofa. She reached for her purse. "How much do I owe you?"

"Nothing," Regina said gently. "I got them as a gift, Zana. For your high school graduation."

"Well, thanks again," Zana said shortly. She crossed her right leg over her left knee, and once again the gold buckle picked up the light.

Long moments passed, with both women silent.

Finally, "Zana, I'd like to use our last session together to learn a little more about your parents. You know, your early life with them and how they died."

Zana sighed and wagged her leg, the gold buckle sending crazy beams of light zigzagging around the room with each movement.

"I already told you. I don't like to talk about my parents."

"I can understand that," Regina said. "I don't like to talk about mine either. Especially since they left me alone to fend for myself."

Zana smirked. "I wish my parents would have just left me alone. It would have been the best damn thing they ever did for me."

Regina was startled by the anger and resentment in the girl's voice, and she pressed on gently, eager to learn more.

"Not everybody is fit to parent a child," she said in an agreeable tone. "I think folks should have to pass a written test and undergo counseling before they can take a baby home from the hospital."

"Or something," Zana agreed pensively, wagging her leg.

Regina watched the young girl's eyes for long, long moments. The glint from Zana's shoe buckle flitted across her forehead and created a fascinating pattern of light and shadows on her face. There was something different about Zana's eyes today, Regina realized. Something different about Zana. A strange aura had fallen over the room. They stared at each other curiously, serenely. Minutes passed, and they seemed to talk without words. Zana looked down at her foot and wagged her leg, and Regina sighed and forged onward.

She spoke softly, her tone tender and hushed.

"I know what he's doing to you."

"Everybody knows what my brother's doing. He's taking care of me."

"How long?" Regina asked softly.

Silence.

"How long?"

She shrugged and conceded.

"Since I was twelve."

"He abused you."

"He *sacrificed* for me. It wasn't abuse. It was love."

Regina felt light-headed. Her palms were wet. The girl's admission had flowed from her lips like it had always been there, just waiting to be released.

"You were a child," she repeated. "You trusted him and he took advantage of you. Your parents trusted him—"

"Oh they did that shit too!" Zana yelled, shattering the still of the room.

"Get in the bed, Zana," the girl whispered in a child-like voice. Trance-like, she swung her legs around and lay back on the sofa, her eyes squinched tight as she replayed the nightmares of her

youth. "Open your legs, baby. Now get on top of her, Zeke. Move around like Daddy showed you. Yeah, just like that. See how much your brother loves you, Zana? It doesn't even hurt, does it? Okay, it's Daddy's turn now. You can do it again later, Zeke. Get off of her, son. Your sister is ready for Daddy now . . ."

Regina sat paralyzed by the emotions playing out on Zana's face. The girl lay with her legs spread wide, sucking in deep breaths. Her lips trembled and quivered. She hunched her shoulders and whimpered, her whole body going stiff with pain. *Okay, Daddy . . . Okay Daddy . . .* She thrashed around on her back, her midsection gyrating and taking a pummeling as she was ridden by an unseen lover. Her legs went up in the air, spread wide, and she held herself by the thighs as she simulated a sex act, whispering dirty obscenities in a little girl's voice. Sunlight pierced the room and collided with the buckles on her blue suede shoes, and Zana arched her back and groaned loudly as her body shuddered in release. Moments later she relaxed and sighed, lowering her legs with a look of relief on her face as her chest rose and fell and sweat beaded her child-like face. She lay there limply, as though she were sleeping, but her eyes were now open and staring across the room.

Regina sat transfixed. It was a very long time before she could either move or speak. When she did, her voice seemed as drained as Zana's young body.

"How'd they—" she asked hoarsely, then swallowed hard and tried again. "Your parents. How'd they die?"

Zana answered in the voice of a very small child. "I killed them."

~

Lincoln Center was a hub of bustling activity, and Regina filed in along with the rest of the folks who had come to witness the proud occasion. Photos were being snapped and video cameras were rolling, and there was a jovial spirit of accomplishment in the air.

Regina searched for her seat as the school band played in the background, and marveled at the rite of passage that was about to take place for some of New York City's brightest and finest young students. Arriving at this milestone in their lives was no small feat, Regina knew. The statistics on high school dropouts were staggering, especially among people of color, and each time a cap-and-gown-adorned young person passed by, she gave them a big, proud smile.

Filing into her row, Regina excused herself and squeezed past a large family who was already seated. They made room for her amicably, and when she sat down an older white woman with bouncy blond hair leaned over asked, "Who are you here for? You certainly don't look old enough to have a child graduating from high school."

Regina smiled and patted the woman's hand. "You're right. I don't have a child this age, but I'm here to cheer on a friend. Thanks so much for the compliment."

Settling back in her seat, Regina took a few moments to reflect on the path that had led her to this moment. Although she'd been intrigued by Zana's case from the very beginning, never could she have imagined the depth of the girl's pain or the scope of her abuse.

"I was four the first time it happened," Zana had told her. After witnessing Zana's regression, Regina had broken the rules again and taken the girl to her apartment, where they curled up at opposite ends of her sofa and drank from steaming mugs of hot cocoa.

"I remember because it was the night of my birthday and I'd had a huge party earlier in the day." Zana's story came out in a rush. As though she'd been waiting her whole life to tell it. "They started me off with Zeke. He was only about eleven, and they made him do it. At first he didn't like it, but after a while, I guess he did."

"Was there anyone you could have told? You know, confided in?"

Zana shrugged. "If there was, I didn't know about it. They were my parents. I did what they told me to do. I thought it was normal. Even after my father started in on me, I still thought it was normal. Me and Zeke slept in the same bedroom. At night they'd start me out with Zeke, then my father would get in my bed and my mom would climb in with my brother. We thought everybody did things that way."

Regina was careful to stay fully engaged in Zana's story but to refrain from asking too many questions.

"I can remember the night I stopped it like it was yesterday. Zeke had already left me by then. And with him gone, Mama and Daddy would just put me in the bed between them and do . . . whatever they wanted to do.

"Our next-door neighbor had been cutting his grass earlier in the day. I saw him put the lawn mower and the gas can next to his front stairs, and that evening, right before Mama called me inside, I stole his gas can and hid it in my bedroom closet.

"Daddy was drinking a lot that night. Shooting dope too. Some of his friends had come over to play cards and get high, and he kept calling me in the living room to bring him this or to go get him that. He'd say, 'Zana comere, baby girl.' And when I went over to him he'd rub me on the butt or run his big hand up my leg. I was eleven! I didn't want his friends to see him touching me like that. A few of them had already tried to touch me themselves, and by that time I had figured out that most girls my age didn't sleep with their damn daddies!

"I waited until Daddy's company left and he called me into the room with him and Mama. I cried, and for the first time I told them I didn't want to sleep in their bed anymore. Mama was real high. She slapped me and called me ungrateful. She said Daddy worked hard to take care of me and to give me every little thing I asked for. She said I owed both of them something for all that and that I was damn sure gonna give it to them. So I did."

Tears streamed from Zana's eyes as she spoke. The mug of cocoa shook in her trembling hands. "But I gave my parents something else that night too. I waited until they were both asleep, then went to my room and got the gas can. I poured it all around the bed, then backed out of the room, pouring the last of it in a trail until I reached the front door."

Zana fell quiet, and long minutes passed with only the sound of their breathing disturbing the air. Regina didn't want to ask, but she certainly had to know.

"What did you do then, Zana?"

The girl looked at Regina like she was crazy, and in the voice of an eleven-year-old she replied in a manner that stated the obvious, "I lit a match."

Chapter SEVEN

The graduation was beautiful, and Regina actually cried as Zana walked across the stage to get her diploma. She'd been startled, and then mad as hell as Zana's name was read and a handsome young man down front stood up and hollered, "Yeah! Zana!" He clapped and whistled. "Way to go, Baby Sis!"

Regina felt sick in the pit of her stomach. She wanted to jump up and scream out for folks sitting near him to guard their little girls. She wanted to curse him out and call him a nasty-ass pedophile. She was dying to call the police and have him locked up and put underneath the jail, but she'd given Zana her word. She'd made a promise to a young lady who trusted her, and there was no way she would break it.

"Your brother has to answer for what he did to you," Regina had told the girl several nights earlier. They were sharing a pizza and sipping iced tea in Regina's kitchen. Zana's confession had been liberating and cathartic. She'd cried all night in Regina's arms, and the very next morning she had moved out of the apartment she'd shared with her brother and was now sleeping in Regina's spare bedroom.

Regina had comforted the girl, using everything she'd learned as a social worker to convince her that she bore no responsibility for what her parents and brother had done. The death of her parents, Regina wasn't going to touch. Word in the hood was that Zana's piss-poor parents had been taken out by local drug dealers, and nothing different could be proven at this point. Regina did feel it was important to report the recent sexual abuse to the police, but Zana had been adamant about protecting Zeke.

"No. Hell no! You're right about what we did being wrong, Regina. And I'm glad you helped me see it and admit it. But Zeke is just as much a victim as I was. He didn't ask for this anymore than I did."

"Maybe not," Regina pushed, "but he was an adult when he took custody of you, Zana. You were a child. He chose to pick up where you guys had left off, when he could have chosen to get counseling for both of you instead."

"We loved each other the only way we knew how, Regina. Zeke did what he'd been taught to do. We both did."

Regina pushed again. "Somebody has to be held responsible for the damage that's been done to you, Zana! Don't you see that?"

Zana nodded slowly, then reached out and took Regina's hand.

"I do see it, Regina. And at the age of eleven, it got handled. *I* handled it. The people who made me and Zeke what we are, are dead."

"You deserve a chance to have a normal life."

"Listen, as bad as life was with my mother and father, it was nothing compared to what I went through in foster care. Zeke came and got me when he could have just walked away. He rescued me from a living hell, and I owe him. I'll *always* owe him. I couldn't have survived another day in the foster system. Not another minute. I was ready to kill myself in there, and Zeke came and got me. Because he *loves* me. You might not be able to understand it, Regina, but my life wouldn't mean a damn thing if my brother went to jail."

Regina placed her hand over Zana's, sandwiching the girl's hands between hers.

Zana's voice went soft. "Zeke's been calling me a lot. He knows I told you. He's scared, and I don't blame him. I gave Zeke my word that I would never betray him, and I need your word too," she said firmly, without compromise. "Leave my brother alone. He's all I have. Let it be."

Regina nodded. "Okay," she said gently. "It's your life. I won't be the one who turns your brother in. But I need your word on something too. I need you to free yourself."

"Free myself?"

"Yes," Regina said, softly. "Free yourself. Accept one of your out-of-state scholarships for college. Leave your brother's house for good. Burn it completely from your memory. Leave New York and run towards your life."

"Do you have your itinerary?"

Zana nodded.

"Your ID and your cell phone?"

Zana laughed. "I have everything. Stop worrying, Regina. I'm ready for this."

Regina sighed and put her arm around the girl's shoulders. She led Zana over to an airline kiosk and got her checked in, then printed her boarding pass and handed it to her. They walked over to the security checkpoint in silence, the air between them heavy with emotion.

"You're at gate C12, okay?"

Zana nodded. "I can find it."

Regina looked at the girl from head to toe and couldn't help but smile. Zana's gear was together. She looked ready for a photo shoot instead of a five-hour plane ride to California.

"Nice shoes," Regina said, grinning.

Zana laughed too. "Yeah," she said, turning her right foot to and fro, admiring the blue suede shoes that had been a graduation gift from a trusted friend. She nodded toward Regina's feet, on which there were an identical pair. "I like yours too."

"Are you excited?" Regina asked. "You're flying for the first time in your life . . . going to a new state, a new school . . ."

Zana grinned. "Yeah, I am. Excited, nervous . . . all that. How about you? You've put off starting your engineering job for weeks. You ready for it now?"

Regina shook her head. "No, I'm not. I think I'm gonna stay put for a while. At least long enough to help a few new clients. In fact, I've already told Tanya to withdraw my resignation. I sent the engineering company a letter yesterday, I hope they'll understand."

"Wow," Zana said. "You're giving up the engineering job with the big cheese and the phat office? I'm surprised, but then again I'm not really surprised. You said you're a social worker at heart, and you really are, Regina. You really are."

Regina reached out and hugged the girl closely. She'd done a lot of that over the last few weeks. Zana had confessed that no woman had held her in years, and during the short time that Zana was with her, Regina had hugged the girl as often as possible.

"Good-bye, Zana," Regina said, fighting the tears that welled in her eyes.

Zana hugged her back, just as hard. "Bye. See you for Christmas break?"

Regina nodded. Zana had become the daughter she would never have.

"I'll be there, sweetie. Believe me, I'll be there."

Zana walked toward security while Regina headed for the airport exit. The distinctive sound of their footsteps could be heard above the din of the crowd. Two identical pairs of blue suede shoes. One pair leading its wearer toward her destiny, the other helping its wearer escape the bonds of her past.

TaRESSA

BREAKIN' DISHES

STOVALL

Blur

Has the jury reached a verdict?"

"We have, Your Honor."

"Will the defendant please rise for the verdict?"

My attorney, Victoria Anthony, lays a reassuring hand on my forearm and squeezes it once, somewhere between gently and hard. Fighting the sensation of being stuck in concrete, I push back my chair, place both hands on the scarred wooden table for support, and force myself into what I believe is a standing position.

These ridiculously high blue suede stiletto shoes, which I am wearing in direct defiance of Victoria's advice, make the trembling of my knees even worse. But these gorgeous, near-gaudy shoes are my good-luck charm, the only hope I have of recovering any semblance of my life.

I am not breathing. Victoria isn't either. My eyes are locked on the jury foreman's mouth, awaiting the pronouncement of my fate. Everything else is a blur.

His words seem to be in slow motion, coming at me through a fog. I strain to quiet the screams inside my head so I can hear. "We, the jury, find the defendant, Monique Estelle Worthington . . ."

Red

It's second nature to keep the red lights on the three studio cameras in my peripheral vision. After twenty-three-years in television, the last dozen as the six and eleven o'clock news co-anchor for WTFS-13, Atlanta's NBC affiliate, I still get a thrill from the high-pressure jazz of each newscast.

My co-anchors and I are the top-rated news team in town. Duke Wankowski, a burly, good-natured Texan who swears he was named after the movie legend John "Duke" Wayne, sits in the center. I'm on Duke's right. Liz Santiago, a stick-thin blue-eyed blonde who claims she's Latina but looks like a straight-up Barbie to me, is on his left. Viewers have nicknamed us the Mod Squad: one black, one white, one blonde.

"And now," Duke is saying, "Monique Worthington has the latest on the fake Botox scandal in a leading plastic surgeon's office. Monique?"

"Thanks, Duke," I say smoothly, relaying the story from the TelePrompTer rolling next to the cameras, switching focus when the red lights change from camera one to camera two and back again.

Exactly fifty seconds later, my story is over and I'm passing the news torch to Liz.

I'm in my midforties, look at least ten years younger, and am at the top of my game: a highly successful, extremely popular star in one of the nation's top markets. I never wanted to go into TV; actually, I dreamed of becoming a lawyer, but a journalism-law internship during my undergraduate years at Howard University led to an emergency fill-in for an ailing reporter. And once I felt the rush of live TV news, my destiny was clear.

Duke is chuckling and gently nudging me in the side. "Atlanta City Councilman Armstrong Worthington is steadily rising in local opinion polls, some say largely to his plan to reduce violent crime," Duke says. "There's even speculation that insiders are testing the waters for a possible mayoral run next fall. I don't suppose you have any special scoop on that, Monique?" he asks with a knowing glance.

Seething inside, I play along. "No scoop at all, Duke," I assure the viewers with my most winning smile. "As for any speculation about my husband's possible plans, I can only say, 'No comment.'" I fake a gentle "ahem," then continue, "While I can't predict our great city's political future, our very able meteorologist Nathan 'Weather Wiz' Sommers is here with this week's weather forecast. Nathan?"

Minutes later, we've wrapped up another newscast. By the time I tie up loose ends in my office, it's past midnight. I rush to my car, a nice-but-nondescript black Lexus, and zip home, eager to debrief with my husband and decompress from my day. On the drive, I replay Duke's query. Armstrong running for mayor? We've joked about it a time or two, but he's never expressed any serious interest. At least not to me.

He's been a member of the Atlanta City Council for nearly eight years and seemingly content with his role in helping manage the Mecca of the Southeast.

I turn into the circular driveway, noting that a few lights are burning in our oversized, overpriced, totally-worth-it dream house in glitzy (and formerly mostly-White) Buckhead. Each successful black person who lives here is like a raised middle finger to those who feel we have no business infiltrating one of their enclaves. Another source of satisfaction in my life.

Speaking of satisfaction, Armstrong is waiting at the door with a drink for each of us. I take mine gratefully: it's a mellow merlot wine, perfect for unwinding from our equally crazy days.

"You saw the newscast?" I ask, settling into my favorite chair.

Armstrong nods, still standing, his eyes on mine.

"Including Duke's little dig?" I ask.

"Oh yes. Of course," he replies in his soothing baritone voice, the one that hooked me the first time it flowed into my ears.

"So?" I inquire. "What *is* the inside scoop anyway, Councilman Worthington?"

We share a chuckle, and I stifle a nervous twinge in my gut. Hate that feeling. It usually means I'm about to be hit with something I'd rather not deal with, rather not know.

I steel myself, then look more deeply into my beloved soul mate's eyes. "You're up in the polls. Your track record is the most impressive in the whole City Council's. The civil rights icons seem to be in your corner. Not to mention some of the Big Money white boys from the north side and outlying suburbs." I take a sip of the merlot, willing it to soothe my nerves.

"Yes," Armstrong says, a smile playing at the corners of his full lips. "You seem to have all of the facts straight so far, Mrs. Worthington. I can't argue with any of them."

I arch an eyebrow and await his response, the gut twinge intensifying.

"What I want to know is, how you would feel about being Atlanta's First Lady?" he asks.

"For real?"

"Yes, Monique. For real."

I set my wineglass down on the table next to my favorite chair, take a moment to survey my flawlessly furnished home and my beloved husband. "I'd have to step down from my job, obviously."

"And how big of a problem would that be?"

I sigh. "It might not be a problem at all, Armstrong. I'm sure there are a hundred things I could do besides the evening news."

Our eyes dance a tense tango. "How badly do you want it, darling?" I ask. "Because if this is truly your heart's desire, you know I'll be behind you all the way. Whatever that means for me."

Armstrong sets down his glass and smiles slowly, then nods.

"Thank you, baby," he says. "Now come over here and gimme some of that sweet, spicy sugar."

I smile at his corny old joke, loving the familiarity of it, and move into his embrace. As I tilt my head to press my lips to his, I find myself bracing for a sneeze.

"Ahhhhhhhhhhhhhhhhh-shit!" I say, covering my nose and mouth with my left arm. "I'm sorry."

"Bless you, baby," Armstrong says. "Are you coming down with something?"

Before I can answer, I'm hit with a wave of sneezes, one right after the other, with no time to speak in between. I sneeze at least ten times, moving further back from Armstrong with each one.

His eyes are downcast now. Mine are blazing. All I can see is red. Because what Armstrong and I both know is that my allergy to cheap perfume is a dead giveaway that he's been cheating. Again.

I snatch up my half-filled wineglass and hurl it directly at Armstrong's head. He ducks, and it shatters against the marble mantelpiece, raining onto the matching marble hearth in front of one of our home's half-dozen fireplaces. The wine pools around the shards of crystal like blood around the bones of a corpse.

Neither of us moves to clean up the mess. The latest in a long line of cleaning women will get it tomorrow, I reason. After all, that's what we're paying whatever-her-name-is for.

"Monique, you're mistaken," Armstrong says softly. "You're getting all worked up over nothing. There's no reason for you to worry. Just calm down."

My response is to rush forward and slap him in the face, knee him in the groin, and stomp on his foot. He gasps, bends at the middle, and groans just a little, almost silently. I freeze, waiting for him to recover. Finally, after a long minute or two, he straightens, wincing with the effort of movement, and speaks again.

"You know I'd never cheat on you, Monique. I love you too much to damage what we have, what we've built, *together.*"

"Liar!" The rage is boiling inside me. I am blinded by another flare of crimson red. And like a crazed bull, I charge him again. I punch him in the jaw, rake my flawless (and 100 percent real) fingernails across his neck. I draw blood.

Armstrong makes no physical move to stop me, no attempt to defend himself.

The look in his eyes enrages and terrifies me more than the cheap perfume and its message that he's screwing another of his whores. His eyes look dead, as if his mind and emotions have vacated his body completely, leaving me an empty shell to attack.

I hate him. I hate myself more. I pound harder on his back, his ribs, his chest, hoping to drum all the hatred away.

He steels himself against my blows, damning me with his silence. I am screaming, cursing like a gutter rat, no longer the "classy and articulate" Monique Worthington whom the public admires, no longer the "exemplary role model" known throughout the community for good deeds and charitable works.

I grab one of my two local Emmy Awards from the mantelpiece and aim it at Armstrong's temple, wanting more than anything to make the pain he feels on the outside match the agony I am suffering on the inside.

Finally, Armstrong grabs my wrist and stops me. He wrestles the golden Emmy statuette from my hand and sets it gently back onto the mantelpiece. "Now Monique, you know you don't want to hurt your favorite award, now do you? The one you got for your ground-breaking special on domestic violence? The one that talks about wives attacking their husbands? You might want to hurt me, but I know you don't want to mess up your precious Emmy."

Armstrong's voice is a full-out sneer now. I punch, slap, and kick, but his taunting words keep coming. I lift my arms in front of my face to ward them off, but they wind their way around my flesh to infect my ears. "What you really want is to break me down, bend me to your will like you do everyone else in your life," he says. "But I'll never give you that satisfaction."

And with that, the last bit of adrenaline drains from my body. The fight has left me. The urge to destroy has been neutralized by my husband's voice.

I stagger upstairs to shower, making the water as hot as my skin can stand. I soap and rinse a dozen times, hoping the shame will run down the drain and leave me forever. I apply lotion to my still-wet skin and pull on a cotton bathrobe. Brush my teeth so hard my gums sting, feel bruised. I want to draw blood.

Exhausted, I moisturize my face, then turn out the lights and move toward the bed. Armstrong is standing at the door, a shot glass filled with straight whiskey in his hand.

"Oh, God, Armstrong, I'm so sorry, baby," I sob, moving toward him. He puts up a hand to signal me to stop, but I keep going. I throw myself against his chest, begging forgiveness.

We stand like this for what feels like five minutes. He doesn't soften, doesn't respond. Just knocks back that whiskey. Then he moves away, undresses swiftly and silently, and climbs into our bed. I join him, moving closer to savor the warmth of his flesh against mine.

"Stay over there," he commands, his voice bigger and deeper than ever. It fills the dark room. "Do not touch me, Monique. I warn you."

And then, he goes to sleep. Closes both eyes just inches from the woman who has attacked him. I know he's asleep because the cadence of his breathing changes. Because the rise and fall of his chest gives him away.

His revenge for my beating? He hasn't washed himself at all. The scent of cheap perfume and dried sexual juices torments me, just inches away. And even sleeping, Armstrong knows that I can't move any closer or I'll sneeze myself silly.

I'll fight for my family, stand against anyone or anything that threatens to come between us. That's what love is to me. That's what commitment means. Armstrong gets weak sometimes, I know that. He's a brilliant politician, with that irresistible charisma, that aura of power, that turns countless women into skank hos. He can't help it. It's not his fault. God just made him that way.

But it's my familial duty to protect what's mine, what's ours, what we've struggled to build together. And, as I swore to God the day we exchanged those eternally binding vows, for better or for worse, *nothing* will get in my way.

Gold

The editing room at the TV station is my sanctuary. Within its dark embrace, I can lose myself in the hypnotic process of selecting bits and pieces of video—pictures and sounds—and quilting them together into a succinct, dynamic news story.

But this is even better: I'm editing an excerpt of "Home Is Where the Hatred Is," my acclaimed documentary on domestic abuse, into a brief excerpt to be shown as part of my keynote speech for the National Coalition Against Domestic Violence conference this coming weekend.

It's harder for me to be objective about this—my pet project and unquestionably my very finest work ever—and not give in to the temptation to simply watch the entire documentary over and over again. This is the work that won my latest local Emmy Award, the one I grabbed to hit Armstrong with just last night.

I shake my head to clear it, returning my concentration to footage of the nation's leading expert talk about the surprising growth in the number of men battered by their wives. I am so engrossed that I jump at the pounding on the editing room door.

"Yes?" I call out, annoyed at the interruption.

"What, you couldn't answer the phone?" asks Sharlita, my executive assistant, with a look of mock annoyance on her face. "Wait till you hear the news!"

"Who's on the assignment desk?" I fuss, still annoyed at the interruption. "I told them I'd be tied up for several hours. This is a priority project, and my stories for this evening are already in the—"

"'Home Is Where the Hatred Is' has been nominated for a *network* Emmy, Monique!" Sharlita proclaims with a wide smile. "I'm talkin' 'bout the big time, boss woman!"

I whirl around to face her. "Say it again, Sharlita. Slowly, so I can savor every word."

She obliges me.

I jump up and we hug, exchange robust high-fives, and dance around the editing suite.

"Sharlita, do you understand what this means? This is the gold medal of television! I am finally, *finally,* getting a shot at the big prize."

She nods, her bouncy straw curls underscoring the affirmation.

"And Monique? The best part is, the media are already calling." She hands me a stack of message slips. "These were too good to go to voicemail," she laughed. "The *Today* show. *USA Today. The View. Da Jet.* And Tyra."

"What, no Oprah?" I ask.

"I keep trying to tell you: Tyra *is* the new Oprah. She reaches a younger, more diverse demographic, and—"

"Chile, please! I love Tyra as much as you do, but until she can get America to put a Black man in the White House, she's still got to bow to the queen!"

"Well, I'm sure 'the queen' will be calling soon. *After* you win the Emmy!" Sharlita assures me. "Oh, and your friend Joyce called to remind you of your lunch appointment in exactly one hour at the Ritz-Carlton, Buckhead. To finalize plans for her charity auction."

I nod. "Thanks, Shar." Joyce's selection of the Glitzy Ritzy, as we call it, means she wants to talk in a place where we won't be likely to run into anyone we know. *Hmmmm. Wonder what's going on with her.*

I race through the media callbacks, setting up interviews to take place after I return from lunch.

As I'm letting Sharlita know I'm on my way out, she hands me a glossy lavender folder.

"What's this?" I ask.

"I wove the news of your new Emmy nomination into your talking points for the Coalition Against Domestic Violence conference this weekend," she says with a crisp nod. "*And* I've sent your new, improved biographical sketch to the woman who's going to introduce you as well."

"Sharlita, you are without question a true gem," I say, smiling my genuine appreciation.

"You're welcome, Monique," she says brightly. "Now, if you wanna show a sistah some appreciation by bringing her back some crème brûlée from the Ritz-Carlton, I certainly wouldn't be mad at ya."

"I'll try to remember," I promise, and we laugh together. Sharlita is my sugar-fiend alter-ego. She's pleasantly full-figured and insists that her man likes it that way. "Dessert not only keeps the curves together, but it makes my disposition sweet," she likes to remind me.

Since life in front of the camera keeps me on a strict physical regime, I live vicariously through Sharlita's sugar jones. Although today I could use something sinfully rich and gooey myself.

~

Traffic isn't bad—a miracle in the ATL, even in the middle of a weekday—so I'm gliding up to the Ritz-Carlton, Buckhead just as my Rihanna CD comes to the end of the song where she wails about breakin' dishes, kickin' ass, fightin' her man.

Humming the song under my breath, I glide into the luxury hotel, a cocoon of high-class comfort that perfectly symbolizes Joyce's commitment to having and enjoying the finer things in life.

We hug and air-kiss hello, taking a table in a corner of the hotel dining room.

The waiter seats us, and we quickly place our orders, eager to get down to the business of catching up on each others' lives. Joyce is my best girlfriend of over twenty years. She's an Atlanta native—a rare breed—a Black southern belle to the bone. Even though she lovingly calls me a "Yankee heifer," she *gets* me in a way that few others do.

Still, even Joyce doesn't know about my dirty little secret, the rages I fly into against my husband. No one knows except Armstrong and me. And God, of course. And I fully intend to keep it that way.

"Monique, I have to admit you were right," Joyce says in a voice so low I have to lean forward to hear her.

"About what?" I inquire, as we sip our mimosas. I figure three or four cups of coffee between now and the early evening newscast, and I'll be good to go.

"Marriage. Even to a man as wonderful as Jeffrey."

"Well, it certainly looks lucrative," I observe, noting the platinum gold earrings, necklace, and bracelet set she's wearing.

"That's exactly what I mean," she says. "These are 'guilt gifts.' When Jeffrey comes home with a Tiffany box, it can only mean one thing: he's been cheating."

"Are you certain? Do you have any proof that he's cheating? Have you asked him point-blank?"

"Monique, a woman *knows*. My instincts are positively screaming at me," she says unconsciously touching one of her new earrings.

"So it's all good as long as he keeps you in the high-class bling?" I ask.

Joyce winces, a grimace creasing her beautiful mahogany face. "That's a bit blunt, but I guess if you want to put it that way—"

"Well, if you're not going to confront him or even get some proof so you'll know either way what's really going on, it just seems like you're giving up everything for a few pieces of gold. And you deserve better than that."

There's a long silence. Then Joyce sighs, and shrugs her shoulders. "This is not what I am supposed to be experiencing. Marriage is not supposed to be this way."

I shrug. "Two things about marriage, girlfriend. One, just like everything else in life, it never quite lives up to our fantasies or expectations. And two, it always, *always* involves compromise." "What did you expect?"

"Well, I don't know exactly, but it wasn't this," Joyce replies, staring sadly at the waiter as he places our orders before us.

We dig—daintily, of course—into our lunches: bluefin tuna for Joyce, and some Moroccan-inspired lamb dish for me. Every bite is exquisite, needless to say. I am definitely going off my diet. But I figure I can compensate by sticking to soups and salads the rest of the week.

"Well, why don't you fight?" I ask. "Why don't you stop accepting the jewelry and tell your husband what you really want?"

"Pardon?" Joyce asks, laying her fork on her plate and dabbing the corners of her lips with the linen napkin.

"Girl, listen. You love Jeffrey. You've made a commitment to him. He's made a commitment to you. Never mind the huge, expensive church wedding that y'all had just a little over a year ago. When you decided to chuck your career as a Realtor and marry a man who wanted you to hold down the home front, you agreed to give this your all, to make it work. I mean, this was your lifelong dream, right? You need to fight for it."

Joyce pushes her plate away. "You don't think this is fighting, Monique?" she says, tears quivering beneath her words. "Making sure that I am in perfect shape, that I look flawless each and every day? Maintaining the 'perfectly run' household, which is a job in itself? Responding to his touch, every time, no matter what I want? Real estate was never this hard!"

"Exactly!" I say, savoring another sip of the mimosa. "Your marriage is more than your career. It's your *life,* Joyce. True love forever. Isn't that what you always wanted? Well, now you have it."

"True love." She rolls her eyes, raising her mimosa glass in a mock toast before draining it.

"All I'm saying, honey, is that you deserve the best," I say, trying to break through her misery. "But to have the best, you've got to *give* it your best shot. And sometimes that means fighting for what's yours."

Joyce shudders delicately. "I know you aren't suggesting that I go after the tramp he cheated with. Because that is simply beneath me. I will *never* lower myself to her level."

"I am not suggesting a physical altercation, Joyce. But I can't stand seeing you just sit back and take it."

She shakes her head. "Monique, we each have our own ways of dealing with life's ups and downs. I appreciate your friendship and words of wisdom, girl, as always. And I thank you for listening."

"But?" I ask.

"But we really need to take care of some urgent charity business," she informs me with a change of tone and the pasted-on smile that signals the end of our personal conversation for the day. She hands me a list of instructions for her charity auction that I'm emceeing the next night. We look over them: everything is flawlessly organized. All I have to do is show up looking glam, move the event along with upbeat quips and a sparkling smile, so that my beloved friend can enjoy the accolades for raising yet another chunk of money for yet another worthy cause.

I wonder when she'll put some energy into doing something worthy for herself.

Joyce insists on picking up the tab, and since her darling hubby is paying, I don't argue. I even let him pay for the Milk Chocolate Pear Opera Cake I'm taking back to the office for sugar-loving Sharlita.

Hell, it's the least the cheating bastard can do.

We hug good-bye, and I stare deeply into Joyce's eyes, hating the resignation I see growing there.

"Fight, Joyce," I say, then turn before she can argue. The valet retrieves the Lexus, and I slide in, buckle up, and turn Rihanna back on, setting the CD player to "repeat."

"I'm breakin' dishes up in here," I sing along, out of tune but with great enthusiasm, at the top of my lungs, car windows up, air conditioner blasting. I'm singing for myself, for Joyce, for all of the women everywhere who need to throw a fit, break a dish, get the madness out where we can see it. Otherwise, the pain and anger of betrayal can eat up our hearts and souls.

"A real woman stands up for what is rightfully hers, ain't that right, Rihanna?" I ask the voice filling my car.

She continues her fed-up anthem in response.

Blue

Back at work, I will the sadness of Joyce's words and eyes from my mind and focus on the euphoria of my network Emmy nomination.

"What inspired you to make a documentary about domestic violence, Monique?" asks the *USA Today* reporter in our phone interview.

"Because love should never, *ever* hurt," I say. "And everyone deserves to feel safe in their own home."

I answer each question while staring at the elegant black-and-white photo of Armstrong and me, the one in the brushed silver frame at the left-hand corner of my desk. I peer deeply into Armstrong's eyes, willing him to stop causing the cycle of pain-and-blame that is tearing us apart.

By the time the interview is over, I have vowed to be the sweetest, most perfect wife in the world. A promise I've made before but truly intend to keep forever this time.

"Honey, how would you feel about a nice long weekend in the Bahamas?" I ask Armstrong over the dinner prepared by Lucie, our longtime cook.

My husband studies me for a moment, then pulls his Treo from his pocket. "Sounds good to me. When?"

"Next weekend. I'm leading a workshop on women's empowerment at the Women's Business Coalition conference. I called them today and insisted that they fly you down with me. And of course they agreed."

"Because you're just that good," Armstrong teases in that sexy voice of his.

"And because, together, we're just that much better," I reply, loving the way his eyes linger at the crest of my cleavage, then wander up to outline my lips with his heated stare. My skin tingles with the first flush of desire.

And minutes later, my darling husband and I are enjoying each other for dessert.

"You know, there just ain't no tellin' what a satisfied woman might do . . ."

I sing along to the Sweet Inspirations' hit from waaaaay back in the day as I wheel the Lexus to Joyce's charity auction, having spent the day being pampered at my favorite sistah-owned spa.

One of the best things about living in Atlanta is the proliferation of Black-owned businesses that one can support if one is so inclined.

I am waxed, massaged, mani- and pedicured, steamed, exfoliated and facialed. My hair is deep-conditioned, washed, and styled, and I leave feeling like a whole new woman.

Especially after the amazing love that Armstrong and I made last night. Even better is the fact that he juggled his calendar so that he can join me in the Bahamas. Though we were working up some mighty tropical heat right in our very own house last night . . .

The memory of it has me glowing and giggling to myself. And singing along about sweet inspiration at the top of my lungs.

~

An hour before the charity event begins, I'm at Joyce's side, helping her to check on last-minute details. The auction items fill the tables that line the room, each more alluring than the last and all designed to bring in the big bucks.

What catches my eye, amid the dozens of huge themed baskets and stacks of goodies is a wild pair of bright blue, obscenely high heels. They're unique, more like short boots, laced up the front. "You like?" Joyce asks.

I pick one of the shoes up, turn it around. "You know these are not at all my style. Too loud. Too gaudy. Too tall!"

"Well, they're certainly mine. And they should be yours, Monique. Lord knows you are way too fly to be wearing those old-lady shoes all the time."

We both glance down at my low-heeled, practical pumps and chuckle. "You are the queen of sexy footwear, Ms. Shoe Diva," I say. "My dogs have to be comfortable 24/7 or you know how they start to growl."

"Ever hear that saying about teaching old dogs new tricks?" Joyce asks as she straightens the fabric covering the table. "Maybe these divine kicks are exactly what you need."

"Tell you what. You buy them, and I'll borrow them one day," I say.

Joyce shrugs. "I don't know about that. You might stretch them out!" She turns one of the shoes over, inspects it with longing in her eyes. "I don't know how much folk will bid for these, but I might have to get in on this one myself."

Laughing, I excuse myself to get some water and take a Benadryl in anticipation of the mix of heavy scents the crowd will be wearing. Don't want my allergies to kick in. I've been to several specialists, and all say they've never seen someone who reacts *only* to cheap colognes or perfumes. But I've been that way ever since I was a child. It's gotten more intense since Armstrong and I wed.

Lord knows this crowd of Atlanta's finest will be all decked out in their most glam attire. But it's an absolute guarantee that several will also be doused in bargain fragrances, and as emcee for the evening I cannot fall victim to a sneezing fit.

Inspecting myself in the ladies' room mirror, I smooth down my elegant gown, pat my newly-styled 'do into place, and flash a quick test smile.

All good. I don't like to admit how hard it is to look at myself, to meet the gaze of my reflection. Something about the expression in my eyes reminds me of my fight with Armstrong, which I want to wipe completely from my mind.

I want to remember only the laughter we share, the life we've built together, the lovemaking that had us exploding together, the highest form of union between a woman and her man.

Joyce's charity auction is a smashing success. The ballroom is filled to overflowing, the atmosphere is festive, and the guests are eager to show what they are willing to spend to support the worthy cause of the day. As always, I'm proud of and happy for my wonderful girlfriend.

Afterward, Joyce and I hug good-bye. I walk past the auction table, looking for those ridiculous blue suede shoes. They're gone. I laugh to myself, wondering how much some fool paid for those completely impractical stilettos and whether Joyce was the high bidder.

My laughter fades as I spot her husband, Jeffrey, whisking the shoes from behind his back and handing them to Joyce. He is smiling deeply into her eyes. She squeals with delight, hugging him with her free arm and kissing him sweetly on the lips. I can't hear their words, but I can read the body language, the energy between them. And I pray those aren't another of his guilt gifts, another compromise my best friend is making as her husband stomps all over her heart and soul.

Grey

All is well on the home front and even better at work. But as I am packing for our trip to the Bahamas, I'm shocked to discover that Armstrong's suitcase is still stored in the back of our double walk-in closet. His resort attire is nowhere to be seen. And I know how he detests getting ready for a trip at the last minute.

"Honey?" I call through the house, wondering where he's at. "Armstrong?"

He's in his basement media room, which is technically ours but in reality serves as his getaway.

"You'd better get started with your packing," I say, trying to keep my voice light, though my gut is starting to feel that ugly twinge.

"Packing?" Armstrong asks, flicking lazily through every channel on the TV.

"For the Bahamas. Our tropical getaway, remember?"

Silence.

"Armstrong, my darling, you know we leave first thing tomorrow. They're sending a car, which will arrive at six o'clock. Which means we have to get up at around 4:30. So it's really best that we get our things together tonight."

"Listen, Monique," Armstrong says, and in those two words, I feel the storm that is about to crash upon our shores.

"Oh, honey, I know you're busy—hell, we're both busy—but this will be the second honeymoon we've been talking about. Once I've finished leading that workshop, my time is my—oops, I mean *our*—very own."

"Something has come up." When Armstrong speaks like that, in short, staccato rhythm, it means he's upset.

"What's wrong?" I ask sharply, hating the raw tension scratching at my throat.

He shakes his head, still looking at the TV.

I inch closer and inhale deeply, afraid that my nostrils will fill with the cheap scent that will confirm my suspicious and set off a sneezing fit. When nothing happens, I feel equally disappointed and relieved. Disappointed because that would at least explain why Armstrong is being so aloof, so cold. Relieved because I am determined never to lose my temper like that again. I simply cannot stand the way that Armstrong looks at me afterward, how he pulls away, torturing me with his nearness. Even worse is the lava of self-hatred and shame that erupts like a volcano from the deepest pit of my soul.

I pour myself a drink, whiskey this time.

"So something has come up, Armstrong?" I echo his words, trying my best to sound softer and sweeter than I'm feeling.

"Yeah," he says in that infuriatingly offhand way of his. "Important meeting. Can't cancel." He is steadily flicking that remote, reminds me of some famous guy's comment—I don't remember which famous guy—who said that men don't channel surf to see what else is on TV. They do it to see what *else* is on TV.

Silly thought. I don't know why it hits me just now. Except that it reminds me of how some men feel about women as well. Never satisfied with what they have, always hungering to taste whatever else is out there. *Who* else.

Of course, Armstrong is not that kind of man, I tell myself, sipping my drink. I study the back of my husband's head, the close-cropped silver-and-midnight hair that caps his elegant skull. My eyes linger on his cinnamon-hued neck, his broad shoulders, all ignoring my love and passion to radiate cool indifference toward me.

Who is it who said or wrote, "The opposite of love isn't hate. The opposite of love is indifference?" I think it was that Jewish author Elie Wiesel, but I'm not sure.

Shaking my head, I finish my drink. No time to worry about citing quotes now. I consider canceling my big keynote speech in the Bahamas. It would be easy enough to tell them that I've gotten sick with something not-too-serious but highly contagious, like a bad stomach virus. I mean, flying all that way to deliver a keynote speech of ten minutes, followed by nearly an hour of question-and-answer from the audience suddenly seems much less exciting if I'm going to be in paradise all alone, while the love of my life is back home.

Armstrong still hasn't acknowledged me, or my plight. "I'll just cancel then."

"Don't do that," he says quickly. A bit too quickly. I bite back the jealousy rising in my throat.

"Why not?" I ask. "There will always be another speech in another sunny place, darling. The exciting part was knowing that we'd be there together. If you're not going, there's really no reason for me to—"

"I'll be tied up in meetings all weekend, Monique," Armstrong says, his voice maddeningly neutral. "Go. Make your speech. Shop. Have fun."

He is *dismissing* me, my inner voice says indignantly. Shooing me away as if I am some kind of pest or servant.

Words come to me, but they are angry, accusatory, suspicious. So I bite them back, swallow them, determined to avoid conflict.

I have no plan or strategy for breathing life back into my marriage, my love, my home. But in the absence of certainty, I elect to give up this battle in hopes of winning the war.

Tropical Rainstorm

It figures that I am in the tropics alone during a deluge of nonstop rain. The famous blue Bahamas skies are the same murky gray as Atlanta when it's being moody. The palm trees seem to droop in resignation as they soak up the pouring wrath of the clouds.

So much for paradise. My speech goes well, delivered on autopilot as the rest of my brain wonders what Armstrong is doing. And with whom.

The audience of women is enthusiastic, soaking up tips for inspiration and empowerment from a woman at the top of her professional game.

They applaud wildly for the excerpt of my "Home Is Where the Hatred Is" documentary, peppering me with earnest questions for nearly an hour afterward. I feed them what they hunger for, unable to stop my brain from imagining Armstrong with that skank ho who wears the $10 toilet water from the bargain section of the corner pharmacy.

It isn't right. He should be here with me, applauding me, craving me, loving *me.* I struggle to keep my anger in check.

There are the usual invitations to special VIP receptions and networking dinners, but I turn them down, eager to be alone. I hit the hotel gym for about an hour, grateful for the distraction of hard-earned sweat. Next I sit in the sauna, hoping to exorcise the anger and frustration through my skin.

And then, because the massage area is right next to the locker room, or maybe because the tall, midnight-hued man with the lilting voice informs me that the cost of a full-body massage is included with my room, I find myself prone, my face relaxing into the hole cut out in the massage table. My arms are at my sides, and a sheet covers the lower half of my body.

Midnight man's strong hands knead my muscles, gently, confidently, pressing here and soothing there. He smells like coconut. It is not an applied scent, but something that seems to rise naturally from his being.

Like a tropical dream.

I recall a recent magazine article about women of all races, mostly forty-plus, who make special visits to tropical resorts to enjoy the pleasures of sex with local men, usually much younger.

The most shocking part is that many of the women said they preferred hooking up *au naturel*—without condoms.

In this age of sexually-transmitted disease, I wonder at the women's daring. What would make someone risk such danger for a few moments of passion? Was it the fear that this adventure would be their very last?

His hands move toward my lower back, my skin rippling with pleasure. I wonder if he feels my response.

Get a hold of yourself, Monique, I scold myself silently. *You are a happily married woman, and too grown to be entertaining such foolishness.*

Unlike my beloved husband.

I sigh.

"Everyt'ing all right?" the man with the magic hands asks in his soothing rumble of a voice.

"Yes," I gasp, noting that his hands are now teasing the top of the sheet, which covers my behind.

"You have a lot of tension," he says.

"Mmmmm." I wonder if he says that to all the women.

"Would you like to extend the session an extra thirty minutes?" he inquires, ever so gently, so discreetly.

"I am not one of those women who is here to—"

He chuckles, a sound as soothing as his amazing fingers, which are pressing the muscles at the top of the back of my thighs.

Gently. Confidently. Dangerously.

"I would prefer that you concentrate on my neck and shoulders, okay?"

"Certainly, ma'am," he replies, his tone polite, neutral, completely professional. But the heat of his touch sends my mind in another direction.

I am embarrassed to note a sudden dampness between my legs. Thankful for the cover the sheet provides, I will myself to think of Armstrong and the pleasure we are so good at bringing each other.

He is kneading my buttocks now, through the sheet. My juices are gathering. My breasts are tingling. My brain is softening, happy to go along with the program.

"Stop. Now. Please," I manage to gasp, trying to sound authoritative.

His hands pause. Lift. "Are you sure?"

I try not to think how many women succumb to the temptation of those talented hands. I do not allow myself to look at the front of his crisp white linen pants, to scope for a hint of what treasures lie beneath.

"I am absolutely certain," I say, regaining some measure of normalcy. "Thank you so much."

I hand him a fifty-dollar tip, wait for him to exit, and throw my clothes on. Then I rush to my room, where I lie on the cool sheets, conjuring the scent of coconut rising from midnight skin while I pleasure myself again and again until, weak with longing, I drift into a hazy dream.

~

Armstrong's features are clear, but the woman's face is a blur. Her body is young, her skin medium brown like mine, taut where I am battling gravity. Armstrong devours her eagerly, with his eyes, his fingers, his mouth, awakening every part of her before filling her with his—

I sit up, heart pounding, stomach burning with nausea. I look around, disoriented, until I quiet myself with a long, steadying breath and remember that I am in a strange, tropical hotel room.

Alone.

Hundreds of miles from my home, my husband, and everything that matters to me.

I have never considered myself a jealous person, I muse as I take a shower. Perhaps a bit possessive, but that is only common sense, only natural to want to protect one's own, is it not?

Joyce flashes into my mind, her rich gold jewelry, those ridiculous blue shoes. *Guilt gifts.*

Hell, I don't even get guilt gifts, I realize with a start. Armstrong doesn't even pretend to be sorry for his transgressions.

"Some men feel entitled to more than one woman."

I was thirteen when I first heard my aunt Cecily saying that to my mother, Leila.

"Some men just move through life feeling this is something they are owed: the chance to fuck around."

I remember how shocked I was to hear that obscenity coming from Aunt Cecily's elegant lips. She had always been so proper.

"Daddy is one of those men, and we both married men just like him," Aunt Cecily continued. "You can live with it, or you can leave. But you can never change it, Leila. No need to kill yourself trying."

I could not see my mother's face, so I couldn't gauge her reaction, except to see the sudden slump of her shoulders, the dip of her head.

I heard her sobs, though, underscored with a kind of moaning whine. The sound sent shivers up my spine.

Aunt Cecily reached over to stroke Mama's hand, trying to balance the harshness of her words with a comforting touch.

Mama died a year later. The diagnosis was congenital heart failure. But at the wake, Aunt Cecily whispered under her breath that the real cause was "a heart broken by her cheating bastard of a husband."

At that moment, I vowed that I would not become my beautiful, tragic, heartbroken Mama. If, by some cruel twist of fate, I, too, ended up married to a cheater, I would stand up for myself and fight like hell for what was mine.

For Immediate Release

Home from the tropics and back at work, the phones are ringing nonstop and my office is a jumble of plants, bouquets, and balloons, all congratulating me on the Emmy nomination.

The swirl of fragrances makes me dizzy. I open a window,

deeply inhaling the fresh air. Sharlita hands me another stack of requests from the media—local, regional, and national. With each interview, I steel myself for the inevitable question:

"Monique, yours is one of the first documentaries to shed light on the high rate of men who are abused by the women in their lives. What led you to call attention to this?"

My answer comes out, smooth but not too slick. "I was shocked by the research, which suggests that female-on-male domestic violence is almost as common as male-on-female," I say. "It's like America's dirty little secret, that women can be just as angry and violent as men."

If they only knew . . .

But I have vowed to change, to take myself out of that despicable category of women who allow themselves to become foolishly out of control. I will continue to fight for my marriage, my family, but now I want to do it in a different, less destructive way.

It's a little strange being interviewed because, like most journalists, I prefer asking the questions to answering them. The whole process is so draining that, by midday, I need a double mocha latte from the downstairs coffee shop just to make it to the evening newscast.

The red eye of the camera beckons me, and I flip the internal switch to top-rated news anchor, all knowing smiles, crisp language, and mindless banter for the faceless crowd.

"Tonight we'll look into allegations of corruption in a local investment banking firm," I intone, comforted by the familiar rhythm of the on-camera dance that defines my public identity and life's work.

Too soon, the red lights fade, the cameras cool, and the dance is done for another day.

"How 'bout that Emmy nomination?" Duke Wankowski asks, his words underscored with professional envy.

"Fingers crossed," I say lightly. "Because a win for me is a win for the team," I remind him with my brightest on-camera smile.

"Absolutely!" Liz Santiago chirps brightly. "Ratings will soar."

"Well, it's out of our hands," I remind my co-anchors. "The work has to speak for itself."

"Ya know, Monique, I've always wondered," Duke asks, his face suddenly serious. "What drew you to that topic in the first place? I mean, domestic violence—it's been done before."

I glance at Liz, then return my attention to Duke. "You're right," I tell him. "It's been done *to death,* Duke. And unfortunately, it will probably be done again, because the problem is still with us and nobody seems to know how to solve it."

"I was totally shocked by how many men are beaten by women," Liz said. "You never expect that to happen."

"Those men are wusses," Duke snarls. "Hell, no real man would—" He stops talking when he sees the expression on my face and on Liz's.

"No *real* man would ever hurt any woman or child for any reason," I remind him coldly.

"So does hitting a man make a woman more of a woman?" Duke asks testily. "C'mon, Monique, you can't be upholding some kind of double standard, now, can you? Good girl, bad boy, for doing the same exact thing?"

I shake my head, which is now pounding. "No offense, Duke, but you're completely missing the point. I have conducted more than two dozen interviews on this topic, from victims to perpetrators to experts of all kinds. The documentary is fact-based, in case you've forgotten. The fact is that some men and some women make bad choices in expressing themselves."

"Yes, and hopefully pieces like your doc will help to make a difference," Liz adds.

"Thank you, Liz," I said. "And on that note, dear colleagues, good night."

As I straighten my office, then gather my things and walk to my car, I remind myself that no one knows about my dirty little secret. *There is no proof that I have hurt Armstrong. No recordings, no documentation of what has gone on in my home. So no one can come forward with damaging information if I do win this Emmy.*

When *I win it, not* if, I correct myself.

Home beckons, yet I drive more slowly than usual, anticipating tension with Armstrong. Since my return from the Bahamas, the energy between us has been cordial on the surface. But a river of tension gurgles beneath our polite words and neutral expressions.

Armstrong greets me at the door. Instead of kissing me, he hands me a glass of wine. I swallow my disappointment and accept the glass, murmuring "Thanks dear."

I take a sip and sink into a seat, kicking off my sensible shoes.

"So what's new?" I ask, hating the awkwardness between us. How can you know someone so well, yet have no idea how to reach them?

"Monique, we need to talk."

Armstrong is looking straight at me, tension compressing his lips and narrowing his eyes. I wait silently, struggling not to drown in fear. *This is it. He's leaving me. Demanding a divorce. Leaving me for her, the woman with the cheap perfume.*

Deep breath. Sip drink. "I am listening, Armstrong. What is it?"

"While you were away, I met with several key people about my mayoral candidacy," he begins.

And what else did you do? Who else did you "meet" with? I wonder silently. Holding his eyes in mine, I nod, encouraging him to continue.

"Everyone agrees that my prospects are good. Better than good, as a matter of fact," he says, taking a sip of his own drink. "'Highly favorable," he adds.

"So it's a done deal?" I ask, eager to cut to the chase.

"I waited till you came back to go public," Armstrong says,

unable to keep the excitement from his voice. "We're holding a press conference tomorrow afternoon."

"You couldn't call me, text me, e-mail me, Armstrong? Hell, an instant message would have been better than this. You couldn't wait until we could discuss, *together,* the biggest decision of your life? And mine?"

Armstrong sips his whiskey once more, then sets the glass down and moves toward me, arms outstretched.

I put up the "stop" hand to halt him in his tracks.

"I guess I should be grateful I didn't learn about it during tomorrow night's newscast," I say, biting back the rising bile of rage.

"C'mon, Monique. You knew this was inevitable. We've talked about it dozens of times."

"We have discussed the *possibility,* Armstrong, yes. But never on the level of 'this will be happening tomorrow.' It seems we've missed some crucial steps, don't you think?"

He takes my hand and pulls me into his embrace. I hear the pounding of his heartbeat in my ear. A comforting sound, the drumbeat of our shared rhythm. After a long, warm moment, I pull back to study his face.

"Have you and your 'key people' given any thought about what will happen to my career?" I ask. "I cannot be the mayor's wife and a news anchor at the same time."

He shakes his head, smiling, planting a warm kiss on my forehead.

"What's to think about? You'll win your Emmy, then retire at the top of your game to become the First Lady of Atlanta. What's not to love about that?"

"I would like to make my own decisions about my career, in consultation with you, my beloved husband," I fuss. "Why can't you do the same? Include me in your process?"

Armstrong doesn't answer. Instead, he lowers his lips to the side of my neck and presses them closely, teasing me with the tip of his tongue. His hands slide to my lower back, tracing circles to make my juices flow.

The scent of coconut dances through my memory, the strong-yet-gentle hands of that other man just the day before: forbidden scents, forbidden hands. I melt into Armstrong, unbutton his shirt with fumbling fingers. My knees weaken, my pulse gallops, and soon we are making the most exquisite love right there on the plush Turkish carpet of our luxury living room.

"I love you, Monique," he murmurs, thrusting deeply inside me.

"And only me?" I gasp, craving reassurance even as I approach the peak of ecstasy.

"Yes, my darling, my sweet," he groans, and I feel the forces gathering for his climax.

"I love you, too, baby," I purr, tightening my muscles so that we come together, our bodies arching and shuddering in exquisite and perfect unison.

After we move apart to catch our breath, just as I am drifting into a satisfied slumber, Armstrong says, "You know, I met with the president of Clark Atlanta University, and they're looking for someone to run their film and television program."

"Yeah, so?" I murmur drowsily.

"So I think an Emmy Award–winning superstar would be the perfect person for the job, don't you?"

"Shut up," I mutter, enjoying the warmth of his strong, hard body as he spoons me from behind. "I have no comment at this time."

Coral

I awaken the next morning relaxed and energized. There is nothing like the feeling of lying entangled with my husband, savoring the intimacy that is our special bond.

There is nothing like the closeness we share.

Or the gaps in our communication, I sigh, realizing that this is the day my ambitious spouse will announce his run for mayor.

What will that mean for him? For *us*?

I roll over to study his face, even more handsome in repose.

I have never been drawn to the blood sport of politics. But that is Armstrong's element. Whereas I am most comfortable as an observer and commentator, Armstrong has to be in the thick of the action, making things happen.

He is a natural leader, I must admit, born to inspire others. I know this. And I must have known, throughout our years together, that he will never be satisfied with less than the top. The recognition he gets as leader of the City Council is good. But not good enough. He sees it as a stepping stone to bigger and better things.

Head Negro in Charge, as he likes to joke. "I was born to be the HNIC," he is fond of saying. "God did not put me on earth to half-step."

What about my work, my career? I wonder. I am on the brink of something bigger than I have ever known with this, my very first national Emmy nomination. This is network, the big time. New opportunities await. Bigger markets. Higher visibility. I, too, am at the top of my game.

We are not so different, Armstrong and I, at least not in this way. We both want to reach the pinnacle of our professions. We are driven to conquer, to win, in whatever we do.

His hand strokes my hip, moving toward my thigh. I shiver with the pleasure of his caress. There is something so hot about loving someone you know deeply, someone whose body is the terrain of your deepest desires.

An hour later, after he has showered and dressed and I have called into the office to remind them that I am taking the day off, I see Armstrong to the front door with a warm kiss.

"I'll be at the press conference," I promise him.

"Early?" he asks, warming my heart with the little-boy expression on his face.

"Definitely," I respond with a warm smile.

"And off-duty," he reminds me, "in supportive spouse mode."

"Of course," I assure him, waving until he's backed out of the driveway and headed down the street.

"Of course," I repeat to myself as I pour a second cup of coffee and wonder what to do with the hours stretching before me.

I don't need a massage after last night's delicious lovemaking. My hair is tight, my nails are flawless, and my face is suffused with a charming post-orgasmic glow.

There are errands I could run, but they feel too mundane for such a momentous day. Drumming my fingers on my imported countertop, I shudder to imagine a life like this, free of red lights and ticking deadlines, enjoying endless spare time, infinite choices, and nowhere urgent to be.

I don't know how Joyce could give up her career for marriage. It's not as if she's raising kids; that would make staying home the logical option. But this desperate housewife scenario feels a little frightening to me.

I put in a call to the head of the Clark Atlanta University Film and TV department, happy to be doing something proactive about my possible change in status. She's not in, so I leave a voicemail.

Then I call Sue Billings-Schwartz, the human resources director at work. More voicemail: "Sue? Monique Worthington here. Today my husband, Armstrong, is announcing his candidacy for mayor. I need to meet with you ASAP, preferably tomorrow, to discuss the actual implications of this as far as my position at the station, since we certainly want to avoid any conflict of interest and such. Please call me right away on my cell."

I leave my number and hang up.

Only 10 A.M.

Too late to laze around, too early to get dressed.

I call Joyce.

"Hey girl," she answers. "What's up?"

"I am home, hungry, bored, and anxious," I tell her. "Can you swing by Starbucks, pick up some sustenance, and come over?"

"Sure," she says brightly. "Give me half an hour."

"Perfect."

I shower quickly and put on my robe, thanking God for friends who accept you without reservation and can hang without pretense.

I step outside to pick up the newspaper when Joyce glides up in her convertible Mercedes sports coupe.

She steps out, carrying the Starbucks goodies, and sashays up to my front door on those bizarre blue shoes. Her long, lean legs are sheathed in skin-tight, low-rise denims, and she's rocking a cashmere twin set that perfectly matches the shoes.

"Heeeeey now! I see you're preparing for life as a lady of leisure," she laughs. "Welcome to my world."

I shake my head as we move to the kitchen.

"Girl, I have been working since I was fifteen years old, and I have got to have something to do. Armstrong told me about a possible opening in the communications department at Clark Atlanta University. I've already called to find out more about it."

"Being first lady could be very demanding," Joyce says, raising her mocha-ccino-whatever for a toast with my pumpkin spice latte.

"Could be," I agree, completing the gesture.

I note the impressive turquoise-in-silver earrings, necklace, and bracelet Joyce is wearing.

"Nice accessories," I say. "New?"

She rolls her eyes.

"And I see you're rockin' those crazy Empire State Building shoes too."

Joyce nods, resignation filling her eyes.

"Things okay at home?" I ask, taking a bite of the carrot muffin she has so thoughtfully provided.

"Things are what they are," she says resolutely. I cringe at the hopeless shrug in her voice.

"Well, here's another toast," I say, raising my venti Starbucks cup and nodding for her to do the same. "To the ups and downs and ins and outs of marriage."

Joyce's smile is rueful as she taps her cardboard cup to mine.

"So today's the big day?" she asks, referring, of course, to Armstrong's news conference.

I nod.

"I'll be watching," she promises, "as both of your lives change forever."

"Maybe," I shrug. "We don't know whether Armstong will win."

Her smile turns a little sad. "Oh, yes we do, Monique. When has Armstrong ever lost at anything?"

I shake my head and un-mute the kitchen television so we can channel-surf through the mid-day news updates and endless talk shows.

"You could do something like that, right?" Joyce asks as we check out Whoopi and company on *The View*.

"Not sure," I answer. "I've called Human Resources to find out exactly what the options might be."

"It would be nice if you didn't have to completely give up your career," Joyce muses. "I'm sure they'll be flexible with you."

"Thanks. And how about you?" I ask pointedly. "Miss selling houses?"

Joyce looks at me, surprised. "Yes," she says tightly. "But you know that Jeffrey and I agreed—"

"I know. But couldn't you do something part-time without threatening his ego?"

"Maybe," she says, draining her latte. "Maybe not."

"So tell me this," I say, contemplating her situation and mine. "Why does it always seem to be the woman who gives something up to make the marriage work? Why are we always bending over backwards to accommodate our men?"

"Good questions, Monique," Joyce says, crumpling the paper that held her chocolate chip muffin and stuffing it inside her Starbucks cup. "Maybe it's because we're more flexible. Or maybe it's just because we're willing."

After she leaves, I check the clock.

Three hours till the Big Event. My phone beeps with a text message.

"Swing by soon," it says. "Something special 4 U. Mitch the Bitch."

I chuckle, thanking God for the other thing every woman needs: the perfect gay male buddy to really put things into perspective.

Mitch Kangelaris is a Greek-American bartender at Dante's Down the Hatch, an Atlanta institution. We've been girlfriends since I moved to Atlanta, and he seems to have a sixth sense about when I need cheering up, calming down, or, as he calls it, "unruffling your diva feathers."

I slip into my designer wifey costume, a chic coral suit calculated to complement Armstrong in the video and still photos that will be taken today and beamed all over the globe at his announcement.

Driving up Peachtree Road to Dante's Down the Hatch, I hum along to Rihanna. "Shut up and drive!" she growls to the man she's seducing. I knew there was something I liked about that girl.

"About time," Mitch fusses as I enter the bar, a popular place where folks come to bolster their nerve, tickle their libidos, and/or drown their sorrows in his expertly mixed drinks. Mitch and I always joke that he put his psychology degree from Emory University to good use as a bartender.

"Great money, no stress, and everybody loves me," he quips. "How many shrinks can say that?"

He surveys the bar, which is nearly empty, thanks to the early hour, and waves me into a corner booth. I love how Mitch always goes on break when I come in.

"How are you feeling about hubby's upcoming announcement?" he asks, cutting right to the chase as usual.

"Excited for him. Worried for me," I confess. "Maybe worried for us."

He nods sympathetically. "Girl, the minute I heard the news, I said, 'Oh, shit! I gots to get Mo-Mo in here and get her head straight.'"

Needless to say, no one else on Earth, including my mother, could get away with calling me "Mo-Mo."

"Well, whatever you have, bring it on, 'cause I damn sure need it today," I say.

"Be right back." Mitch sashays off to the kitchen and I chuckle, thinking of Joyce's sky-high blue suede shoes and wondering how they'd look on Mitch. Not that he's a cross-dresser. He's just so gloriously gay that sometimes I want to dress him up like a big, hairy Greek doll.

Who is at least as feminine as I am.

Mitch returns in minutes with a tantalizing slice of broiled salmon, some rice pilaf, and almond green beans. My favorite.

As I murmur my thanks and realize how hungry I am, he switches off to the bar, engages in his signature hocus-pocus, and returns with a concoction the same coral hue as my outfit.

"Isn't it kind of early to be imbibing?" I ask.

"Not to worry," he assures me. "Minimal alcohol content—you could even pass a field sobriety test, I swear to God. This is just a lil sumthin' sumthin' for those famous nerves of yours."

"If you say so," I say, and take a sip. "Mmmmmm. Soothing."

"Bartender voodoo," he assures me. Then I notice a look of concern on his face.

"What?" I ask, between bites of my delicious lunch.

"How are things?"

"'Things' are fine, I guess. Why?"

He shrugs, lets his gorgeous olive-black eyes with the ridiculously long, thick eyelashes roam the wall above my head for a moment, then looks right at me.

"I just think you need to stay on top of 'things.'"

"Don't play games with me, Mitch," I say. "We know each other too well for that. What exactly are you talking about?"

"Your man."

"What about him?" I ask, dropping my voice to a whisper, though we're still the only ones in the bar.

"Do I really have to tell you?"

"You really have to get to the damn point," I hiss, hating the sudden gallop of my heart. "Because, as you know, in less than two hours, I will be in front of cameras and microphones, every pore and facial expression being recorded and scrutinized, as my husband makes the biggest and most significant announcement of his life. So if there is something you have to say, Mitch, then get to it."

"He's fucking around on you, Monique."

I cannot meet his eyes.

"All marriages have room for improvement," I respond finally, annoyed at the undercurrent of tears threatening to ruin my face.

"You can bullshit yourself, but I love you too much to bullshit you, Mo-Mo," Mitch says, covering my hand with his. "I've seen him with this woman—"

"I know about her," I break in. "And it's over between them."

"You sure about that?" He raises a skeptical eyebrow. "Because I've seen them recently and she looked—"

"Look, Mitch," I push the plate away, take a hefty sip of the delicious drink, and lean forward, keeping my voice low and steely. "I love you and I appreciate your concern. But you know I'm not a quitter. Armstrong and I have challenges, no question. But so does every couple. And I can't give up on him because women throw themselves at him, now can I? What would that make me?"

Mitch studies my face intently. "I don't want to see you hurt," he says gently. "That's all."

"Which I appreciate. Just as I appreciate this wonderful meal and this strange but tasty beverage," I say, arranging my face into a grateful smile. "Thank you, Mitch."

I pull out my wallet. He reaches out to stop me, shaking his headful of shiny ebony curls. "Won't hear of it. This is on the house, girlfriend."

"Well, thank you. I deeply appreciate it."

"All tips, however, will be gladly accepted," he cracks. I reach into my billfold and pull out a fifty, tossing it at him.

"All this without a lap dance?" he purrs. "Honey, you are way too good to me."

"Ditto," I say, giving him a hug and a kiss.

"Text me later?" he asks. "After the big shindig?"

"Definitely," I say. "Thanks again, darling."

"No prob," he drawls, handing me a large 'to go' version of his 'voodoo' drink. "In case of emergency," he says.

I thank him again. He nods, then waves me away. "Get out of here."

Before I hit the door, his voice rings out again. "Mo-Mo?"

"Yessssss?" I turn to peer at him over my shoulder.

"Denial is not just a river in Egypt."

"Thank you, Cleopatra," I say. "And you can kiss my asp."

Green

The reporter in me dreads the thought of being the subject of Armstrong's big news story. Well, more like the sidekick, I tell myself as I ease into the traffic onto Peachtree Road, but still . . .

My phone rings. Number unavailable. Could be a telemarketer, but then again, it could be work-related. "This is Monique Worthington," I answer. "How can I help you?"

"I have a hot news story for you," says a woman's voice, raspy, husky, unfamiliar.

"Who is this?"

"Let's just say someone you need to know," the voice promises.

"Uh-huh. And what is this alleged news story?" I ask, annoyed.

"I can't tell you over the phone," she says. "Meet me in the parking lot of the Atlanta Civic Center in fifteen minutes. I'll tell you everything then."

"Is this a joke?" I ask. "I'm not working today. If this story of yours is so hot, you need to call it in to the station tipline. That number is—"

"Fifteen minutes, Ms. Worthington. Civic Center lot. Come alone. No cameras. No friends. And don't worry. You won't be late for your husband's press conference. I only need a minute of your time."

Click.

Who is this calling me? Must be a reporter or political groupie. Who else would know about the press conference? I review the phone call. Can't place the voice at all. What kind of news story could this be? And how the hell did this woman get my personal cell phone number, which I guard like a national secret? It's a little more than an hour until the news conference. I don't want to be late. Though it's just a couple miles away, midday traffic can be nasty, especially downtown.

I drive toward the Atlanta Civic Center, weighing my options. The parking lot isn't really visible from any major streets. Will I be safe? What sane person goes to a semi-secluded place to meet a cryptic stranger?

Armstrong hasn't even announced his candidacy, and the crazies are coming out already.

The lot is deserted, except for a lone green BMW convertible. I haven't seen that color before; must be a custom paint job. I park several yards away, and wait.

A woman gets out. The first thing I notice is that her pantsuit perfectly matches the color of her car. The second thing I notice is that she is quite pregnant.

She appears unarmed.

Her car appears empty, and I don't see any signs that she's with the media.

I take a deep breath and exit my car, wondering whether I should surreptitiously dial my cell phone to 911 so maybe an operator can hear whatever is about to go down.

"Monique?" she asks in that raspy voice.

I bristle at being addressed in such a familiar fashion by someone I have never laid eyes on before.

"Monique, it is so good to meet you," she says, striding towards me.

I shoot her a hard stare. "And you are?"

"Ivy," she says, tossing her auburn weave, which cascades over her slightly rounded shoulders in unnaturally symmetrical waves. "Ivy Green."

Yeah, right. Sounds like a bad stripper name.

"So what's the story?" I ask brusquely.

She extends her hand.

I keep mine at my side.

We study each other's faces. I am struck by the bright green eyes in her copper face. Eyes the same color as her pantsuit and her car.

They are mesmerizing. I shake my head. "Look, I'm in a hurry, so if you're going to—"

"My baby is due in two weeks," she tells me.

My gut is jumping. I take a deep breath, and something tickles my nose. My nostrils start to twitch. I turn my head to exhale, then breathe in again to calm my nerves.

"And you are telling me this because?"

"Armstrong is the father," she says flatly, no hint of emotion in her startling eyes.

I cannot breathe. My throat feels as if it is closing. I shake my head for what feels like a long minute. She watches impassively.

"That is impossible," I say when I regain my voice. "I'm sure you are mistaken."

"He said you would say that," she says.

I feel as though I'm naked on national TV.

I sneeze.

Once, twice, three times without pause.

I step back from the funk of her cheap perfume, recognizing the scent that caused my last episode with Armstrong.

"That's why I brought evidence. You're a reporter. You like proof? Here it is," she says fishing a manila envelope from a sleek Gucci tote and stepping forward to extend it toward me.

I let the envelope hang in the air, knowing that to take it will change my life forever. I don't know what the change will be, but I'm not ready for it at this moment.

"Do you love him?" I ask.

She nods. "I do. And I believe he loves me too." She watches my face intently, those green eyes seeming not to blink.

"Believe what you like," I say, with more confidence than I'm feeling. "Armstrong has had affairs before. You're not his first, and you may not be his last."

She places one hand on her stomach and rubs it in a slow circle. I sneeze three more times.

She pushes that manila envelope at me again. "There are things you need to know," she says. "For your own protection."

I am frozen in place, not ready to know what those 'things' might be.

"Why are you doing this?" I ask. "Even if that is his"—I can't bring myself to say the word "baby"—"what's your point or your goal or whatever?"

"You want answers? Everything you need to know is in here," she says, pushing that envelope at me again. "All the reasons that Armstrong really belongs to me."

I grab it, reluctantly. And then I sneeze again.

"Bless you," she says. "You're gonna need it."

She turns and walks back to her car, swaying from side to side with the weight of her pregnancy. As she drives away, I memorize the license plate: IVY 313.

Figures, I say to myself as I return to my car, thinking of the old Bell Biv DeVoe hit. "That girl is poison . . ."

I am shaking. I throw the envelope into the backseat, prolonging the moment when I have to cross over into knowing, a place I can't go until I have finished smiling for the news cameras and delivering lovingly supportive sound bites into a phalanx of microphones.

It simply will not do at all.

~

The press conference unfolds like a well-rehearsed play. Everything happens on cue: Armstrong's announcement that he is the next person to lead Atlanta to greatness.

The inevitable questions from reporters.

The way his arm feels draped across my shoulder.

I am numb inside and out, as though I am watching myself from afar, assessing my own performance through a haze.

"Monique," shouts a colleague from a rival TV station. "What will this mean for your career?"

I smile and pat Armstrong's hand. "It will mean that I have pledged Armstrong my full and undivided support," I say. "We don't yet know just what form that will take. But we do know that this is great news for the people of Atlanta. I know that he will do a wonderful job."

Armstrong draws me closer and plants a kiss on my cheek.

The cameras unleash a frenzy of clicks and flashes.

My smile is frozen into place as my minds wanders to that manila envelope tossed into the backseat of my car. I'd like to wish it away. But the need to know trumps all, and my heart races at the thought of sneaking out to discover its contents, though I am absolutely certain they'll change my life in undesirable ways.

My co-anchor Liz "Barbie Doll" Santiago waves until I catch her eye. "What will you bring to the position of first lady of Atlanta?" she asks crisply.

"Well, Liz, I will bring the utmost support for my husband, my commitment to helping Atlanta reach its full potential and glory, and I will definitely bring my unwavering faith that God will steer us toward selecting the very best person to run Atlanta. And that person can be none other than my very own husband, Armstrong Worthington."

Liz nods. The crowd applauds. My cheeks hurt from smiling so hard. I hate being the one having to answer questions on camera. Much better to be the reporter, much better to be the one in control.

For the millionth time, I wonder what drives anyone to seek public office. The heat of constant scrutiny is my idea of Hell on Earth. But it's obviously Armstrong's idea of Heaven.

I find myself scanning the room for any sign of Ivy Green. There is none. But every five minutes or so, my nostrils twitch and

I sneeze, as discreetly as possible, into a lace-edged white cotton handkerchief that someone has pressed into my hand.

~

"I'll see you at home in a few," Armstrong whispers as he kisses the spot between my earlobe and my neck that makes my knees quiver.

I nod, savoring the electricity between us before I remember the sight of that green-clad belly. "A few minutes or a few hours?"

"Not too long," he assures me. "I just have to swing by the office for a few."

"I could go with you," I suggest in what I hope is a lightly flirtatious tone. Armstrong glances at me, then shrugs.

"That you could," he agrees. "But I'm afraid you'd be bored out of your mind."

I am struggling to trust my husband. I am wishing I knew how to do that. I am disgusted with the insecurity and jealousy twisting my insides. I am desperate to know what's in that manila envelope, even while wishing that I could ignore its existence forever.

With all of that churning inside, I kiss Armstrong's cheek, pat his shoulder, and turn back to schmoozing my way across the room, my best award-winning news anchor smile plastered across my face. That sinister envelope may be beckoning, but duty and protocol take priority for the moment.

~

Finally, with the room having been thoroughly worked on Armstrong's behalf, I make my way toward the door, chatting, shaking hands, smiling and nodding at everyone, knowing that I cannot postpone confronting the contents of that manila envelope for another moment.

I brace myself for the walk to the parking lot, striding toward my car and all but diving in, locking the door behind me as if I am being pursued. I breathe in a moment of blessed solitude, wondering what turn my life is about to take. Closing my eyes, I will myself to forget what drew me here. I review the press conference, wondering how it will play on tonight's news.

I fortify myself with a hearty sip of the "to go" version of Mitch's voodoo drink. Reach for the envelope.

Open it.

Shake the contents out on the passenger seat.

There are three eight-by-ten-inch color photos. I pick those up first. They are photos of Armstrong and that woman, Ivy or whatever-her-name-is, having sex.

Who does that? I wonder. *And for what purpose? What woman has herself photographed with her married lover? Does Armstrong know about the photos? And what they can do to his bid to become mayor?*

Well, she obviously doesn't love him or care about his well-being, I think with a grimace.

Or, for that matter, her own. Or that thing in her belly.

For all I know, there's a full-fledged sex tape floating around, playing all over cyberspace and God-knows-where-else.

Beneath the photos is a small white paper, rectangular. I pick it up, smooth it out. At the top is a doctor's name, address, and telephone number. Then, in a nearly illegible scrawl: Ivy Green. HIV test—pos.

This could be fake.

It could be real.

It cannot be happening to me.

I take another sip of Mitch's voodoo drink to steady my nerves. From the corner of my eye, I see Armstrong's car gliding down the ramp toward the exit.

I turn the key, let another couple of cars come between us,

then set off toward his office. I want some answers. I deserve them, don't I?

Rihanna's CD begins to play. The breakin' dishes song, all about how she's gonna fight her man for leaving her alone. Singing along helps me breathe. The road dances in front of my eyes, and I focus on keeping the car steady.

The ring of my cell phone breaks my concentration. I glance at the screen: Joyce. I let it go to voice mail, too distracted by the contents of the envelope to talk to anyone just yet.

HIV positive?

Her? Him? Both of them?

The baby?

Me?

We are at the intersection where Armstrong must turn left to go to his office. But his car is in the far right lane. Keeping two cars between us, I move into that lane. He turns right without signaling.

I am still singing with Rihanna, her song becoming my anthem as anxiety builds inside me. For nearly fifteen minutes, I follow my husband, who is obviously going somewhere other than work or home.

Soon we turn onto a street in Southwest Atlanta.

My phone rings. I turn the music down.

"This is Monique," I say, my voice quivering.

"Hey girl, It's Joyce. How'd it go?"

"I'll have to call you back," I say, noting that my back teeth feel fused together, my jaw locked with tension.

Armstrong pulls his car onto a steep side street. I pull onto the same street, behind a huge SUV, to lessen the chance that he'll see me. God knows there are a zillion black Lexus sedans in Atlanta. Just to be safe, I slide most of the way down in my seat.

He parks at the bottom of a steep driveway. Exits the car, then walks toward the house. Not even looking around.

It's a generic bungalow, white with green trim. The same green as the car. Her outfit. Her eyes.

What kind of evil witch is she? Ivy Green, my ass. What's that bitch's real name anyway?

I'm staring so hard, with such focus, that my eyes burn from not blinking. I close them briefly, take the deepest breath I can manage, then open them.

Ivy and Armstrong are standing on the lawn, talking. She has one hand on her lower back and is gesturing with the other. His arms are folded across his chest. I can't see the expressions on their faces.

I roll down the window and crane my neck to hear what they're saying.

"You told me you were leaving her, Armstrong," Ivy says.

"You know my situation," Armstrong says, reaching out to put his hand on her shoulder. What the hell does he mean, referring to me as his "situation?"

"This baby is going to be here soon," she says. "Then what are you going to do?"

"I've told you, I just need more time. I've got to do things the right way. There's too much at stake to act rashly," Armstrong says. "Especially with this mayoral campaign starting up now."

Ivy rolls her eyes. "I've heard all your excuses before, Armstrong. I got rid of two babies when you asked me to. You swore that I'd never have to go through that again—"

"And I'm keeping that promise, aren't I?" he asks, looking at her bulging belly. "I'll take care of y'all. I just need you to stay on the low until the mayoral race is wrapped up."

I can't take it anymore. Caution be damned. I get out of my car, grabbing the envelope and photos to take with me. I vaguely notice the driver of the huge SUV I'm parked in back of getting in and driving away. But my entire focus is on warning Armstrong about this evil, conniving woman.

"Watch out, baby!" I yell to him. "Get away from Poison Ivy before it's too late!"

Their heads whip in my direction.

"Did she tell you she's HIV-positive, Armstrong? 'Cause I've got the doctor's note." He looks from Ivy to me with disbelief.

"Oh, yeah," I continue. "She gave me pictures of you two fucking like animals. Guess what, Armstrong? She doesn't want you to be mayor. Because you can bet she's got more copies of these and she'll take them to the media, put them on the Internet, if she hasn't already!" I thrust the photos toward Armstrong.

He looks at them but doesn't move. It's as if he's frozen, not knowing what to do.

Ivy grabs his hand.

He moves away from her, walking toward me.

See, you skank, weave-wearing, fake-named ho? This is *my* man, and he wants to be with *me.*

I rush toward Armstrong, embrace him.

He grabs the tops of my arms, both of them, right below the shoulder.

"What are you doing here, Monique?"

"That woman has AIDS, Armstrong! And you kissed her. You screwed her. You've put everything in danger: my life, your life. And your precious mayoral campaign."

He tightens his grip on my arms.

"Honey? Stop it. You're hurting me," I say in a low voice.

Armstrong looks deeply into my eyes and shakes his head.

"This doesn't concern you, Monique. This part of my life does not concern you. Do you understand?"

Suddenly, she is standing at his side. As if they are husband and wife, a family, and I am the unwanted intruder.

I hear Rihanna singing the breakin' dishes song. Is it in my head, I wonder, or coming from my car?

Armstrong looks behind me, startled.

I break free of his punishing grasp.

Ivy Green takes a step toward me.

I sneeze, too many times to count. Too many times to catch my breath. Feel like I'm going to pass out. The envelope with the photos and the doctor's note slip from my hand.

I can see only red. Hear only Rihanna. Their voices—Armstrong's and Ivy's—are being hurled at me, but I can't hear or understand what they're saying.

I sneeze again. Can't catch my breath. Starting to fall. Reach out to Armstrong for support. Fall into him. He stumbles. Ivy grabs for him, gets the sleeve of his jacket. This knocks her off balance. Together, they tumble onto the sidewalk.

Rihanna's singing becomes louder.

I turn to see my car moving toward Armstrong and Ivy Green, who lay tangled on the concrete. He is struggling to get up, but his leg is twisted at an odd angle beneath him, his face contorted in pain. She is lying on her side, clutching her belly, moaning.

Funny, I could swear I'd put that car into park. Maybe I forgot to set the emergency brake?

The car rolls toward them. Now I'm the one frozen in place.

Rihanna's chorus mingled with their screams.

Then all is quiet, except for their moans and my cell phone, which is ringing. I stumble toward the car, which has run into a high hedge and stopped moving, though the engine is still on. I move toward it, yank open the door, pick up the phone.

"It was an accident," I say, breaking into hysterical sobs. "It wasn't my fault, I swear."

"Monique? What's wrong? Where are you?" Joyce asks.

I try to describe the hell I've found myself in.

"I'm on my way," she promises. "Whatever you do, don't move. And don't say a thing to the cops except that you want a lawyer."

Mood Indigo

Silence, for what seems like forever. Then, sirens. Cop cars. Two ambulances. A fire truck.

I put my hands over my ears, close my eyes against the flashing lights.

Powerless to stop the rush of nausea rising from my guts, I lean over and puke right onto a police officer's dull black shoe.

By the time Joyce arrives, I have been given a field sobriety test, and ended up in the back of a police car.

Some baby-faced officer is yammering on about blood-alcohol content and holding the cup with Mitch's voodoo drink in his hand.

Other words shoot at me like verbal bullets: *Driving under the influence. Assault.*

I watch my husband's body on a stretcher, being loaded into one ambulance. Ivy Green's on another, going into the other ambulance. Together, they speed away, lights and sirens splitting the night air.

Everything hurts. I open my eyes to see Joyce talking with the police officers. She is gesturing animatedly. Offering to take me home and be responsible for me.

I hear the whir of a news helicopter. Open my eyes again to see news vans from all of the local network affiliates as well as CNN.

Liz Santiago steps out, scanning the scene.

The enormity of the situation hits me.

I vomit again, out the window of the police car. I can't imagine how I look, how I smell.

"Monique?" Liz's normally calm voice is a screech. Joyce hurries over, tries to turn Liz and her cameraman, Tony, around. The reporters from the other networks move toward the two of them.

A tow truck is hooking up my car. I wave to Joyce. "The pictures and doctor's note fell out of my hand. I don't know where they are. But you've got to find them."

Joyce frowns at me, looks around the chaotic scene. "What kind of envelope? What does the note look like?" she asks frantically.

"Big yellow envelope—what do they call it?"

"Manila?" she asks, turning to look at the concrete beneath her feet. "Is that what you mean?"

I nod. "And the doctor's note is small, bluish white paper. That's all I remember."

I'm so intent on talking to Joyce that it takes a minute for me to notice the police officer talking to me.

His mouth is moving, but the words don't reach my ears for a long minute.

"We have to take you downtown and book you, Ms. Worthington," he says.

I hear the shouts from the reporters, see microphones pushed toward my face. Liz Sangiago's voice rises above the others. "Monique? Can I get a comment, please?"

My only response is to sneeze.

Blank

I am the top story, beating out Armstrong's mayoral announcement on all of the networks, including CNN.

For some reason, perhaps because of who I am (or was), or maybe because I am the subject of said news story, I am allowed to watch the news on a small, funky TV outside of my jail cell.

My jail cell.

It is hard to comprehend where I am and how I got here. What I did to deserve this humiliation. My brain hurts as much as the pit of my stomach, after hours of vomiting until there is not even bile left.

Joyce has stopped by to update me on Armstrong's condition.

And Ivy's.

We are allowed about ten minutes, twice a day, to talk, the officer outside my jail cell informs me.

Has he no empathy?

"Do you have that paper?" I ask Joyce under my breath.

She shakes her head. "I never found it. I looked everywhere for as long as I could, but the police kicked me out of there. And I couldn't get behind that yellow tape of theirs. I tried, girl. Sorry."

"I am so screwed without it," I say bitterly.

"Tell me again what it said."

"That Ivy Green, or whatever her name is, in addition to being obviously pregnant, is HIV-positive."

Joyce closes her eyes tightly for a long moment, then takes a long, shuddering breath. "Look, Monique. I think the best thing I can do right now is find out everything I can about this woman."

"She's been released from the hospital, right?" I ask.

Joyce shakes her head. "Not according to the news reports. Armstrong is in a rehabilitation center, recuperating. He'll need intensive physical therapy, but he should be okay in a few months. Ivy is still being checked out."

"I wonder whether the hospital has been notified of her HIV status," I murmur. Joyce looks at me like she's not quite sure I've got all my marbles on this one.

Before I can say anything else to persuade her, the officer moves toward us to signal that our visit is over. Joyce blows me a kiss and stands. "I'll be back tomorrow with whatever I can find out," she says, a look of determination on her face.

A few days later, Joyce has called Victoria Anthony, the kick-ass attorney I've interviewed for dozens of stories over the years. In Atlanta, we jokingly call Victoria the female Johnnie Cochran for her superior ability in successfully defending high-profile clients who seem to have the deck stacked against them.

First thing, I tell Victoria about the doctor's note that Poison Ivy gave me along with the photos.

"Do you recall the doctor's name?" she asks.

I close my eyes and breathe deeply, trying desperately to recall anything about the printed information at the top of that small piece of paper. But my memory has been overtaken by the handwritten words scrawled across the center of the page.

"I need an HIV test," I whisper to Victoria after telling her, again, what the note had said.

"That's a good idea," she agrees. "Let me arrange for you to have a complete medical work-up while we're at it."

Victoria brings messages from the office. Amazingly, my Emmy nomination is still intact, though of course I am no longer doing interviews.

About anything.

Joyce is saving all of the print articles about me, about my situation, but she won't let me see them until I am ready. Whatever that means.

Victoria wants me to use a "crime of passion" defense.

Problem is, I'd started drinking before the news conference. Before I even heard from Ivy Green. The blood-alcohol test results had confirmed that.

"We have to consider all reasonable options," Victoria said. She is pretty in a straight-A-student, church-choir-member, always-follows-the-rules kind of way. Her cologne is expensive, a subtle blend of rose and jasmine. It never makes my nose itch, never makes me sneeze.

I notice a slender gold band on Victoria's ring finger.

"I didn't realize you were married," I say to her.

"I'm not," she replies with a soft smile. "I did just become engaged, though."

"Congratulations," I say, wincing at the hollowness of my voice.

"I've seen your documentary," Victoria says to me. "It's not just good, Monique. It's great. Powerful. Very moving. And that's a tough topic, too," she continues, searching my face for a response.

I struggle to reclaim just a shred of the good feeling I used to enjoy about my work. Nothing comes, just more emptiness inside.

"What motivated you to focus on that aspect, men who are beaten by their women?" she asks, looking quickly into my eyes, then down at her legal pad, where she is already writing.

When I don't answer for several minutes, Victoria looks at me again, her eyes piercing mine.

"Listen, Monique. We have to prepare for arraignment, figure out whether we want to enter a plea bargain. I need all the information I can get."

I stare at my fingernails, then meet Victoria's steady gaze.

"When Armstrong and I fight, there have been a few incidences of violence," I say in a voice so low she has to learn toward me to hear.

I want Victoria to look surprised, but she doesn't.

"Tell me more," she urges softly. "Did he hurt you badly?"

"He broke my heart each time he cheated," I reply. "So in that way, he hurt me very, very seriously, yes. But the truth is that I hit Armstrong. I struck out at him."

"Police reports?"

I shake my head.

"Medical treatment? Hospital admissions?" Her pen is flying over her legal pad now.

I shake my head. "I know you are aware that Armstrong outweighs me by nearly a hundred pounds and towers over me in terms of height."

"So tell me more about your spousal altercations," she says.

Since I am paying Ms. Victoria Anthony, counselor-at-law,

approximately $500 per hour, I figure she can listen for as long as I feel like talking. I have no access to a therapist to help me cope with my current crisis, so I look deeply into her eyes, fill up with a huge gulp of oxygen, and reach back in hopes of digging up something that can save my troubled behind.

Memory

I have heard it said that scent is the strongest sense tied to memory. Daddy smelled like Bay Rum cologne and Dixie Peach hair pomade. I loved sitting on his lap, resting my head on his chest.

Feeling his heartbeat.

Of course, Daddy was my hero.

Except when he was breaking Mama's heart.

"I hate it when you come home smelling like one of your whores!" Mama would shout, the only time she raised her normally sugar-sweet voice. Her cries would be ragged with sobs, torrents of misery and betrayal.

"I'm a grown man," Daddy would always say. "Work every day. Bring it all home to you. Grown man deserves some fun every once in awhile. And hell, least I don't beat ya like your friend Sylvia's man, George, does."

His logic never quieted Mama's crying.

I wanted to hate Daddy in those moments, but then he'd turn and catch my eye, shoot me that special smile, and scoop me up in his warm, strong, fragrant arms. And each time I'd pray that this would be the last time he made Mama cry out to Jesus as she wrung her hands and paced the floor at night.

I was twelve when I first saw it for myself. Mama had let me go downtown shopping by myself, with enough crisp bills tucked into my new purse to buy a sweater for the cooler weather that was coming with the start of the new school year.

I felt so grown-up, looking at everything in the store, taking my time.

I smelled Daddy before I saw him. In the women's fragrance department. Figuring he must be buying something special for Mama, I tiptoed up behind him, preparing to surprise him.

Then I saw *her.* She was young and slender, with killer curves, long legs, and the glamour of just-styled hair and too much make-up. Her lips and fingertips blazed bright red; her caramel cheeks were outlined with blush.

I couldn't breathe.

I stood behind Daddy, forgetting about surprising him. He reached out and pulled this flashy woman to him. She pressed her body against his, right there in public, in Mama's favorite department store in broad daylight.

For the first time, I understood the meaning of the word *brazen.*

I wanted to kill her.

I reached up and grabbed Daddy's elbow from behind. Not knowing I was there, he jerked his elbow away, which knocked me off balance. I fell to the ground.

His face turned ashen when he saw that it was me.

"Come home with me, Daddy!" I shouted, not caring that I was making a scene, though I knew it would shame Mama terribly if she knew. "Come home with me now!"

The brazen woman's face was frozen, a grotesque mask of bright paint and horror.

"This yo' babygirl?" she asked Daddy, her voice an evil slur.

I stood and hugged Daddy from behind, holding on as tightly as I could, anything I could do to pull him from her nasty clutches and bring him back home, back to redemption.

"Let go of me, Monique," Daddy commanded, his voice cold.

I held on more tightly.

"Dammit, let go of me this minute, girl, or I'll beat you senseless!" he said, his voice a low growl.

I removed my arms and backed away. He had never spoken to me like that. Mama neither. Not in that low thundercloud of a voice that shook the air like a growing storm.

I ran all the way home, forgetting about the sweater and the sweet perfume I'd wanted to buy for months so that Jimmy Swanson would notice me and ask me to the first dance of the school year.

I ran home, sobbing and gasping, the cloying smells of the department store fragrance counter overpowering Daddy's Bay Rum and Dixie Peach. My twelve-year-old heart was breaking like shattered glass.

Like the dishes Mama threw when I told her what had happened.

Like the shards of my life that lay scattered on a jailhouse floor.

Jailhouse Blues

I spend most of my waking hours pacing the tiny jail cell because moving is better than sitting still for countless hours while my brain runs in endless circles of anger and frustration, wondering what led me to this unimaginable low.

How could Armstrong do this to me, to us, to our dreams and our futures? For what? Some sex?

What is the deal with men, anyway? I wonder, varying the speed of my pacing to keep my sanity intact. Why do so many of them destroy their lives, their families, the love their wives and children have for them, just to chase another piece of tail?

Joyce and I ponder these questions on her next visit. She is, of course, rocking some new jewelry.

"Oh, honey," I say when she walks in sparkling at the ears and throat. "Nice bling. But is it really worth it?"

Her mouth tightens at the edges, and she shakes her head. "I'm starting to think it's just the way they're all made," she says, her voice tinged with sadness. "Makes it easier to believe that all men are dogs. That way you figure it's best to keep the one you've got rather than going after another heartbreak with a different face and name."

I tell her the story of when I was twelve in the department store. I tell her about my mama dying of a broken heart. I wonder aloud why we even bother to love them when it brings so much pain, so much destruction.

"Armstrong is hanging in, doing his therapy," Joyce reports. "And my hospital sources say that Ivy Green is doing okay. Though she lost the baby."

My heart sinks, even as I wonder why I care. "I'm sorry to hear that. That's a lot to deal with, on top of being HIV-positive and all that," I say. "Does the woman have a job? Medical insurance? How can she afford the meds?"

Joyce shakes her head. "I have no idea. But she's stable for now. That's all we know. So, Ms. Monique Estelle Worthington, let's focus on you."

My Emmy nomination has been rescinded since I have been charged with a felony: assault with a deadly weapon.

I hadn't put my car all the way into park. Left the ignition on. Hadn't set the emergency brake. But hell, I hadn't known what I was doing. Who could blame me, after the news I'd gotten and the scene that was unfolding before my eyes, right on the heels of Armstrong's life-changing news conference?

I can't watch, listen to, or even read the news anymore, which is why I am relying on Joyce to sift through it and tell me what I need to know. Or, to be honest, what I can handle.

Which isn't much.

As she prepares to leave, Joyce hands me a blue suede drawstring bag. "Here," she says with a tiny smile.

"What is that?" I ask.

"These are my magic blue suede shoes," she says, pulling one out and handing it to me. "Here, try it on."

"Joyce, you have lost your natural mind!" I say. "Where in the hell am I going to wear these skyscrapers? To pace my cell? Girl, I'd be crippled in less than a week!"

"I don't care when you wear them," Joyce said. "You'll know when it's the right time."

"I have to dress conservatively for the trial," I muse aloud.

"You sure that's the right way to go?" she asks.

"Joyce, I am not guilty!" I cry. "You know that better than anybody. Don't even think about suggesting that—"

"Hey, the decision about whether to plea-bargain is up to you and your lawyer. I ain't in it. I just brought these as kind of a good-luck charm."

"You're joking, right?"

"No," Joyce says, "I'm not. It came to me in a dream that I was supposed to bring these shoes to you and that you're supposed to wear them during your trial. That's all. Message delivered. Do with them what you want."

She sits back, folds her arms, and gives me a serene smile. But the resignation that still shadows her eyes tells me that she's going through some struggles of her own.

Inside Out

Mitch stops by every few days to check on me. "I wish I could bring you something good to eat," he fusses. "You are getting way too thin in here."

I shrug. "No appetite."

"Yeah, but darlin' you've got to keep up your strength," he reminds me, doing his best imitation of a mother hen.

I smile. My feet throb from the constant pacing on icy concrete; my joints ache from half-sleeping on a hard, child-sized cot. As for the rest of the cell, it's standard issue and every bit as cold and inconvenient as it was designed to be.

"What are the doctors saying?" Mitch asks.

"The diagnosis: clinical depression," I reply. "Whatever that means."

Mitch gives a harsh chuckle. "Honey, I can tell you all about 'clinical depression.' They'll prescribe meds. Take them and see if they help. But don't get used to them."

"Why not? What else could go wrong at this point?"

"What they don't tell you, Mo-Mo, is that depression is anger turned inside-out. Taking the meds helps you to function more 'normally,' but it can also keep you from getting in touch with the anger that's morphed into the depression. You've got to deal with that before you can get better."

"Anger?"

"Yeah, anger. Root cause. Trust me, I know," Mitch says with a quick flash of his one-sided grin. "If you don't handle it, it'll kick your ass."

"More than it's already being kicked?"

"Much more."

Something makes me reach for the blue suede bag with the shoes that Joyce left. I hold it out to Mitch.

"What is this?" he asks, peeking inside. "High fashion in the city jail?"

"Just check them out, okay?" I ask. "As a favor."

He pulls out one of the sky-high blue suede stilettos, turning it over and examining it closely. "Sweet!" he exclaims. "But how did you sneak these things in here? The heels alone constitute a lethal weapon."

I share the story behind the shoes: Joyce's charity auction, the "guilt gifts" that Jeffrey doles out to buy her acquiescence for his chronic cheating, and how she brought me the shoes because of a dream message.

"So what do you think?" I ask.

"I think messages that come in dreams should be paid attention to," he says with that wry smile. "And shoes as divinely fabulous as these just might have some mojo."

I sigh, taking the shoe back and returning it to its matching bag. "Yeah, right. Maybe I can rub them like Aladdin's lamp or something."

"At this point, I wouldn't rule out anything," Mitch said, standing to blow me a kiss as he turns to make his exit. "Believing in a little magic might do you more good than some damn pill."

~

Back in my cell, I ponder Mitch's words. I've been stewing in a cycle of rage since I've been in here. My mind races in endless loops, fuming non-stop about how I'm the one who's been wronged, wondering why I'm being treated like a criminal when it's my heart that's been broken, my marriage violated, my health endangered, and my dignity burned on a public stage. And all through the actions of others, through no fault of my own.

I walk in the same circles that my mind travels, around and around the cell, as though the repetition will bring insight or at least a moment of peace.

It never comes.

And Mitch isn't the only one to hit the nail on the head.

~

The last person I expect a visit from is my Aunt Cecily. I haven't seen her for I-don't-know-how-many years. But here she is, as statuesque and glamorous as ever, sitting in front of me as though we're meeting for lunch.

"I came as soon as I heard," she says, fanning herself with one flawlessly manicured hand. I sit on my raggedy, nail-bitten hands in shame.

"I just returned from Europe," Aunt Cecily continues. "I sing there, you know. Jazz. For six months each year. The rest of the time I live in New York City."

"How'd you find out about all this?" I ask, finding it hard to look her in the eye.

"I have a Google alert set to your name," she says with a wink. "So I found out when it happened. But I had to finish my stint at the jazz club in Paris. That's my bread and butter, after all. God knows no one wants to pay a living wage for jazz vocals in the states."

I am numb with shock. Aunt Cecily's words are conjuring a world I can barely imagine from this concrete hellhole. I wish it would open and swallow me alive.

"Who is your attorney?" she asks.

I tell her about Victoria Anthony, give her the contact information.

"And she's recommending that you go to trial with this?" Aunt Cecily inquires sharply, sounding like an attorney herself.

I shrug. "I refuse to plead guilty. I was not in the car. I was not operating the car at the time of the accident. I had no intention of harming anyone."

Aunt Cecily studies me, her eyes compassionate as she takes in my words and expressions. Her deep brown skin is unlined; her long, auburn-tinted dreadlocks gathered into a stunning upsweep.

She has always been elegant, a free spirit. And the sight of her makes me miss my mother so much that my chest aches.

"She was a slave to love, your mother," Aunt Cecily says. I

jump a bit, shocked at how easily she has read my mind. "Some women are simply made that way."

"And me?"

"I don't know, Monique. Are you?"

Her simple inquiry opens a floodgate. I tell her everything, rushing my words to finish before the guard comes to tell us that our time is up. For some reason, he takes longer than usual to show up and tell me that visiting time is over.

"You look like Leila now that you're grown," Aunt Cecily observes, gesturing as though she is smoking a cigarette, though she gave them up decades ago. "And from what you're telling me, you're just as passionate as she was, too."

"I always swore I wouldn't be like her," I said. "Making a fool of myself over some cheating man." I sigh, disgusted with myself. "But I guess that's exactly what I've done now, isn't it?"

Aunt Cecily's eyes soften. "Don't be so hard on yourself. When you live as long as I have, you realize that nothing in life matters near as much as love. Even if it hurts, even if it goes to hell, it's the experience that makes us who we are.

"My sister—your mother, Leila—was neither a fool nor a failure. She was, as I said earlier, a slave to love. Believe it or not, I admired her for that. Even envied her a little, truth be told."

"But why? She let her love for Daddy kill her before she was as old as I am now. What good did it do her?"

"God makes some people to do the loving, and others to be the recipients of the love. I've had both. And nothing beats the experience of loving someone with your whole being."

"That's how I ended up here, Aunt Cecily," I say. "So what good has loving Armstrong done me?"

"You wouldn't be so angry with him if you didn't care," Aunt Cicely says.

I squirm in my seat. "Who said I'm angry?"

"Oh, you're angry. Righteously pissed off, if you ask me," she says, chuckling to herself. "You know, you're more like me than you realize. You've got the Carmichael temper. Your mama didn't have it. So I guess you inherited it from me."

"Did you ever hurt anyone?"

"You mean hit them?" She looks me square in the eye.

I nod.

"When I was young and hotheaded, I swung my fists at a man or two, especially after they'd done me wrong."

"Did they hit you back?"

She shakes her head, reaching up to pat a dreadlock into place. "Honey, from what I've seen, a man who's inclined to hit a woman knows how to find the one who will take it. Don't ask me how. Just like a pimp can walk into a room of a hundred women and sniff out the one or two who he'll be able to turn out and trick into the life. It's just an instinct.

"And those men, the batterers, they're not attracted to women like us. We don't have the right vibe."

"What kind of man lets a woman beat him?" I ask her. "What does that mean if he just takes it and never raises a hand?"

"Honey, you'd better find a shrink for those questions."

She stands, doing the invisible cigarette gesture thing again. "I've got to go. I'll be back tomorrow. Get some rest, hear?"

I nod, sorry to see her leave. I do a double-take when I notice that Aunt Cecily, who has to be seventy-five if she's a day, is rocking some high-heeled blue suede pumps. The style isn't as outrageously high fashion as the pair that Joyce has lent me, but the color is identical. And the heels damn near as high.

"Nice shoes," I say.

"Thanks," she says with a wink. "I call them my power heels. Got them in Italy years ago. I wear them when I have something special to accomplish."

"Do they work? Do you get what you want?" I ask, thinking of the crazy shoes that Joyce has lent me.

"They certainly do, Miss Monique," she says with her enigmatic smile. "I'll see you in a few days. Meanwhile, just think on the things we've talked about and ask yourself this: if you have to be a slave to something, what do you want it to be?"

Purple

Joyce comes by every other day or so—one of the perks of her not having a full-time hustle, I tease as she takes a seat and pulls out her notepad full of scribbles with the latest news.

Some young Asian woman is taking my place on the newscast. "They're not mentioning your name at all, unless it's in the context of the news story," Joyce says sadly.

"And how are those going?"

She shrugs, rolls her eyes. "No new developments, so they milk the juicy parts again and again."

"Any mention of Poison Ivy's health status?" I ask, wondering for the zillionth time where that damned doctor's note went. It was the best evidence I had.

Joyce shakes her head. That's when I notice the sterling-silver-and-jade earrings adorning her lobes.

"Let me ask you something," I say to my friend, my heart twisting at the sight of her latest accessory acquisition.

"Shoot," she says, looking for something in her soft leather tote bag.

"Do you own stock in a jewelry company?"

"Don't start with me, Monique," she warns.

"No, seriously," I continue, ignoring her frown. "Damn near every time I see you, you're rocking some fab new gems. They can't all be Jeffrey's 'guilt gifts,' can they? How much extra-marital screwing around is your husband doing anyway?"

"I don't have to take this from you," she says angrily. "I'm going to chalk that little comment up to your circumstances. But please do not go there again."

"Hmph," I say, not willing to agree to any such thing.

Joyce takes a long, shuddering breath to calm herself, closes her eyes, breathes deeply again, smoothes her hands down the front of her linen pants. "Right now, I am focusing on getting you through this trial. I have hired a private investigator to track down Ivy Green's doctor."

I nod stiffly, afraid to allow myself any hope.

"Big surprise—I sold a house today. Yes, even in *this* economy. The commission was decent. I'd love to cover your bail and get you out of here." Her smile is lit with desperate hope and false cheer.

I shake my head. "Thanks but no thanks, Joyce. I truly appreciate the offer. But maybe this is where I belong, at least until the trial."

"Are you crazy? Yes, you obviously are," Joyce answers her own question before I can speak. "This hell-hole has caused you to lose all perspective!"

"Where will I go?" I ask. "Home? To an empty house that reminds me of what I've lost? I'm not ready for that yet."

"You'll come to my place, then!" Joyce says brightly.

I shake my head. "I don't need to bring all of my negative karma into your house. Thanks anyway. Victoria said the trial is supposed to start next week, week after that at the latest."

"I still think you'd be better off out of here."

I change the subject by telling Joyce about Aunt Cecily's surprise visit, ending with a mention of her fabulous blue shoes. "She called them her 'power heels,'" I said. "Said she wears them when she has something special to accomplish."

Joyce's eyes widen. "That's like the message I got in the dream about bringing my blue suede shoes to you."

I nod. "Yeah. But where am I supposed to wear those bad boys up in here? They are not made for pacing on concrete, that's for sure."

"Signs are all around you," Joyce said. "I'd advise you to pay attention to them."

"I could say the same to you," I say, pointing to her shiny new earrings. "I guess we believe what we're ready for, right?"

Joyce looked sad as she rose and waved good-bye. "Maybe so, Monique. Maybe so. It's always easier to tell someone else how to handle their business than to focus on what you should be doing for yourself."

I pace and fume and pace and fantasize about getting out of here, pace and curse out Armstrong and that pathetic Ivy Green over and over and over and over again in my mind, hoping to exhaust myself so I can get at least a few moments of peace.

That night, I, too, dream of the blue suede shoes that Joyce handed to me. I am wearing them with blue jeans and a crisp white shirt, strutting up a downtown sidewalk among fabulous boutiques and shoppers who looked like they don't have a care in the world.

The shoes seem super-powered—no matter how tired I become, my feet feel energized, ready to walk a hundred miles if need be. I have the bounce in my step that comes from being carefree and on top of the world.

Just like I felt when I heard about the national Emmy nomination.

No telling whether I'll ever feel that way again.

I awaken before that little streak of dawn is showing through my miserably small, barred window, wondering at the symbolism of the shoes.

I put them on, turn my ankle this way and that to get a good look, then wait to see whether there is any special energy coming from the blue suede stilettos.

Not a thing.

I stand, wobbling more than a little, until I steady myself with one hand on the jail cell sink. Can't pace in these monsters, but I can step carefully, quietly.

As I move tentatively around my cell, I think about waiting for the results of my HIV test. The first results were "inconclusive," according to my lawyer, Victoria Anthony, who said that's what the lab told her. So they took more blood to test again.

Prognosis: scared as hell.

I admit that I've never given much thought to what it would be like to be HIV-positive. Sure, I've interviewed my fair share of folks with HIV and AIDS for news stories, but I never imagined I would be the one going through this madness.

How ridiculous is it that I might have a fatal disease simply because I slept with my husband? Nobody uses protection once the relationship is established, once you're talking about love and forever and signing your names on legally binding documents.

I could do a documentary about how single women might be more protected from STDs than married women because at least single women *know* that they have to use protection every time. When you're married, you get comfortable. Lazy. You trust. You relax. Then *bam!* You find that you might have relaxed a little too much or in the wrong way or with the wrong person. And all it takes is one damn time.

Waiting for a test result isn't much different from waiting for a verdict. You hold your breath, waiting to see whether you're headed for Heaven or Hell.

Yellow

"The good news," says Victoria Anthony, "is that I've managed to get the trial date pushed up. We start tomorrow."

"Tomorrow?" My foot taps nervously.

"Yes," she says sharply. "There's already been too much media coverage, and it's best to get things in motion within the courtroom. Overspeculation is rarely a good thing. Especially in a case like ours."

I like that she says "ours" and not "yours." It at least gives me the illusion that I'm not in this alone.

"Okay," I say, taking a deep breath. "What's our strategy?"

"Tell the truth," she says. "You have nothing to hide, Monique."

"Except the fact that I've, um, beaten Armstrong in the past."

"Do *not* use that word! You did not 'beat' Armstrong. You were driven to anger and frustration by his repeated philandering, and you hit him a few times."

I close my eyes, unable to imagine what this news getting out will do to my public image. My career prospects. My life in general.

"He never called the authorities, never pressed charges, did he?" Victoria asked. "Reach way back. Make sure you remember clearly."

I shake my head. "Never. Armstrong is too proud for that. Of course, I learned in making the documentary that men are far less likely to report domestic violence than women."

"I like that angle—that your private battles with anger led you to research and make this documentary, which was motivated by your drive to better understand what was making you behave in this way." Victoria scribbles something on her legal pad.

"Did you ever seek counseling or any kind of help with your anger issues?" she asks.

Startled, I bite back the curse words that race to my tongue. "No, never," I admit. "Didn't see the point. And I don't think I have anger 'issues.' Wouldn't anyone be upset by a cheating spouse?"

Victoria stares at me a moment without answering, then goes on to her next question. The conversation goes on as I try not to feel as though the roller coaster I'm riding has taken another huge, unexpected dip. The kind that makes your stomach lurch and twist into knots.

Victoria reaches down for a garment bag. "I've taken the liberty of bringing you something to wear. It's new," she says. "And perfect for trial."

She shows me a conservative shirtdress in powder blue. Combed cotton. Belted at the waist.

"I'll look like a 1950s housewife," I say. "Are you sure? I mean, people are used to seeing me on television every night looking totally different. I'm not sure this will work."

Victoria fixes me with a long stare. "Exactly! You want to be as different as possible from the know-it-all news anchor. I want you conservative. Demure. Humble. Remorseful. Vulnerable. And this dress says it all."

"Are you buying me new outfits for each day?" I ask, incredulous. "How much is this costing you?"

Victoria smiles at me. "The answer is yes, I am. Image is everything, and I believe in ensuring that my clients look the part when they go into a courtroom. As for cost, not to worry. I'm billing it all to you!"

"Fine," I shrug. "I'm all for staying out of prison, *by any means necessary.*"

"Good," she says. "Now let's talk strategy."

I wear the powder blue shirt dress, which feels like a straitjacket. And the ridiculous shoes that Joyce gave me. "Those will not do," Victoria announces when she sees them.

I tell her of Joyce's dream and Aunt Cecily's nearly identical "good-luck" shoes from Italy.

"I *have* to wear them," I tell her. "They're the only security blanket I have."

She shakes her head. "Whatever. Let's go."

I feel the jury staring at me, but Victoria has instructed me not to do more than glance at them, keeping my face neutral at all times. "You don't want to seem overly anxious or confrontational," she says.

Yeah, right.

The words of the attorneys and witnesses seem far away. I focus on the court reporter's hands, flying over the keys of her strange machine to record the proceedings. I feel disconnected as I listen, doodling sometimes on a yellow notepad in front of me.

We have a few breaks ("recess" the judge calls them, though we're not having any fun), then it's back in court. I feel as though I'm onstage. Problem is, I'm not an actress, I'm a news anchor. Where is my script, my TelePrompTer?

Of course Victoria has rehearsed my testimony with me a zillion times. We try to anticipate the prosecutor's questions and respond in the most favorable way.

"This whole process is so manipulative," I complain to Victoria one day as we split a sandwich and fries.

"Kind of like TV news?" she asks, smiling.

"This is worse," I say. "And the stakes are much higher."

Then we're called back into court.

~

Joyce comes to the trial. So does Mitch. Sharlita, my assistant from the station, even shows up once or twice, always sending me smiles of encouragement. There aren't too many other folks I care to see right now.

I'm obsessed with news on the medical front. My test results came back negative. I paid for two more tests from different sources, just to be certain. Victoria thought this was a good idea.

"It shows how terrified you are," she says.

"That's not a strategy," I tell her grimly. "I am truly scared to death."

Armstrong is still undergoing intensive physical therapy to regain his strength and mobility. For now he's in a wheelchair. "Will he walk again?" I ask Victoria.

"The prognosis is hopeful," she says. Spoken like a true lawyer.

The skank ho known as Ivy Green is still in the hospital, with damage to her pelvis. Joyce's private detective hasn't found Ivy's doctor.

A seemingly endless stream of medical experts testify, throwing around complex medical terms.

"Will Ivy Green be able to bear another child?" the prosecutor asks one doctor.

The doctor shakes his head. "Unlikely, due to the extent of pelvic damage," he says.

The jurors' eyes swing toward me, sit on me hard, then return to the doctor on the witness stand. Today's dress is soft pink. Still 1950s TV-wifey style. Still with the crazy shoes.

On Friday, we're released for the weekend.

"What's your analysis?" I ask Victoria as we walk to her office.

"It's time for me to talk with Armstrong," she says, surprising me. "And Ivy Green."

"It's a necessary evil," she assures me. "We're at a disadvantage if I don't have some face time with each of them. Alone," she adds. "And I don't want you disadvantaged in any way."

I hug Victoria, wondering how much she is driven by the urge to have her name in the news as the lawyer of record for the scandalous former anchor.

"We're gonna win this thing," Victoria assures me, patting my back. "Because I definitely do not believe that serving an extended prison sentence will help anyone."

"Sounds good to me," I say, wondering when it will be safe to allow myself to taste just a single bite of hope.

"You're positive that you stumbled into Armstrong, which caused him to fall down with Ivy, right?" Victoria asks, studying her notes.

"Yes. I was sneezing from her cheap perfume, and I fell into him. Then he lost his balance and she lost hers."

"Uh-huh," she says, studying me as she writes a note to herself on her ever-present yellow legal pad.

"I need you to lose those blue stilettos," she instructs me. "I've left some more appropriate pumps for you back in your cell."

My feet would love the pumps, which are bound to be more comfortable than the blue-suede torture chambers on my feet.

I shrug. "Whatever will work, Victoria. I have placed my trust and my future in your very capable hands."

"I know," she says, scribbling like crazy on her pad. "That's why I want those interviews with Armstrong and Ivy Green, ASAP."

Fog

You would think that, being a journalist, I would remember every word, every detail, every nuance of my own trial.

But it's all a blur. I'm so scared and anxious that my brain is like mush. The harder I try to focus, the more I daydream. About how life used to be. About loving Armstrong. About our gorgeous home. My great career.

Even Armstrong's run for mayor.

How could we have tumbled from the top of our world to this place in an instant? And whose fault was it anyway?

I tune in as my attorney, Victoria, grills a psychologist about my state of mind.

"Minutes before heading off to her husband's press conference, Ms. Worthington met with Ms. Green, who informed her that she was pregnant, then gave her photos of herself and Mr. Worthington having sex. Ms. Green also gave Ms. Worthington a doctor's note saying that Ms. Green is HIV-positive," Victoria says crisply. "What would you expect her state of mind to be under those circumstances?"

The doctor shifts in the witness seat. All jurors' eyes are on him, which I prefer to them being on me. "I would expect her to be very agitated. Quite upset. Worried about her health. Distraught. Yes, definitely distraught," the doctor replies, clearing his throat, which makes him sound even more pompous.

I struggle to maintain the neutral face I've perfected from years of interviews and newscasts.

"So would you say this has the hallmarks of a 'crime of passion'?" Victoria asks the doctor.

"Hard to say for certain," the doctor says. "But that dynamic could be present."

"Thank you," Victoria says.

The prosecutor stands to fire dozens of questions at the doctor, each sounding the same to me. Without flinching or breaking a sweat, the doctor maintains that my state of mind was deeply affected by the preceding events, and this should be taken into consideration.

I want to blow the doctor a kiss. Instead, I look down and write on my legal pad.

"Am I crazy?" I scribble. "I'm the victim here and yet I'm on trial for an accident that wasn't my fault. At least not completely.

Our legal system is too black and white. It doesn't allow for the many variations of human behavior that happen in the real world."

The night before I am to go on the witness stand to explain my side of the story to the judge and jury, I am awakened by a noise outside my cell. Not that it's hard to wake me, since I don't really fall completely asleep in here for long.

I notice the cleaning lady, brown-skinned and stout, with shiny hair pulled into a tight ponytail.

She is watching me closely, mopping noisily right outside my cell. This hasn't happened before, so I figure maybe I'd better pay attention.

"Can I help you?" I ask, struggling to sit. "Do you need something?"

She shakes her head. "You want to go to prison?"

Her accent is vaguely Spanish. "Of course not," I answer. "Why?"

"My name is Gabriella," she says. "A beautiful name for an ugly old woman. But I was beautiful when I was young. Beautiful like you. They call me Gabby now."

I stare at her, wondering whether I have finally drifted off into real sleep and am dreaming.

"Hello, Gabriella," I say. "I'm Monique."

"I know you," she says. "News Lady. Watch you all the time."

"Or you did," I say.

"Yes," she says. "So you want to go to prison?"

"I already told you. No. Of course not," I snap. Then I sigh, ashamed. "Sorry. I didn't mean to be rude."

"It's okay," she says. "I served fifteen years," she says. "Used to be a seamstress. Made beautiful dresses for beautiful women. I wore beautiful dresses, too. Not anymore. Prison kills the deepest part of your soul."

"I do not need to hear that, Gabriella," I say. "Please don't make me more frightened than I am."

"Are you guilty?"

I shake my head, remembering Victoria's stern orders to never answer that question aloud or in any way that can be documented.

"Were you?" I turn the tables on her.

She nods. "Killed my husband. I didn't want to. It was an accident. He was trying to murder me. He said it over and over again: 'I will kill you, Gabby, so that nobody else can have you.'

"I grabbed for the knife to take it from him. We got all tangled up, and the knife ended up in his chest. Right through the heart. If I did it, I don't remember. But the jury figured I must have been guilty." She shrugs, looking me dead in the eye. "And just like that, fifteen years. *Hard* time."

There are words floating somewhere inside me, but none connects with my brain.

"Yours was an accident?" Gabriella prompts, still moving her mop around on the nasty cement floor. I don't know how she can tell whether it's clean. No matter how hard or how long she mops, it always looks the same: dingy and cold.

I nod. "Definitely an accident. No question."

"I've been watching about your case on TV," she says. "I don't think you're guilty."

"Thanks. Too bad you're not on the jury," I say softly.

"Most of the women I did time with? They were in prison because of some man. Because of loving some man. Either we stop loving first or they do, and then things get out of control. And *bam!* Locked up."

I roll my eyes. "I really don't need to hear this. I'm anxious enough as it is. Can't sleep. Don't want to eat. It's such a nightmare."

"Tell your lawyer you want to testify," Gabriella advises. "I didn't want to, was too scared. Big mistake."

We hear a clanging noise not far away.

"Oops, gotta go!" she says with a quick smile. "I'll be praying for you."

"You mean you still believe in God?" I ask.

She nods quickly, moving her mop and bucket on down the hall. "You have to believe in something. And God seems a better bet than human beings in my book. Good luck!"

I stand at the bars of the jail cell, looking down the hallway long after she leaves. Think about praying. Certainly seems like a good idea. But it's hard to feel any kind of connection to a holy and almighty God in this pit of waste.

I stumble back to my cot, curling up into a fetal position, hugging myself as tightly as I can.

Wondering what Victoria Anthony will say when I inform her that I want to testify on my own behalf.

Soul

To my surprise, Victoria suggests that I prepare to testify before I even have a chance to let her know that's what I want to do.

We spend hours anticipating questions from both sides and rehearsing my answers. "Which can't sound rehearsed," Victoria warns me.

"I can do this," I assure her. "Of course it would be easier if I had a TelePrompTer to read from."

"You'll do fine," she says with a warm smile. "Just tone down the anger."

"Is that how I'm coming across?"

She nods. "It's subtle but unmistakable, yes. Even so, every woman on the jury and in the courtroom feels sympathetic anger. Unless, of course, they're a mistress or a baby mama. Then they may be sympathizing with Ivy Green."

I shudder.

We practice some more.

I sleep with the programmed answers dancing through my brain.

I sit through the trial holding my breath, trying not to become distracted. But the loudest voice of all in my brain is the one that screams nonstop: but what about *me*? Armstrong and his ho turned my life upside down. And I'm the bad guy?

That must be the "anger" that Victoria was talking about. That Mitch described as the basis of clinical depression. The anger that Aunt Cecily said I had inherited from her. Funny, I always thought of it as having a backbone. Sticking up for myself and fighting for what belongs to me.

I am on the witness stand, wearing a mint green shirtwaist dress and the sensible beige pumps that Victoria insisted upon.

"You can*not* strut up there in those blue suede skyscrapers," she instructed me sternly. And when I tried, she whipped out those pumps and handed them to me with the Black woman evil eye.

I complied.

After I swear to tell the truth, the whole truth, and nothing but the truth, the prosecuting attorney stands a few inches away and fires questions at me.

It feels like a verbal beating, but I stay cool. Give the right answers. Keep my face together. Aunt Cecily blows me a kiss from the back row. Joyce sends smiles of encouragement. Sharlita nods when I speak, as if affirming the truth of my words. And Mitch sits stoically, his high-wire energy coiled tightly, eyes never leaving my face.

Then Victoria questions me. We reenact our rehearsals. All goes as planned, until Victoria delivers something I haven't anticipated.

"Monique, would you say you have anger management issues?" she asks.

I hesitate, trying to recall the answer I'm supposed to give. We haven't addressed this topic. How to play it? Deep breath. Quick prayer.

"I am not an angry person," I say calmly, slowly, measuring my words to balance the tone and inflection. "But I am human. And it was very disturbing to see my husband with that woman, as if they were a couple and I was—the trespasser."

"So you were 'disturbed'?" Victoria asks.

"I was upset, yes. At the allegations that Armstrong had fathered this woman's child. At the doctor's note saying that she is HIV-positive. And at the fact that he was at her house right there in public view right after his press conference to announce his plans to run for mayor of Atlanta."

"Upset? That's what you were?"

"Yes. Very."

"And you were, according to the toxicologist's report, legally drunk as well, were you not?" Victoria asks.

I fix my face to stay neutral. Don't know what she's doing, but I hope it works. "I had had a couple of drinks, yes."

"So you weren't really yourself at the time of the incident, is that correct?"

I nod once. "I guess you could say that. I was under the influence of stress, and I had had a bit to drink."

She asked a few more questions in that vein, then said crisply. "That's all. I have nothing more."

"The defendant may leave the stand," the judge intoned.

I sit and turn toward the judge.

"Ms. Worthington?" I heard the annoyance in the judge's voice.

"Um, Your Honor?" I ask, feeling like a schoolgirl talking to a principal. "May I say a few words to the court? Please?"

Victoria looks alarmed. I return my eyes to the judge.

He weighs my question on his mental scale of justice, then nods briskly. "You may have a minute or two. Please keep it brief, Ms. Worthington."

"Thank you, Your Honor," I say.

I stand, facing the jury. I tell the story of seeing my father in the department store at twelve years old. I tell them of my allergy to cheap perfume. I confess my decision to not be like my poor dead Mama. I tell them of losing my temper with Armstrong and how horrible I always felt afterward.

"I never thought of myself as angry," I explain. "I thought of myself as fighting for my marriage, my family, my home. I thought of myself as defending my most intimate property. I believed that's what a wife was supposed to do.

"Ivy Green wasn't the issue, and I knew that," I said. "But she called me, as the cell phone records have verified. I met her in a secluded spot, fearing for my safety but wanting to know what she had to tell me.

"She gave me photographs of her and Armstrong having sexual intercourse. And a doctor's note saying she is HIV-positive. She gave me this information minutes before my husband's press conference where he told the world that he was going to be the next mayor of Atlanta."

I pause, take a deep breath, and look around the courtroom, then at the judge, then back at the jurors. I smooth my sweaty palms on the front of my Brady Bunch mom dress.

"I never intended to harm anyone. I was very upset when I saw Armstrong with that woman and she was pregnant, and then there was the information she'd given me just a few hours earlier. I did follow them to see where they were going. And yes, I had had a drink or two. Two, to be exact. Which was probably a bad idea, but the press conference alone was very stressful, not to mention everything else that happened that day.

"I didn't mean to attack anyone. Her perfume made me sneeze, over and over again, so hard that I lost my balance and fell into Armstrong, who fell into her. And I guess that maybe I hadn't properly parked my car . . ."

I glance at Victoria, who is staring at me intently, obviously holding her breath. And I continue.

"I love my husband. I would hate for my marriage to end. But if he doesn't want to be with me, then I have to let him go."

To my surprise, I begin to cry. "Armstrong is a wonderful man, the man of my dreams, but like many men, he cheats. That hurt more than anything—to give your whole self to the person you love most in the world and to have them disrespect you in that way. And publicly! But I am not guilty of intentionally committing a crime. I want everyone to know that. If I am guilty of anything, it is loving my husband and wanting to protect my marriage, my family, and my home."

I look around once more, nod my thank-you to the judge, step down, and return to my seat next to Victoria's.

"Well, well," she whispers, putting a comforting hand on mine. "That was quite a speech. Now let's see whether it does the trick."

Clouds

Back in the funky jail cell, I wonder whether my little speech will help me. Or hurt me. Too restless to sleep, I slip off the sensible pumps and strap on the blue suede stilettos.

I don't remember lying down, but I must have drifted off to sleep, deeply enough to dream. Because the shoes are on my feet, guiding me down a strange street. I protest that I can't walk so far in them, but the shoes have a mind of their own. I walk and walk until finally I come to a cemetery.

And then to my mother's grave.

I visit this place every year on her birthday, on Christmas, and on Mother's Day. I bring flowers, leave them, often shed some tears. But in this dream, I arrive to find my mama sitting on her headstone, legs crossed at the ankle as always, looking gauzy and opaque but otherwise normal.

"You need to practice forgiveness," she instructs in a kind of breezy whisper.

"But I was the one who was—"

"No question about that," she agrees. "Forgiveness is the only key that can free you from imprisonment."

I look down at the blue shoes. "Oh, Mama, that doesn't make any sense."

She smiles that slow, slightly melancholy smile that means she agrees but has to share her wisdom anyway. "That's the way of life, Monique," she says. "What makes sense in one realm is nonsense in the other. Forgiveness is the most powerful weapon you have. Without it, you can't win. And babygirl, please believe how much I want you to win this one."

This time her smile is happy and glowing. She blows me a kiss, waves her hands in my direction, and suddenly she is gone. The shoes start tingling: then they march me back to a building that has several front doors, each one a slightly different shade of blue.

I awake with a start to see Gabby mopping the floor. "How are you?" she asks. "Some dream you were having, huh?"

Why does she sound as if she knew what it had been about?

I nod, still pondering my mother's words. I can't really remember her talking much about forgiveness when she was alive. But maybe there was something to her message. I wasn't above a little motherly advice, especially when it came from the other side.

"Yeah, some dream," I agree, looking down at my feet. The

blue suede looks like a summer sky. Or a perfect expanse of tropical water. Cool and warm at the same time.

"Did you ever forgive him?" I ask Gabby, too tired for preamble.

"Hardest thing I ever did, but yeah. No," she corrects herself. "Second hardest thing. Took the longest time. But yeah, I did it. Finally."

"What was harder than that?" I ask. "I don't understand."

Gabby looks at me for a long minute, then smiled. For a minute, she looks like my mother. "The hardest thing in the world isn't forgiving the person who did you wrong," she says. "The hardest thing is forgiving yourself."

"Well, how do you do it?" I ask, wishing I had something with which to take notes.

"You just picture that person and say 'I forgive you.' You can say it to yourself, or silently even. Nobody has to know."

"And if I don't?"

She shrugs. "You learn, the way some of us have to, that refusing to forgive is the greatest punishment you can give to yourself. And agreeing to do it is the best gift you can give yourself."

I thank Gabby, wondering if I'll ever see her again. As far as the trial is concerned, all of the arguments have been made. All of the strategies have been laid out and executed. Each tactic deployed. Now the rest of my life is in the hands of a dozen people who know nothing about me besides what any fool with a computer can access and whatever they gleaned from the probing of two attorneys.

We're expecting the verdict tomorrow. There isn't much time. I force myself to picture Armstrong, pretending that I forgive him until it seems that an eternity has passed. "I forgive you, I forgive you, I forgive you," I say, trying not to gag on the words, which feel fake and lumpy in my mouth. My stomach burns with nausea, but I force myself to keep going.

"I forgive you. I forgive her. I forgive myself, totally and completely, right now."

I spend the rest of the nighttime hours hunched over, repeating the words "I forgive you. I forgive her. I forgive myself."

Soon the words are just a hum; then they melt into my insides until I feel the tiniest, most subtle little shift somewhere deep inside me, in a place I can't name but know well.

I grab my legal pad and write over and over, until my fingers are tattooed with ink stains and cramping with the effort, "I forgive you, Armstrong. I forgive you, Ivy Green. I forgive myself."

I can't say I believe a word of it. But somehow the process clears just a bit of my mental fog. I write until there is no paper left, not a single blank inch to fill. With nothing left to do, I pace my cell in those blue suede shoes until the sun comes up. And for the very first time, though I've nearly worn a pathway in the cold concrete floor, my feet don't hurt in those crazy shoes at all.

Scales of Justice

Has the jury reached a verdict?"

"We have, Your Honor."

"Will the defendant please rise for the verdict?"

Victoria Anthony lays a reassuring hand on my forearm and squeezes it once, somewhere between gently and hard. Fighting the sensation of being stuck in concrete, I push back my chair, place both hands on the scarred wooden table for support, and force myself into what I believe is a standing position.

These ridiculously high blue suede stiletto shoes, which I am wearing in direct defiance of Victoria's advice, make the trembling of my knees even worse. But these gorgeous, near-gaudy shoes are my good-luck charm, the only hope I have of recovering any semblance of my life.

I am not breathing. Victoria isn't either. My eyes are locked on the jury foreman's mouth, awaiting the pronouncement of my fate. Everything else is a blur.

His words seem to be in slow motion, coming at me through a fog. I strain to quiet the screams inside my head so I can hear. "We, the jury, find the defendant, Monique Estelle Worthington, on charges of aggravated assault with a deadly weapon: not guilty.

"On charges of driving while intoxicated: guilty."

The courtroom erupts in pandemonium. Victoria hugs me. People rush at me from all directions. I don't know where to look, what to think, or what to say.

Later, when we return for the judge's sentencing, my head is still spinning. But I am wearing my own gray suit with teal pinstripes and Joyce's ridiculously wonderful blue suede shoes.

I walk into the courtroom, not with arrogance but with genuine humility and gratitude. I don't know what to expect, but I feel ready to face my destiny.

"Ms. Worthington, based on your speech and on letters from your husband, which support your testimony, I sentence you to two years' probation, along with a fine of five thousand dollars, and five hundred hours of community service, to be performed in service of the disabled."

I nod.

"And I am also requiring that you take—and then teach—an anger management course." Victoria hands me a brochure. I glance at it and back at the judge.

"Are there questions?" he asks with a weary smile.

"No, Your Honor. Thank you very much," I say. "I don't know whether I'll be returning to television. But I thank you for your fair and just sentencing. I couldn't ask for anything more."

After Victoria and I have said our good-byes, I rush to the car with an urgent task in mind. I find my Rihanna CD, press it once against my forehead, then toss it into the nearest trash can.

This girl will not be breakin' any more dishes, thank you. And every day, no matter where I am or what I'm doing, I will take a few minutes to do some forgiving. And then I will thank God, Gabrielle, Victoria, my mama, Aunt Cecily, Mitch the Bitch, and most of all those ridiculously beautiful, outrageous, healing blue suede shoes. Which I will return to Joyce ASAP and replace with some classic, comfortable low-heeled pumps with which to stride into the next chapter of The Life and Times of Monique as I find a brand-new tune for whatever awaits me on the road ahead.

ELIZABETH

THE WRONG SIDE OF MR. RIGHT

ATKINS

Chapter ONE

This magic moment was the answer to Charmaigne Carson's dreams and prayers. On the deck of a yacht, she was celebrating with friends and acquaintances . . . nibbling Brie and sipping wine . . . and standing beside her future husband. She savored every second, never wanting this to end.

"Show us the ring," commanded the grand dame of Detroit's black bourgeoisie. Mrs. Renée Jacobs squeezed her pampered fingers around Charmaigne's trembling left hand. "My, my, Marcus, very impressive!"

Mrs. Jacobs twisted Charmaigne's hand to make the emerald-cut diamond—from Tiffany on Fifth Avenue in New York—sparkle in the soft evening sunlight. Charmaigne beamed, loving this attention. Loving the affectionate gaze that Marcus was casting down at her.

"This lady stole my heart like none other," Marcus said, his deep voice booming with pride.

"Sometimes you just *know,*" said Marcus's business partner, Anthony Jacobs. "If anybody else had met a woman and gotten engaged six weeks later, I'd tell that fool that he had unequivocally lost his mind. But you"—he patted Marcus on the back, making a deep thump on the broad shoulders of Marcus's custom-made navy blue pin-striped suit—"you never waste time on 'maybe' or 'mediocre.' When you strike gold, you know its value and you stake your claim."

Charmaigne closed her eyes as Marcus's soft lips pressed into her cheek.

"Gold," Marcus said. "My golden girl, with a golden heart, a golden glow, and a future that guarantees a golden anniversary."

She smiled up at Marcus, who stood a full six inches taller than her. He was inexpressibly handsome tonight. So youthfully radiant. So excited. So loving.

To stare at that man for life would be any woman's dream. With his creamy cinnamon-brown skin that, thanks to the superior genetics that made his grandmother look sixty at age ninety-five, was smooth and clear and flawless. The small gap between his large white teeth gave him a distinctive look in all the business brochures that attracted millions of dollars' worth of deals every year. And his tall, slim build, with the broad shoulders and tennis player's legs, along with elegant fingers with manicured nails, made him picture perfect. The epitome of black male bourgeois success. Except that, unlike his Ivy League partners, he'd earned his degree at Street University.

Charmaigne's head spun. "Thank you, all of you, for sharing our happiness. Two months ago, you couldn't have *paid* me to believe this opulent whirlwind named Marcus Robinson would sweep me off my feet like this. Feet that are still firmly planted on solid ground."

Marcus's eyes seemed to sparkle with her every word. The tenderness radiating from his clean-shaven complexion was unmatched by any of the disappointments she had dated through her twenties and into her midthirties.

"Her humility is what got me," Marcus said. "Beautiful, intelligent, a little too sassy sometimes"—he chuckled, arousing playful laughter amongst the circle of a dozen business associates—"but most of the time, she's a good girl. My princess for life."

Marcus kissed her cheek.

"Princess for life," his business partner said, "and in two weeks, your wife," Anthony said, clasping Mrs. Jacobs's hand. "Welcome to the best club in the world, my brotha."

Charmaigne loved the powerful beam in Mrs. Jacobs's eyes . . . the pride on Anthony's face . . .

And the glimmers of happiness and mischief and genuine delight that danced over Marcus's face. She studied the knowing stares of the women and men around them, many of whom had been married for decades, some of whom were newlyweds or new parents.

What did it all mean?

That she and Marcus would live happily ever after? That they were doomed to the secret misery of marriage, even though they'd been taught from birth that it was what they had to do to legitimize themselves as individuals, as a couple, as successful business people, as citizens of a civilized world?

Mrs. Jacobs's regal stance commanded Charmaigne's attention above all others. How could this woman, with her dramatic silver hair that swirled so elegantly against her head, and her beautiful, nearly sixty-year-old chocolate satin face, and her slim but aging body, exude such power, such confidence?

Didn't she worry that the man at her side—so distinguished as older men were praised for the fine lines that fan around their eyes and the white streaks in his combed-back waves—had succumbed to the temptation that surely must have been placed before him for their whole marriage?

How did Mrs. Jacobs maintain her queen-like demeanor when just minutes ago, Charmaigne had seen a beautiful young woman at the seafood buffet hoist her cleavage upward as she all but batted her eyelashes and shook Anthony's hand?

"You, Charmaigne," Mrs. Jacobs said, as if reading her mind, "are about to blossom into the woman that you're meant to be."

Marcus's deep chuckle punctuated the wisdom in her voice with something defensive. "Oh, my girl has been blossoming. I wanna keep her just the way she is. A perfect flower."

Mrs. Jacobs's velvet brown eyes glinted with a dignified yet defiant expression. Her smile expressed a thousand words that were best left to Charmaigne's interpretation.

"A toast!" Anthony exclaimed as a waiter brought a tray of champagne flutes. "To the bride and groom! May your lives together set a new standard for wedded bliss!"

"Yes, yes!" Marcus agreed, handing a glass to Charmaigne. He tapped the rim of hers with his. "Thank you, Princess, for making me the luckiest man on the planet."

His hazel eyes sparkled down on her with such intensity that everything and everyone around them faded to black. Her heart pounded, her palms dampened, and her whole body felt like liquid opium. He stared at her during moments like this in a way that every woman dreams a man will look at her. As if she were the most beautiful lady he'd ever seen. As if he had no desire to ever look at another woman. As if he could never, ever look at her any other way.

Anthony's voice boomed over the chorus of cheers as the yacht passed the sparkling lights of the downtown skyline. Pink and orange swirls in the sky, glowing around the dark yellow disk of the setting sun, cast a surreal beauty on the city, the white and black yacht, and the faces of folks around them. Nearby, a band played soft jazz.

The moment felt cinematic, as if she had stepped into the pinnacle moment of *The Story of Charmaigne.*

That was all she could think about right now, while Anthony was raising his glass to the heavens and calling on God to bless them with eternal happiness.

"May all your days fill you with the fulfillment of family and wholesome values," Anthony said, his gold cuff link shimmering in the soft light. "May you take the good with the bad, the sickness with the health, the challenges with the celebrations."

Mrs. Jacobs raised her glass. "And may you always maintain a strong sense of self so that your union stands on two solid pillars. A man. And a woman. Together as equals."

Her glass clinked on Charmaigne's; their eyes locked for a moment that crackled with such potency that Charmaigne felt goose bumps rise beneath her blue silk dress.

"To a match made in Heaven and a marriage that keeps you there," Anthony said.

A dozen glasses rose around them.

Marcus stared down again with those I-love-you-forever eyes. And Charmaigne smiled so big, her cheeks felt like they'd crack. He pressed his glass to her mouth; the sweet bubbles on her tongue went straight to her head. She felt dizzy with happiness as he sipped from the same glass. Her arm lowered with her fingers grasping the untouched flute of champagne.

"I love you, baby girl," Marcus whispered.

"I love you," Charmaigne said, her eyes welling with tears of joy. The dreaminess of *now* felt so good, after she had suffered so many agonizing years alone, that she thought only of the absolute euphoria of this moment. Not a single inkling of doubt twinged in her gut.

She gazed at her Mr. Right.

If her best friend, Lisa, had told her two months ago, during one of their late-night chats about the dearth of eligible bachelors for professional black women, that Mr. Right and a wedding were sparkling on the horizon, Charmaigne never would have believed it. That night, after yet another disastrous date, Charmaigne had nearly given up on having it *all.*

She had almost resigned herself to the reality that having a spectacular legal career precluded her from qualifying for a phenomenal husband as well. As if the universe had decided that such professional bounty had exhausted her personal buying power.

Now Marcus bent closer, pressing a feather-soft kiss on her trembling lips. Everyone around them exploded with cheers. He pulled her close for a hug. His large hands on her small waist, the warmth of his body, the spicy scent of his cologne, all ignited her desire to celebrate this beautiful moment by making love. It had been a week, and her body was craving his touch. But with his trip to Chicago to open the new offices and his late nights working on the Kenner deal, she'd hardly seen him.

Tonight would make up for that stretch, the only one in six weeks, that had prevented them from being together nearly every day. Lunch, dinner, even a coffee break on busy days had highlighted the weeks since they'd met. They'd already taken two weekend trips, one to New York and another to Florida. That's where, on a yacht docked off Palm Beach during sunset, he had slipped the diamond engagement ring onto her finger and asked her to marry him.

Charmaigne grinned at the memory of that fairy-tale moment. Right now, she wore the dress that he had bought her during that trip for this occasion. It was blue silk with a shirred neckline that he said framed her face like he was looking at a portrait of a princess. And the shoes—Marcus loved to help her pick shoes that showed off her feet that he kept pampered with her weekly pedicures at the spa. Yes, tonight she was wearing the stiletto-heeled silver sandals that wrapped so delicately around her slim ankles. He had bought them for her during their trip to New York. They cost as much as some folks' monthly mortgage payment, at a designer boutique on Fifth Avenue, no less.

"Only the best for my princess," Marcus had announced as she'd modeled them.

And then, that night, after seeing *The Color Purple* on Broadway and having dinner at an associate's Park Avenue penthouse, Marcus had been the epitome of romantic, attentive, and affectionate. And loving her shoes. In fact, back at their suite at the luxurious Peninsula hotel, he had slowly and carefully unbuckled each silver sandal, kissing the arches of her feet, the curves of her calves—as a prelude to the most tender intimacy they had ever shared.

Tonight will be an encore, even better . . .

It seemed that every time they made love, their passion deepened and intensified her feelings and confidence that she could feel this happy forever. Marcus's love seemed to have a Midas touch on her already spectacular career as well. Since they'd met, she'd enjoyed new heights of mental clarity, concentration, and physical endurance while working, preparing for trial, running meetings at her firm, and arguing cases in court. In the past six weeks alone, she had won two trials and settled three difficult cases, inspiring her clients to lavish praise of her talent and dedication to justice.

"I can hear you thinking," Marcus now whispered, smiling. "You're absolutely stunned at the magic that love makes in every area of your life."

Charmaigne stared into the enchanted sparkle in his eyes.

"You're still shocked that this is happening so fast," he said, "that the serious, analytical Charmaigne Carson would contemplate the pros and cons and give it time, but now that the glass slipper fits, there's no question that the happily-ever-after is yours, with me, forever."

Marcus took her hands, kissing each one. He gazed at the people around them, the water, the city skyline, the pastel-streaked sunset sky.

"Welcome to our life," he whispered. "Our life of love and luxury."

Charmaigne felt dizzy with happiness.

"Anything you've ever seen or heard," Marcus said, nodding

toward several male colleagues near the rail, "about the downside of marriage will never happen with us."

Charmaigne glanced at the cluster of prominent men. All of Marcus's associates were married; they often cited the benefits of stability, fulfillment, and partnership that marriage afforded. And that, they said, enhanced their reputations and productivity in the business world. Even though Charmaigne knew that half of them—starting with Harry over there, with the cigar smoking beneath his thick black mustache—were notorious adulterers. Just last week, Charmaigne had seen him driving in his convertible Benz by the river, with a young, big-haired beauty in the passenger seat. The same seat where his wife, Denise, had sat tonight as they pulled under the marina's valet tent behind Marcus and Charmaigne.

Rumor had it that Denise didn't care as long as he provided her with a wallet full of credit cards, their country club membership, and a new Jaguar every year. And she was always boasting about her long weekends away with her best girlfriend at resorts and spas and on shopping trips.

"Charmaigne, you are absolutely glowing tonight," Denise said, walking up as if Charmaigne's thoughts had summoned her. In a plump hand adorned with an enormous diamond ring, she held a plate piled high with chicken wings, cheese cubes, crab dip, and crackers. "You and Marcus make the most beautiful couple."

Charmaigne beamed at Denise and the well-wishers around them.

"Beauty and brains, times two," Denise said, her diamond stud earrings sparkling behind her black Farrah Fawcett hairstyle. The breeze forced her shapeless black dress against her body, whose round middle made Charmaigne think of Humpty Dumpty. To be so rich, living a life of luxury in society's upper echelon, being photographed in *Ebony, Jet,* and *Town & Country* with her husband—yet being imprisoned in fat and a food addiction . . .

Charmaigne smiled to mask the sadness that she felt for Denise, even while Denise was beaming and kissing her cheeks, then Marcus's cheeks.

"You two make an outstanding team," Denise said, reaching for a chicken wing. "I'm so happy for both of you."

Marcus took Charmaigne's hand and raised her five-carat diamond into the evening sunshine. "See this rock?" he asked Denise. "Every glimmer in there represents a reason that I love this woman to death."

"Spectacular ring, girl," Denise said, her wispy hair shifting over her forehead as she bent to take a closer look. "Did you say you two designed it together?"

"Absolutely," Marcus said. "Had to put a one-of-a-kind creation on my princess's hand. Let the world know she is unique, I am unique, we are unique."

"Girl, you got a good catch with this Romeo," Denise said, grinning. "Remember tonight and all the good times in the beginning. You'll need them someday, to remind you why you said 'I do' in the first place."

Charmaigne's freshly waxed brows furled. She exhaled with a bit of frustration and said, "With all the stress of planning this wedding, I've been feeling that way already. The florist, the caterer, the alterations on my dress. Honey, this is more than a notion."

"That's the fun part, sweetheart," Denise said, biting into the chicken wing and holding it over the pink china plate. "I'm talkin' about when the honeymoon is over. Oh-verr! And you wake up next to this joker and say, 'Romeo who? What the hell did I just do?'"

The bitter twinge in Denise's voice as she laughed made Charmaigne stiffen.

"Harry," Marcus called. His voice was playful but tinged with annoyance. "You better come show some charm to your wife. Show us how you keep the love alive."

Harry raised a "just a minute" finger as he chatted with a congressman and the mayor.

Denise shrugged. "I don't mean to sound harsh. But marriage definitely has its moments."

Marcus laughed and said, "Spoken like a veteran of this thing called marriage." He put his arm around Charmaigne. His fingertips tenderly grasped her bare shoulder. "I guarantee, my girl will never have a moment of regret, remorse, or doubt. Happily ever after is the name of my game, baby girl."

Marcus's eyes sparkled down at her. Charmaigne's heart fluttered, and her mind spun with déjà vu. He'd spoken those same words just three days ago, at the brunch hosted by the Jacobs at their sprawling lakeside estate. A Sunday brunch for the bride and groom to be, with fifty of their closest friends and associates. That, and this evening, were just a few of the many celebrations that their pending union had inspired.

Each one, it seemed, was an excuse for a party. And a way for the hosts to remind themselves of the goodness in marriage. As each host lauded the merits of matrimony more loudly and eloquently than the one prior, Charmaigne got the feeling that she was about to join an exclusive club that would bestow her with privileges and perks beyond her imagination.

Prior to that golden revelation, Charmaigne had sometimes looked down upon marriage as a ploy to convince women that they needed "Mrs." in front of their name in order to be legitimized, celebrated, and valued by society. And throughout her life, she had witnessed plenty of proof that for many women, being celebrated and valued was hardly what happened behind closed doors. Affairs, alcoholism, abuse, depression, addictions—she'd heard it all, especially when handling divorce cases at her firm. It always amazed her how two people could start off in love and then, years later, radiate such hatred in her law offices and in the courtroom.

We'll be different. Those are OPP. Other People's Problems.

"Baby girl," he said now, "dance with me. Let me show you off to everybody here tonight."

He pulled her onto the parquet square in front of the band. Then he whispered to the lead singer, and they began *One in a Million* by LTD. Their theme song.

Denise took their champagne flutes. And Charmaigne loved every minute of being on a yacht, under the setting sun, in the arms of her Mr. Right.

Chapter TWO

Marcus's gleaming black Bentley pulled up under the valet canopy.

"Congratulations!" called a cluster of their friends who stood on the electric blue carpet. They looked like a Shakespearean chorus of courtiers, applauding the king and queen as they departed for an adventurous journey.

Charmaigne hated to leave the spotlight of their adoration, but she knew that Marcus would whisk her into yet another charming dimension tonight. A private, passionate one where they could physically express all that their eyes had spoken this evening.

A valet opened her door and she stepped inside.

"The night has just begun!" Harry cheered as the valet opened the driver's door for Marcus. Charmaigne loved the way the butter-soft leather seat hugged her body; it was an affirmation that she was now, as Marcus had promised at the party, cradled in the lap of love and luxury.

"Beautiful evening," Marcus said softly as he buckled his seatbelt. "Your class and poise are unparalleled, Princess."

Charmaigne beamed. She grasped his hand. "Thank you, love."

"Everybody is so happy for us," Marcus said. "If I had known how much love I'd get for getting married, I would have done it a long time ago."

"No, you wouldn't," she said with a sultry voice. "You hadn't met me yet."

He let out a low, sexy laugh. "My bad. Let me correct: if I had met you say, ten years ago."

"Clean it up now," she teased.

"You and I both agree, Princess," he said, while driving on the dark, tree-lined road as classical music played on the stereo, "that it was smart of you to wait until thirty-five, and me to wait until forty-two, before locking down for life."

Charmaigne leaned back against the headrest; her head spun with the euphoria of champagne and romance and anticipation of making love.

"Absolutely," she said. "It takes this long to find out who we are, what we want, and why we're here."

"And we've still got time on your fine-ass clock for babies," Marcus said. "Plus I've had enough time to play"—he paused, as if catching himself—"I mean, to appreciate the virtues of all that a marriage can bestow upon a man's life. One woman, one man, one home."

"Like I said," Charmaigne teased, "clean it up now."

"Let's clean up something else while we're at it." Marcus's tone hardened as he turned to her and said, "If I ever hear you complain about the so-called 'stress' that planning our wedding is causing your poor little soul," he said with a mocking tone, "I'll fire the planner so you can see just how stressful it would be doing it by yourself."

As Charmaigne turned, her eyes widening with the shock of his angry tone, he faced the road. She stared at his profile, her cheeks stinging as if she'd been slapped. His words replayed in her mind as proof that yes, he had just spoken to her like that.

This had never happened before.

She was so shaken she couldn't decide how to confront him.

"Marcus, what—"

"If you think I'm paying that flaky bitch Jo—what's her name?"

"Josette."

"A small fortune to coordinate some cake and flowers," Marcus snapped, "just for the fuckin' fun of it, then you need a quick lesson on appreciation."

Charmaigne's cheeks burned, the same way they had when her father would scold her for getting a B or letting a droplet of spaghetti sauce stain her dinner dress. Then, and now, she remained stiff and silent. As a child, she had come to expect Daddy's tongue lashings. As a grown woman, with this seemingly perfect man, it was shocking.

"Let's see how well you can run a law firm, Counselor, and plan the wedding of the year," Marcus said. "The wedding that will be attended by dignitaries from the White House and a multitude of continents around the globe. Not to mention your mother."

His words hit the air with such brutal coldness that Charmaigne thought of a frigid winter wind that sucked away her breath and stung her skin.

"I'm sorry, Princess." His voice was as soft as a summer breeze. He hit his palms against the steering wheel as they approached a red light on the city's main, traffic-clogged boulevard. "I'm doing this for you. For your special day. For you to be my wife. But that hurt me. You made it sound like a strain, a pain—"

"I'm sorry," Charmaigne whispered. "Denise was—"

"Stay away from that obese bitch," Marcus said. "Bad influence. Nothing but negative. If you need a marriage mentor, Mrs. Jacobs is the one."

Charmaigne stared at the red tail lights on the Corvette ahead of them. She did not, at all, like meeting this side of Marcus's personality. If a client or opposing attorney had snapped at her like that in court or in her office, she would have immediately instructed him or her to speak to her with a respectful and appropriate tone of voice. That was a point she always made when mentoring the dozen female law students through the Women Lawyers Association. While hosting monthly chats with the young ladies, Charmaigne epitomized Miss Confident Career Woman, who shared stories about how she'd clerked her way through law school, graduated with top honors, and now ran a very successful law firm with her name and her name alone on the door.

But right now, something about Marcus kept her still and silent. Was she afraid? Did she hope that his outburst would blow over so that they could get on with the magic of the evening? Was this worth addressing? Maybe he was even right. Maybe her comment about all the work involved in planning a wedding had come off as ungrateful or even bitchy.

Charmaigne felt three inches tall, as if she had taken one of those shrink pills that Alice in Wonderland had popped. Charmaigne's confidence deflated into a mini mockery of the woman who just this afternoon had commanded one of the firm's best stockholders' meetings ever.

She was a winner in her professional life. And she would be the same in her personal life. So tonight, she would let him have his one little snippy comment. Compared to the grandeur of their candlelit dinners and intelligent debates about current events and like-minded viewpoints about work ethics and success, this was nothing. Nothing at all.

I want a husband. I want a man of his caliber as my husband. Nothing less.

And there was plenty of less out there. She knew firsthand. All the duds that she had dated prior to Marcus bobbed in her head like goblins.

There was Luke, the lawyer who talked big game about his romantic prowess but kissed like a drooling Saint Bernard and had barnyard table manners to match.

Barney, the internist who had turned out to be married to a woman in St. Louis.

Willie, the entrepreneur whose business was a front for laundering his brother's drug money.

Sebastian, the musician who—six months into the relationship—told her that he was bisexual and could never commit to one woman, one gender, or one type of genitals to keep him happy.

Oh, and she couldn't forget Fred, who—despite the successful real estate company and civic-minded reputation in the community that made him appear a perfect catch—had three baby mommas and all their drama! One had even confronted them in the city's finest restaurant, calling Charmaigne a "gold digger" and Fred a litany of insults such as "pimp" and "player."

After that embarrassing night, Charmaigne had decided that she wanted *all* or *nothing*. Either a man had it *all* and would become her *all*, or she would have *nothing*. No dates until Mr. Right came along.

Three months later, Marcus showed up.

And he was definitely *all*.

Intelligent conversation. Appreciation of her success in building a highly respected law firm bearing her name. In fact, it was his visit to Carson & Associates that precipitated their introduction. He had heard about her specialty in contract law, and he needed to retain an attorney who could craft such documents for his various business ventures.

While both had maintained a professional decorum during their first three meetings, the electricity crackling around them had been undeniable. At first, though, Charmaigne was cautious.

He had the look of a man who could get any woman. The kind of man who radiated success and confidence—and attracted female admirers everywhere.

But subsequent time spent with Marcus disproved that fear. At receptions and in restaurants, he focused his attention on her and only her. When female colleagues stopped him to chat, he kept the encounters brief and professional. And he always said, "Now pardon me, I'm here with Ms. Carson."

His aggressive pursuit of her made it difficult to resist him. Not that she wanted to. She loved the way he treated janitors and judges with equal respect. And how he volunteered time with and donated money to many organizations around the city and country that helped children. Whether he was donating to a school breakfast program or a sponsoring a new playground in a blighted neighborhood or personally mentoring young men, Marcus put his money behind his mouth when he pledged to "give back."

He attended church and had Sunday dinner with his mother; he was always helping his siblings stay afloat in the choppy seas of the ghetto life that he had so gratefully escaped.

That was the man who, in just six weeks, had wooed her heart and won her hand. The man she would marry fifteen days from now.

"From now on," he said sternly, "you are to project only the perfect image of happiness. I don't care if you're having the worst day of your life. You represent right, you hear?"

Charmaigne nodded. "I didn't think—"

"Then think." His voice whipped through the dark air like a February wind.

"As my fiancée and as my wife, you represent me. That is a weighty responsibility to shoulder. I've worked my ass off to build my empire and keep my reputation sterling. Now, as Mrs. Robinson, you will maintain and enhance that hard work but always, always, shine bright for me."

Charmaigne's stomach churned.

"Marcus," she said softly, "I am so sorry."

Because he did have a point. It wasn't right for her to gripe about the wedding that he was paying for. Especially since the planner was doing all the work. Many times, when the planner had called Charmaigne's office on busy days, Charmaigne had felt so grateful that she was not shouldering the responsibility of wedding planning on her own. It seemed like a full-time job!

And the expense—

"Lavish" was the only word that could describe how Marcus had instructed the planner to orchestrate the day. Flowers flown in from Tahiti . . . lobster and filet mignon for dinner . . .

"Just remember tonight," Marcus said. "Life is all about learning. Tonight we learned something about my expectations for you."

"I appreciate this insight," Charmaigne echoed. "It won't happen again."

"Good. Now, one more thing," Marcus said sternly. "I saw you scarfing down all that Brie with a stack of crackers. Baby girl, smart as you are, don't you know cheese is almost pure fat?"

Charmaigne's eyes widened. "Excuse me?"

She had spent an extra thirty minutes on the StairMaster this morning at the gym, just so she could indulge in her favorite cheese tonight. She worked out six days a week and counted calories to maintain her firm, size-eight figure. A figure that Marcus had raved about two weeks into the relationship, when they'd first made love.

"I don't need the Diet Police to patrol my plate," she said playfully yet dismissively. "I'll take the one about the wedding planner. But food? I'm doing just fine."

This reminded her of when her father would scold "Gluttony is one of the seven deadly sins" if she took a second dinner roll or requested more of Momma's famous macaroni and cheese.

"Marcus, I just had my dress fitted yesterday," Charmaigne said. "It is utter perfection."

"Let's keep it that way. But think about the honeymoon too. I don't want your ass bustin' out all over the beach."

Charmaigne's eyes bugged. "I haven't gained a single ounce in ten years. I resent that you're not giving me credit for the discipline that I exhibit every single day."

"Don't want you to let yourself go," Marcus said. "Some women—"

"I'm not *some women.*"

"Don't interrupt me."

"Marcus, we have to talk."

"We're talking. And I don't like what I'm hearing."

"My assertive communication skills are what impressed you," Charmaigne said. "At least that's what you told me after our first three meetings at the firm."

"At least that's what I told you? Are you implying that I lied? That I have some ulterior motive in wanting to marry you, so I have to fabricate reasons for my choice of you as my partner for life?"

Charmaigne exhaled loudly. "Marcus, I'm going to attribute this whole conversation to pre-wedding jitters on both our parts."

"That's fair," Marcus said in a tone that reminded her of the man she'd adored back at the party. "I'm sorry, baby girl. But the representin' thing, that's for real."

"Point taken." Charmaigne wrapped her arms around herself. The chilly tone of their exchange, even though it was warming up, had frozen her romantic feelings. Now she did not even want Marcus to come up to her condo to share a glass of wine or make love or even talk. This emotional roller coaster had her so drained, she didn't know how she'd get up and out of this seat.

And if she did, the thought of curling up on her couch with a cup of chamomile tea, in her fluffy pink robe and thick socks, with the latest *O* magazine in her lap, sounded divine.

"Marcus, can you promise me something?"

"What, Princess?"

"That you'll send the Diet Police packing on their merry way. I am not about to blow up now or when I become Mrs. Robinson. I work hard at the table and in the gym to look and feel my best. For me. For you. So relax. I plan to get better with age."

"Denise said something like that before she married Harry. She let herself go, the fat cow. Had no shame, popping those fried chicken wings in her mouth like that."

"I'm not Denise."

"She was just like you when they married. Slim, always wearing tailored suits. VP at Deltech. Gorgeous. Once the kids came, *whoosh*. Went to pot."

"Not me, ever. Rest assured."

"I will. But the Diet Police are still on patrol." His tone was playful but defiant as they pulled up to her downtown high-rise condominium. The doorman opened her door.

"Good evening, Ms. Carson."

"I'll come up," Marcus announced.

Charmaigne stepped out of the car quickly, so that if any disappointment or annoyance flashed in her eyes, he would not see it. Part of her loved his take-charge personality. He was a gentleman, treating her like a queen. Part of that old-school style of being a gentleman gave him the clout to order for her in restaurants or choose the best wine on the list or insist on the hottest place in town—even though she had requested her favorite meal at a nice but less celebrated eatery. It thrilled her that he was exposing her to new things; she was grateful for someone who was so generous and knowledgeable about the best places to go.

"Marcus," she said, turning toward him as Rex replaced him in the driver's seat.

His hazel eyes sparkled at her with that look that said he would give her all the tender loving care she needed, as soon as they stepped into the privacy of her twentieth-floor condo. That look—

it melted her inside. Her whole body hummed at the thought of his magic touch.

"I have a fresh bottle of Dom," she said happily. "I bought it just for this occasion."

He offered his arm as another doorman welcomed them into the vaulted marble lobby.

"Perfect, my Princess."

Chapter THREE

Marcus had transformed into sizzlin' hot in July. And that made Charmaigne euphoric, as if his love had pumped her veins with opium. Her every cell hummed with happiness.

"I love you with all my heart and soul," he whispered beside her in bed. He kissed her forehead.

"I love you too," she told him, tilting her chin up so that she could kiss his lips.

But he turned, rose from bed, and motioned with his hand for her to follow him into the bathroom. "Time to brush our teeth. Cheese, champagne, a nasty mix for sour mouth."

Charmaigne tensed. He hadn't eaten any cheese at the party. So was he telling her that she had bad breath?

"My dentist just gave me a new mouthwash," he said, flipping on the bathroom light. "It's state-of-the-art stuff when it comes to killing the bacteria that cause dental odor."

Her stare in the mirror probed his face for confirmation that he was criticizing her breath. But he merrily brushed his teeth, evening humming "One in a Million," which would mark their first wedding dance.

She studied his I'm-so-perfect aura. She stifled the urge to squirt toothpaste at him and make him apologize. Charmaigne had excellent dental hygiene. Brushing several times a day, including after lunch. Flossing. Getting checkups and cleanings every six months. Even forgoing her favorite foods that were known offenders, like garlic, onions, and other spicy dishes, when she knew she'd see him. The cheese tonight, yes, she had indulged. But so did the rest of France—every day! And the French were known for romance, so it couldn't be that bad.

Besides, Marcus never seemed to think twice when he ate garlic or onions or cheese. Charmaigne squeezed the toothpaste tube. Blue gel squirted out. Onto her brush. Onto the white marble countertop.

"Careful," Marcus said. "I can't stand toothpaste globs in the sink."

Charmaigne flashed forward to living with him. This was the kind of moment that everyone warned would get on her last nerve. Little irritating things that weren't even worthy of talking about but annoying enough to add up to an argument. Or the silent treatment. Or avoiding the other person by staying in distant rooms.

She'd seen this firsthand, with her parents' idiosyncrasies clashing in close quarters. Her father was domineering, and her mother let him be that way but suffered in silence.

A recipe for disaster.

Marcus bent over to spit with perfect precision into the running water in the sink. Why was he always so neat? Even when he ate an omelet, every forkful cut with laser sharpness, so that his omelet stayed perfectly intact. The cheese did not ooze out, the mushrooms didn't spill, the spinach didn't slide. His plate always looked like a gourmet food magazine was about to come photograph it, even in the middle of his meal.

All the while, Charmaigne's omelets were a mess from the first bite. Oozing cheese, spilling innards, little pieces of egg dotting the plate. Besides, she liked to indulge in the best bites, from the middle first, so she could enjoy the most delicious morsels without eating the whole thing and consuming all those calories. It was a trick she used to keep her calorie count in check. A messy trick, but the payoff on her waistline was worth it.

Now, with her chin high, she left the bathroom. She went to the hall utility closet for a towel to clean up the mess. Not that they ever talked about it, but Mr. Neat probably had a special way to wipe his butt. Then again, he would probably impose that on her someday too.

He yawned, stepping out of her way so that she could wipe the counter. As he left the bathroom, she caught a glimpse of herself in the mirror. The fiery euphoria that she'd seen in her eyes during the party was now dull disappointment.

At this moment, Mr. Right felt like Mr. Wrong. But no one was perfect. She certainly wasn't. So why should she expect to love every facet of her fiancé? In the context of all that was right about him, tonight's negatives were far from major enough to question a lifetime of happiness with him.

"Baby girl," Marcus called from the bedroom. "Come let me hold you while you sleep."

She closed her eyes, wishing that he would always speak so tenderly and say the words that she had waited years to hear. Yes, she had prayed for a loving man who would hold her while she slept. A man who could do that in a way that made her feel safe, cozy, loved.

Right now, that man was laying in her bed, calling her. And, as her mind quickly flashed back over so many years of lonely, cold nights alone, so many disappointing dates, so much wishing and waiting for love, Charmaigne went to this man who—despite the irritating moments—truly was the man of her dreams.

Chapter FOUR

Charmaigne's stomach cramped as Lisa shook her head with disapproval. She needed her best friend to provide some affirmation that she was doing the right thing by marrying Marcus and that last night's drama was just pre-wedding jitters, not a red flag to call it off.

"You got me worried, Charmaigne," Lisa said with her trademark rasp over the screams of seagulls. She strode even faster along the RiverWalk as the dark blue water chopped angrily on the other side of the silver rail. "Any problem you have now will multiply by a bajillion once you're married."

"That's exactly what I was thinking in the bathroom last night when I wanted to smack him," Charmaigne said as they speed-walked past benches, trees, and flowers. "Men have this superior attitude that just oozes out of them. Like we're here to cater to them. Like what they say goes."

Lisa pumped her toned, nutmeg-hued arms as they dashed past two young mothers pushing baby carriages. "We're the ones who create life," Lisa declared. "These dudes act so superior. But it's our bodies that bring them into the world."

"Here we go," Charmaigne teased, loving the sight of a silver-haired couple, probably in their seventies and married a half-century, as they laughed and ate sandwiches at a picnic table by the water. Would she grow old with Marcus and look that happy? A crampy feeling in her gut shot question marks through her core.

"Seriously, Charmaigne, you gotta make a decision. Were you having a close encounter with a side of this man that makes him Mr. Wrong? Or was your Mr. Right just acting out because he's nervous about getting married?"

Charmaigne watched a rust-colored tanker slice through the river.

"I don't know the answer to that question right now." Charmaigne shrugged, mesmerized by the huge boat's power despite its heavy load of ore. It was going to get where it needed to go, with nothing stopping it. She had felt that way about getting to the altar—until last night.

"In your heart, you know the answer," Lisa said. "Your head is just not letting you listen."

"This is the perfect relationship for me," Charmaigne said. "You and I both know that a man of Marcus's caliber is every woman's dream. My dream."

Lisa said, "Life ain't a fairy tale, girl. You know that."

"But I'm thirty-five. My clock is ticking. I want kids. Who in the world do you get with after having Marcus Robinson? I mean, the man has been on the cover of *Forbes* for his entrepreneurial prowess."

Lisa tapped her fingertips to her chest. "Look at me. I got an ordinary guy. A firefighter. And he treats me like a queen."

"So does Marcus."

"But my guy has never come at me from left field like Marcus did you last night. If my husband *ever* told me 'Don't eat cheese' or 'Don't make such-and-such comments'!" Lisa rolled her eyes. "That's called Control 101."

"Part of what he said made sense."

"Girl, your head's so high in the clouds, it's hard for you to see," Lisa said, tightening the drawstring on the sky blue sweatpants that hugged her toned waist. "There's a certain line you don't cross in a relationship when it comes to telling someone what to do or how to act. Each person has to accept the other as they are. Not inflict some *My Fair Lady* scheme to remake the other person."

Charmaigne loved the level-headed confidence glowing on her best friend's face. "Lisa, how come you never second-guess yourself? When you left corporate and started your business . . . when you left Johnny . . . when you opted for a holistic cure instead of chemo—"

"God." Lisa glanced up at the roiling gray sky. "I always get the right answer, and make the right decision, when I ask Him for guidance." The explosion of tight black corkscrew coils around her narrow face bounced with every step, as if punctuating her words.

"I do pray," Charmaigne said with a confused tone.

"But you let your brain get in the way of the answers. Pray like I do, keep the answer line silent and still, and you'll hear loud and clear." Lisa's dark green eyes glowed with wisdom as she stared at Charmaigne. They were the same age, but in matters of the heart, somehow Lisa always seemed older, more experienced.

"We look like that," Charmaigne said, staring at a couple walking toward them. Both wearing business suits, holding hands, gazing at each other. Just like she and Marcus often did.

"Looks like a perfect match," Lisa said. "But I've seen that dude three times this week in my building. Having lunch with a different hot babe every day. And it ain't business."

Charmaigne wondered whether Marcus had other women. His reputation implied a loud Yes. But his availability and accessibility to her, in person and by phone, text, and e-mail, made it seem like his schedule revolved around seeing her.

"I enjoy my sanity," Charmaigne said. "I can't sit and wonder what he's doing every minute away from me."

Lisa high-fived her. "That's my girl. When I was dating Rufus, I refused to think about it. And I still maintain that. 'Cause it could make you crazy. You either trust, or you don't."

Charmaigne strained to hear the couple's conversation as they strode past.

" . . . so beautiful today," he said.

"For you," the woman answered.

Both their eyes glowed with happiness.

"Do you think every couple has issues?" Charmaigne asked. "I mean, won't there be some conflict with anybody?"

"Of course," Lisa said. "But you have to be honest with yourself about that issue. Is he bisexual on the down low, playing Russian roulette with your body every time he points a potentially loaded gun between your legs?"

"Yuck," Charmaigne said.

Lisa shadowboxed the cool, humid air. "Is he a boxer? Physically abusive?"

"That would definitely count him out."

"Is he perfect on the outside, with a few flaws on the inside?"

"Bingo," Charmaigne laughed.

"Now you gotta decide if those flaws will make you walk up that aisle and say 'I do'—or make you walk away."

"Last night I wanted to," Charmaigne said. "But then he turned tender on me. And I've ached for love so bad, for so long, I just melt when he does that. I don't want to go without affection anymore."

Lisa smacked her hands together. "Case closed. You'll keep him!" She stopped to stretch her leg on the silver rail by the river. Bending over her knee like a ballerina, she turned to Charmaigne and said, "It's all give-and-take. If you want to take the good, you have to give in to the bad. Just roll with it."

Charmaigne rested her ankle on the rail to stretch, facing her friend. "But I feel like I'm ignoring a big part of myself that's unhappy when he's nitpicking about what I eat or my toothpaste. It made me feel like I'm a prop that he expects to be perfect for his performance in life."

Lisa switched legs. "Sounds like you're answering your own questions. You gotta listen to your gut, girlfriend. God and your gut. They never lie." She laughed. "But when you find out the truth, let me know if me and Grams still have a date to the Mayor's Ball Friday night."

Charmaigne laughed. "Of course you do!"

Lisa stretched lower. "Grams has been talking about this all day, every day."

"Grams has that fire in her eyes," Charmaigne said. "Eighty-eight years old and eyes blazin' with life."

"You should've seen her mother," Lisa said. "A priestess back in Jamaica. Scared the hell outta me with all those chants and chicken blood. I only knew one person who fell prey to her spell. And he drowned in Montego Bay."

Charmaigne thought about Grams's ageless ebony face and shock of silver hair, and the way her floral dresses swished around her sturdy build in sync with her determined gait.

"She always walks like she's heading to a board meeting," Charmaigne said. "Like she's the CEO ready to take charge."

Lisa smiled. "Then imagine her getting ready for the Mayor's Ball. We got her a new dress, a hair appointment in the morning, even a manicure. You'd think she's meeting the president."

As Charmaigne reached for her ankle to stretch, her diamond engagement ring glimmered. When Marcus had first given her the ring, she would stare into it and let it mesmerize her. She'd look up, and twenty minutes would have passed because she'd been daydreaming about life as Mrs. Robinson.

"Suddenly what looked like a fantasy is starting to feel very different from that," Charmaigne said. "I don't want to wake up one day and feel like I made a terrible mistake."

"Charmaigne, go home tonight, get quiet, find your center. And you'll hear the answer, loud and clear."

The problem was, Charmaigne wasn't sure she wanted to know the truth. She cast a questioning glance at Lisa, whose eyes locked on her hard.

"I can see the answer in your eyes, girl," Lisa said. "The pretty package isn't so pretty once you remove the bows and look inside the box."

Charmaigne's stomach gurgled with worry. "In my practice I feel confident, in charge. But after last night I realize that with Marcus, he's the boss. At the expense of my feelings. And I'm so caught up with feeling loved and getting affection that I let it happen. Then I brood about it—until he charms me back to this spineless, subservient person who feels like a stranger in my own brain."

Lisa stood with her feet shoulder-width apart and raised her hands gracefully over her head to stretch.

"Charmaigne, you got some work to do," she said playfully. But her eyes were hard and serious. "You have to either decide this is how it is and you're okay with that. Or you need to return that rock and walk away before you make a huge mistake."

Charmaigne wanted to crumple to the sidewalk. Her whole body suddenly felt tremendously heavy. Her heart pounded. A sad fog rumbled through her head.

"Everything comes with a price," she said. "But is giving up such a big part of myself—for the reward of being Mrs. Marcus Robinson—worth it?"

Lisa's eyes widened as if the answer were obvious. "Ask any woman you know, and they'd say it's a no-brainer. He's the perfect catch on paper. But only you know if he's the perfect catch for Charmaigne Carson."

Lisa took her hand and pulled her to face the railing over the river. The huge Caesars Windsor casino, with its gleaming blue glass, caught her eye across the water.

"A gamble," Charmaigne said. "This wedding feels like I'm about to bet my life on the elusive jackpot. Happiness."

Lisa shrugged. "Hey, Thomas Jefferson was onto something when he said, 'Life, liberty and the pursuit of happiness.' Pursuit, as if it's something we're always chasing but never reach."

Charmaigne marveled at how the water flowed downriver, toward the Ambassador Bridge, with such an unrelenting pace. Lights on the bridge's arches, which resembled a smaller version of San Francisco's Golden Gate Bridge, sparkled against the evening sky.

"But have you found happiness with Rufus?" Charmaigne asked. "Looks like you have. But deep in your heart—"

"Every morning my first thought is 'Thank you God for blessing me with the real thing.'" Goose bumps danced on Lisa's bare, toned arms. "But I had to love me first and know what I would and wouldn't stand for. I had to get right to find Mr. Right."

Lisa pointed to the bridge.

"Rather than a gamble," she said, "think of marriage as something that takes you across a bridge. Are you stepping into an enchanted new world that's better than you ever imagined? Or are you entering hostile territory?"

The nauseating burn in Charmaigne's gut seemed to answer that for her.

Chapter FIVE

The sun shooting through the wooden slats on the conference room window created just enough natural light to soften the mood of the tense negotiations. Mr. and Mrs. Branford, sitting at the head of the long, polished table, radiated wealth and power. In black suits and starched white shirts, they were the kind of long-married couple who actually looked alike. They seemed to speak for each other and even shifted simultaneously in the high-backed leather chairs.

With her elegant, jet black French twist and the freshly barbered lines around his close-cropped Afro, their matching diamond wedding bands, and a twinlike intensity in their dark eyes, their demeanor announced, "power couple extraordinaire."

"Mr. and Mrs. Branford," Charmaigne said from the opposite end of the conference table as their corporation counsel sat facing the lawyer for the company that they were acquiring. "I have reached an agreement with representatives from Lindstrom Industries that satisfies each and every one of your requirements."

The authority deepening Charmaigne's voice energized her with confidence. This was the person she loved. The person who knew exactly why she was here on the planet and what she was supposed to do. Law was her purpose, her passion, her safe space, where she always shined.

This law firm, on the thirty-fifth floor of the tallest building in downtown Detroit, was her turf. The place where she had no questions about who she was or how she felt. Save for the sun catching on her engagement ring and Mrs. Branford's split-second glances at the diamond, Charmaigne did not think of Marcus. She focused on business and her confident ability to handle it with intellectual stealth and skill.

I have the power. Charmaigne's lifetime mantra, learned from her mother when she was a second-grader worried about a spelling test, checked in her mind. *I have the power to do and be the best at all times.*

Commanding $400 per hour and representing some of the city's most powerful and prosperous business leaders, Charmaigne's brains and hard work had earned it all.

And this meeting symbolized that like none other. She had spent years wooing Mr. and Mrs. Branford away from the silk-stocking firm of Miller and Jones, founded decades ago by some of the city's first black lawyers.

It was her highly publicized victory in the Smith trial—a wasp's nest of corporate fraud, sex, and back-stabbing deception between brothers—that had inspired the power couple to jump ship and trust the negotiations for their future fortunes with Attorney Charmaigne Carson.

She had spent many late nights and weekends crafting the perfect deal, which they would sign on the dotted line today and make millions.

"I must say, Ms. Carson," Mr. Branford said with a voice that sounded as elegant and stage perfect as that of Harry Belafonte, "you have handled this matter with exquisite skill. Brilliance, even. For that I must thank you."

Mrs. Branford nodded, her heart-shaped, red-painted lips pulling back in a slight smile that raised her beige-powdered cheeks and sparkled in her wide set eyes lined in thick black, Sophia Loren–style.

"Indeed," the matron said with the deep voice of a smoker. "You are a shining example of all that a woman can be. Your mother told me at our Links dinner that she couldn't be more proud of you."

Charmaigne beamed. "Thank you, Mr. and Mrs. Branford. I'm here to serve you. Allow me to share once more the honor that I feel for the privilege of handling this momentous affair for you."

She turned toward the lawyers representing the company that the Branfords were acquiring. She tapped her gold pen on the stack of contracts before her.

"These papers epitomize a win-win for both you, Mr. and Mrs. Branford, and everyone at Lindstrom Industries," Charmaigne said. "Not to mention the environmental considerations that we have included in the agreement."

"Of utmost importance," said the lawyer for Lindstrom Industries. Zachary Hill rubbed most people the wrong way; Charmaigne would never forget how he'd made a female attorney burst into tears with his razor-sharp criticism of her negotiation skills. She'd also seen Zach reduce veteran male lawyers to quivering, bumbling wrecks.

Perhaps his power to intimidate rested in the upward tilt of his chin and the more-brilliant-than-thou tone in the faux English accent that he'd copped at Cambridge University. He'd tried that on Charmaigne years ago in federal court, but her articulate brilliance under pressure had lobbed an intellectual argument back at him that zipped his lips and dimmed the ferocity in his eyes.

And the judge loved it. Charmaigne had won—both the case and Zach's respect.

"Ms. Carson, let's proceed," he said impatiently. "My clients have a small matter to resolve."

The Branfords shifted slightly. Charmaigne remained still but furled her brows slightly. "Yes, and what is that?"

"We need to amend the contract to include a clause about water use at the downriver plant," Zach said. "My clients are concerned that only the most environmentally stringent procedures be in place."

Sweat prickled across Charmaigne skin beneath her tailored beige suit and crisp white cotton blouse. No way was she going to fall for Zach's last-minute nitpicking.

"I can assure you, Mr. Hill, that we have consulted the most reputable water-processing firm to ensure that under the Branfords' ownership, the plant will not spill a single drop of unlawful toxins into the river."

He slid a document across the table toward Charmaigne. "I need these specifications written into the contract, or the deal is off."

Charmaigne hated the arrogance in his voice. The what-I-say-goes tone, as if he owned the world. It inspired a feeling inside her body as if her blood were turning to acid, burning angrily through her veins, making her heart pound with resentment.

This was her firm, her turf, her deal, and months of hard work that had carefully reached each and every term in the contract. Including water processing.

"With all due respect, Mr. Hill, I believe that the meticulous consideration that we have given water use in this agreement—"

"My clients have reconsidered," he said with a louder tone. "They do not want the company that they built to leave carbon footprints on the earth if it can be avoided. I need you to amend the contract accordingly."

Charmaigne breathed. She focused on inhaling deeply to disperse the string of expletives that were tickling the tip of her tongue. His arrogance roused in her a trembly sense of rage that made her want to shout across the table.

"Mr. Hill," she said with a calm, smooth voice, "I assure you that this contract requires the most stringent procedures for—"

He stood. "Your disregard for my client's concerns indicates that perhaps we should rest the future care of Lindstrom Industries in the hands of more environmentally conscious owners."

The panic in the eyes of Mr. and Mrs. Branford, despite their poker faces, switched the adrenaline pump inside Charmaigne's body.

"Mr. Hill, please allow me a few minutes with my clients," she said, standing.

"Certainly," he said.

Charmaigne pushed a button on the phone on the conference table. "Mark," she said, calling her secretary. "Will you please escort Mr. Hill to the lobby for a brief recess."

Charmaigne stood, giving a single nod to Zach. "I assure you we will resolve this immediately."

"I know that you will, Ms. Carson, exactly to my specifications." Something about the way he said that reminded her of her mother, telling her to do a better job cleaning her room as a child.

His domineering, almost spiteful expression made Charmaigne's cheeks sting for a split second. But her confidence, and her commitment to pleasing her watchful clients, no matter what kind of bullish egomaniac was in the room, overruled any reaction except for diplomacy and grace.

As she stared at him in the tense silence, she suddenly felt punched in the stomach.

He is just like Marcus.

This is exactly how I feel when Marcus is telling me what to eat or criticizing what I say or telling me to brush my teeth.

Charmaigne's stomach lurched. She swallowed a heave.

Because under Marcus's condescending glare and criticisms, she crumpled. Here in her office, however, she stood tall and refused to allow any man's child-like treatment of her to diminish her self-worth.

Why can't I stay strong with Marcus?

Mrs. Branford's right eyebrow raised as she stared at Charmaigne.

"Never let them see you sweat," she could hear her father saying as she expressed anxiety about her role as prosecutor in the moot court trial during law school.

"Mr. and Mrs. Branford," Charmaigne said, thankful that her voice belied her sudden internal meltdown. "I assure you that we will resolve this to your liking."

Mr. Branford's shoulder twitched. "We've already spent a small fortune on the environmental consulting. That is over and done with. We have already agreed to the most stringent emissions."

He cast a fiery look at Zach.

"This is a minor technicality," Charmaigne said, hoping that her confident tone would calm any testosterone clash that was brewing between Zach and Mr. Branford.

"I would hardly call global warming and the industries that cause it 'minor,'" Zach snapped, turning dramatically on one heel away from the table.

His demeanor cast a chill over the room. Even the sunbeams through the wooden blinds seemed to dim.

Charmaigne's heart hammered. Her reputation with the Branfords was on the line. She had to handle this with exquisite skill to resolve Zach's sudden and silly macho posturing. She was no expert, but her consultants had assured her that this was the most environmentally friendly deal she could craft.

Perhaps Zach was motivated by resentment that Charmaigne

had wooed the Branfords away from the firm owned by his dear friend. Maybe he was jealous that Marcus had far more money, power, and prestige than he did. Whatever the reason, Charmaigne was not about to let him win.

I have the power, she repeated in her brain, even though her body was trembling.

Because on top of everything, Marcus would be furious if she lost the Branfords as her clients. He had helped facilitate this lucrative relationship by lauding Charmaigne's legal brilliance to the Branfords over an elegant dinner at the mayor's mansion.

Charmaigne hated that her motivation to perform right now included pleasing her man. Then again, without Marcus, the Branfords would not be sitting here in her conference room.

Suddenly her mind spun with the complexity of it all. If she were to opt out of marrying Marcus Robinson, what professional disaster would she create? Would he be vindictive?

Popular rumor had it that when ChemCorp pulled out of his mega-million-dollar deal to merge with three other pharmaceutical companies, it suddenly became the IRS's favorite company. Two months later, facing bankruptcy and charges of tax evasion and securities violations, the CEO was indicted and later imprisoned.

That's what happened, according to whispers at cocktail parties across town, when someone crossed the mighty Marcus Robinson.

On the romantic tip, it was no secret that his previous girlfriend, who owned an upscale dress boutique downtown, went out of business and moved home to Iowa after a mysterious fire that followed her break-up with Marcus. The reason? She'd been pressuring him to marry and have children. Not only did she leave a ruined business in her wake, but Sheila B.'s reputation festered with rumors that she was a lesbian, that she had a gambling habit, and that the former runway model maintained her lithe figure by puking up gourmet meals from Paris to Tokyo.

He would ruin me, too. Especially if I left him on the eve of our wedding. A wedding that's been announce in *Town & Country, The New York Times,* and at the most celebrated gatherings of the business world from California to Cape Town. Landing one of America's most eligible bachelors, said a feature on marriage in *Essence,* was the ultimate honor and privilege—

A privilege bestowed on me.

A privilege that would destroy me if I walk away.

Charmaigne's head spun. She felt like a whirlpool of panic was swirling inside her chest, her gut, sucking her breath and body into oblivion.

She steadied herself by pressing her fingertips to the table.

If I leave him, I'm ruined. Professionally, personally.

The polished wood double doors opened; Mark stood regally in a brown suit and waved an open palm toward Zach. "Mr. Hill, may I get you some coffee or tea?"

Zach's polished oxblood loafers shone as he stepped across the plush beige carpet, through the double doors into the black marble lobby. "No thank you. An office where I can make phone calls in private would suit me fine."

Mark grasped the doorknob in Zach's wake.

"Ms. Carson, Mr. Robinson has phoned three times. He said it's urgent, but I said you were not to be disturbed."

Charmaigne could feel the curious and tense stares of the Branfords. She knew they could tell something was already wrong. But the word "urgent" regarding Marcus's calls made the blood leave Charmaigne's face. Was he mad about something? Was he even more furious that she would not take his call?

"Excuse me," she said, squaring her shoulders, raising her chin, and donning a mask of confidence over her withering spirit. "Mr. and Mrs. Branford, I will return in a moment to discuss Mr. Hill's concerns."

Her legs trembled as each black stiletto pump pierced the carpet. Every tap on the marble lobby floor put her one step closer to her office, where she could close the door and collapse into her chair. Into her driver's seat. Into the place where she felt most confident. Where she could collect herself, call Marcus, and handle the Branford case with her trademark skill and expertise.

Mark stepped into her office and closed the doors behind him.

"You look like hell," he said. "Are you sick?"

She slumped into her big black leather chair behind her wide, polished cherrywood desk.

She laid her ear on her folded arms on the glass top. She breathed deeply, closing her eyes. That made her head spin more. Her stomach cramped as if some wicked fist were gripping it, squeezing it with ruthless fury. She burped, as if she were about to throw up. But her stomach was empty, as she'd been too jittery this morning to eat her usual oatmeal, egg whites, and fruit.

"Charmaigne?" Mark asked, his blue eyes and suntanned skin contorting with worry. His straight blond hair swayed slightly as he dashed to her side. "Should I call the doctor?"

She stared into space as the whirlpool inside sucked her deeper into oblivion.

Mark pressed the backs of his manicured fingers to her hot cheek. "You feel feverish. I'll call Marcus to tell him you're sick."

No, not Mr. Never-Miss-a-Day-of-Work. The man who never caught colds or even had a single cavity. The man with perfect blood pressure and cholesterol.

"Aches and pains are for the weak," he would say to blow off a twinge in his knee after an especially competitive tennis match.

Mark touched her forehead. "Definitely a fever. I'll tell the Branfords we have to reschedule—"

Charmaigne sat up.

"I'm fine. Just a little overwhelmed. The wedding, Zach's sudden nitpicking—" She breathed deeply.

"You need water," Mark said, dashing to the small refrigerator built into the wooden shelves. He retrieved a bottle and stepped toward her.

The phone on the desk rang; a red button flashed. Marcus Robinson Enterprises appeared in the ID screen.

She pushed a button for the speakerphone. "Marcus, love, I was with the Branfords—"

"Take me off speaker."

Mark froze, bottle in hand. His eyes widened. He gently set the bottle on the desk, turned, and tiptoed out.

Charmaigne's heart hammered as she picked up the receiver. His voice shot through the phone like darts into her ear: "Why did you overrule my decision? The planner just called to get approval for the price of crab cakes as the appetizer, when I specifically requested foie gras."

The thought of brown liver paste made Charmaigne's gut churn. As did the rage in Marcus's voice.

"Last week," she said softly, "when you were in Chicago and we couldn't reach you, she called to confirm the appetizer. You know I love crab cakes, and—"

"Our chef prepares the most celebrated foie gras this side of France," Marcus said. "It is the appetizer for our wedding dinner."

His voice slammed her like a gavel. He was the judge, the jury, the decision maker, period.

"Any more surprises you need to share, my dear Princess?" Rage rang in his voice as he said "princess."

Charmaigne pressed her palm to her flat, gurgling stomach.

"Crème brûlée," she said flatly. "Josette insisted that the dessert table include my favorite because I'm—" her throat burned with tears. Her lips quivered as she said almost silently, "the bride."

"Crème brûlée is not on the menu cards that are already engraved with eighteen-karat gold script!" Marcus declared. "And if you think I want to spend time away from running my empire to police your sudden culinary whims—"

"Stop," she whispered. That single word seemed to sap her every cell of energy. She wanted to slump in her chair, but she squared her shoulders and summoned a strong voice. "Marcus, why are you suddenly so angry with me? Where is this coming from? Why are you outraged over something so frivolous?"

Silence.

Her heart pounded. Had he hung up?

"Frivolous," he repeated. Never had she heard the word spoken with such disdain. "The day that I make you my wife, that I care enough to plan everything down to the most perfectly minuscule detail. And you call it frivolous."

Charmaigne closed her eyes. Anything she said or did right now would definitely be used against her in the court of Marcus.

"I'm sorry," she said. She opened her eyes, which immediately focused on her law school diploma, framed on the wall alongside a dozen awards and an article about her that had been published in *Time* magazine after she negotiated the high-profile eighty-five-million-dollar cable merger that made history in the industry and launched her firm into the spotlight.

All that, and this man who was supposed to cherish her for life was instead furious at her about crème brûlée and crab cakes.

"Marcus, the Branfords are in my conference room. Zach Hill is having conniptions. And quite frankly, I'm stunned that you're having a tantrum—"

Click.

Charmaigne's eyes bugged. Shock sizzled through her. She couldn't believe this was the same man she'd fallen in love with over the past six weeks. Had he really just hung up on her? Unbelievable! That was the ultimate act of disregard for her opinion. And her feelings.

Dread numbed her body. They were scheduled to attend the Mayor's Ball tonight at the Detroit Institute of Arts. Did that mean putting on a happy face? Would he go without her and say she was ill? Would he call to apologize?

Either way, Marcus had just done irreparable damage to their relationship.

And she had a serious decision to make.

Now.

Chapter SIX

N*o, I can't leave this man.*

Charmaigne twirled in his arms under the chandeliers of the ballroom. The scent of his cologne, the adoration in his eyes, and his stunningly handsome appearance in his black tux made her head spin all the more. As did the champagne she had been drinking. And the intoxicating triumph of convincing Zach Hill to sit down and shut up this afternoon, so that the Branfords could sign the deal and acquire the company exactly according to the brilliant contract she had crafted for them.

Everything always works out for the best.

Charmaigne closed her eyes, loving the moment.

Marcus pressed his lips to hers as they danced to the live jazz band. Surely his outburst this afternoon was just a symptom of retiring from bachelorhood and making the leap into being a husband. He did everything with 200 percent commitment and intensity. Marriage, and even the menu at the wedding reception, did not escape the perfectionism that had made him a global leader in business.

"We are going to have the time of our lives in Fiji," Marcus said. His deep voice close to her ear, and his lips tickling her neck, made her shiver with happiness. "I spoke with the resort owner today. He never lets me forget how I prophesied my honeymoon at the Global Summit in Rio. Three years ago, I said I'd see him next time with my bride, within five years."

Charmaigne beamed. "Fiji. The most exotic place on the planet. With you! A dream."

"VIP treatment every step of the way," Marcus boasted. "Our overwater bungalow even has a glass floor so we can watch the fish swim below as we lay on the massage tables."

Marcus cupped his hands around her jaw. "Princess, please accept my deepest apology for turning into Groomzilla this afternoon. I just want our day to be perfect."

Charmaigne smiled. "I understand. Usually it's the woman who loses her mind before the wedding."

As soon as the words escaped her lips, Charmaigne's heart skipped a beat. She braced herself for him to interpret that as an insult—

"Lost!" Marcus declared. But his tone was jovial. "I was like, 'Man, get a grip on yourself here. If your Princess wants crab cakes, then crab cakes it will be. With foie gras!'"

A waiter appeared, offering a tray of champagne flutes. A tall, muscular hunk with smoky bedroom eyes, he nodded respectfully at Marcus as he took two glasses.

"Lucky man," the waiter said, casting an admiring glance at Charmaigne.

"Yes," Marcus nodded, smiling, "Yes I absolutely am. I will toast to that." He clinked his glass to Charmaigne's as the waiter offered bubbly to the next couple.

"Well, if Mr. Mandingo thinks I'm lucky, then it's official, baby. Damn lucky!" Marcus tossed back his head, laughing so deeply that it vibrated through Charmaigne. Was he really amused? Or was that a sinister twinge in his laugh?

"That just makes my night, Princess," he said, chuckling now, pressing his cheek closer to hers. "Thank you for inspiring such candid moments, my love." He kissed her cheek and twirled her until she giggled.

Yes, Marcus was about to chill out. He was just nervous about tying the knot. Soon he'd be back to mostly charm, most of the time. He pressed his cheek to hers and twirled her to the music through the crowd of sequined gowns and tuxedos. She closed her eyes, savoring a lifetime of this.

Yes! I'll keep him.

A short time later, after Marcus said he needed to chat with the CEO of Better Media, Inc., Charmaigne retreated to the opulent ladies' room. First she stood looking in the mirror, loving the radiant glow on her face. As bejeweled women and their rustling dresses entered and left the mirrored lounge, she sat at a vanity examining herself. Her oatmeal complexion appeared pinkish, peachy, thanks to happiness glowing from within.

Wow, I've never looked better.

Her cheekbones appeared sharper than usual, thanks to this morning's loss of appetite. Her lips—full and bow-shaped—sparkled with peach gloss. Her side-parted, shoulder-length bob, whose ends curved forward, looked as silky and sassy as usual. Not a frizz or kink dared mar its smoothness, especially now that Marcus had connected her with a stylist who flew in from Los Angeles to give her the most potent relaxer perm she had ever had.

"Oh, honey," a woman in the next mirror announced, "I've had this dress for twenty years. I said, 'Let me see if it still fits.'"

The woman's friend squealed. "I'd gone up twenty sizes in twenty years. From a six to a twenty-six. Literally. But now I'm down to an eighteen and still shrinking."

Another lady clapped. "You go, girl. A moment on the lips ain't worth a second on the hips. Nothing tastes as good as a size eight feels."

"Amen to that," Charmaigne chimed in.

"Congratulations on the wedding," one lady said. "Girl, you are the envy of women around the world, let me tell you!"

"Marcus Robinson is the ultimate catch," another woman added. "The man is fine, rich, charming. The epitome of success. Power. Hmmm, all that a man should be!"

"And a heartbreaker," said a woman as she strode in from the toilet area, opening her beaded purse to remove lipstick. "I tried to lure him with my feminine charms," she said, puckering to spread red lipstick on her plump kisser. "Girl, you is one lucky sista."

Ebonics. Charmaigne smiled. No wonder Marcus didn't want her. Speaking the King's English meant everything to him, especially since he had taught himself how to use proper English by studying white people on TV as a child.

"Hard for one woman to keep a man like that happy, though," the heavyset woman said. "All that temptation—"

"Enjoy the newlywed phase," one woman said. "You're the one he'll call his wife and take on trips and keep in the mansion."

Charmaigne didn't like the way that sounded. *The one,* as if there were twenty others.

"You're that lawyer Carson, right? You did the cable merger," the young temptress with red lipstick said. "We learned about you in my business class. You a bad sista!"

"Wow," Charmaigne smiled. "Thank you. What was the lesson?"

"About females in business," the woman said. "How just 'cause you got a uterus, don't mean you can't understand complicated business contracts. And make a shitload of money while you doin' it."

The women all laughed.

"Congratulations," the heavyset woman said. "Glad to see you got it goin' on by yourself first. Then you get all the trappings of marriage to a powerful man, and you truly have it *all.*"

"And you got a bangin' body," the young woman said. "Damn, you my hero, Attorney Carson."

"Thank you," Charmaigne said, loving that they were appreciating her individual accomplishments in addition to her status as Marcus Robinson's fiancée. She shared a laugh with the ladies, who continued their chatter about diet and exercise.

Charmaigne was so glad that she had maintained a strict regimen that kept her weight stable and her body firm. Including her face. She was thirty-five, staring into proof that "black don't crack." Not a wrinkle in sight, thanks to years of sunscreen and shunning the sun. Plus genetics. Her mother's superior complexion showed no sign of being sixty. And Daddy was routinely mistaken for fifty-five even though he was seventy. A lifetime of activity and excellent diet—including salad and vegetables every evening with dinner—paid off.

Charmaigne studied the results in the mirror. Black eyeliner and mascara framed her doe eyes to accentuate the sparkle in her coffee-bean brown irises. The arcs of her brows accented her happy expression just right.

Even the sprinkling of freckles on her little mushroom nose—freckles that she had loathed while growing up—looked cheerful as they peeked from beneath a silky smooth layer of foundation and powder.

The v-shaped shirring of her red dress framed her oatmeal-hued cleavage and hoisted her breasts just enough to look beautiful but still classy. The dress tapered to hug her waist, where a sequined belt cinched the floaty, filmy red chiffon that elegantly graced her slim hips and round behind as she walked and danced. The fabric whooshed around her ankles and the strappy red satin sandals that Marcus had bought her at Nordstrom. They pinched at the toe, but they were so beautiful, the way the thin straps showed off her shiny red-polished pedicure.

I feel like a Princess.

She needed to tell Lisa about her new revelation, about her decision to go through with the wedding. Her best friend was supposed to have arrived. Her date was not Rufus, who had to work tonight, but her grandmother. One of the most elegant women Charmaigne had ever met, Miss Baxter could have been a queen in another life. Her hardscrabble childhood as a sharecropper's daughter in Alabama and her subsequent adulthood as a seamstress had never dimmed the stellar sparkle in her eyes, even now that she was nearly ninety and living in the carriage house behind Lisa and Rufus's home in historic Indian Village.

"Where are they?" Charmaigne glanced at the diamond-faced Cartier watch that Marcus had bought her for her birthday. MY PRINCESS FOR LIFE, it said, engraved on the back.

They were a full hour late. She pulled her cell phone from her red crystal-covered clutch. A push of the 2, and the phone speed dialed her best friend.

"Girl, Grams and I are walking up now," Lisa said. "We had a situation. But we're fine."

"I'll meet you at the entrance."

Charmaigne hurried out of the ladies' room, dashing up the stone steps to the main ballroom gallery. Just a quick stroll through there, and she'd be at the entrance where she could meet Lisa and Grams, then introduce them to the who's who.

She felt so happy, like Cinderella, as people smiled and offered congratulations as she walked through the crowd.

She grinned at the sight of Marcus, standing with outstretched arms as she made her way through the well-coiffed couples, including Harry and Denise, Anthony and Renée Jacobs.

Marcus was smiling, welcoming her toward him.

But his eyes roiled.

Dread shot through her as she floated, dream-like, toward what felt like a devilish dance. The rage in his eyes contradicted his mask of charm and his genteel posture.

Twenty minutes ago, she had grasped his hands for an enchanting twirl. Now she was grasping his hands, exactly the same way, for a tongue-lashing.

He pulled her close, kissing her cheek. "Where the hell have you been?" he demanded through gritted teeth hidden from the crowd by her hair as his lips touched her ear. "I needed to introduce you to one of the most powerful men in media—"

She pulled back, smiling, feeling Mrs. Jacobs's stare.

"You said you needed time alone with him, so I thought—"

"There you go, thinking again."

Charmaigne smiled to stop the tears from welling in her eyes. Her shoes suddenly pinched her toes.

"You made me look like a jackass. Boasting about my bride, who was nowhere to be seen."

"I went to the ladies' room," she said flatly.

Marcus guided her by the arm through the crowd, to the entryway. He led her behind a huge stone archway, into a stone alcove a short distance from the hostess table. Couples continued to trickle in as hostesses took their tickets and welcomed them to the Mayor's Ball.

Charmaigne, sobered by Marcus's sinister mood swing, refused to allow his unwarranted anger to ruin this enchanted evening.

"Marcus, I was in the ladies' room. I had my cell phone. Just call or text me. You're suddenly so concerned about how I look. I was making sure that I look picture perfect for you."

He pinched her elbow, leaned close, and glared hard. "What took so damn long?"

"I was chatting with some ladies—" Charmaigne stiffened. She shook her head. "I refuse to justify this with an explanation."

"You will," Marcus snapped.

She crossed her arms and raised her chin away from him. "You need to get a grip."

He grasped her elbow, pinching her skin. "I got a grip on you. My future wife. But for all I knew, you could've been off bangin' Mr. Mandingo."

Charmaigne froze. "I couldn't have heard that right."

"You heard me."

She blinked, widening her eyes at him.

"Since you're always asking me for it. Maybe I don't satisfy you—"

She closed her eyes, wishing she could wake up from this bad dream. But his rapid breath on her cheek and the angry energy bursting from his body let her know this was real.

And wrong.

"Marcus, if you think—"

"I don't know what to think about you anymore."

"Obviously." Charmaigne took a step. But his grip pinched her elbow. "Let go of me. I'm going to take a cab home so you can cool down. We'll talk in the morning."

"You will not abandon me at the premier social event of the year."

"The charming man I agreed to marry has abandoned me. So when you find him, I'll come back."

The expression in Marcus's eyes made her heart pound with terror. His fingertips dug into her arm. And her toes throbbed in her strappy sandals. Even her heels ached, balanced atop the three-inch stilettos on the stone floor.

Was he on the verge of becoming physically abusive? As if his emotional torment weren't vicious enough? Did he have a split personality? Was this why he hadn't married? Because women who got close to him met his dark side—then ran for their lives?

"Let go. I'm leaving."

Charmaigne yanked out of his grip. On throbbing feet, she stepped away. But he slipped beside her, took her arm in the most gentlemanly way, and forcefully escorted her toward the arch leading into the party.

Her cheeks burned. Her heart hammered with fear. And anger. She hoped that no one had witnessed this most vile moment. Actually, she was sure that no one had, because Marcus would never allow anyone to observe him with less-than-exemplary behavior. Except for her, of course.

That whirlpool sensation, the panic, the dizziness, the overwhelming thoughts made Charmaigne's knees feel weak. She walked on wobbly legs, guided by Marcus.

It felt as if she had no choice but to return to the party and pretend that they were the happy couple, celebrating their wedding two weeks from tomorrow.

But everything felt so wrong.

"Marcus, let go. I'm going home."

He grasped her arm tighter.

And she gasped.

Because, standing in a stone archway that would have enabled them to witness the entire drama, were Lisa and Grams. Tears glazed Lisa's eyes; Grams cast a stare of warning that made Charmaigne go numb.

Chapter SEVEN

Charmaigne stared at the grape-sized bruises on her right elbow. She looked away, then glanced back, expecting them to be gone. That couldn't have happened. Marcus could not have put marks on her body like that. He could not have implied that she would actually have sex with a complete stranger at the Mayor's Ball. He could not have looked at her with such hate in his eyes.

But he had.

And if it had not been for Lisa and Grams coming back here to her condo to literally tuck her into bed last night, with a hot toddy of something potent to knock her into a deep slumber, Charmaigne was sure she would have stared at the ceiling all night.

Without Marcus, of course.

Lisa and Grams had escorted her out of the party, leaving him in stunned silence as the three women turned their backs and stepped into the night.

Now, in the bright light of day on her terrace overlooking the city, she sipped her hazelnut-creamed coffee and let this last Saturday of May drench her in warm sunshine. In a white satin robe, she sat with her still throbbing feet on the faux-suede seat of a white wicker chair.

On the glass table, her diamond engagement ring sat on a black cloth napkin. She stared into the sparkling square as if it were a crystal ball.

Even though she already knew what she had to do: use last night as her reason to call off the wedding. Now, before he found a way to woo her back.

He'd been calling all morning.

Rex, the doorman, had called to say that a truckload of red roses had been delivered, but Charmaigne had asked that they be taken to the closest hospital to cheer up the patients.

She needed to talk to him on her time.

"His behavior doesn't even warrant the courtesy of an explanation," Lisa had said last night.

But Charmaigne felt strongly that withdrawing from a wedding was such a momentous decision, she owed Marcus an explanation. Even though he offered none for his outrageous antics.

Lisa had insisted that Charmaigne call with an update later today. After she finally told Marcus the wedding was off.

She pulled her cell phone from her bathrobe pocket and pushed the number 1.

"Princess," he gushed with 100 percent charm. Why couldn't this be one of the countless Saturday mornings when she'd phoned him to talk happily about their plans for the afternoon or evening or eternity for that matter?

Why did he have to go and turn her dream into a nightmare? A nightmare that in so many ways could be ignored, explained away, forgotten, by focusing on the absolute fantasy of it all. A nightmare, too, that could be erased by the absolute horror of the alternative: being alone. Sitting here on Saturday mornings by herself, after a dateless Friday night, facing another solitary Saturday night, searching, seeking, wishing, waiting for Mr. Right to show up. Only to meet dud after dud, then one status-seeking poseur or arrogant playboy after another.

Her insides ached with sadness at the thought of being alone again.

"Princess, I promise to spend the rest of my life making up for every split second of sadness I have caused you."

His voice was pleading, humble. And powerful.

At least she would hear him out.

Even though her intuition was screaming:

Don't.

He won't change.

He'll get more abusive.

You'll regret this.

Being alone and safe and sane is better than being a victim.

You're too smart to let this man manipulate you.

All the luxury in the world isn't worth it if he treats you like this.

You will be signing your death warrant—figuratively, if not literally—when you write your name on that marriage license.

Don't!

"Princess, two weeks from now you'll be my wife," Marcus said with his most charming voice. "And I will spend a lifetime, a lifetime, that's a good forty—maybe fifty years—celebrating you as my Princess."

Two hours later, Charmaigne was in his private jet, slicing through the afternoon sky toward Florida. She kept thinking about

Lisa and Grams, how they would be furious if they knew she had succumbed to his charms once again.

It's my life. My decision.

A short time after that, they were sitting on a yacht in Boca Raton, behind his home there, watching the sun lower toward the ocean as a tuxedoed waiter served crab cakes, sea bass, garlic mashed potatoes, asparagus, and crème brûlée for desert. All washed down with Cristal and a super sweet dose of Marcus's best charm.

"I spoke with the concierge at the resort in Fiji today," he said. "They're having a special reception in our honor when we arrive. And for our first night, we'll have a candlelight cruise around the islands."

She smiled. "That sounds like a dream."

"But it's real, baby girl," he said, taking her hand. "And that guy last night, I promise that I have laid him to rest. I have a lot of pressure right now. Three companies with urgent issues. The wedding. And trying to tame this demon inside."

"Demon?" Charmaigne asked.

"I shouldn't say that," he said, piercing a piece of fish on his fork. "Sometimes I just snap inside. That works in business. But it's wrong to sic my inner piranha on my Princess. You deserve nothing but TLC and respect."

She probed his eyes for answers. Lisa came to mind. Charmaigne's cell phone was still off from the plane ride. It was inside her purse hanging from the back of her chair. Lisa would be worried sick if Charmaigne didn't call her soon. But she'd no doubt explode if Charmaigne told her where she was and what she was doing—listening to Marcus explain and plead his way back into her heart.

"You deserve the best," Marcus said. "And I'm afraid my behavior has not shown that."

She hated that he said the word "snap." That sounded so ominous and uncontrollable.

"Is there something you can do to nip it in the bud when you feel it coming on? I mean, your comment about the waiter last night really hurt me."

He dropped his forkful of fish. "I know, baby girl. I am so sorry. I guess, as successful as I am, we all have a complex when we come face-to-face with the classic Mandingo warrior. We know the ladies all fantasize about dudes like that."

"Not me," Charmaigne said. "You are physical perfection and my intellectual match. I need for no other man to touch me. Ever."

Marcus beamed. "I promise to keep you so happy that you'll always say that. I will keep you drunk with pleasure." He raised his glass and toasted her, reaching into his pocket at the same time to pull out a small robin's-egg blue Tiffany box.

"For you," he said. "For the wedding."

Charmaigne stared at the box. The small fortune's worth of baubles from the world's most famous jewelry maker could not make up for the emotional devastation and physical pain that she had endured last night.

But taking the box, feeling the heart-pounding anticipation of it all and beholding two emerald-cut diamond stud earrings—sure made it easier to forgive and forget.

She squealed. But her gut cramped.

"Oh, Marcus! These are so beautiful!" She held them next to her engagement ring. "They match perfectly."

Wearing a white linen shirt and trouser set, with a cream alligator belt and matching loafers, Marcus came around the table to secure the diamonds in her ears.

"Three carats each," he said proudly.

Lisa's face popped into her thoughts, as if her best friend were her conscience that had been turned off. She could hear Lisa warning, "Girlfriend, don't do it . . . he's slick as oil."

She held up an ornate hand mirror from her purse. He pulled

her hair behind her ears as she watched the diamonds sparkle in the evening sunshine. If only her eyes were sparkling as brightly.

Oh, she looked happy. But she was totally conscious of what was going on. She knew this was classic abuser behavior.

Act crazy angry, then pour on the charm to make up for it. Over and over and over, year after year. Grinning and bearing it. Just like her mother did. And now, after the kids are raised, the reward is to retire and settle into retirement with a mellowed-out man at her side, so she doesn't have to be alone.

Alone on my terrace, as opposed to dining oceanside with the man of my dreams. At least he is most of the time.

Yes, he had a sinister side. But the highs of this roller coaster were so high, so glorious. And they afforded her a life that few women even dared to imagine, much less experience. That made it so easy to forget the treacherous, terrifying valleys. If only she could have some guarantee that her physical safety would never be jeopardized during those plunges into Marcus's dark side.

"Princess," he said, taking his seat and putting his white cloth napkin back in his lap. From there he set a second Tiffany box on the table. It was the same size as the first. But his expression was different. Less celebratory. More serious.

"I'm about to do something quite unconventional," he confessed, handing the box to her. "Open this. Please, Princess."

"What is it?" Charmaigne asked without reaching for the box. He'd laid on the charm thick enough already.

"Please," he said with pleading eyes.

She took the box, opened it.

"Your ring," she said, recognizing the diamond wedding band that they had picked out for him. She tensed. "Why'd you bring it here?"

He grasped her hand across the table. "Princess, I want you to put that ring on my finger right now."

She drew her brows together. Yes, her agreement to come

on this makeup trip must have affirmed to him—if he'd had any doubt when she walked out on him last night—that she would still marry him.

"But what about the wedding?"

"Two weeks from now feels like eternity," he said. "I need to do something to symbolize my commitment to making you feel happy. Forever."

Something about that word "forever" always made her melt. Her muscles loosened. Her gaze softened.

"How will you wearing this ring change anything now?" she asked. Now Lisa's voice was shouting in her head. *Ain't this some melodramatic B.S.!? Charmaigne, you're a damn fool if you fall for this sensitive-man act!*

"It will serve as a visual reminder of how precious you are to me," he said, staring at her with tender eyes. "It will help me maintain this demeanor, this persona, at all times—"

She drew her brows together. "Why do you need a physical reminder of something that's supposed to be in your heart, your mind, your soul?"

He leaned closer. "Princess, I have to confess something. I am nervous as hell about getting married."

"I signed the prenup," she said.

"It's not about money," he said. "It's about me. I'm a stellar success in business. Everything I touch turns to gold."

He held her left hand in his palm and caressed her knuckles with his other hand.

"Baby girl, my piranha-style rules in boardrooms," he said. "But on a personal level, I'm finding it hard to turn off my inner control freak. The past few days have made me take a hard look in the mirror."

Charmaigne's heart welled for him, even though her mind kept front and center the memories of how terrible he'd made her feel this week. The corners of her mouth rose in a slight smile.

How impressive that he had actually diagnosed his own personality disorder. Perhaps that meant he could repair it just as easily and quickly.

"I apologize for trying to micromanage you, our wedding, the reception menu," he said softly. "I feel like a perfectionist maniac who's on a rampage to ruin what we have—"

"Oh, Marcus," she sighed. "Can we see a counselor to work this out?"

He closed his eyes, as if her words hurt him. "I'm already seeing someone. The best in the business. Had an emergency session with me last night after the ball."

"Wow," she whispered. Daddy never got help. Just got old and mellowed out. "That takes a lot of courage."

Charmaigne closed her eyes to give a moment of thanks. The first step to ending alcoholism or drug addiction or a gambling habit was to first admit and face the problem. The same went for abuse.

Her lips trembled. Her throat burned. And Marcus's face blurred as tears filled her eyes.

"I love that you're man enough to do this," she whispered, "for the sake of us."

Lisa couldn't argue with this. This was real. And Charmaigne believed him enough to give him one last chance.

"I love you, Princess," he whispered with eyes aglow with affection. He raised her knuckles to his lips and kissed them for a long moment.

Then she stood, sat on his lap, took the ring out of the box, gently held his hand, and slid the channel-set diamond band onto his left ring finger.

"It's a deal," she said, looking deep into his eyes for proof that he could uphold his pledge.

"I am now your official Prince Charming. We can live happily ever after."

Charmaigne closed her eyes and kissed him so that the delightful sensations would numb the twinge of doubt in her gut.

Chapter EIGHT

Charmaigne wanted to cringe in the corner of the dressing room to escape the silent disapproval in her mother's eyes.

"Do you really want it that snug against your hips?" Mother asked. She tugged at the lace overlay on the white satin mermaid-style gown with long sleeves and an explosion of frothy lace and satin below the knees. "Seems like another style might be more slimming."

The seamstress turned Charmaigne on the carpeted pedestal so that she could secure pins along the side. "Not too tight," the seamstress looked up from pinning the side of the gown. The woman's Eastern European accent sounded even more confusing as she spoke through lips clenching a half-dozen pins. "She lose weight. I take in one inch, one side each."

Mother crossed her arms. "I don't know. I thought you'd have a princess style or a more traditional look."

"Is beautiful," the seamstress said with a tone like Mother was insane.

"Thank you," Charmaigne said, loving the scalloped edge that framed her cleavage and the row of satin-covered buttons down her back. "This is the style that I always dreamed about."

Now Charmaigne remembered why she had not, until today, allowed Mother to see her wedding gown.

"Are they finished with your dress?" she asked her mother without looking at her.

"My weight is stable," Mother snapped. "It fits the same as when I tried it on six months ago."

"What about your shoes?" Charmaigne asked.

"I have them," her mother answered. "Charmaigne, do you have something borrowed?"

"Yes, Mrs. Jacobs gave me the most beautiful tiara. See?" She pointed to the veil and tiara on the mannequin nearby. The opalescent fabric of the veil was rather heavy, difficult to see through from the outside. Charmaigne liked that literal veil of mystery. She liked that she could see clearly from the inside out, while observers could see only a silhouette of her nose, if that. "I had my veil custom made to fit it."

"Isn't a tiara rather juvenile? Like a teenage prom queen?" Her mother's tone was like a baseball bat, smashing Charmaigne's words in mid-air.

"Lady Di wore a tiara, and she epitomized elegance," Charmaigne answered. "It's what I want on my wedding day."

Her mother crossed her arms tighter against her slim waist, cinched by a fabric belt that matched her plain green dress. She wore beige pumps with a small heel, nude panty hose, and no jewelry except for a gold wedding band and tiny gold hoops in her ears. Mother never wore perfume or make-up. Just hand lotion, the cherry-almond-scented Jergens kind, a scent that always took Charmaigne back to childhood. Though it smelled sweet, it roused bitter memories of feeling not-good-enough as her mother radiated that scent and her disapproving glare. Like now.

"What about something blue?" her mom snapped as if she were asking if Charmaigne had scrubbed the toilets.

"The bridesmaids' dresses are baby blue," Charmaigne said.

"I mean for you," her mother said. "For the bride."

"Yes, Lisa's grandmother—" Charmaigne glanced toward the door. "Mother, can you please go find them? I should actually try on the shoes with the dress."

"Smart girl," the seamstress mumbled.

"You're wearing blue shoes?" Disgust punctuated Mother's tone.

"Lisa says they're very pale blue, but they're lucky," Charmaigne said. "Three generations of women in her family have worn them down the aisle—and lived happily ever after."

Her mother exhaled loudly. "I suppose they clicked their heels when they said 'I do' and the Wizard of Oz worked some magic on their marriages."

Charmaigne glared at her mother. "Something like that."

Her mother shook her head. "Marcus is very traditional. He will not approve of blue shoes."

"They won't show," Charmaigne said with a dismissive tone. "All the frothy fabric of my dress will hide them."

"Marcus doesn't miss anything," Mother said. "I think you're making a mistake."

"Mother, can you please find Lisa for me? She should be finished with her alterations by now. She's wearing the prettiest blue gown."

Her mother uncrossed her arms and stepped to the door. "I've never seen a maid of honor look so disgusted about her best friend's wedding. Is there something you need to tell me, Princess?"

"No." Charmaigne turned back to the mirror to admire her dress. Lisa would get over it. She would see that Marcus was committed to changing, and that last week's outbursts were history that would never repeat itself.

Yes, Lisa had given her an earful of warnings, but Charmaigne had to make her own decisions, and this was it.

A wedding. And becoming Mrs. Marcus Robinson.

The door opened.

Lisa and Grams walked in; Mother resumed her cross-armed post against the white wall of the dressing room.

"Those are beautiful!" Charmaigne exclaimed.

Grams held the prettiest pair of slippers. Pale baby blue suede, embroidered with swirls of clear crystals, with beige satin inside. Small heels, maybe one inch high, gleamed with satin that looked new.

"They're like princess slippers!" Charmaigne gushed. "I love them!"

Grams's onyx eyes glowed with something that Charmaigne could not pinpoint. Mischief? Forgiveness? Empathy? She handed the shoes to Charmaigne, who admired them close to her face.

"How can these be three generations old? They look new."

"I don't think it's appropriate to wear blue shoes with your wedding dress," Mother snapped. "Suede shoes at that. I don't think it's appropriate at all."

"Charmaigne looks happy," Lisa said, smiling and stepping close to admire the shoes in Charmaigne's hands.

"These shoes are doing something right," Charmaigne said, mirroring her friend's grin. "They made Lisa smile at me for the first time all week."

Charmaigne probed Lisa's eyes for answers. "Why do you suddenly look so happy?" "I'm sorry, Charmaigne," Lisa said. "I've been pretty hard on you lately. I trust you can make your own decisions about life, liberty, and your own pursuit of happiness."

"Thank you," Charmaigne said. She stared into her friend's eyes, thrilled to see happiness reflecting back.

"Put dem on," Grams ordered with her Jamaican accent.

"How do you know they're your size?" Mother demanded. "What if they don't fit?"

"Dey will," Grams said.

"Here," Lisa said, taking a shoe in each hand. Grams lifted the dress; Lisa slipped the shoes onto Charmaigne's bare feet.

A silky tickle enveloped her feet. She squealed with delight.

"Wow!" Charmaigne exclaimed, raising her dress to stare at the perfect fit and dainty appearance of these borrowed blue shoes. "Thank you, Grams."

The older woman grasped Charmaigne's hand. "You'll tank me anotha day." She winked and smiled.

"I still think it's a strange choice," Mother said, "Borrowed, old shoes seem unsanitary. And blue?"

Grams turned to Mother. "The guhl is happy. Nuttin' else mattas."

"This wedding is the social event of the year," Mother said. "My daughter should dress accordingly."

"She is," Grams said, lifting the veil from a mannequin nearby. Lisa stood on the pedestal and placed it on Charmaigne's head.

"Picture perfect," Lisa said. "From head to toe."

The tiara sparkled. The white veil fell over Charmaigne's face. She wiggled her toes. Her mind spun back over Marcus's sweetness this morning; he'd had her favorite breakfast catered to her condo, where he'd joined her on the sunny terrace for veggie omelets and fruit salad. Ever since she had put that ring on his finger, he had been the epitome of charm. And that was a full week ago.

Now, her eyes welled with tears.

I'm really going to do this. And live happily ever after.

Charmaigne closed her eyes, savoring the euphoria of the moment. The relief that she felt so certain about getting married.

She felt still and centered, the way Lisa had said she should feel in order to listen to her inner voice. Only then could she hear what her intuition was telling her about becoming Mrs. Marcus Robinson.

You won't do it.

Her own voice spoke in a matter-of-fact tone what she needed to hear. But that was not what she wanted to hear. She wanted to believe that everything would work out fine. That all this pomp and circumstance would open a golden doorway to eternal happiness with her husband. She wanted what most women wanted: love.

She studied the women around her. Grams was still admiring the dress. Mother still looked constipated. Lisa was fluffing the fabric of the mermaid pouf. And the seamstress was still pinning. Everyone was silent.

Except that voice inside Charmaigne's head.

You know Marcus is a lying, manipulative control freak. You'll be miserable as his wife.

Charmaigne drew her brows together. Her inner voice spoke with such confidence and authority.

But why now? This was the most excited and hopeful she had felt about the wedding since Marcus's wicked outburst at the Mayor's Ball.

Yes, I am going to get married. Everything will work out fine.

Charmaigne focused on that thought.

But the other voice spoke louder:

Walk away.

"No!" Charmaigne said aloud. The women in the dressing room turned and stared at her with curious expressions.

"No, what?" Lisa demanded.

"I poke you?" the seamstress asked.

Grams flashed a mischievous smile.

And Mother cast a cold gust of disapproval.

"I was just—" Charmaigne shook her head. She was just what? Hearing things? Hallucinating? Letting her intuition tell her what she didn't want to hear in the dressing room of the bridal boutique?

"I was just thinking out loud," Charmaigne said. "About the menu. The planner was trying to talk me into adding another appetizer, but—" the ladies around her looked perplexed. "Never mind." She laughed. "Every bride is entitled to act a little whack for a minute."

"Well, you've had your minute," Mother said.

Lisa snickered playfully. "She's had many minutes!"

And Grams just smiled, as if she knew a juicy secret.

Chapter NINE

Marcus stepped into the restaurant after Charmaigne and her parents were already seated. Their table overlooked the river; but her parents' disapproving eyes looked only at their daughter.

"Punctuality is a virtue," Daddy snapped as he stood. Marcus strode quickly toward them, stopping briefly at several tables to shake hands.

Charmaigne noticed that as he approached, he was adjusting his wedding ring. Was he adjusting it or putting it on?

"My deepest apologies," he said, bowing slightly to Daddy and Mother. He kissed Charmaigne's cheek. "Hello, Princess."

She enjoyed the warm feeling of looking at Marcus while he shook Daddy's hand and kissed Mother's cheek. But what was that beige smudge on his white collar? Dirt? Never. Marcus didn't let dirt mar his beautiful custom-made suits that hugged his body just right. Nor did he allow food or her make-up or lipstick to stain his crisp white dress shirts. But what else could cause a brown streak like that besides a woman's foundation? It looked just like the smudges that Charmaigne's own make-up made on her blouses if she removed them too quickly and they brushed her cheek.

Her heart pounded at the suspicious smudge on her man's collar. But sometimes even an innocent hug from a male acquaintance covered her with his cologne—for the whole day—and if questioned about it, she would feel terrible. So she would give Marcus the benefit of the doubt right now. Perhaps a female colleague had hugged him in a most innocuous manner, caused a smudge, and—

"Why are you wearing your wedding ring before the ceremony?" Daddy demanded as they sat down.

Marcus beamed and grasped Charmaigne's hand. "It's part of a special pledge I made to your lovely daughter."

"That's quite odd," Mother said. "I've never heard of a man wearing a ring until the wedding."

"I'm an unconventional kind of guy," Marcus said playfully. "I think way outside the box. In business and in life."

"Well, so does our daughter," her father said. "That's the secret to her success as well. We are so proud of both of you."

Charmaigne loved the glimmer of pride in her father's dark eyes. Such an expression was not freely shared; that proud radiance and words spoken along with it were reserved for graduations, career accomplishments, and now. She never took them for granted.

"Thank you, Daddy."

"Now, I suppose you should get right to work on having a baby," Mother said. "After all, thirty-five is no spring chicken."

Charmaigne hated that her mother's iciness had just obliterated her father's loving words. "My doctor says I'm in perfect health with several years left for motherhood."

She wanted to add that she had been taking notes her whole life on how not to be a mother.

"Marcus, I trust that you want children?" Daddy asked.

"Of course, sir. After we enjoy the honeymoon phase for a few years. We both decided that two or three years down the road should be plenty of time to enjoy as a couple before we hear the patter of little feet."

"I'd like to see my grandchildren before I go to glory," Daddy said. "And since Charmaigne is an only child—" He glanced down at the table.

Charmaigne grasped his hand. "You're not going anywhere, Daddy." Her heart swelled with hope and sadness and the sudden realization that her father could very well die before she had children. He was in great health, but he had been in his forties when she was born. Now, at his age, anything was possible.

A sudden urgency to marry and get pregnant made her heart pound. "We'll be calling you Grandpa before you know it."

"That's my girl," her father said proudly.

Charmaigne beamed at him, then at Marcus. Thank goodness he had cleaned up his act and Charmaigne had dismissed all thoughts of canceling the wedding. This wasn't just about her. It was about her parents' hopes and dreams for grandchildren.

"I'll make you proud," she said over a hot lump in her throat. "I promise."

Marcus squeezed her hand. "All this love! It's a beautiful thing. I'm absolutely honored to join this family."

"And we're honored to welcome you in," Daddy said. "Now, I've taken the liberty of ordering for all of us. The lamb chops earned this place the honor of being restaurant of the year."

Charmaigne shook her head; Marcus bristled.

"Oh, Daddy, we're eating light this week," she said, "with the wedding and all."

"One decent meal won't ruin your girlish figure," Daddy said with a tone that dismissed her words.

"With all due respect, Mr. Carson, I prefer something lighter. I usually get the grilled salmon with mixed greens and rice here."

Daddy shook his head. "You've got to try this. I've already made special arrangements with the chef. Lamb chops for four. French onion soup with sourdough and four cheeses. Baked potatoes with the works. And for dessert—why, that's a surprise."

Charmaigne stared at her father's proud and determined smile and Mother's expressionless face aimed toward him. She said nothing, even though Charmaigne knew that her mother suffered stomachaches every time she ate lamb. And Marcus—his eyes roiled with a brainstorm on how to proceed with diplomacy. This was definitely a "pick your battles" kind of moment. Would refusing to indulge her father's domineering dinner order be worth the angry fallout?

As she sensed Marcus's intense contemplation of how to respond, her brain buzzed with an epiphany.

Now he sees how it feels when he takes control and orders my dinner. He hates it. And he won't allow it.

Marcus grinned. "You're right, sir. One night of indulgence will not expand our waistlines. My mouth is watering already."

Charmaigne almost gasped.

She was being double-teamed by the two most important men in her life. And she hated it. They had no regard for what she wanted, how she felt, or what she thought.

Nor did Mother, sitting there like a zombie. No feelings. No opinions. No power.

I will never be like her!

Charmaigne looked back and forth between her father's domineering arrogance, his all-powerful aura of authority, and Marcus's radiant glow of it's-a-man's-world and I-know-when-to-defer-to-an-elder.

She wanted to scream at Mother, "Don't you see what's happening? Why have you let it kill you inside?"

A nauseating burning sensation rippled up from Charmaigne's stomach, into her throat, making her mouth taste like vomit. No way could she eat disgusting lamb. She was glad that Marcus had retired the diet police, but this was the opposite. Endorsing a heavy meal—

His eyes cast an all-knowing warning at her. As if to say, "Just go along to get along."

Mother's completely zoned out demeanor announced that as well.

Charmaigne wanted to scream.

Especially when the waiter arrived to confirm that the dinner preparation was already under way now that all four of them had arrived.

She gasped. *Yes, I could end up like Mother. An attractive prop. Silent. Emotionless. Bitter.*

Never!

Charmaigne shot to her feet. "Excuse me," she said, "I have to wash my hands in the ladies' room."

She dashed away, her mind spinning. How could she have her cake and eat it, too? How could she marry Marcus and enjoy that dream—but maintain her voice, her choices, her power? Was that even possible?

She barely reached the ladies' room before tears filled her eyes and spilled down her cheeks. Thank goodness she had eyedrops and make-up in her purse.

"Never let them see you sweat," her father's voice echoed in her head.

"Charmaigne," a deep woman's voice called out.

Panicked, she dashed to the sink. "Something is irritating my eyes," she said, bending over to splash running cold water into her eyes.

"It's me, Renée. Renée Jacobs."

Charmaigne's heart pounded. Mrs. Jacobs was the last woman on the planet she wanted to see right now. Not looking and feeling a mess. Not in the throes of doubt or at least disappointment.

"Honey, are you all right?" Mrs. Jacobs placed her hands on Charmaigne's shoulders. "Let me see."

"I think it's the smoke from the kitchen. I came face to face with something that I must be allergic to."

"Come here," Mrs. Jacobs said, guiding her to the couch. "Let me see."

She peered into Charmaigne's eyes, dabbing the corners with tissue. A knowing half smile raised the corners of her mouth and made her eyes sparkle.

"I see," Renée said. "I see very clearly. You're afraid."

Charmaigne shook her head.

"It's alright. Anthony and I saw you with Marcus and your parents. We were going to stop by your table after our dessert."

Renée squeezed Charmaigne's hand. "Fear is a natural feeling to have before your wedding. But I guarantee, you will be just fine."

"I don't want to lose myself behind the 'M-R-S.'"

"Anything you do give up or lose," Renée comforted her, "will be replaced with someone far more beautiful and powerful."

Charmaigne studied the elder woman's eyes, which radiated sincerity and wisdom.

"I'm having trouble with the realization, on a whole new level, of just what a man's world it is. And becoming a 'wife' casts me in an inherently subservient role."

The elegant matron nodded. "On one level, yes. But in truth, we hold all the power."

"How?"

"Men are motivated by the love of a woman more than any other factor. We legitimize them. We provide the strong foundation of home from which they can go out into the world to hunt and kill and conquer." She smiled. "Pardon my reference to the caveman days—"

Charmaigne laughed. "I guess the same could be said for the business world."

"No matter what they do," Renée said, "It's ultimately for us. Think Helen of Troy, Napoleon and Josephine. Some of the greatest love affairs ever inspired war and acts of bravery."

Renée's platinum watch, with diamonds glittering at each hour, caught her eye.

Charmaigne gasped, remembering the disaster at the Mayor's Ball when she had spent too much time in the ladies' room. "They're going to wonder where I am. See, this is what I mean. My time is no longer my own."

"But your time is so much more full and fulfilling," Renée said. "Everything in life, especially marriage, is about what you tell yourself."

The ladies stood.

"If you tell yourself your time is not your own, you'll feel cheated," Renée said. "If you tell yourself your time is enhanced by a wonderful man to share it with, you'll feel happy."

She pulled Charmaigne into her soft cloud of perfume for a hug. "You can call me anytime. In fact, I'd like to take you to lunch after the honeymoon."

Charmaigne felt warm inside. She smiled.

"I can't tell you how much I appreciate this," she said. "I admire you so much. Your confidence. The power that you exude."

"Why thank you," Renée said humbly. "I see in you what I felt too many years ago. And I want to see you through it so that someday you can help another young bride."

Mrs. Jacobs escorted Charmaigne back to the table, where her husband was sitting in Charmaigne's chair and chatting sociably with her parents and Marcus.

Charmaigne hated that she felt such a huge sense of relief that her prolonged absence had been "legitimized" by her matronly escort. No chance of being accused of sneaking off with a waiter. She hated, too, that such a thought even crossed her mind.

But for now she would enjoy the happy sparkle in Marcus's eyes. She would nibble some of the lamb that her father had ordered. And she would never become a clone of her dead-inside mother as Mrs. Marcus Robinson.

Chapter TEN

I knew it was too good to be true.

Charmaigne cringed in the passenger seat of Marcus's Bentley as his wicked side roared out from its weeklong retreat behind charm.

"How dare you question why I was late to dinner?" he snapped as they drove around Detroit's answer to Central Park—an island of grass, trees, fountains, a golf course, a beach—called Belle Isle. As he looped the six-mile, one-way drive that provided sweeping views of the city skyline, Windsor, and the water, his anger seemed to intensify.

"I am working my ass off to maintain and build my empire for you, the future Mrs. Robinson!" he shouted. "So don't you ever question me if I'm fifteen minutes late, an hour late, or a day late, for that matter!"

Charmaigne wanted to ask him who had smudged her makeup on his collar. And why had it looked like he was putting his ring back on as he approached the table. He didn't smell like perfume. Or anything else that she could detect with his clothes on.

But something wasn't right.

And she was sorry she had asked, because it roused his demon inside.

"The river looks pretty," she said, staring out the window, wanting him to shift gears back into the charm zone.

"I hate the shoes you're wearing," he said. "They look frumpy. Don't wear them again when we're together."

Charmaigne glanced down at her black pumps. Low heels, perfectly broken in, they fit like a glove. So comfortable, she forgot she was wearing them. Unlike the painful, pinchy red stilettos she'd worn to the Mayor's Ball that made her feet throb the rest of the weekend.

"I wasn't trying to look vampish for dinner with my parents," she said. "My father is pretty conservative when it comes to my clothes. That's why I wore this black business suit from work, as opposed to a dress." She ran her hands over the skirt that extended past her knees. The glimmer of her diamond corresponded with the worried cramp in her gut.

A cramp that only worsened when Marcus's sinister tone sliced through the soft light: "You're not Daddy's little girl anymore. You're about to be my wife. So dress accordingly."

Charmaigne crossed her arms. The act reminded her of how her mother had crossed her arms in the dressing room at the bridal boutique. And she thought of the words that popped into her mind when she modeled the dress, the veil, and the shoes all together.

Marcus would hate those shoes. Low heels, not really sexy but very pretty. They would hardly show.

I'm going to wear them. If I walk down the aisle at all.

"Tell me, Marcus, the top five reasons you want to marry me." Her confident, assertive tone surprised her. "One week from now—"

The tires screeched as he pulled to the curb. The river churned in the breeze; someone honked and yelled, "Cain't drive bourgeoisie motha fucka!"

Marcus's eyes were like laser beams, aiming to slice her confidence to shreds as he turned to glare at her. At that moment, she hated him. Her whole body hummed with disdain, with loathing, with contempt for this man who made her feel so good and so bad in a few minutes' time.

That song about there being a thin line between love and hate came to mind. Was that the feeling that motivated him to treat her as he did? Did he love her one minute, but hate her the next? Even though he pursued her, asked her to marry him, told her he wanted to wear his wedding ring early?

Was he realizing that his own desires to marry were stifling him? Making him feel trapped? Vulnerable?

"I will not justify my marriage proposal one week before the wedding," Marcus growled. "But I will demand why the hell you need to know right now. Sounds like you're the one with second thoughts." His accusatory tone struck like a punch in the stomach. "How dare you sit there, covered in diamonds, and ask such a ludicrous question?"

"I need to know," she said softly, with courage that she didn't know she had. "Because for the last week I've felt like I cause you more misery than happiness."

"You're damn right! You do, when you ask silly-ass questions!"

Suddenly her feelings shut down. Turned off. As if the look in his eyes had flipped a switch on her inner fuse box and cut the power. For a moment, she felt a twinge of horror: this was her mother all the time, except for the disapproval that always shot from her silent stares. Charmaigne could not spend another moment turned off by the man who was supposed to turn her on. She most certainly could not spend a lifetime this way. No matter how brightly or heatedly she glowed when he turned on the charm.

"Take me home," she said flatly. "Please take me home. Now."

Marcus exhaled, shifted into drive, and followed her order.

Inside her condo, alone, Charmaigne took a long hot shower that left her skin tender and warm as she slipped on a white cotton nightgown. She craved comfort: curling up on the couch, drinking tea, reading a magazine. As she walked through her bedroom, past the dark cherry four-poster bed with its fluffy white duvet and eyelet sheets and mound of pillows, her wedding accessories caught her eye. The beaded purse, the tiara and veil, the blue suede shoes. All sat on the dressing table beside her perfume bottles, make-up, and jewelry box.

The shoes. Charmaigne had loved the immense comfort that she had felt in those shoes at the bridal boutique. And the tiara; Renée Jacobs's wisdom seemed to sparkle from each diamond.

She pushed the combs of the tiara into her hair, securing it. The veil exploded behind her head.

Then she fingered the incredibly soft suede of the new-looking but ancient shoes. She slipped her toes, then her heels, inside.

"Oooh," she squealed, feeling the first bit of happiness all evening.

The tickling sensation made her smile. It was as if the shoes were shrink-wrapping to fit her. She removed one to search the inside for a size. The beige interior suede had no markings. They didn't even smell old; in fact, a rosy scent rose from the shoes. Even her hand tingled as she held the shoe to her nose.

"Bizarre," she whispered, slipping the shoe back onto her foot. She stepped to the floor-length mirror in her walk-in closet. She had not walked in the shoes at the bridal boutique.

"Wow," she whispered, loving each cushiony step. Even her house slippers were not this comfortable. She almost felt floaty.

An overwhelming sense of peace tingled through her. Suddenly the questions chugging through her head like a run-away freight train and the images of Marcus's angry eyes—and the horrifying realizations that she could easily seek an early death inside like her mother.

All of it stopped.

Quiet and stillness calmed every synapse of her brain.

"Wow," she whispered. "This feels so good."

It was the first time in weeks, perhaps months, that Charmaigne had felt this relaxed. A week or two ago, when Lisa had urged her to get quiet and find her center, and then she would know the answers . . . well, Charmaigne had not taken that advice. Years ago, she used to meditate—during law school and the years when she was a "baby lawyer" and needed the solace of getting quiet to listen to her intuition. But somehow the hustle and bustle of opening her firm and growing it to the prominence she enjoyed today had stymied her commitment to meditation, as magical as it was.

Her inner voice would always speak loudly and clearly. Telling her not to attend the party and to study instead. Reminding her that the pressure of law school and a new career would someday reward her immensely—financially and emotionally—with a deep sense of fulfillment. And her intuitive voice would always be right on when advising her about dates.

Whether that voice warned her that a man was a user who wanted to get close to her to borrow her notes when he skipped class—or that another guy was gay or that yet another date was dishonest about his background and marital status—her inner voice was always correct.

She relied on it to make every decision, which instilled in her a great sense of confidence and divine guidance. Because that intuition, she believed, was God talking directly to her. Guiding her to follow His divine plan for her life.

Plus, meditation always left her feeling refreshed, even after a few minutes of closing her eyes, crossing her legs, and letting her mind go blank. She had been so good that she could do it anywhere. In the law library. In a bathroom lounge. In a classroom. In her office.

Why in the world had she stopped such a powerful ritual?

"Now's the time to begin again," she said. Because this moment, though she was standing, made her feel just as good.

Leave him.

Her own voice spoke with authority and clarity, just as it had in the dressing room of the bridal boutique.

You'll be miserable with him. No high is worth the lows. No romance or opulence or social prominence is worth the toll that he will take on your self-esteem. Think of Mother.

Charmaigne shook her head. Yes, tonight Marcus had been a jerk. But thirty minutes out of a whole week's worth of charm was hardly cause for leaving him at the altar. Or was it? Was this just a taste of worse to come?

Yes.

What about Renée Jacobs's reassurance that she would triumph as a wife? That she would find power despite the fact that it was a man's world and being a wife was an inherently subservient role?

She has to justify her life. If Renée sat there and told you that it was hell being wife to a prominent man who probably had affairs and who was the star of the couple, she would be confessing her misery to you and to the world. But Renée has to justify her existence. She radiates power and confidence because it's a practiced survival skill.

Charmaigne stared into the mirror. Her eyes were wide with amazement. Why couldn't she always think this clearly? What was happening right now that—

Was it the shoes? The tiara? The veil?

Those were the only common variables between now and her similar moment of clarity in the bridal shop. She kicked off the shoes.

The phone rang. She dashed into the living room to grab the cordless from its base. The caller ID said MARCUS ROBINSON. She stared at his name, pulling the veil back so that it did not obscure her face. She did not want to talk with him again tonight. He had lost that privilege in the car when he'd spoken so cruelly to her. So she let it ring. The machined recorded and amplified his message:

"Hi, baby," he said with his best humility and charm. "I apologize about tonight. That whole thing with your dad ordering dinner for me, it set me off. I had just come from a meeting where Mick Wilson tried to strong-arm me into a deal, and I was tired of the world trying to force its will on me. For me to take that out on you"—his voice cracked—"I'm looking down at this ring, and I broke my promise."

He sounded so pathetic. Was she being too harsh? Her heart swelled with sympathy, empathy. What must it be like to be a man, always having to radiate power, make decisions, be in control? What was it like to feel that pressure, to dominate in the business world, then somehow shift gears with a woman in a romantic relationship or at dinner with her parents, to tailor one's speech and behavior and emotions into the most appropriate, sensitive demeanor possible?

"Baby girl, I'm sorry. I want to see you tonight. To make up for it."

Charmaigne reached for the phone. "Marcus," she said.

"Princess," he gushed. "Let me come see you."

"I'm here," she said flatly.

"I'll be right over."

After hanging up, she returned to the bedroom, humming with relief that Marcus was on his way, that he would make things right, that she would be happy and have her wedding as planned. But she had to figure out what was causing her inner voice to speak to her with such amazing authority and insight. Was it the veil? The tiara? Or the shoes?

She removed the tiara and veil.

Could the blue suede shoes be the source of power, as Dorothy's red slippers helped transport her home to Kansas from Oz? Was it possible—in real life—for an inanimate object such as a shoe to possess such power? In college she had met a woman whose family practiced voodoo in Louisiana. Said it worked all kinds of magic when the right person cast the right spell over a doll or other object.

The shoes were from Grams, the daughter of a Jamaican priestess.

Never superstitious or even curious about ghosts, Charmaigne had heard enough convincing accounts of voodoo powers that she believed her friend—and the real potency of spells, charms, and mysterious powers afforded to things.

So she held each slipper in her hands. She studied the crystal beads, carefully hand-sewn into the butter-soft, baby blue suede. She analyzed the satin heels and suede interiors. She stroked the shoes. Smelled them. Bent them. Twisted them. Looked inside them.

All the while, she glanced repeatedly at the clock, knowing that it would take Marcus at least twenty minutes to arrive from his house in a gated multimillionaire's community on the river.

The slippers looked like normal shoes.

She didn't care that Mother had criticized them. She was right. Marcus would hate them. But wearing them would be her single act of rebellion, to do something her way during the wedding. Marcus was micromanaging every other detail. And he was always buying her shoes, telling her which shoes to wear with a particular suit or dress or criticizing her independent choice, as he had tonight.

Still, she was so glad that he was coming over. They could enjoy a romantic talk or something even better, to erase the sting of his angry explosion in the car on Belle Isle.

She would meet him at the door, embrace him, forgive him. And believe, once again, that he would work hard to control his temper so that they could enjoy the wedding of the year and the marriage of a lifetime.

You're fooling yourself, Charmaigne. You know the cons outweigh the pros. You can't marry that man.

Her intuition was speaking loudly and clearly. She had to listen. And act accordingly. Charmaigne dashed back to the phone. She would call Marcus to tell him not to come over—ever. That she wanted to erase him from her life as quickly and as easily as when she highlighted a chunk of text on her computer and pushed the DELETE button. But just as her fingertips touched the receiver, it rang.

Just tell him to go away. This relationship has had nine lives. He killed every one and then some.

"Hello?"

"Ms. Carson," Rex said cheerfully, "Mr. Robinson is on his way up."

Most times, those words from her doorman would elicit a smile or a shriek or a sigh of happiness and relief at any hour. But now she barely recognized the somber, strong voice escaping her lips:

"Tell him to leave, please."

The line was silent.

"Pardon me?" Rex asked.

"I said tell him that I don't want to see him."

"Yes, ma'am. But I'm afraid he's already boarded the elevator."

"Then follow him and tell him to leave." Charmaigne loved the geyser of energy gushing upward through her bones and veins and skin, fueling this new determination to liberate herself from the emotional clutches of Dr. Jekyll and Mr. Hyde.

Knock, knock, knock.

She stared through the shadowy living room, toward the white marbled vestibule where she had kissed and hugged and beamed at her fiancé so many times.

Rex would follow him to the door and escort him out. Charmaigne sat on the couch. Her fingertips caressing the beaded shoes in her lap shot a tingle up her arm.

Knock, knock, knock.

"Princess, are you in the shower? Answer the door." Marcus sounded upbeat but confused. She never made him wait at the door. She was always ready when he arrived. Dressed, made up, smelling good, smiling, ready for a visit or romantic adventure—or an emotional wallop.

A deep voice in the hallway joined his. Rex.

The voices grew louder.

"I need to hear that from her," Marcus said angrily. "You're excused, Rex."

A muffled male voice said something else.

"I just played golf with the man who owns this building," Marcus said in a threatening tone, "so if you value your job, you will return to your post."

That punk Rex was probably shaking in his shoes knowing that Marcus had the power to get him fired.

Knock, knock, knock.

Charmaigne shot to her feet. He was not going to intimidate her doorman or bully his way into this condo that she had purchased with her hard-earned money in this building where she paid an exorbitant monthly association fee so that she could enjoy the safety and protection of a door staff, valet service, and excellent security.

Her bare feet tapped the white marble foyer floor. She crossed her arms behind the white door.

"Marcus," she said firmly, "I want you to leave. I'm tired of this roller coaster. I'm getting off. And I want you to leave. For good."

Silence.

No footsteps. No words. He was still there, probably stunned. She did not have to look through the peephole to confirm.

"Princess, stop talking nonsense."

"Leave, please."

The golden doorknob shook. "Unlock the door!" he shouted. "Open up!" He shook the doorknob even more.

Charmaigne exhaled.

"It's over, Marcus. Good night."

She turned on a heel, stepped softy back onto the white carpet, and padded to her bedroom. She yawned, ready to sleep now that she'd done the final deed to free herself from his emotional torment.

She pulled back her blankets and slipped between the white sheets.

Bang, bang, bang!

"Charmaigne! Open this door! Now!"

Bang, bang, bang!

"You will not shut me out like this!"

Panic shot through her. *He's not going away.*

"Open up, Charmaigne!"

Scared but still determined, she got out of bed, made her way back to the apartment door, and opened it.

He towered over her in the doorway, his eyes glowering like an angry wolf's.

Panic exploded inside her like a red flare, sending hot sparks through her core, down her arms and legs, into her head.

Her brain told her to shut the door. But she couldn't. Because he was charging through, slamming it behind him. Locking it.

"I come over here to apologize to you, and you tell me to leave, that it's over?" His lips were wet; his eyes were wide with a crazed-angry wildness. "Princess!" Her name passed over his lips with flying spit and the most disgusted tone of rage she had ever heard him spew.

He stepped close, face-to-face, staring down at her. He smelled like nervous sweat, like a dog that'd been running outside in the park.

His hands grasped her arms. His fingers wrapped around the tapered spaces above her biceps. He squeezed hard. Harder than when he'd taken her elbow at the Mayor's Ball. That had left grape-sized bruises; this would leave black-and-blue bands, she was sure, around her arms.

She hated that her first thought was not the pain, physically or emotionally. Instead she felt fear that bruises would show with her wedding dress on Saturday, one week from now. Then she hated even more the sense of relief that her gown had long sleeves and that surely the bruises would fade in a week's time, anyway, so that they would not show on the honeymoon in Fiji.

I am just as sick as he is. Thinking about how to cover up and hide the evidence of his abuse. Because her insides were already brutally bruised from being jerked like a yo-yo . . . up, down, up down . . .

"Marcus!" she screamed. "Let go of me!"

He shook her.

"You've been bad!"

She panted. Her mind spun forward onto all kinds of wicked scenarios. Rape. A pummeling by his large fists. Ring marks on her skin from the wedding ring that he wore a week before the ceremony to symbolize his commitment to charm and living happily ever after. All the while striking her cheek, her stomach, her back—symbolizing his brutality and demonic heart instead.

Naked under her nightgown and barefoot, she thought of escaping her own home to get away from the man who was supposed to love her, cherish her, protect her.

What would Renée Jacobs have to say about this?

Business Week's Entrepreneur of the Year . . . *Forbes* magazine cover story . . . one of *Time* magazine's 100 most fascinating people . . .

Exploding in a monstrous rage in his fiancée's luxury condo, a lawyer no less, reverting to the Neanderthal that lurked inside some men.

"You're hurting me!" she shouted.

Someone had to hear her. Someone above, beside, below, or in the hall. Where the hell was Rex? He would call the police, surely. He would know that her shouts were not normal and would not be tolerated.

Especially with that growling and yelling on Marcus's part.

Marcus stormed into the bedroom.

"Where is he?"

"Who?"

"Your man. The Mandingo-dicked motherfucker who turned you against me."

"Marcus, you've lost your mind!"

He stomped into the dressing room. "I know he's here. A man is the only reason you could turn on me. A woman does not turn on Marcus Robinson."

Charmaigne stared in disbelief as he peered below and behind rows of suits and dresses, then dashed into the bathroom. He turned on the lights, staring at the countertops, into the bathtub and glass shower, as if she would be stupid enough to hide a man in the bathroom.

"Marcus," she pleaded. "Stop."

"No, you stop. Stop talking about the most insane idea you could ever have."

"And what is that?"

"Calling off the wedding. One week before the who's who of American business is expected to gather at our church and watch us pledge our lifetimes to each other."

"That was the idea," Charmaigne said. "But your actions have caused a quick change of plans. I can't do it."

He shot into the bedroom, snatched the veil and tiara off the bed.

"Put these on," he said, shoving the items into her hands.

"No." She crossed her arms.

"Put these on!" he growled.

Charmaigne stepped to the door. "You need to leave. Now."

He grabbed her arm, pulled her toward the bed.

Charmaigne's heart pounded with terror. Was he going to rape her? No, she would fight for her life, fend him off by any means necessary.

He pulled her into the reflection of the mirror over the dresser. "Marry me, now."

She stared at him like he was crazy. Because he was.

"Stand here and say, 'I, Charmaigne Carson, take you, Marcus Robinson, as my lawfully wedded husband.' Say it now."

"I won't, because I don't. I will not marry you, Marcus. Anything you say and do now will only be used against me in the marriage, only much worse."

He fell to one knee. Rage glazed his eyes. His chest rose and fell as he breathed loudly and quickly. He grabbed her hand, pinching her engagement ring between his fingers.

"Please, Charmaigne. Don't make a fool of me in front of the whole world. It would kill me."

She glared down at his pathetic face. He didn't understand

that his behavior—his abuse—would kill her, emotionally, spiritually, and possibly physically.

"It's all about you, isn't it?" she shouted. "It always has been all about you. You don't care that you've somehow killed my love. You don't care that your behavior has smashed my heart to bits. All you care about is your reputation. What everybody will think if a woman dares leave the mighty Marcus Robinson at the altar."

"You will not."

"As far as I'm concerned, you can call the church, the caterer, the concierge in Fiji, right now, and tell them all that the Carson-Robinson wedding is off!"

Her bare feet dug into the carpet, to ground her from the lightening and thunder that she knew were about to strike. Marcus knelt there, breathing hard, glowering at her, his grimace aglow with disbelief that she would dare think, utter, and actually carry out such a decision.

"Women all around the world want to marry me," he boasted through gritted teeth. "I was named by *Black Enterprise* and *Ebony* and even *Time* magazine as one of the most-sought-after and eligible bachelors in North America."

Charmaigne shrugged.

"My net worth could sustain a small country," he said angrily. "I am offering you the chance to share my empire. The princess of my empire that is celebrated in every media—"

She crossed her arms. Her body felt numb. She knew she should be scared, but she wasn't. She had gotten dizzy on his roller coaster ride too many times. Now she was off, for good.

"I fell in love with the fantasy image of you," she said, "the fantasy, the lie, that the rest of the world sees and celebrates and perpetuates with every news article and magazine cover and TV report."

"That's me! You love me!"

"I *loved* you. Past tense. You killed my love every time you glared at me, criticized me, hurt me inside and out."

"I did not. I made up for my mood swings—"

Charmaigne shook her head. "Mood swings," she mocked.

Standing straighter, taller, stronger, she inhaled deeply.

He rose.

"Princess, please."

"I think you should leave now." She loved the flatness of her tone. It boomed through the room with authority, yet sounded feminine and heartfelt. "Marcus, stand up and be a man about it. I am not going to marry you."

No, she would not become Mother. She would not become Renée Jacobs, playing a role to convince herself that it just wasn't that bad. She would not become Denise, overweight and content to fill her void of marital love with food and a lavish lifestyle. And she would not become the woman she had been, too many times, loving the highs of this luxurious relationship so much that she psyched herself into enduring the emotional anguish of the lows. And she would certainly not become the woman who allowed his physical abuse—as minor as a pinched elbow or snatched hand or grabbed arm might be—from escalating into a punch, a slap, a kick, a broken bone. Or death.

No, she would not become any of the above.

But Charmaigne Carson would become the powerful woman who had the courage to speak up for herself. To make wise decisions with her mind, without the subjective influence of her body or heart. She would proceed with clarity and confidence, from this day forward.

She stared hard at Marcus as he stood facing her. His shoulders slumped. Weariness pulled his face and cast a sickly pallor over his cheeks. His eyes were dim.

"Please, Charmaigne. Don't do this."

She stared blankly at him. She'd heard one too many apologies. Accepted one too many opulent "make-up" gifts, dinners, trips, and promises.

She turned toward the door. "I'll see you out."

"No!" Marcus lunged at her.

His hands sliced the air, aiming for her neck.

They struck her throat.

She wanted to cough.

But the force stunned her.

Knocked her over.

He caught her, holding her up with his hands around her neck.

His eyes bugged.

Her eyes widened with terror.

She could not breathe.

In or out.

She could not think.

She could not die.

Chapter ELEVEN

Charmaigne remembered what she'd been taught in a self-defense class during college: if ever grabbed by an attacker, go for his most vulnerable spot.

Between his legs.

Kick.

Grab.

Claw.

Marcus gritted his teeth and stared with hate into her eyes.

"Suddenly not so sassy, are we, Princess?"

Her hand shot to his crotch.

She grabbed a handful of soft flesh. But the fabric of his

trousers bunched in her palm. Had she gotten a grip on him at all?

He squeezed her throat harder.

A grotesque sound shot from between her trembling lips.

He slammed her against the wall. The back of her head slammed into the drywall so hard, she was sure that it had cracked and crumbled. Both her skull and the wall.

She tried to scream.

But Marcus's eyes seemed to delight in this deadly anguish. His face actually lit up with every horrible sound that shot up from her constricted throat. Her eyes burned. Her heart hammered. And she felt dizzy, light . . .

Her hands hung at her sides. Limp. Numb.

She wanted to scream, "Don't kill me!"

She wanted to appeal to this egomaniac by shouting "If you think being left at the proverbial altar will tarnish your precious reputation, think about a murder conviction!"

A canceled wedding would be nothing compared to prison for first-degree murder! All your hard work, all your fortunes built, will be for naught. All because you can't control your rage.

Your anger destroyed my love. Now it's about to destroy your whole life!

"Kill or be killed."

Charmaigne remembered the credo that warriors used in battle. And that her law professor once said about the courtroom. Fight to the death—or at least until you won the case in front of the judge or the jury.

Now she had a choice between *killing and being killed.* And it looked like she would be dead in a matter of minutes. Wouldn't have to worry about dying inside as a wife. She'd be dead as a fiancée first.

"Princess, I'm sorry," he groaned. "You're making me do this."

Tiny black spots danced through her brain. Her ears rang. She would black out soon . . . loss of oxygen.

Then death . . .

"If you don't marry me," he said, his face inches from hers, his eyes bugging with insane rage, "I will kill you."

She half nodded. Those tiny black dots became spots, obscuring his face as if blots of ink had been splattered behind her eyes.

"You hear me, Princess? Marry me, or you will die."

Chapter TWELVE

Charmaigne thought Lisa and Grams would be furious. She imagined them calling the police and the jack-up crew from the old neighborhood to administer the kind of conflict resolution that always worked and left no evidence.

"We'll take care of this," Grams said after she and Lisa took Charmaigne to church Sunday morning. Before leaving, they had photographed the purple-black splotches on her neck. Then, with make-up and a pink satin scarf, they covered the bruises.

Bruises that had been inspected by one of the city's best doctors, whom Marcus had called to her condo last night after laying her on her bed so lovingly. All the while, he had whispered, "You're going to remember this forever. When you're my wife, the mother of my children. You'll know what you're here to do. Love me. Act right. Or else."

He smiled, but his eyes glinted with hate. "Yes, Princess, my brilliant attorney. This is a clause in our marriage contract will endure ad infinitum. Forever. Till death do us part. Only you have a big say in when your death will occur. Naturally, fifty or sixty years from now. Or whenever you get too sassy and I have to enact this secret clause."

Her brain had spun over every conceivable solution to save her life. Run. No, he would hunt her down and kill her. Go to the police. No, he was so powerful that he would find a way to discredit her story. His creative vengeance had no limit, she was sure; he was capable of hiring people to plant drugs in her purse. Or fabricate a lover and an extortion plot that she was working with him to marry Marcus, steal his money, then run away.

She thought of the devastation that had plagued Marcus's previous girlfriends when things didn't work out. No coincidence. Just pure vengeance.

Death, destruction—

Now, as she picked at her cheese omelet, Charmaigne shivered at the raw memory of his words scraping over her psyche. Tension clenched her muscles in a way that made her whole body ache.

"Stop t'inking 'bout 'im," Grams said with the same authority that had emboldened Marcus's threat. Sitting across the table in the sunny restaurant where she and Lisa were treating Charmaigne to brunch, Grams cast a loving gaze and said, "I have a plan that will get 'im where it hurts de most. In public."

The excitement and confidence twinkling in Grams's eyes made Charmaigne almost smile. And by the time Grams finished describing her plan, a calming sense of relief seeped through her, soothing her mind and relaxing her muscles.

"I can do that," Charmaigne said. "It'll be the final chapter of this fairy-tale romance that has become my own personal horror story."

Chapter THIRTEEN

The wedding day was as picture perfect as any little girl and grown woman prayed it would be. A cloudless blue sky. Temperatures in the mid-seventies. A slight breeze. No humidity.

And all the trimmings of the most opulent celebration. National media, including a few bridal magazines, were on hand to document the nuptials of the great Marcus Robinson, the successful lawyer Charmaigne Carson, and the who's who of business, government, and social circles nationwide.

Even Mother looked happy here in the luxurious hotel suite where Charmaigne was dressing. The seamstress from the bridal shop was making last-minute adjustments to her dress, thanks to the additional pounds she'd lost this week.

Charmaigne was playing along as the perfect bride as Lisa and Grams shared knowing smiles. In less than an hour, it would all be over.

Charmaigne beamed. "I am so excited," she said softly, glancing at the reporter for *Beautiful Bride* magazine.

"Tell me the story about your unusual choice of shoes," the reporter said. "They're stunning."

"A secret," Grams chimed, "dat we can share after de ceremony."

Charmaigne smiled, choosing instead to share the story of her diamond stud earrings and the private jet ride down to Florida for dinner when Marcus had given them to her. The reporter's enchanted stare as she took notes filled Charmaigne with a nauseating bittersweetness.

But playing along for just a little bit longer was part of the plan. Her gut cramped as she slipped into her dress. The beautiful dress she had so carefully chosen to mark her debut as a wife.

Charmaigne sat looking into the three-paneled mirror at the vanity. Lisa, in a column of baby blue taffeta, stood beside her as the hairstylist swooped Charmaigne's hair upward in an elegant twist and secured the tiara. It sparkled in the sunshine pouring into the suite. Then the veil fell gracefully over her face, obscuring her just enough to create a mysterious silhouette. In a short while, the groom would raise the veil, and her life would begin anew.

Lastly, Charmaigne slipped into the blue suede shoes. Their power had stayed with her; but that tickle-tingle and the shrink-wrap-to-fit sensation made her every cell hum with excitement. Her brain popped with epiphany.

This is what it's all about.

The ultimate power.

The bravest decision and action.

The only way to save my life.

Chapter FOURTEEN

Charmaigne's stomach fluttered as she took her father's arm at the foot of the long aisle. Hundreds of people in the church were standing, turning back to glimpse the bride in her white glory. The organist and four-piece orchestral ensemble played "Here Comes the Bride."

Tears burned her eyes. This was the moment that every girl, every woman, wished for. But neither happiness nor bliss registered on Charmaigne's emotional barometer. While her legs trembled with each step, she felt strong and determined, as if she were walking into a courtroom to defend a case that she knew she would win.

She stared at the defendant, her groom. Stunningly handsome in his white tuxedo. Beaming with pride. He stood at the end of the pink petal–strewn aisle, past the explosions of flowers marking the ends of the pews. The guests, who would become the judges and the jurors, composed this beautiful crowd of hundreds: the mayor, business leaders, lawyers, socialites, and friends like Renée Jacobs. Charmaigne's parents sat near the front. Lisa, her maid of honor, stood at the altar opposite Marcus's best man, Anthony Jacobs.

The preacher stood in the middle, holding the black Holy Book, ready to seal this union before God forever. Two television cameras focused on her, following her every step, along with several cameras from local newspapers, the bridal magazines, and Detroit's upscale lifestyle magazines. Today they would record a far more dramatic and newsworthy wedding than they ever imagined.

Charmaigne shivered. She listened to the rustle of her dress, felt the smoothness of the satin-covered stem of her bouquet of pink roses, and savored the wonderful comfort of her special wedding slippers.

As she and her father marched past the guests, Grams beamed with an angelic aura that made Charmaigne grin. Beside her sat a lawyer and two men in dark suits.

Charmaigne had no doubt that her best life awaited. No fear. No worries. No abuse.

I have the power.

She radiated this as she floated past the twelve women from the young lawyers' mentoring program. In just minutes, she would show them the importance of finding their inner power and using it fearlessly to overcome any problem. They beamed and waved, no doubt envisioning themselves as the perfect brides on their wedding days.

Charmaigne smiled at them as she and her father passed.

"You're a tremendous role model for them," he said. "I'm so proud of you today."

Charmaigne squeezed his arm and cast tear-glazed eyes up at him. She was certain that he would place her well-being before his yearning to enjoy grandchildren anytime soon.

Moments later, they arrived at the altar. Marcus's eyes sparkled the way they always did when he was being charming. His face was radiant, healthy, handsome. He was the picture of the dream husband.

For a split second, Charmaigne imagined his face morphing into that malicious, sweat-sheened scowl as he'd choked her.

That vision sent a bolt of confidence through her. She tilted her chin up. And faced her groom. Staring through her veil, she looked into his eyes as he grasped her hands. She smiled as she and Marcus faced the preacher.

"Dearly beloved," the reverend began, "we gather here to witness the true meaning of life—when God unites two souls in love and in law forever and ever. And today we have before us a stellar and shining example of the perfect match made in Heaven."

Marcus smiled, glancing at her as the preacher continued. Charmaigne tuned out; it was pointless to listen to this holy man speak words that held no truth in her heart. Instead, she reviewed the plan. And she tuned back in when she heard "Do you, Charmaigne Carson, take this man, Marcus Robinson, as your lawfully wedded husband?"

Charmaigne glanced at the preacher. She turned to Marcus. And she pulled back her veil.

"Hell, no!" she said with a strong, loud voice that echoed through the silent church.

Shock flashed in Marcus's eyes. The reverend started.

And the guests let out a collective round of gasps and whispers.

"Ms. Carson," the reverend said. "Perhaps you misunderstood. Do you take this man, Marcus Robinson, as your lawfully wedded husband?"

She turned to the preacher and repeated, "Hell, *no*."

Chapter FIFTEEN

Every bride was supposed to love the expression on her groom's face during the most dramatic moments of the wedding. Today, Marcus did not disappoint.

Because his face literally twitched as he struggled to maintain a mask of cool confidence over the ugly rage that was surging within him.

From his perspective, there could be no worse offense than to expose his wicked secret in front of everybody who mattered—and the media—right here, right now.

"I refuse to marry Marcus Robinson," Charmaigne said with the steady, strong voice that she used when addressing a judge and jury in court. "You may all still believe the perfect façade of charm and intelligence and goodwill that he works hard to maintain every day. But beneath his mask of perfection lurks a violent, abusive man."

The rows and rows of guests were as silent and still as a freeze-frame video shot. The red lights atop the TV news cameras glowed; the only sounds were the clicking of cameras.

Charmaigne looked at her parents. Mother had turned three shades paler. Her father squinted and scowled as if he wanted to charge the altar and give Marcus an old-fashioned whoopin'. The young female lawyers stared with shock.

"This is the most disappointing yet empowering moment of my life," Charmaigne said. "And I want to serve as an example for all the women here today, to show that nothing—not reputation, not money, not prestige, not a wedding, not the seemingly perfect husband—*nothing* is worth sacrificing or jeopardizing yourself, your peace of mind, or your personal safety. Nothing."

Charmaigne's voice quavered. She took a deep breath.

"Ladies and gentlemen," Marcus said, stepping in front of her. He sounded confident and charming. "Clearly my bride is having a wedding day melt-down. I apologize. Please, give us a few minutes." He stood with his back to the church. He gripped her wrists and glared down at her. Through gritted teeth he said, "Whatever the fuck you're doing, stop it and marry me."

"No more!" Charmaigne snatched her wrists from his grip. She side-stepped. Her father rose. So did the two undercover police officers at the back of the church and the uniformed officers at the sides of the altar.

"Marcus tried to kill me this week," Charmaigne said, looking at the mayor and business leaders and the Jacobses. Renée looked horrified while Anthony radiated anger. "He choked me. He said if I didn't marry him, he'd kill me."

Gasps and whispers echoed through the church.

Her throat burned with sadness. "When I met Marcus"—she glanced at his face, that was distorted with a disgusted expression—"I was sure that I had met the man of my dreams. I was sure that finally, after building my successful career, I would get my reward with the perfect husband."

Charmaigne focused on the young ladies she mentored. "But all that glitters is not gold. And if something seems too good to be true, it is." She made eye contact with people throughout the pews as she said, "I'm sorry that you've come here to watch us *not* get married today, but I hope you can take away the power that I feel right now, standing up for myself, speaking out, and watching justice get served."

The police officers approached.

Marcus's eyes grew huge as he glared down at her.

"You will pay for humiliating me!" he growled. "I will ruin you!"

Charmaigne's father stood nearby as the officers grasped Marcus's arms and escorted him back down the aisle. Without his bride.

Halfway through the church, he turned back and glared at her.

Charmaigne stared back, tilting her chin upward and loving the power pulsing through her body.

I did it. I am free.

EPILOGUE

Charmaigne and Lisa stretched on the lounge chairs facing the turquoise water behind Grams's house near Montego Bay, Jamaica.

"I'm proud of you," Lisa said, raising her piña colada to toast Charmaigne's glass. "That took more courage than most people have in a lifetime."

Grams came out, rubbing a satin cloth over the blue suede shoes.

"What are you doing?" Charmaigne asked.

"Getting de shoes ready to help anotha guhl in need," Grams said with that special twinkle in her eyes. "Dese shoes give powa."

Charmaigne shook her head. "Those shoes feel good. They look pretty. But the power is up here." She tapped a finger to her temple. "I changed my mind. And that gave me the power to walk away from a disaster."

Grams smiled. "Believe what you want, guhl. We love ya all de same." She turned to Lisa. "Now, who we gonna give de shoes to next time round? Gotta keep de magic movin'."

Lisa patted the lounge chair beside her. "Sit down, Grams. I'd say you just worked enough magic for the week."

Grams set the shoes on Charmaigne's chaise. "I pass them to you. A guhl you know, maybe she need some powa like you got now."

Charmaigne smiled. "I promise, Grams. Thank you."

Her father had called earlier to say that Marcus had been charged with assault. Charmaigne wasted no time going to the police station to take out an order of protection against Marcus. Whether he was proven guilty in a court of law didn't matter so much with Charmaigne. Because she had convicted him in the court of public opinion, and he would serve a life sentence of shame and dishonor.

Charmaigne stared at the water, vowing to live passionately and love herself first. If she were blessed with romance again, she would embrace it. But only if the man respected her and cherished her the way she desired and deserved.

"Let's toast," Charmaigne said, raising her glass. "To the power of love! Love for Lisa, love for Grams, love for Charmaigne!"

ACKNOWLEDGMENTS

Tracy Price-Thompson

As always, I give eternal thanks to God for blessing me with roads to travel that are straight and peacefully balanced. I give many thanks to my husband, Greg, and my son, Kharel, for their invaluable support and assistance with my work. You guys are the best! Thanks also to my literary manager, Ken Atchity, for his tireless work on my behalf, and to Emily Bestler and Sarah Branham for making this process painless and joyful and for providing the vehicle for our versatile voices to be heard as one. My love and thanks go out to my literary sistah-friends TaRessa, Elizabeth, and Desiree, for being such brilliant and wonderful women and writers. It has been a long haul for the four of us, and I'm proud to have taken this journey with you ladies by my side. Finally, to my beautiful and precious line sisters in the most devastating, most captivating sorority in the world, Delta Sigma Theta Sorority, Inc. Libra Forde, Regina Williams, Anitra Albea, Marisa Moore, Denise Rogers, Ursula Sellars, Chandria White, Altese Cabiness, and Aisha Lubin . . . I love you! Peace and balance, T!

TaRessa Stovall

First and foremost, endless praise and gratitude to Mother/Father God, the Almighty Creator, for the incredible blessings of family, friends, and the opportunity to work with such a brilliant and talented group of sister-authors on a cause that is very near and dear to our hearts.

Special acknowledgment to my father, George Louis "Kelly" Stone, who was both a victim and perpetrator of domestic violence, perpetuating the cycle and driving me to work to want to break it and begin healing for all members of the human family who are caught up in this vicious pattern and pain.

Special thanks to my mother, Rosalyn Weisberg Stone, for having the heart and courage to move my brother and I away from our father so that his abuse of us was minimized. I will be forever thankful that my mother was one who always put her children first, even before the love of her life, when he proved to be detrimental to our well-being.

Reported statistics of all forms of domestic and intimate abuse are disgustingly high, and we can assume that those numbers represent a mere fraction of the real numbers, which will probably never be fully documented or known. The Information Age makes us more aware than ever of the many types of abuse running rampant through our society and around the world. Knowledge is not just power, we can turn it into fuel to work together to move toward healing, which we all so richly deserve.

Special kudos to all of those who are working to heal and move from wherever they are in the cycle of abuse to a stronger, healthier place. You are the light at the end of the tunnel for those who see your example and gain a new vision of possibility for themselves.

Big love to our wonderful team at Atria for working above and beyond to support our mission and bring these stories to life.

Ashe!

Desiree Cooper

I am lifted by the arms of my foremothers, who, through their sacrifice and perseverance, have enabled me to give voice to oppressed women everywhere. Thank you to Tracy, TaRessa, and Elizabeth for their commitment to the transformative power of fiction, and to the women who lived and died without ever having shared their stories. Mom, you taught me that there's no human force greater than a mother's prayers.

Elizabeth Atkins

I want to express immense gratitude to Tracy Price-Thompson, TaRessa Stovall, and Desiree Cooper, for enabling me to participate in this collaborative creation to empower women everywhere.

To our editors and supporters at Simon & Schuster, thank you, thank you!

And to my mother, Marylin Atkins, and my sister, Catherine Greenspan, I am overwhelmed with appreciation for your infinite love and encouragement.

ABOUT THE AUTHORS

Desiree Cooper is a journalist, author, and former co-host of American Public Media's *Weekend America.* A 2002 Pulitzer Prize nominee for her column in the *Detroit Free Press,* Cooper graduated Phi Beta Kappa from the University of Maryland with degrees in journalism and economics and earned a law degree from the University of Virginia. Cooper has been published in *Best African American Fiction 2010* and is a founding board member of Cave Canem, a national residency for emerging black poets. Cooper was born in Japan to a military family and now makes her home in suburban Detroit.

Tracy Price-Thompson is the nationally bestselling author of the novels *Black Coffee, Chocolate Sangria, A Woman's Worth, Knockin' Boots, Gather Together in My Name*, and *1-900-A-N-Y-T-I-M-E.* Tracy is a highly decorated Desert Storm veteran who graduated from the Army's Infantry Officer Candidate School after more than ten years as an enlisted soldier. A Brooklyn, New York, native who has traveled extensively and lived in amazing places around the world, Tracy is a retired Army Engineer officer and Ralph Bunche graduate fellow who holds a bachelor's degree in business administration and a master's degree in social work. Tracy lives in Hawaii with her wonderfully supportive husband and several of their six bright, beautiful, incredible children.

TaRessa Stovall is a Seattle native and playwright and the co-author of *A Love Supreme: Real-Life Stories of Black Love* and *Catching Good Health: An Introduction to Homeopathic Medicine* and the author of *The Buffalo Soldiers.* TaRessa released her first novel, *The Hot Spot,* with BET Books (2005). She resides in New Jersey with her two children.

Elizabeth Atkins, a former race relations reporter for *The Detroit News,* is the author of the bestselling novels *White Chocolate, Dark Secret,* and *Twilight,* which was co-authored with actor/painter Billy Dee Williams. A motivational speaker with the American Program Bureau, Elizabeth has written for *The New York Times, Essence, Ms.,* BET.com, *Black Issues Book Review, HOUR Detroit,* and *The San Diego Tribune* and has contributed to a national tribute program for Rosa Parks. She lives in Detroit with her husband and son.